Praise for *Eaves*

"With arresting detail, Alexandra Kivowitz ̇
of a dangerous, sinister time in our nation's political history through the intimate, droll voice of Sara Green, our fourteen-year-old narrator, whose eavesdropping habits gradually expose the complicated lives of her protective parents. Harrowing situations unfold, and Sara's passionately idealistic mother must ultimately and bravely confront the hysteria of McCarthyism, creating challenging consequences for Sara as she faces her own adolescent worries and troubling questions about the world. This is moving, intelligent, entertaining storytelling that resolves in a beautiful metaphorical finale of growth and understanding."

–Leslie Monsour, author of *The Alarming Beauty of the Sky* and *The House Sitter*

"*Eavesdropper* is a tender exploration of identity, courage, family dynamics, and the complexities of growing up in the tumultuous era of McCarthyism and the Rosenberg case. With a deft hand, Kivowitz draws upon her skills as a psychotherapist, raising themes that resonate powerfully in today's political landscape, reminding the reader that, despite seemingly insurmountable hurdles, standing up against injustice is timeless. In an era where activism is again vital, this engrossing novel inspires readers to reflect on their own roles in the ongoing fight for truth and equality."

–Dora Levy Mossanen, bestselling author of *Harem*, *The Last Romanov*, and *Love and War in the Jewish Quarter*

"Our coming-of-age eavesdropper hides under the dining room table or in her bed listening to her mom and dad's memories and fears. Jews escaping shtetels in Eastern Europe. Full-bore hunts for communists in America. She takes the bus alone to piano lesson, smells her grandfather's cigar. She wants her parents and grandparents to talk to one another. She reminds us that history is the stories, not memorizing dates."

–Eve Hoffman, author of *Memory and Complicity* and *Red Clay*

EAVESDROPPER

A Novel

Alexandra Kivowitz

Montpelier, VT

Eavesdropper: a Novel copyright 2024 Alexandra Kivowitz

Release Date: February 25, 2025

Printed in the USA.

Published by Rootstock Publishing,
an imprint of Ziggy Media LLC
Montpelier, Vermont

info@rootstockpublishing.com
www.rootstockpublishing.com

Paperback ISBN: 978-1-57869-296-5
eBook ISBN: 978-1-57869-192-0

Library of Congress Control Number: 2024926341

This is a work of fiction. Names, characters, businesses, events and incidents are the products of the author's imagination. Any resemblance to actual persons, living or dead, or actual events is purely coincidental or used fictitiously.

Cover and interior design by Eddie Vincent, ENC Graphic Services.

Author photo by Monona Boatright-Simon.

All rights reserved. No part of this book may be reproduced or transmitted in any form or by any means, electronic or mechanical, including photocopying, recording, or by an information storage and retrieval system (except by a journalist or reviewer who may quote brief passages in an academic or editorial review) without permission in writing.

For permissions or to schedule a book club visit or reading, contact the author at alexkivowitz@gmail.com.

EAVESDROPPER

CHAPTER ONE

That early summer dawn in 1953, I heard Uncle Arthur's old Chevy skidding and grinding up our gravel driveway and scrambled out of bed to pull the curtains aside. My mother, whom I'd always called by her first name, Libby, was back from New York City, where she'd gone with friends to a demonstration to stop the execution of the Rosenbergs.

They must have driven all night through thunder and lightning storms to get back here to Goshen by morning. My father, Hank, had stayed behind to babysit me, even though I'd turned fourteen in January and now was fourteen-and-a-half.

The rain had stopped. Aunt Dorothy, who wasn't really my aunt, but an old friend of my parents, gave the handbrake a mighty yank to hold the car on the incline, and the three of them piled out. After Uncle Arthur climbed out of the shotgun seat, Libby unfolded from the back seat, looking rumpled and exhausted, but beautiful. As always.

My first glimpse was of her long, shapely legs, crisscrossed with the laces of those rope-soled Spanish shoes she insisted on wearing. I saw she was wearing one of her peasant blouses, too, and a skirt, hand-embroidered from somewhere in Central America.

Libby once told me she wore peasant clothing to demonstrate her sympathy for the downtrodden of the world, and the espadrilles were from when she was a student and had gone to Spain. All my life, I'd been in awe of my mother's beauty and original tastes. Dark, wavy hair, a wide forehead, and heavy-lidded hazel eyes. But now that I was a teenager, I cringed at those embarrassing get-ups of hers, above all, the espadrilles.

Still, I was relieved to see her home again and safe, and so was my dad. "Sara, they're back," Hank called to me from the hallway, his footsteps pounding past my bedroom door.

From my window, I watched Libby and Arthur and Dorothy trudge toward our front door, looking defeated. A wave of fear washed through my body.

I felt I almost knew the Rosenbergs: Ethel and Julius. My parents referred to them by their first names, as if they were family. They'd been unfairly convicted of passing secrets about the atomic bomb to the Soviet Union, which was the enemy of the US.

Being Libby and Hank's child, I knew things that ordinary kids didn't. Our government was always hurting innocent people. US soldiers had nearly wiped out the Indians. The government had put Japanese Americans in camps during World War II, wrongly suspecting them of disloyalty. Although they were released when the war was over, I'd overheard talk in my house that the government was saving those camps for other people suspected of disloyalty. I'd seen pictures of the camps in Libby's special newspapers that our mailman, Mr. Washington, delivered in brown paper wrappers.

Sometimes, before I fell asleep, I pictured the three of us—Libby and Hank and me—in a desolate barracks in the desert behind barbed wire, with nothing to do all day but sweep the dust around and play softball.

Just then, my favorite chickadee that I'd named Tensing, landed on the metal tray mounted outside my window. I'd named him after the Sherpa who climbed Mount Everest with Sir Edmond Hillary just a month ago. Tensing cocked his head at me, then began scratching and pecking away at the bird seed I replenished every day with a dedication I showed in few other areas of my life, as my parents liked to say.

Chickadees were my favorites because of their little tuxedos and because they stayed all through the winter.

I climbed back into bed, burrowed under the covers, and lay still, listening to the water pipes groaning and clanking, as, one by one, Libby and Uncle Arthur and Aunt Dorothy took showers.

My mind filled with pictures I'd seen in the newspapers of the Rosenberg kids, two little boys dressed in shorts, suit jackets, and ties on their way to visit their parents in Sing Sing Prison. I closed my eyes, curled into a fetal position, and tried to tamp down the idea of never seeing my own parents again. Soon, I had to run to the bathroom.

Judging from the sound of doors opening and closing, Libby and Hank and Aunt Dorothy and Uncle Arthur had by now adjourned to the back yard to what we grandly called the lawn, actually just a bunch of grass tufts and fallen pine needles. Hank liked to say he'd carved the lawn "out of the wilderness."

By wilderness, my dad meant the second-growth pine forest that had grown back after the farmland had been allowed to go fallow and cows stopped grazing the pastures. For more than a year before we'd actually moved, from the city out to Goshen, Hank had been secretly building our new house in the woods—with his own hands and help from Uncle Arthur who drove out on weekends.

The aroma of coffee and bacon was in the air, and I pulled on a t-shirt and dungarees. I approached the lawn by way of the breezeway between the house and garage. The crooning voice of Billie Holiday wafted from the windows of Hank's back-of-the-garage office.

Out on the lawn, Uncle Arthur and Aunt Dorothy and Hank sat on green-webbed lawn chairs, their freshly shampooed hair, wet and combed, gleaming in the sun. Steam rose from their Styrofoam coffee cups, and glazed donuts lay half-eaten on paper plates in the damp grass, even though ordinarily Libby didn't allow unhealthy food in the house.

I advanced slowly and silently, the better to hear what they were saying. Arthur, with his corduroy cap and rimless eyeglasses pushed back on his shiny, bald head, had his face in his hands and was staring down into a coffee cup wedged between his knees. Dorothy, who was short and a little zaftig, as she said herself, with short, dark hair around her pink face, sat hunched over, looking sad.

"You're lucky you didn't come," Arthur said to Hank as he slapped the front page of the morning newspaper with the back of his hand. "Five Thousand Red Sympathizers Fail to Save Spy Couple," he read aloud.

"We chanted our hearts out, but it all came to nothing. At eight o'clock, when no pardon came from Eisenhower, they pulled the switch. I swear, you could hear it, thirty miles away, up the Hudson at Sing Sing. Everyone said they felt it."

"People were crying and wailing, throwing up on the sidewalk," Dorothy added in a hoarse whisper.

There was no doubt left. The Rosenbergs were dead. Robert and Michael were orphans. A gruesome picture took shape before my eyes of Julius strapped into the throne-like wooden chair—I'd seen pictures of the electric chair in the newspaper—wires attached to him, being jolted with electricity until he was dead. Then, Ethel.

The Rosenberg family nightmare composed itself like a jigsaw puzzle from everything I'd been overhearing since I was eleven, and now it haunted me as if it were my own. Light-headed, I sank down at the edge of the patchy grass. A twig snapped under me, and the conversation died, as it often did when I appeared unexpectedly.

They all looked at me. Arthur waggled his eyebrows at me. "Good morning, Sweet Pea. Up and at 'em early, I see."

I gave him a withering look like the one I'd seen Libby use with overly friendly men on the street, a look I'd practiced in front of my bathroom mirror. "It's the only way to be sure of getting the worm," I answered him.

"That's true. You see, we got your mother back home all right. She's in the kitchen making more coffee. And, if my nose doesn't lie, firing up some bacon, too."

Uncle Arthur called me Sweet Pea, the name of Popeye's adopted daughter, maybe because he and Dorothy had no children. According to my parents, during the Depression, Arthur had helped himself to the equivalent of a college education in the Roxbury public library. After the War, he worked in a government lab until, a few years ago, he'd been let go—something about a loyalty investigation.

"Yes, back safe and sound," Hank said with obvious relief. Utterly devoted to my mother, my father was tall, dark, and handsome, although he was losing some of his hair on top.

"I saw her from my window," I said. "She looked…tired."

"Yes, well," Hank said, rubbing his eyes with his fingers, "things didn't go well down in New York City. Eisenhower didn't grant clemency or stop the execution. He showed no mercy, I'm sorry to say."

At that moment, Libby stepped out the kitchen door with a fresh pot of coffee that sent a plume of steam into the cool morning air. The phone on the wall in the kitchen began to ring, which she seemed to ignore. It rang three times, then stopped, something peculiar that had been happening lately, but I couldn't be sure.

"You're up," Libby said, looking at me. Her large, heavy-lidded eyes were surrounded by pink from not sleeping, but she was still beautiful. Libby was always beautiful.

She kissed me on the forehead, put her free arm around my shoulders, and hung it there for a moment, her breasts pressed against my still almost nonexistent ones. I could smell her lipstick. It felt good to be close to her, but I felt an awful tension in her body.

"In the long run, Ethel and Julius will be vindicated," said Arthur. "They'll get hold of the Soviet's files and find out they were never spies at all."

"Witch hunts have to have their victims," Libby said in a matter-of-fact tone.

"Yes, they do," Hank said.

"It's been crazy," Arthur said, shaking his head. "We breathed easy for a couple of years after the war. But when Truman lost Congress in '46, and they started accusing him of being soft on communism? The Soviets test their bomb a few years later, and Joe McCarthy's off to the races."

Hank added, "He stands up in front of the Republican Women's Club of Wheeling, West Virginia, no less, and says 'I hold in my hand…blah, blah…a list of 205 communists in the State Department.'"

"No wonder the whole country thinks the government is infiltrated with Commie spies and subversives," Arthur said. "Fear spreads like polio. And now *this*."

This meant the Rosenbergs. A chill of fear passed through me. I picked up a racket and a birdie lying in the grass and moved down to the pine needle-covered clearing we called the badminton court. From there, I'd still be able to hear what they were saying.

With a series of whacks, I kept the birdie aloft and in motion, the little fledged ball rising, battered feathers-down, then reversing in mid-air and dropping, feathers-up, to my waiting racket.

Dorothy spoke in a low voice. "When Julius was already dead, they kept offering to spare her life, if Ethel would testify against him. They thought she'd relent, instead of leaving her children alone in the world, but she still refused."

"I still don't see how she could have left them—two young children," continued Dorothy.

"Betrayal all around," Libby said. "How could Ethel's own brother accuse Julius of recruiting him? And how could her own sister-in-law claim Ethel had typed up the information when *she* did it herself? Ethel is so brave and adamant…or was."

"What will happen with Robert and Michael now?" asked Dorothy.

Libby closed her eyes, and the sun showed the devastation on her face. "I hear the Meeropols want to adopt them."

That name rang a bell. Abel Meeropol, I knew, had written "Strange Fruit," a song about lynching, sung by Billie Holiday on one of Hank's records. Lynching was one of those things that lodged in a part of my brain reserved for the unthinkable, terrible things I'd heard about because I was Libby and Hank's child.

I willed my birdie to veer left, as a way of moving closer to the lawn where I could hear better, but in the process of retrieving it, I tripped over the ropes that anchored the net poles, nearly pulling the whole thing down.

My landing was muffled and painless, padded by inches of dry pine needles, warm from the sun. I lay where I'd landed, turned onto my back and spread my arms out wide like a snow angel. I looked up through the tree branches at the dense blue sky and wished I were a bird.

A car horn—three toots—one long, two short, familiar and demanding, sounded from the front of the house. My parents exchanged a look. Libby jumped up from her webbed chair on the lawn. "Isn't today Saturday?"

"It sure is," Hank said with a nervous chuckle.

"Did you tell my parents I was going to New York?" Libby demanded.

"I haven't talked to them," he shrugged.

"Maybe *I* did," I said, rising from the pine needles and approaching the lawn. "Grandma called on Friday afternoon."

Libby rolled her eyes and groaned, "The bacon!"

"Probably you should hide the bacon *and* us in the basement," said Arthur.

"Stay right where you are," Libby ordered and headed into the house.

"Don't worry," said Hank to Libby's retreating figure. "We'll take care of them."

He meant Grandpa Joe and Grandma Rose had arrived, even though it was Saturday, Shabbos, which they always spent in their synagogue.

Before we moved to Goshen, against my grandparents' wishes, we'd lived right across the street from them in one of the houses Grandpa had built. When I was younger, I'd even gone with them to the schul. With his head and shoulders covered in a huge tallis, Grandpa and his brother, my real

Uncle Izzy, would prostrate themselves on the steps of the bimah, Libby said, "like Moslems."

They would argue and plead with God on the platform in front near the ark, while Grandma Rose, with me glued to her side, jabbered in Yiddish with the other ladies in the women's section, where you had to sit if you were female.

Since we'd moved out to Goshen, Grandpa Joe, who was a successful house contractor in the Mattapan section of Boston, had periodically taken what he considered a long, arduous journey to do inspections of our forever unfinished house in the woods. He was convinced that Hank had made some fatal mistake in building it and that, sooner or later, the house would, without his oversight, come crashing down on our heads.

Still, they never came on Saturdays.

Our single-story modern house stood out like a sore thumb in colonial Goshen. Perched on a partly exposed blue granite ledge, surrounded by pines, it was long and low with a gently sloping roof that overhung huge picture windows in front.

In the fall, when the angle of sun made the glass into perfect mirrors of the woodland scene outside, birds got confused and flew into the glass, breaking their necks. I had to set up a bird cemetery a little way off from the house, in a little clearing where lady slippers came up in the spring.

"Okay, Sarah, you go out front and greet them," said Hank. "Hold 'em off as long as you can, get them into a good mood, then casually bring 'em around back " He nudged me in the direction of the front of the house.

Grandpa's big celery-green Nash, which looked to me like an upside-down bathtub, was still inching slowly up the driveway. I was excited to see them. As much as I believed what Libby and Hank believed—that there was no "God," that the old, traditional ways, including the kosher food rules, were based on ignorance and superstition, and that "the system" was badly in need of overhaul—I adored Grandpa Joe and Grandma Rose.

Their ideas might be all haywire, but they were as solid as the huge, dark granite boulders that still hulked in the open fields and pastures and in the woods of Goshen. Meanwhile, Grandpa Joe and Grandma Rose doted on me as their only grandchild and did their best, despite strained relations with Libby, to spoil me rotten.

Grandpa's short, thick frame, packed into a brown, three-piece suit with pinstripes, came around the car to open the passenger door for Grandma Rose. Her thick, nylon-stockinged legs dangled over the edge of the plush seat as she slid out and landed on the rutted dirt driveway, her legs wide apart for balance. She wore a dark flowered dress, and around her neck, her summer fur stole—which was really a dead fox with a pointed, dried-out face, its jaws clamped down on its own tail, its beady glass eyes pleading with me for help.

"Did your mother get home?" Grandpa Joe growled.

"Yes, Grandpa" I said. "She's in the kitchen."

Grandpa lit a cigar, filling the air with cherry-scented smoke, and looked warily out into the amber shade beneath the pines. "You still like hiding out here in the sticks with the wild Indians and the goyim?"

"We're not hiding, Grandpa," I laughed. "We're staying away from polio. And there are no Indians anymore."

Grandpa liked to kid me about the Indians, but it wasn't really funny.

"Polio is only in the swimming pools. You can stay on dry land." Grandpa looked up into the trees, then scowled at Arthur's car with its road dirt and faded paint job. "And, who belongs to that jalopy?"

"Uncle Arthur and Aunt Dorothy are here, too," I said.

A dark look crossed Grandpa's face. "Never mind those pinkos." He gestured dismissively at the car and came toward me, the cigar clamped in his teeth, arms spread wide. "Who's my best girl?"

I stepped forward to accept the honor. Grandpa Joe continued to approach, his jacket open, his gleaming watch chain encircling his vested stomach like the equator. I let myself be taken into the cloud of his cigar and be scratchily kissed. Then Grandma enclosed me in her fussy hug, all cologne and floral-scented face powder.

"She's too busy to come out and say hello?" Grandpa grumbled.

"She doesn't know you're here yet, Grandpa," I said, accustomed to running interference for my parents. I knew I was Grandpa's best girl by default. At some point my mother had fallen from grace because of her meshugeneh, crazy politics, and because it was her idea that we move out to the sticks in Goshen.

"Joe," Grandma prompted, "show her the present."

"Come, look what I have in the machine for you, Sara." Even the two simple syllables of my name, which had also been his mother's name, too, worked their way from his throat, around his cigar, and emerged in a rough tsimmes of Russian, Yiddish, and English.

He led the way back to the trunk of "the machine," which is what he called each of the Nashes he bought new every three years. He unlocked the trunk, and I waited eagerly for my gift to be revealed.

One of Grandma's schmatte tablecloths was wrapped around a small television set of blonde burl wood with a round five-inch screen and a gold ring aerial attached to the top. "It's a Philco," Grandpa announced proudly.

My subversive joy was mixed immediately with dread. Grandpa and Grandma had a big Motorola console in their house, with the works—radio, phonograph, and television screen—but in our house, television was anathema. Libby said television was a corrupting, commercial influence and, so far, she'd refused to allow even one small TV to cross our threshold.

I gazed into the Philco's milky, gray-white screen and felt its allure of delicious hours spent in front of it.

I helped Grandpa carry the Philco inside, where the smell of bacon still hung in the air, and we set it down in the living room on Libby's prized Noguchi coffee table. Grandpa wrinkled his nose in disgust and quickly lit up a fresh cigar. He strode among the modern furniture Libby had scrimped and saved to buy—molded plywood chairs, the teak and walnut pieces, and a Herman Miller bench—squinting at them as if they were animals in a zoo.

He stopped in front of the Nelson love seat, made up of brightly colored, marshmallow-shaped leather pads on a wrought iron frame, for which he reserved special contempt.

I sat down on one of the leather pads and bounced up and down. "Look, Grandpa," I said, patting an adjoining cushion, "It's really comfortable. Come try it."

Grandpa shook his head. "It's not safe. What do I tell you, Rosie? In this house, there's no place to sit down."

"It's her house," Grandma scolded. "You'll sit down when we get home."

Grandpa Joe went to the piano, his cigar clenched in his teeth, and struck a single loud note with his thick middle finger. "When are you going to play for us, Sara?"

"Next time. I promise," I said. In ascending to best-girl, I'd unfortunately also become Grandpa's great new hope for the piano, since Libby hardly played anymore. To avoid having to do a command performance, I hurried them on through the house and outside.

Hank intercepted us as we stepped onto the lawn. "Hi, Pop. Hi, Ma. You remember Arthur and Dorothy."

Grandpa Joe acted as if he didn't even see Arthur's hand extended for him to shake. He walked quickly past him to the outer edge of the lawn and peered sourly out into the woods. Poor Arthur put his ignored hand in his pocket, pulled out a bandana and began to polish his glasses.

"I can't believe you chose this god-forsaken place," Grandpa said, as if he were speaking to the trees.

"Don't forget, Pop," said Hank. "Once this was the frontier of the America you love so much. The first people, besides the Indians, were also immigrants from the old country. They cut down the trees, built the stone walls, planted crops, pastured their flocks, and practiced democracy in that meeting house down in the center of town."

Grandpa blew cigar smoke into the air.

"Our people busted out of Catherine the Great's Pale of Settlement," Hank went on, suppressing a smile, "where she wanted to hem us all in. We crossed the ocean, came to these shores, and landed in Mattapan, continuing a direct line out to Goshen where houses are still popping up in the woods like mushrooms."

"You talk nonsense," Grandpa said.

I pictured my pioneer grandpa in a racoon hat with a striped tail, like the ones that were all the rage with the kids at school. I had to smile.

"And luckily," Hank laughed, directing the rest of his speech to Arthur and Dorothy, "grumpy old Mr. Tooey, who owns most of the land around here, despised his neighbors enough to sell some of it off to me!"

All I knew about Mr. Tooey was that he was mean. He wore a beat-up felt hat and farmer's overalls, lived in a hermit cabin halfway down to the creek behind us, and sometimes came over our back stone wall to scatter corn in our yard for the pheasants and their chicks.

Hank said it was his way of reminding us that our land had once belonged to him and that he still ran things around here.

Grandpa turned suddenly on Hank, "How many wild Indians live out here?"

"If you mean Goshenites, about seven thousand."

"Same as my little town in the Ukraine." A faraway expression crossed Grandpa's face.

"Ah, there you are." Libby burst out the screen door from the kitchen. Had she seen the TV already? She went from Grandma to Grandpa, kissing them on their cheeks. "And on Saturday!"

"We came right after schul," said Grandma.

"I think your Dad was worried about you—afraid you got blown away in the storm," Hank told Libby.

"As you can see," Libby said, doing a little curtsy, "we survived."

Grandpa paced the lawn like Napoleon, a shortened cigar clenched in his mouth. "So, what are these Reds doing out here on the frontier? Making plans to throw over this beautiful country? Maybe you're sitting shiva for Uncle Stalin. Maybe you're in Philbrick's book, too?"

I cringed. "These reds" were Arthur and Dorothy. Sometimes Grandpa dropped the word like a bomb, an insult. I knew who Stalin was, more or less, but I had no idea what "book" Grandpa was talking about, when he was practically illiterate in English. I'd heard the name, Herb Philbrick, who was a stool pigeon, although *that* was a bird I didn't know.

"We're Progressives, Pop." Hank pulled Libby close beside him. "Believe me, nobody here is in mourning for Joseph Stalin."

"He was a bum," Grandpa growled.

"Your grandfather," Hank said, looking at me, but for the benefit of Arthur and Dorothy, "is so conservative, he voted against Roosevelt the second time! And the third time."

"I don't go for nonsense about unions or special privileges for schwartzes," Grandpa said.

"He says that word just to make me crazy." Libby broke away from Hank, turned sharply on her rope heels, and headed into the kitchen, letting the screen door slam.

"Pop!" Hank pleaded. "You know that kind of language upsets Libby. And it's not healthy for Sara to hear either."

Schwartze meant "black" in Yiddish, the language my grandparents spoke with one another. But it was a slur, and my parents wouldn't have it.

Grandpa paid no attention. He was studying our roof. "It's my constitutional right." Grandpa Joe shook a finger in the air. "I'm an American citizen now. Freedom of speech. I can say what I want."

"You can't yell fire in a crowded theater," I said.

Grandpa gave me a puzzled look. "What is she talking about?"

"You have the right," Hank said. "But remember, *your* Declaration of Independence says all men are created equal, and *your* Supreme Court just said we have to treat everybody equally."

"What do they know?" Grandpa Joe spit out the words. "A bunch of goyim in choir robes."

"What about Justice Frankfurter?" I said, feeling Grandpa had gone too far and wanting to show I knew something about the government, too.

"Never mind him," said Grandpa, waving his hand like he was batting away a mosquito.

Grandma struggled out of her chair. "I'll go help her get something to eat."

"Don't worry, Rosie," Grandpa called after her. "They can get it for free from a collective farm." With that, Grandpa went down to the badminton court, he said, to look around.

Although I was used to the ongoing battle between Grandpa Joe and Libby, I was beginning to worry that maybe I was old enough now to speak up and argue with Grandpa about Reds and schwartzes, to stand up for what we—Libby, Hank, and I—believed.

Grandpa's gold watch chain caught the sun, and I imagined what it would be like not to be his "best girl" anymore, not to have Grandpa and Grandma as my back-up, my refuge, in case anything ever happened to *my* parents.

Grandpa's body in his dark suit was framed against the pines. Once I'd asked Hank how Libby had come from her short, round parents. His answer was that in the old country people often didn't have enough to eat, but in America where there was plenty of food, their children's generation grew strong and tall.

Libby had added, "Yes, and when you take two undernourished teenagers out of a god-forsaken, muddy, Polish village, send them in steerage to America, and tempt them with perfume, face powder, shiny new cars, and cigars—what you get is the petty bourgeoisie."

Grandpa strolled back. He stood at the edge of the lawn and gazed out toward our property line marked by a low fieldstone wall. "What's a kid supposed to *do* out here with nobody to talk to?" he thundered.

Hank winked at me. "Oh, Sara knows how to entertain herself. She knows these woods like a regular Sacagawea."

"Lucky we brought 'er a television," Grandpa said.

Hank's eyes darted toward the kitchen. "Pop," he said quietly, "you know Libby—we—don't approve of television."

"It's the future," Grandpa said. "Half of America has one." He pointed up to the roof. "Your aerial will go right up there next to the chimney." My eyes followed his finger up to the chimney Hank had built using the blue green stone from the excavation for the house.

Hank collapsed onto a lawn chair. "Pop," he said, "we're not about to put an ugly antenna up there."

Arthur patted Hank on the back. "There's nothing you can do. Your father-in-law's got hold of the American dream like it's some golden pigskin. He's running like hell down field with it, and nobody's going to stop him."

Libby burst out the kitchen door. "It's not staying!"

My heart sank. She'd seen the Philco.

Grandpa turned on Libby. "With no TV, how would we know they finally took care of those Jewish traitors with the electric chair?"

I was shocked. As much as I loved Grandpa, it was cruel to rub it in about the Rosenbergs. He must know they were innocent victims. The Rosenbergs were brave. They'd refused to betray their consciences and their principles.

Libby glared at him. "The government had its Jewish prosecutors and its Jewish judge. Up to the last minute, rabbis were pleading with the prison authorities to execute them *before* the scheduled time, to get it over and done with before sundown, so their execution wouldn't befoul the sabbath." She bit the edge of her lip and turned to go back into the house.

"They betrayed the beautiful country that took us in," Grandpa called after her.

Libby turned on the doorstep. "Ethel resisted to the end. She refused to die on time for them, even after three two-thousand-volt jolts. It took a fourth one to kill her at 8:16 p.m. Three minutes *after* sundown. She showed those rabbis."

The image of a defiant Ethel Rosenberg slowly, painfully "frying," as I'd heard it called, left me limp with horror.

"They deserved what they got," Grandpa said. "They were traitors."

"You have no idea what you're talking about," Libby said, seething, her hands clenched. "And don't forget to take that *thing* with you when you leave."

"She's always been meshugeneh," Grandpa fumed. "From now on, Rosey, we don't come to this house. They want to see us, they'll come to us." Pulling a fretting Grandma Rose along by the arm, he stormed through the breezeway, through the house, and out the front door which closed with a bang.

The Nash was rolling slowly around the loop of the driveway by the time I ran across the driveway circle, dodging trees and rhododendron bushes. I positioned myself at a spot where they would have to pass me and would have to say goodbye.

As their big green bathtub of a car lumbered closer, Libby appeared beside me, out of breath, with the Philco in her arms. She stepped in front of the approaching Nash and stood, head cocked, defiant, flushed, and beautiful.

The machine lurched to a stop. She stepped around to the driver's side. "I'm putting it in your trunk," she told Grandpa and carried the TV around to the back of the car.

Grandpa glared over his cigar at me. "So, you agree with *her*? That the Rosenbergs are heroes, not traitors? That schwartzes aren't schwartzes? That TV is no good?" The end of his cigar was red hot.

Fear washed over me. Maybe he was angry at me, too. I couldn't lose them. Where would I go if the government someday took Hank and Libby away and electrocuted *them*?

From behind the car, Libby called, "The trunk is locked. Sara, get the key from your grandfather."

Grandpa smiled at me. "Come on, girl, what do you say? You're old enough to have your own opinion."

I couldn't speak, pulled in one direction by my fear of alienating Grandpa and Grandma and in the other by my parents and their noble beliefs.

"And, Sara, don't enjoy too much the taste of trayf," Grandpa said slyly, referring for the first time to the bacon. With that, he let up on the brake, and the Nash resumed its slow creep down the driveway, leaving a silently fuming Libby and me and the Philco in its exhaust.

As Grandpa and Grandma and the Nash disappeared up Guernsey Road, Libby marched the rest of the way down the driveway with the TV in her arms and set it down in the weeds by the road where the people who collected trash would pick it up the next time.

Next day, in the wee hours of the morning, when all was dark except for a half-moon that lit up the trees in the driveway circle, I crept down to the road. The little TV reflected moonlight from its round glass screen. Torn as I was, there were whole other worlds inside that little blonde Bakelite cabinet, and I wanted to know them.

I picked the Philco up out of the weeds and lugged it up the driveway to my room. I wiped the cabinet and screen off with a towel and buried it behind the hanging clothes and junk on the floor of my bedroom closet.

CHAPTER TWO

Hank, Libby and I lazed over the Sunday papers, sitting at our chartreuse Formica kitchen table—a color Hank joked didn't exist in nature, forgetting what I'd told him. The female painted bunting is a startling yellow-green, although she's dull compared to the multicolored male. They're only found far south from here.

The telephone on the wall rang once, rang again, and then stopped.

"Who's that?" asked Hank from behind the sports pages.

"I don't know," Libby said. "There've been some peculiar noises on the phone lately and hang-ups, too."

"That's what you get with these rural party lines," Hank said.

I put down the comics pages. "That was for me. Two rings means Mary's back from Mass and getting changed. She and I are going birdwatching at the college today. She'll ring again when she's ready, and then I go meet her."

"Ah, so it's your secret code," Hank said.

They returned to the paper, and I went to my room. I pulled on an old, red-checked flannel shirt of Hank's I liked to wear on rambles in the woods, grabbed the binoculars, my bird guide and notebook, and went back to the kitchen to keep my parents' company until I could leave.

"So," Hank said, "the gruesome twosome is off on an expedition, eh? But are you allowed to go in there? Doesn't the college have no-trespassing signs posted?"

"Mary says the Jesuits don't care, as long as you don't leave anything but footprints."

"I'm sure these nature jaunts are good for you," Libby said, her eyes still on the paper. "As long as you don't go alone. Mary does seem like a smart, fine young girl."

"Yes," I said. "I'll be with Mary."

"Just be back before dark," Libby said.

I was still fidgeting and waiting for Mary's call, when Libby remarked to Hank, as if I'd already left, "Ted Bramhall was telling me there are some books they've removed from the high school library because somebody, maybe the school board, considers them improper."

She paused. "He agrees with me that there might be enough people in town who would agree that censorship is undemocratic, and that we should try to get them reinstated."

Ted Bramhall was *Mr.* Bramhall to me, my English and social studies teacher. Soon after we'd moved to Goshen, and Libby started teaching civics at Goshen High, Mr. Bramhall and his wife, Amanda, had become friends with Libby and Hank. They were of "like minds," Libby said.

I prayed for Mary's signal to come soon. The idea that Libby and one of my teachers might work together on anything, but especially something controversial, unsettled my stomach.

"But mi pasionaria," Hank said, "I thought we moved to Goshen for a little peace and quiet. Pasionaria was the pet name he sometimes called her. He'd once explained it was the nom de guerre of some heroine from the Spanish Civil War, famous for saying: "It's better to die on your feet than live on your knees."

This was exactly the kind of sentiment, especially when connected with Libby, that scared me.

Hopefully, like it so often was when something happened to stir Libby up, Hank with his tongue in his cheek would be able to calm her down about the books.

"Just think about it," Libby said. "You can't get Hemingway, Steinbeck, or even Huckleberry Finn in any of Goshen's school libraries now."

Hank folded the newspaper and picked up his coffee cup. "I forget, what's supposedly wrong with Huckleberry Finn?"

"They say it's un-American," Libby said, "to have Huckleberry Finn and Jim be friends. And Steinbeck sympathized with migrant workers, and Hemingway, of course, drove an ambulance for the republican side in Spain."

"That's ridiculous and it's bad for you kids, too," Hank said, turning to me. "Steinbeck was always good for a last-minute book report, as I recall."

"I don't mind longer books." I was busy rearranging some refrigerator magnets. The telephone rang. Finally. "Okay, I'm leaving," I said.

I grabbed the binoculars and notebook, closed the kitchen door quietly, and tore across the back yard, afraid they might change their minds about letting me go. Passing my bird cemetery, I climbed over the stone wall that marked our lot, then past Mr. Tooey's little green house, which looked like it was thatched with dry pine needles and skidded down the steep decline into the glen.

The water in the creek was low, and it was easy to step from hummock to slithery stone, then back up the other side to dry ground. I clambered up the hill, dashed across another open pasture, and came out onto Merriam Street. I had to cross the Boston and Maine train tracks at a place where, a week before we moved to Goshen, an entire family in a car had been wiped out by a train. The signal was out that day.

I checked up and down the tracks where heat phantoms of the dead family sometimes hovered above the rails, and darted across, anxious to find Mary.

Mary O'Reilly became my first and best friend in Goshen, when she came up to me on our first day of home economics class. She introduced herself, and told me how much she despised cooking and sewing. We ate lunch together at school that day, and every day after that. Later, when we both got our periods, they synchronized after two months.

Mary liked birds, too. She'd promised for a long time to take me birdwatching at the college, a Jesuit seminary on a hundred-and-fifty acres. Today was the day.

Why birds, you might ask. My interest in birds began as an escape from practicing the piano. I'd sit at the keyboard of Libby's old Chickering Baby Grand, trying to concentrate. Libby almost never played herself, but she was often after me to practice. She'd been accomplished on this very piano when she was young, and a couple of years ago, she'd enlisted her childhood duet partner, Muriel, to be my piano teacher.

From my perch on the piano bench, my focus on the sheet music would wobble, then stray out to the wall of our picture windows, out through the tree branches, and down the pine-covered slope. There was so much life going on out there.

Beginning then, I watched the birds—the wrens, white-breasted nuthatches, black-capped chickadees, flickers, red-headed woodpeckers, blue jays, and yellow-bellied sapsuckers, which actually do suck tree sap from holes they drill in trees. I knew this because on my birthday, my parents had given me my own copy of *Peterson's Guide to Eastern Birds* and a pair of Zeiss binoculars, in spite of my grandparents' private ban on German products.

Mary sat waiting for me on a low wall that marked the perimeter of the college land along Merriam Street. With her knees drawn up under her chin and one of her brothers' gray sweaters stretched down over her legs, she looked like one of the gray squirrels that stole food from my bird feeders.

Mary had the habit of biting her fingernails, had reddish hair and freckles, and was as gawky in her shorter, plumper way, as I was in my taller, skinnier, dark-haired way. She was Catholic, though "lapsed," as she said, and was, like me, in the grip of a need to escape her parent's scrutiny and mind control.

When she saw me coming, Mary released the gray sweater and sprang from the wall. Her blonde-orange hair was the color of the turned maple leaves around us. "I have to be home no later than four o'clock to practice," she announced as we got closer and fell into lockstep along the edge of the road.

"Big Patrick said we should be on the lookout for the pig farm in our wanderings. Nobody knows whether the seminarians slop the pigs or if the pigs have gone completely feral, but one way or the other, the priests get their bacon and their Easter hams."

Mary loved to mimic Big Patrick's way of talking, and I felt a certain pride that Mary had started referring to her dad by his first name, even adding epithets. Like my parents, Mary's parents made her study music, in her case, the violin. The difference was she loved the violin and practiced, not only to avoid a "good licking," but for its sheer pleasure.

In my house, of course, there was no corporal punishment. Spanking children was a relic from an earlier stage of historical development when children were economic assets and valued primarily for the labor they could provide. So said my parents.

I winced at the memory of the clink of Big Patrick's belt buckle, the first time I'd been invited to the O'Reillys' for supper. He'd noisily undone his belt right there at the table as a warning to Mary's misbehaving older brother, Pat, who dared to take a bite of food before grace.

I wondered what it would be like to have a good "thrashing" hanging over my head, instead of the impossible aura of "goodness" that prevailed in my house.

Two brick gothic buildings of the college stood on a hill overlooking acres of woods, fallow fields, little ponds, and one large, five-acre pond, an apple orchard, a collapsed barn or two, and, somewhere, the ruins of an old pig farm.

Mary led the way along the sandy shoulder of Merriam Street, bordered by goldenrod and fallen leaves, until we arrived at a break in the stone wall that led into the network of paths, kept open all year round by the seminarians who walked long distances, praying and meditating. A rusty chain hung between two iron posts on either side of the entrance path, with dangling metal signs reading, Private Property. Entry Prohibited. No Hunting.

A gray '49 Plymouth—I knew my car-makes then the way I knew my bird species—heading in the direction of Goshen Center. It passed us, then slowed and pulled over to the side of the road, fifty feet beyond us. Two men, one tall and slim, the other shorter and stout, both wearing dark suits and fedoras, climbed out.

"City people," I said to Mary, "out for a Sunday drive." We often saw them on weekends, with every seat in the car filled, the kids making faces out the back window.

The two of them took off their jackets, threw open the car's hood, and peered in. When they noticed us, the taller one, who had draped his jacket over his arm, walked in our direction. "Say, ladies," he called out, as he came closer, "maybe you can help us out. How far into the center of town?"

Mary held up two fingers. Her parents must have warned her not to talk to strangers. Mine had never instructed me on the issue, although they tended to take the good Samaritan approach to strangers in distress. People were put on this earth to help one another.

The tall guy next loosened his tie and pushed his hat back from his forehead, gleaming with sweat. "You ladies live around here?"

Mary and I shrugged at one another.

"Just asking." He jerked his thumb back towards the car. "Looks like we're gonna need somebody to take a look at the car." He smiled at each of us in turn, taking what felt like a few extra moments to study me. The extra scrutiny stuck with me, maybe because I was new to the feeling of being looked at as a female, feeling the thrill and the fear that went with it.

"Anyway," the tall guy continued, "we'll just sit here a while. If nobody comes along pretty soon, I guess we'll just have to walk into town and find a service station—which you informative ladies say is two miles up this way, right?" He squinted into the sun. "Hope something's open today. It's a nice day at least."

"Tony's is open every day," I volunteered, which I knew because Hank had plenty of car trouble with the Heap, which is what we called the junky old 1935 Ford with a rumble seat, which he used sometimes as a truck. I came close to offering to run back to my house to get Hank to help, but out of selfishness, I didn't.

If Hank and Libby saw me back so soon, they might change their minds about letting me out of the house with men on the loose. The guy tipped his hat and turned back to the car. "You ladies mind your Ps and Qs today, okay?"

By the time Mary and I approached the chain across the entrance path, the two men were sitting on the running board of their car, smoking, apparently in no big hurry to be on their way.

"That was weird," I said, stopping at the chain.

"It was," Mary agreed.

"Forgive us our trespasses," I intoned to the signs in our way, a phrase from the Lord's Prayer we recited every morning in school.

"It's alright," Mary said. "The priests don't care." She jumped over the chain. She crossed herself—forehead, heart, left, right—and laid her fingertips in solemn benediction on my brow. "Now we're absolved from trespassing, anyway—and you, for talking to strangers."

I crossed myself ineptly and stepped over the chain after her.

Mary jogged ahead of me, down the entrance way that soon turned from tire ruts into a narrow, wooded trail. The deserted path, still littered with twigs and branches downed by a recent storm, was arched by oak and maple saplings, aflame with sunlight filtering through the pines.

"All this belongs to *them*?" I said.

Mary turned around. She puffed herself up and pinched her mouth to do Big Patrick in an Irish brogue, complete with flicking an invisible cigar. "We Catholics love our whiskey and our politics, we do, but we also have quite the nose for real estate. Bleedin' Yankees can call us upstarts and dumb micks, but the archdiocese owns more land in wee Goshen than anyone else."

I chimed in with my impression of Mary imitating her father. "St. Annie's wee steeple rises straight up, smack in the center of town, higher than all the others, giving the bloody finger to the Yankee Protestants who look down their noses at the Papists."

"That's a pretty good Big Patrick." Mary laughed her crackle of a laugh.

I was flattered, but also a little worried. If that's what the Protestants in Goshen thought of Catholics, I hated to think what they thought of Libby, Hank and me, the only Jews, as far as we knew, in town. These were not misgivings I ever shared with my parents. To them, all prejudices were wrong, and shouldn't be compared to one another—as in, which group had suffered the most?

We moved deeper into the woods, crossing a crumbling stone wall and an unused pasture, then, picking up the path again, back into sun-dappled trees. In the sprays of sunlight, particles from the maple leaves underfoot floated up in the air like gold bubbles in water. In the gilded light, objects appeared as hazy, eerie, half-seen mirages. Magical things, even ghosts, seemed possible here, even the presence of something or somebody like "God," silently watching.

I moved my arms as if swimming underwater. Mary followed, and we swam together, taking turns leading, then following, through imaginary depths. Somewhere, a bird was alternately whistling and singing. It was a wood thrush.

We didn't see him at first, but then spotted him thrashing in the dead leaves, on the hunt for insects and grubs. My bird guide said the male thrush could sing in harmony with himself because he has two voice boxes. We stopped so I could record the sighting in my notebook.

Someone or something was coming along the path from the other direction. I reached for Mary's arm. "It's okay," Mary whispered. "There aren't any wild animals out here."

A young man, blond and dressed completely in black, was coming toward us, his stride smooth and easy in the amber light. His lips moved and his eyes, behind small, frameless glasses, were cast down at the pages of a small book he held open in both hands in front of him. With each step he kicked the hem of a long black garment away from his ankles.

I stepped in behind Mary to make way for him. As he passed us, his straight blond hair caught the sun, and his face, which was otherwise pale, showed a red flush on his cheeks. I saw that he was handsome, like a Greek statue, or a Christmas angel.

He never looked up.

"Good afternoon," said Mary in annoyance when he was already too far down the path to hear.

"Aren't they allowed to talk?" I whispered.

"Of course. He can stop praying for two seconds to say hello," Mary scoffed. "He's just a snob. And frus-*trated*, I bet you. Probably he can't stand to even look at a girl now."

"We're trayf to him, right?"

"Traduction, s'il vous plait," said Mary, who was good in French, the best in our class.

"Trayf means not kosher, or not in accordance with Jewish dietary laws," I replied. "My Grandma Rose says it means 'poison'." I probably knew five words in Yiddish, my people's language. I knew Catholic priests were celibate, too, and was stirred by the newly dawning idea of being forbidden fruit.

"At least we're not choosing of our own free will to be virgins the way he is," Mary laughed.

"A boy can be a virgin? Why do priests wear those skirts?"

"Sure, a boy can be a virgin. It just means he hasn't—you know—done it with a girl. And that skirt of his is a cassock. They're wool and scratchy to mortify the flesh." Mary's face flushed under her freckles. "To punish them for forbidden urges."

"They have forbidden urges?" I murmured.

"Of course. When you see a cute guy like that, don't you get a funny feeling?" Mary threw her head back, closed her eyes. "I have forbidden urges all the time when I'm around my brothers' friends. Of course, they won't even look at me."

I pictured Mary's rambunctious brothers and their friends, being shooed out of the O'Reilly kitchen by their mom, Annie O., snapping her dishtowel. I felt nothing. I wanted to feel what Mary said she felt.

I was also afraid. It was almost comforting that she and I were still the only two remaining girls in our grade who showed almost no outward signs of maturing. Between us—Mary with her baby fat and I, already too tall—we had none of the kind of curves we were supposed to be acquiring.

"How do you know about—the urges?" I asked cautiously.

Mary laughed. "I've known about wicked urges since first grade catechism class. Catholic kids learn about mortal sin before we even feel anything we shouldn't. People say they're naked under the cassocks like Adam and Eve." Mary flashed her wicked girl smile.

"A good Catholic girl shouldn't even think about that," I teased her.

"I'm lapsed, remember?"

Mary questioned everything about Catholicism, to the dismay of her parents who, despite Big Patrick's occasional cracks about the priests, were loyal laity of the church. Annie O. had even once considered becoming a nun, and Mary's grandmother had hoped Big Patrick would go into the priesthood. Luckily for Mary, one of her mother's sisters and one of her father's brothers had devoted their lives to the church.

For me, even the thought of Mary never being born gave me an awful, lonesome feeling. "Maybe *I* should become a Catholic," I said.

"Oh, sure," Mary said. "Why would you want to be Catholic?"

"Then I'd have somebody up there in the sky telling me what to do. I'd have freckles—and brothers, or at least a sister or two, for company."

"I don't recommend it," said Mary. "But if you do decide to convert, you can have my place in heaven. I won't be needing it. I have a feeling I'll be going to the other place."

I couldn't understand how Mary, who was the smartest, best person I knew, actually believed in heaven and hell. Didn't she see that religion was a myth, the "opiate of the people?"

Meanwhile, I was learning about Catholic ideas, and maybe half believing them. Heaven, hell, original sin, redemption, confession, immaculate conception. It all sounded wonderfully fantastic and imaginative.

From what I could see, Judaism, the religion of my grandparents, could never measure up to the liveliness and drama of Catholicism, nor could the absence of religion, which was our faith—Hank, Libby's, and mine.

"Atheists view the world scientifically," I said.

"Catholicism is scientific," Mary answered. "Did you know the seismograph was invented by a priest? The one they have up at the college registers earthquakes from all over the world."

"What about vibrations from nuclear tests?"

"Yes, those, too. We need seismographs, since we and the Russians both have nuclear bombs now."

"And one day those bombs are going to blow us all to smithereens."

"Now, there's a good reason to believe in God," Mary said.

"I guess," said I. "So. Do you believe in God? Really?"

"Do you really not believe in God?" Mary laughed.

"I don't know," I said.

We clambered over a stone wall and moved into darker, denser woods. We walked closer together and spoke in a hush. "Libby wants the books they banned from the libraries put back," I said.

Mary picked up a big stick from the ground and brandished it, as if fending off unseen attackers. "Well, I agree with her, don't you?"

"I just don't want her to make a...spectacle," I grumbled. "She always attracts a bunch of attention to herself. It's embarrassing."

"That's a very immature, selfish attitude, Sara Green," said Mary. "Especially when she's right."

"Well, you don't have a mother like her."

"You're right, I don't. Your mother's an idealist, kind of like the way Jesus was," Mary said.

"I hope she doesn't end up the way he did."

"Touché. But you should be proud of her, not embarrassed."

"Everything she does bothers me," I said.

"If I even *think* of arguing with Annie O., Big Patrick loosens his belt."

"Well, I wish my mother made soup and baked stuff from scratch and would knit and crochet," I said.

"Yah, Annie O. knits—*fiendishly* like Madame Defarge." Mary mimicked the cramped motions of knitting and screwed up her face like the woman who never missed a beheading in *Tale of Two Cities*, which we both had to read in Mr. Bramhall's class.

Mary put down the stick and picked up a pinecone, half-eaten by squirrels, and examined it, saying, "I hope your mother gets those books put back in the library. I want to read *Catcher in the Rye*. It's about a teenager who uses a bunch of bad words. The Church has put it on their list."

"They have a list?"

"It's printed in *The Pilot*."

I shrugged. "Libby believes whatever she reads in *Partisan Review*."

"I wish my mother had gone to college," Mary said.

"I wish mine didn't teach right upstairs in my school and take on every cause she sees. She could stay home and knit me just one tiny sweater. It wouldn't even have to have fancy cable stitches or anything."

"Where's your idealism?" Mary said.

"It skips generations, I guess."

Mary laughed, and then we both laughed. Wind in the pines whispered over a chorus of scolding squirrels, nagging crows, twanging tree frogs and cicadas. A Great Horned Owl, camouflaged in mottled foliage, glided silently down from on high in the trees. It hovered momentarily above us.

We stopped in our tracks, hearts pounding, and lowered our heads, giving the owl time to realize we were too big to carry off. He flew back into the woods. When he was gone, the sight of his predator face and his talons, poised to carry us off by the scruff of our necks, left a chill. We stopped so I could write him down in my notebook.

The path skirted a small pond, just visible through the foliage. About thirty feet across, its surface flecked golden from the sun. On the far side, stood a decrepit cabin, maybe a fishing shack once, with a deck extended out over the water, its dark wood tinged with a green patina of lichen and moss.

The sound of a splash stopped us cold. We crouched down behind some junipers that bordered the path. An animal? A person? Something thrown in? After the splash there was silence.

From behind the bushes, we watched water circles spread from the spot where something or someone had gone in. Light-colored fur—no, wait, human hair darkened by the water—broke the surface, then sank back underneath.

We both recognized him at the same moment. It was our novitiate. We doubled over giggling, shaking silently, holding our stomachs. At a nudge from Mary, I handed her the binoculars just as he resurfaced. He took three long, straight-armed strokes to one side of the pond, then to the other. After another lap, he began making his way out of the water, wincing at sticks and muck near the edge.

His head and shoulders emerged first, hair slicked back, his pale back, his narrow behind streaming with water. Excitement tinged with fear ran through me. He turned in our direction, stretched his arms out to the sun with an ecstatic taking-in of breath.

Mary smiled and handed me the binoculars, but I pushed them away, afraid to see up close what, even in paintings, was covered with leaves. Shivering, our priest stepped up onto the deck of the shack and picked up his glasses from where he'd left them, unfolded them, and put them back on. Then, tender-footed, he went inside the cabin.

Bent over, Mary and I scurried back like rats along the path and retraced our way back.

At the first stone wall, Mary turned, covering her mouth. "You look like you've seen a ghost."

"Wasn't that a ghost?"

"That, my friend, was our seminarian in his birthday suit." Mary danced backwards along the path, grinning back at me. "Oh, that's right. You don't have brothers. I keep forgetting."

I hurried after her, breathing hard. No brothers. No sisters. "Libby says this is no world to bring children into."

"Well, they had *you*, didn't they?" Mary giggled, as we scrambled over a ruined section of the next wall. "Which means Libby and Hank did it at least once."

"Yes," I conceded, although I tried not to imagine that between my parents, as necessary as it might have been to my existence. "Anyway, we're all God's children, right?"

"I guess so." Mary wasn't sure where we were, but we followed a path that took us over more walls, some laced with rusted barbed wire. It was getting late, but we continued wandering so our priest would have plenty of time to leave the woods.

"Okay, now I see where we are, come on," Mary said. The path opened onto a field. After the deep shade of the woods, the sun was blinding and felt warm. We waded through high, silver grass. "Now we'll *both* be going straight to hell," Mary laughed. "We looked upon a man with lust in our hearts."

"Maybe *you* did," I said. But I'd felt something, too, I thought. Lust—just a word I'd read in books until now. I felt it again, a lovely tugging, low and insistent, deep in my body. "Luckily," I added, "we don't have to worry, since there's no such thing as hell."

"Just because your people don't believe in heaven and hell doesn't mean those places don't exist," Mary said cheerfully.

"Even a vengeful, eye-for-an-eye God could see blaming us isn't fair. Our priest knew he was taking the risk of being seen, swimming naked where people sometimes walk," I said. But, I thought, what if one day Mary joined up with her church again?

She said they'd always take you back. She'd go to confession, take communion, do the penances, and be forgiven. Then, if we died, we would go in opposite directions. The thought made me very sad.

"Let's make a pact," Mary said. "Wherever we are when we lose our virginity, we have to call the other one on the telephone, even if it's long distance."

"It's a deal," I said, although it seemed very far off.

The two men with the car were still there when we came out onto Merriam Street. They were still sitting on the running board with their shirt sleeves rolled up, eating sandwiches from waxed paper spread out on their knees, like they were having a picnic. When they saw us, they both got up and walked toward us, with smiles on their faces.

These guys were giving me the creeps. I had the urge to just take off running, but I didn't want to split up. I waited with Mary to see what they would say.

"So," said the tall one, who'd done the talking before, "you ladies finished with your little secret meeting?"

Neither of us answered, it was all so odd.

"Say, Sara," the short one said, looking straight at me. "Maybe you can ask your parents to call this Tony's place when you get home? Looks like all that was wrong is we ran out of gas. Maybe they can bring us some in a can? What do ya say, Sara?"

My heart started to race. He knew my name?

Without waiting for my answer, they both turned and walked back toward their car.

"I don't like them," Mary whispered, as we walked away on the road toward our homes. "How do they know your name?"

"I have no idea," I said and felt a chill of fear.

* * *

"What were you two *doing* out there all this time?" Hank demanded when I burst in the kitchen door, breathing hard from running all the way. "And don't tell me 'nothing.'"

Libby was still in the kitchen, too, still reading, buried now in her copy of the *Partisan Review* which came every month in a brown wrapper.

"I have to call Tony's," I said.

"What for?" said Hank.

"There were these two guys who ran out of gas on Merriam Street right near the path into the college."

"You talked to them?" Libby asked, looking up.

I opened the Goshen phonebook, which was only about an inch thick, to look up the number for Tony's.

"What did they look like?" Hank asked. Libby was listening and looking intently at me.

"They were city slickers," I said. "They had suits and hats like they were on their way back from church or something. One was pretty tall and skinny, the other kind of short and round. They wore those felt hats. They were just too lazy to walk into town, I guess."

Hank's face darkened. "Sounds like Mutt and Jeff from the funny papers."

"What kind of car were they driving?" asked Libby.

"A 1949 gray Plymouth sedan," I said and began to dial the phone. "They knew my name," I added.

Hank jumped up from his chair, took the phone receiver roughly out of my hand, and hung it up. "Let them find their *own* way downtown," he said, as he and Libby exchanged a look.

CHAPTER THREE

I rested my head against the rain-spattered window of the overheated Trailways bus, focused on the thick folds of skin on the back of Mac the driver's neck, and settled in for the forty-five-minute trip to Boston. In yellow slicker and rubber boots, I was headed to my first piano lesson after summer vacation.

Most teenagers in Goshen didn't ride the bus alone into the city. Goshen was small and rural and, for most kids, self-contained. Libby, though, said taking public transportation developed street smarts and opened you up to the wider world. Although she did instruct me to sit right up front, close to the driver.

Mac, who drove the Wednesday-three-o'clock into town, as well as the six-o'clock outbound, smiled at me in his rearview mirror as he muscled the big silver and blue bus out onto the Old Post Road. "So, did'ya have a good summer, dolly?"

"It was okay," I admitted. "I added quite a few birds to my list." I knew enough not to bring up the Rosenbergs, whose fate had been the big news of the summer at our house.

"If memory serves me," Mac said, "the real question is: did'ya practice the piano over the summer?"

"I refuse to answer on the grounds of my fifth amendment rights against self-incrimination."

Mac laughed into the mirror. "I'll take that as a no," he said, as he sped up to pass a slow-moving school bus, dawdling along and spewing smoke.

Dark and somber trees, mostly stripped of their leaves, flicked by. Rain drumming on the windshield and the wipers set up a soothing rhythm. Most of my fellow passengers were already dozing.

Muriel Rubin had taken me on as a piano student as a favor to Libby. She and Libby had grown up in the same neighborhood, walked to school together, and attended Miss Lubbett's Music School together, after regular school. For some reason, Muriel, who had never married, and my mother had drifted apart. They'd spoken only infrequently over the years.

"Your mother was gifted and very accomplished," Muriel told me at my first lesson, imagining this would encourage me. "She had wonderful technique," she said wistfully. "I'm sure you can hear it when she plays."

I nodded ambiguously. I knew Libby was good, but I'd only heard her on rare occasions when she mistakenly thought no one else was in the house. So far, I hadn't told Muriel that Libby didn't play anymore. It felt like tattling.

This would be Libby's third year of trying to make me into a serious music student. She'd begin each fall with gentle prodding. By Hallowe'en she'd be writing out elaborate schedules for me to fit piano practice in amongst breakfast, school, dinner, and homework—fifteen minutes here, fifteen minutes there. By spring, both of us would be longing for the summer break.

The giant neon City Service sign was my signal, high above Kenmore Square, perpetually filling, then erasing, bright Kelly-green lines. We had arrived in Boston proper. It was almost dark. My stop was next, at Mass. Ave., a wind-blown corner off the Charles River, where a bundled-up policeman stood upon what looked like a garbage can painted white, directing traffic with elbow-high white gloves. "Maa—ss Avenue!" Mac called out.

I pulled up the hood of my slicker and stepped down from the bus.

"Don't take any wooden nickels, dolly," Mac called after me.

"I won't."

I faced an eight-block gauntlet of the darkening city in the rain. People struggled against the wind, hunched over and gripping their umbrellas. Gross things flowed in the street gutters. Rain spilled off the buildings in sharp driplines.

There wasn't anything to be afraid of, really, but even in good weather, when the days were longer and the city sparrows and pigeons were out and about, that stretch of Massachusetts Avenue seemed long and bleak.

As light faded, vague and threatening things popped up in my peripheral vision, in the darkened storefronts and swirling in the eddies of water I had to cross. Several blocks farther along the avenue loomed the Fenway Theatre, its grand marquis studded with unlit milk-white bulbs, overhanging a marble plaza stretching out to the street.

It was four-thirty. The early show, *From Here to Eternity*, wasn't on until seven o'clock, but I caught sight of a small figure, propped against the dark ticket kiosk. It was a man without any legs, sitting like a doll in empty trousers, holding a cardboard sign: Pencils, 5¢.

I was appalled by the sight of a person with no legs. There was still time to avoid him. All I had to do was turn around, go back to the previous traffic light, and continue walking on the other side of the street. He was like a troll under a bridge, keeping me from the green grass on the other side, even though the grass was a piano lesson I hadn't practiced for.

Out of some sudden desire to be a braver, better person, I resisted the temptation to retreat and made myself continue forward until I was on the theater's marble plaza. In that moment, my troll came to stand for all the unfortunate and wounded of the world. These were people familiar to me mostly by way of my parents' dinner-table conversations.

Misfortune had obviously touched this man, and he was asking so little of me. I'd wanted desperately to avoid him, but he suddenly became a test of my goodness. My revulsion served as punishment for being the over-protected, skittish, and now, uncharitable child that I was.

The steady sound of rain spattering on the hood of my slicker stopped short as I stepped under the marquis. I walked close to the curb, avoiding the spray from passing cars and taxis, but giving my legless nemesis a wide berth. I negotiated with God, offering an extra fifteen minutes of piano practice, before breakfast, if I could pass by him without his noticing me.

I then changed the rules on myself. I had to look straight at him as I passed—at least for a moment. He was obviously harmless. In fact, it was his helplessness and the obscene pictures that came into my head of where exactly his legs had been severed from his body that made this so hard. Focusing down at my boots, I walked quickly and forced myself to raise my chin, turn to the left, and look at him.

As I did, his crusty old voice came to me over the traffic noise: "A nickel for a veteran, little girl?" He held out a fan of yellow pencils. My heart thumping, I faced forward again and sped away, pretending I hadn't heard him.

* * *

Muriel pulled aside the gauze curtain over the glass of her mullioned front door. Her hooded gray eyes were soft as she let me into her Victorian house. Glasses in a breakfront cabinet tinkled from nearby trolley vibrations. There was a grandfather clock and velvet chairs with lace doilies. Muriel, who was only a few years older than Libby already had crepe-papery pale skin.

"It's wonderful to see you, Sara. You've had a relaxing summer, I hope."

I thought she was about to hug me. But no, thank goodness, her smile flickered and then was gone. I was back, back to push the limits of her patience and her old friendship with Libby.

I nodded, but toward Wolfgang, her parakeet in a cage, hanging in a corner of the living room. I heard him rustling fallen seeds on the cage floor and felt a surge of pity. He was so cooped up, only allowed to fly around the kitchen once a week when his cage was being cleaned.

I set my piano books on the music stand. Muriel sat down with perfect posture on a velvet chair at the end of the piano's keyboard. I played some scales and arpeggios, then stumbled through Bach's *Two-Part Invention*, the only piece she'd asked me to practice over the summer.

"Concentrate on playing legato. Make whichever hand carries the melody sing," she said.

Within a few measures it was obvious. The old mistakes, including wrong fingering, remained firmly entrenched. Far from Muriel's advice to practice meaningfully, with care, concentration and enjoyment, I had barely touched the piano all summer.

Muriel's pale hands, the nails clipped to exactly the right length for playing the piano, rested in her lap. Her polite, rose-scented cologne added to the lady-like aura around her.

"Alright," she breathed after I'd struggled through the piece. "Let's try it again, this time at a much slower tempo." She slid the counter-weight of her polished cherrywood metronome higher on the pendulum, which then swung back and forth very slowly and made me think of a time bomb.

My mind drifted to a short story I'd been required to read over the summer in which a rebellious young girl flatly refused to play with a metronome, the difference being that girl was her teacher's very best and favorite student. I played poor Bach through again. Even at a sluggish tempo, fumbled notes, missed accidentals, accumulated like snow on a frozen pond.

As I made my bumpy way along, the air in the room grew heavy with Muriel's—and I imagined Libby's—disappointment. My fingers moved mechanically, but what I heard was the cadence of another misspent year in music, crawling toward spring.

"Sara, dear," Muriel interrupted me in mid-measure. "Let's stop here." She drew a deep, silent breath. "Let's just sit and talk for a minute." She stopped the metronome.

My heart drummed faster. The grandfather clock tolled the half hour, the lesson not even half over. I could hear a trolley car shearing along wet metal tracks out on Commonwealth Avenue, the sweet clanging of their bells softening the sound.

"Maybe you didn't have much time over the summer to practice?" Her attempt to give me the benefit of the doubt made me feel even worse. Was I supposed to fib to preserve Libby's and Muriel's thread-bare friendship? I felt trapped and desperate to be somewhere—anywhere—else. Maybe in the woods listening to birds, who didn't have to practice to get the notes right.

"Actually, I *did* have time," I said, perversely refusing to lie.

"So you *did* practice?" Muriel asked, looking doubtful.

"Well, not exactly. I had the time, but I didn't practice."

"I see." Muriel shifted in her chair to face me. "Sara, dear, I think you know I care for you almost as if you were a daughter."

I looked down at my hands, which carried scratches, chewed nails, and chapped skin from doing the things I preferred to do *rather* than practice the piano.

"The piano has been my life," Muriel said, "but I think we need to face the fact that it may not mean the same thing to you."

"I'm sorry," I murmured.

"No need to apologize. It's partly my fault. Maybe I thought if I could get you to love the piano, I would have passed something on. And your mother! I suppose neither of us wanted to disappoint her." Muriel gave me a mischievous smile.

"I suspect it's harder for me to think of having to 'graduate' you, than it is for you to think of being 'graduated.'"

"Grad-u-ated?" I mouthed the word under my breath.

"Yes," Muriel said softly, "I think, come June, unless things change quite a bit, it's best if we plan to end our lessons."

My heart pounded hard, although I felt relief, too. Being released from what had become a thankless chore should have had me leaping in joy from the piano bench, flinging my sheet music out the window, watching the loose pages blow across the trolley tracks. But I couldn't enjoy the possibility of liberation.

I didn't want to disappoint Libby. "You mean, stop forever?" I said.

"I'm afraid so, yes. Of course, if by chance, you are able to change your… habits," Muriel smiled hesitantly, "then, of course, we could reconsider. That's fair, don't you think?"

"It's fair," I said.

She closed the cover of the metronome, and I couldn't help seeing the resemblance of the polished wooden obelisk to a grave marker. "You know, Libby doesn't really play the piano anymore," I said, adding tattletale to a lengthening list of my character flaws.

Muriel regarded me in silence, broken only by the tinkling of the crystal in the cabinets resonating with the trolley bells from the Avenue. She massaged the top of one hand with the other. "Not even for your father?" she asked. "He used to love to hear her play. It was part of their romance, I think."

"Well, she plays…if she thinks there's nobody else in the house."

"What a shame," Muriel said. "She was good. But, I guess, once your mother started going to college—your grandfather could afford it even in the Depression—she found other more compelling interests. We didn't get together to play anymore. And then, of course, she went to Spain."

"Spain? What was she doing in Spain?"

Muriel's hand fluttered to her mouth, as if she'd spoken out of turn. "Well, she learned some…Spanish, of course."

"Yes," I said, "she wears those funny shoes from there and she cooks Spanish food sometimes."

"Your mother was very interested in Spanish culture…and politics, I guess you could say. *So* interested, she dropped out of college to go there."

"She dropped out of college?" I asked.

"Well, your grandfather didn't want her to go to Spain…and your father and I tried to talk her out of it, but your mother is a determined person.

She went back to college later, though."

"Yes, she is strong-minded," I said. Stubborn, I thought.

The front doorbell sounded. Muriel glanced at her watch, then at me and stood up, signaling the end of our lesson time.

Glimpses of Libby's past, like the one Muriel had just given me always left me hungry for more. I was curious about Libby *before*—Libby before me, Libby before her trouble with Grandpa, Libby before Hank even. One thing was clear. Libby, who was so generous with her opinions about almost anything, was miserly and secretive about the story of her own past.

If I "graduated" this spring, one of my few potential sources of information would be closed off. "I promise to try harder," I told Muriel.

"I'm very glad to hear that." Muriel smiled as if she actually believed me, as she walked me to the door. The rain had let up, and the streets were gleaming and dark, as I made my way back up Mass Ave in a rush to catch the six o'clock. I stepped onto the plaza of the Kenmore Theatre and heard my troll's voice, loud and clear.

"Girlie, hey, girlie. Come on, buy a pencil."

I sped up, then slowed. I made myself turn toward the human sack with the whiskery face, his overseas cap studded with patriotic pins, his mouth spewing condensation into the cool evening air. "Come here." His bony troll finger beckoned me.

I took a step toward him. He stuck out one gloved hand with a fan of yellow pencils, then the other, a gloveless claw ready to take the money. "Only a nickel for one," he croaked.

I reached into my raincoat pocket where I kept my bus fare plus some extra coins, and moved closer, close enough to put a nickel into his hand. I glanced quickly at the place where his legs should have been, then away.

The coin slipped out of my grip, wobbled across the tile, rolled in a miraculously stable course across the marble plaza and jumped the curb into the gutter. I followed it, bent down and, taking off one glove, reached into the dark rushing water to fish it out.

I wiped the coin off on my raincoat and made my way back to him. I pressed the nickel into his cold, grimy palm and, for an instant, our skins touched.

I snatched a pencil and hurried away, half running, to catch my bus. With the pencil secure in my pocket, my little self-test of righteousness passed with shining colors.

CHAPTER FOUR

Immediately after the Pledge of Allegiance and the Lord's Prayer, which I only mouthed, and just as I had almost finished Paul Coleman's algebra homework, ear-splitting electronic horns began blasting in the school corridors. The sounds easily penetrated the thick, metal-clad classroom door. I thought my heart would burst, it started beating so hard.

"That's the three-minute warning," said Mrs. Z., her dark eyes big, her voice breathless, but straining for calm. "It means an attack is imminent. No time to go downstairs to the shelter. Duck and cover immediately. Close your eyes. Cover the backs of your necks with your hands. The flash will be coming in seconds."

Like a flock of panicked Canada geese, with chairs scraping across the floor, choked screams, crying, and praying came from all corners of the classroom, we students scrambled to obey. Even Mary, who sat to my left, was already under her desk, crossing herself in cramped, little motions for father, son, holy ghost.

Bucky, to my right, was trying to stuff his big thick body into the cramped space under his desk. John L., the tallest kid in our class, folded himself like a daddy longlegs to fit under his.

I looked up at the clock and remained where I was, seated at my desk in a daze, not budging.

Mrs. Z., stood at attention at the head of the class, beside her desk. "Duck and cover," she said sternly. "Remember your training."

Our training. In the event of nuclear attack while we were in school, we would hear an alert—a horn blast every ten seconds. We would file down to the school basement where the windows were taped to keep out radioactive fallout, and blankets and food rations were piled against the walls in big blue plastic bins.

But this was a three-minute warning. A nuclear attack was imminent. The next thing we'd see would be the flash of an atomic bomb exploding. And that would be it. We were all going to die. We would all be vaporized. The world was coming to an end. I would die. I 'd never see Libby and Hank again. Or Grandma and Grandpa. Or Mary. Or any bird, or anything, ever again.

"Boys and girls," said Mrs. Z., looking straight at me. "I cannot take shelter myself until you are all safely under your desks."

I was glued to my chair, unable to move. Time had stopped. The horns blasted their honking again.

Our training had included a short film featuring a reckless cartoon monkey dangling a stick of dynamite next to Bert the Turtle in a civil defense helmet, who performed "duck and cover" by withdrawing into his shell.

Even with all the honking, praying and weeping, I felt a strange calm coming over me because Libby and Hank believed that the mutually-assured-destruction theory would save us. We and the Soviets *both* had the bomb. We were like two scorpions in a bottle, circling one another. They were as afraid of nuclear war as we were. Neither country would launch a nuclear "first strike," because, then, everybody dies.

Still, I was afraid. The bleating of the horns was giving me a headache. I waited for the blinding flash. Behind my eyelids, a Russian bomber, with a red hammer and sickle painted on its side, silently opened doors in its fuselage, releasing a bomb, which tumbled down, end over end, and landed at the exact center of Goshen's perfect town green.

A gigantic splash of liquified soil and bright green grass rose, forming a cloud like a gigantic, churning mushroom, vaporizing everything.

I'd seen pictures in the newspaper, the day after Halloween, of a little Pacific atoll called Elugelab, blown to smithereens and swallowed up by the ocean when the US tested the first hydrogen bomb.

"Sara Green," Mrs. Z. hissed from the front of the room. "Get under your desk immediately."

The sky outside the floor-to-ceiling classroom windows was a silent, deep blue; a perfect fall day. I pressed my fingers into my ear canals and stayed as I was.

"Sara!" Mrs. Z. raised her voice between horn blasts. "The sooner you take your position under your desk, the sooner I can take cover myself." She rested the fingers of one long, manicured hand lightly on the front edge of her desk and glared at me.

I understood. The ship was going down, and the captain had to be the last one to abandon it. Now that Mrs. Z. was making me directly responsible for her own survival, I relented. Slowly, very slowly, I pushed my chair back and ducked under my desk. Maybe Hank and Libby were wrong.

"Thank you, Sara," came Mrs. Z.'s edgy voice. I heard her chair roll back as she, too, finally took cover.

The minutes crawled by. No flash came. For the moment, at least, there was no nuclear attack. Hank and Libby were right this time, and this had been just a drill. My heart slowed almost to normal. I closed my eyes. The honking horns continued.

Between their blasts came a rhythmic metallic tapping. It was John L., one row back, bent over under his desk, looking straight at me. His long basketball legs were doubled up under him, like a frog's, and he was tapping on a metal leg of his desk with two pencils, his braces-clad teeth clamped down on his lower lip like a drummer in a jazz band.

"The Commies are coming, the Commies are coming," he sang softly in time with his tapping, apparently for my benefit.

John L. was called "John L." because there were always at least two Johns in every classroom. Mr. Bramhall referred to him as John the Lank, to illustrate the use of an epithet. John L. was famous for his large and sudden growth spurt at the end of seventh grade. He'd become so exhausted, he had to stay home in bed for almost two months.

John L.'s father was a Goshen selectman, who voted the opposite way from my parents on almost every town issue.

"Silence," Mrs. Z. commanded from under her desk. The drumming stopped. I faced front and closed my eyes. Grit on the floor was irritating my bare knees.

Soon, the drumming started up again. I poked my head out into the aisle and looked around. Thinking John L. might still be looking in my direction gave me a melting feeling, laced with excitement. I kneaded a cramp in my right calf.

John L. was watching me with keen, dark eyes. One of his great grandfathers on his father's side was a descendant of Chief Massasoit of the Wampanoag,

Squanto's tribe. His parents didn't like him to talk about that, especially his mother who was a Daughter of the American Revolution.

Now John L. was making odd hand signals in my direction. Could it be Indian sign language? I pulled my skirt down over my knees and, in the process, bumped my head on the underside of the desk.

John L. pointed first at the middle of his chest, then at me. He made the gestures of strumming a guitar. Next, he plucked at the strings of an imaginary bass fiddle. He swayed with eyes half-closed to music in his head. He stretched his arms out into the aisle and pretended to be dancing with a partner.

Then I remembered. If a nuclear bomb wasn't going to wipe us all out today, tomorrow was Saturday night, and the fall junior-high sock hop would take place. Was John L. maybe inviting me to dance with him at the sock hop? A jolt of excitement ignited in me—although the possibility that he, or anyone, had that kind of interest in me came as a shock. I had no idea if this was something I wanted, or something I wanted to avoid at all costs.

The bleating of the horns stopped abruptly, leaving my head still pulsating and my ears ringing. Mrs. Z. emerged slowly from under her desk, straightened her slightly mussed clothing, and began patrolling the aisles. "Even though the alarm has stopped," she said in her Dictaphone voice, "you must remain sheltered in place until Principal Peele gives us the all-clear, which will be three short, regular school bells."

John L.'s crackly, unreliably low laugh came from behind me. He uncoiled, pushed his desk chair back and stood up. He stretched his newly-sprouted six-foot-two-inch frame and groaned with pleasure.

The clicking of Mrs. Z.'s stilettos on the asphalt tile floor stopped short. "John L., get back down immediately. The all-clear has not sounded."

"Since we're all dead," John L. said, with another voluptuous stretch, "why can't we come out of our holes?"

A giggle burst out of me, and I quickly covered my mouth. John L. was being bad. I didn't have his courage, but his defiance was contagious and, of course, I agreed with him. These drills were ridiculous.

I unfurled my numb left leg into the aisle, and prepared to climb out from under my desk, unleashing a storm of pins and needles.

Mrs. Z., coming down my aisle, stopped and glared at my leg, which buzzed painfully as the feeling came back. She was known by the students as "the chicken," because of the way she walked in long, stiff strides on three-inch, patent leather heels in the tight, straight skirts of her shantung "business" suits. She had a "Better Dead than Red" bumper sticker on her car.

"Sara. Let this be a warning to you and some others who don't appear to be taking civil defense seriously. You are being very irresponsible and—" here Mrs. Z. selected her word carefully—"un-patriotic."

Patriotic. The word confused me. Did it mean love of country? I glanced up at the American flag that drooped from a short staff at the corner of the blackboard, to which we pledged allegiance every morning. Is that what patriotic meant? But the country—the government—so often got things wrong. It took people's rights away and was always making or preparing for war. It had killed the Rosenbergs.

How was I supposed to love a country like that? And how could Mrs. Z. know what was in my heart? With Libby's blood flowing in my veins again, I swallowed hard and left my leg exactly where it was, out in the aisle, still tingling, until the all-clear bells sounded.

CHAPTER FIVE

"We're so glad to hear you've changed your mind about going to the school dance," said Libby.

"Sock hop," I corrected her.

"Alright, sock hop." Libby studied me from across the kitchen table. "We could find time for a little shopping trip tomorrow," she said. "Maybe you'd like something new to wear to this …sock hop?"

"Not really," I said. You see, instead of telling them about the bomb drill, which would have given my parents fits, I had announced, as a diversionary tactic, that I wanted to attend the fall sock hop, something I'd flatly refused to do up to now.

Hank stood in front of the open refrigerator, grinning at both of us. "Your mother suffers from occasional eruptions of a retro-bourgeois shopping gene."

"That's not funny," Libby said severely and shot him a look. "And don't pull that just-a-country-boy routine with me. Although your father did grow up on a farm, which he likes to hold over my head sometimes."

"Well, it's true," Hank protested. "The government funded chicken farms for refugees from Europe during the Depression. My parents ignored me and my brothers and sister, while we all took care of the chickens."

"Then you just happened to go to M.I.T.," Libby said dryly.

"I had construction experience, building the chicken coops."

The point was the Green family didn't participate in crass consumerism. Hank's frugality was unquestioned, but Libby did occasionally make an assault on some of the fancy stores in downtown Boston. One of those jaunts appeared likely to happen now.

"We can find something for you to wear to your…sock-hop," Libby said, "and we'll also have a chance to…talk."

That night I barely slept. Shopping trips with Libby, though rare, were ordeals for me due to my extreme self-consciousness. I was emerging from my tomboy stage but was still far from a butterfly. As much as I yearned for time with Libby, I dreaded being out in public with her, playing ugly duckling to her swan.

Bonwit Teller & Co. occupied an old pink brownstone building that had once been Boston's Natural History Museum at the corner of Newbury and Exeter. Life-sized, pigeon-blotched lions slouched on either side of grand, wide steps.

"Do we have to go to such a fancy place?" I whined.

"It's not so fancy," Libby said, taking hold of my arm. She was dressed to the bourgeois nines—flared gray skirt, darker gray cashmere sweater, which she kept in a cedar drawer with mothballs, a charcoal Chanel-style jacket, and black leather pumps, thankfully rope-less.

In one of my slightly snug school skirts, I lagged behind. With a backward glance at the lions, I followed Libby, who mounted the steps and swept through the revolving front door, and across the echoing marble lobby to the elevators.

"Good morning," she said loudly to a white-gloved elevator operator, whose name badge read, "Washington." We stepped into his car. "How is your family, Mr. Washington? I remember you told me your mother had been sick."

"She's better, thank you, Ma'am," he replied in a near whisper. "Your floor, please?"

I wanted to disappear. Libby prided herself on extending common courtesies to those people that many people, as she put it, didn't even see. She was trying to act as if the world already was the way it *ought* to be, but anything that attracted attention was torture for me.

Within seconds of our stepping onto the Young Sophisticates Floor, sales ladies hurried over from three separate directions. "Good morning, madam," the troika of salesladies chirped, almost in unison. I tried to shrink into Libby's shadow.

Giving one of them the nod, Libby swept to the clothing racks, eyes squinty and darting like a military commander surveying a battlefield. She began working her way through the hangers, while I stood by, arms dangling, useless and miserable.

Libby piled skirts and sweaters on one of the saleslady's outstretched arms. When the stack reached the poor woman's chin, we adjourned to the fitting rooms, the real chamber of horrors for me.

On the way, I snatched an aqua felt skirt from a nearby rack. Appliqued on the front was a large white poodle connected by way of a bejeweled leash to an open parasol. "Can I try this, too?" Despite Libby's dubious expression, we took it in with the rest.

Surrounded on three sides by mirrors, I saw only faint hints of the woman I was supposedly becoming. I slipped out of my clothes, an awkward girl-woman, neck too long, feet too big, shoulders too broad. Libby helped me into one after another of the things she'd selected, while saying to the saleslady, crowded into the room with us, that we had chosen.

Libby expertly adjusted the waistbands, zipped the zippers, and cocked her head to study me in the mirror. She bit her lower lip and maneuvered me around by my undefined middle. The touch of her fingernails and her wedding rings was cold on my skin.

When we had made our choices, my poodle skirt remained on its hanger. I slipped into it without her help and looked squarely in the mirror. Even I could see it looked somewhat ridiculous, but I also saw in the silly tableau of glued-on poodle rhinestones a small protest against Libby's dominance, my entrée into mainstream adolescence. I decided it looked fine.

The poodle skirt went into a Bonwit Teller bag, together with a green and black tartan kilt, McGregor clan, and a mint green cashmere sweater.

"Why don't we celebrate with a little ice cream?" Libby said, as we stood at the top of the stone steps, the shopping bag looped over my arm.

"Did you ever go shopping with Grandma?" I asked, bidding the stone lions farewell and looking out over Copley Square.

"Yes," Libby said, "but not around here. In those days, we didn't go very far from our neighborhood."

"Why not?" Sara asked.

"Well, I don't know. Maybe we were a little scared...."

"Of what?"

"Well, I guess we weren't sure we were welcome…the children of immigrants. Our parents worried about acceptance, so we kids did, too, I think."

Hank and Libby had an ongoing debate about which Boston ice cream parlor was the best. Libby, who never had to worry about her weight, preferred Schrafft's. Hank was inclined to Brigham's, which, he said, was more down-to-earth ice cream for the working man. It's where the soda jerks, as soon as Hank walked in the door, started making his chocolate frappe, which he drank to soothe his stomach ulcer.

Cold green marble, high mirrored ceilings, and silver plate utensils, plus the racket of the frappe machines, created a fussy din as Libby and I settled into one of Schrafft's green leather booths. We reached with long-handled silver spoons into a banana split, cradled in an oval bowl between us. "This is nice, isn't it?" said Libby, snagging one of its two maraschino cherries.

She looked across at me with her large, heavy-lidded eyes. Having Libby's full attention—she was so often preoccupied with more important things—felt good, although I was nervous about what "talk" was in store for me.

"By the way," Libby said. "Muriel called me."

"She did?" Uh-oh, I thought. I didn't just want Libby's attention. I wanted her approval. "What did she say?"

"She wanted me to know that you and she agreed that you would stop your lessons if you didn't start practicing. *Did* you agree?"

"Well," I shrugged, "I didn't have a choice."

"You don't enjoy the piano that much, do you?" Libby said.

"I like the piano alright, but practicing is…boring."

"It can be, yes, but it makes it possible to play beautiful music…beautifully."

"But you don't even play anymore, so what was the point for you?"

Libby looked surprised. "Well, it's because I don't have time to practice…. If I can't play it…beautifully, I don't want to play at all." Libby gazed dreamily into the banana split.

"But why did you stop?"

Again, Libby looked taken aback by my questioning. "I'm not sure I can answer that. I think it just happened."

"Did it have anything to do with you going to Spain?" I asked.

"Spain?" Libby looked hard at me. "What do you know about my going to Spain?"

Floundering, I felt like I was swimming now in murky waters and wanted to retreat. "Well, you know. The espadrilles, the Spanish food."

"Well, there weren't a lot of grand pianos floating around over there," she laughed. "Their instrument is more the guitar. But I don't think being there had anything to do with my quitting the piano."

A waitress appeared to fill our water glasses, and Libby took that opportunity to shift the direction of our conversation. "I'm assuming," Libby said, as she slid a spoonful of chocolate ice cream with nuts and chocolate sauce off the spoon with her lips, "your Human Reproduction class already covered it, but I think it's time I said at least something to you about sex."

"Miss Shepard explained everything to us," I said quickly. "At the end of last year."

"She's the physical education teacher, right?"

"Yes, but she teaches Human-Rep, too. She showed us charts and posters and slides…."

"Human-Rep?" Libby said. "Oh, I see…. In my day this talk was called the birds and bees conversation. It was never in school, and your grandmother and I never had it."

I twisted my legs into a pretzel underneath the table, wishing I could melt into the cold leather. Miss Shepard had spent more time in Human-Repclass on proper tooth-brushing technique than anything resembling birds or bees. Still, I knew where babies came from and, more or less, what was required to get one started.

"There are certain biological realities," Libby said. "That men and women make love—have sex—in order to procreate. That is, have babies."

"I know all that," I half-whispered, desperate for this "talk" to be over with.

"I'm glad to hear that," Libby said, undeterred, "but sex is also, you know—" here Libby looked momentarily uncomfortable, but pressed on, "for pleasure."

This statement sent me to deeply exploring the mounds and crevices of the ravaged banana split between us. The second maraschino cherry and some almonds were awash in half-melted ice cream, while chocolate sauce flowed like lava in the crevices, and red juice from the cherries ran like blood over remnants of the banana.

Libby wasn't finished. "We don't have anything to say about the way nature made us. But society has to deal with sex, just like it has to deal with every other aspect of human nature—violence, selfishness, competition and everything else."

The frappe machine roared, and Libby raised her voice to be heard.

"Unfortunately, our society has chosen to ignore the fact that people are animals. It still offers no fool-proof way to prevent unintended pregnancies, nor ways to deal with them if they occur."

I shrank further into the green leather. Until now, the only time sex, pregnancy, or childbirth had even been alluded to in our house was when I, at age five, had innocently asked for a baby brother or sister. "The world is not a good place to bring children into," had been my parents' answer.

"Getting pregnant" was simply the expression Mary and all girls our age used for the terrifying, no-exit situation we had better *never* get ourselves into. If we failed at this, we risked being sent "away to the country," to one of the "maternity homes" run by nuns that Mary had told me about.

"The best thing is to simply wait—put off sexual intercourse," Libby said, "until…later. Until you're ready, until you are—in love," said Libby with an uneasy smile.

She reached into her handbag and pulled out a paperback book with the symbols for male and female on the cover. "This is for you," she said. "Published by Planned Parenthood. It should explain anything you may be unclear about. Women have been fighting for their right to control their own reproduction decisions since 1916."

"It's primarily the Catholic Church, you know, that wants to keep us in the dark ages. When you're older we can talk about prophylactics. The good news is, they're working on a pill to prevent conception so none of this will be a problem."

"That's good," I mumbled.

"I don't mean," Libby said quickly, "that you *should* have sex, even if pregnancy could be prevented…not right now. You're too young." She blotted her mouth with her napkin, leaving lipstick marks. "Maybe you have some questions?"

The scoops of ice cream were turning into soup as I poked with my spoon and struggled to find something to ask that would satisfy her. "Why did you have me, since you say what a terrible world this is to bring children into?"

Libby looked startled. "Well, you were…unplanned."

"Like a…a mistake?"

"Not exactly a mistake," Libby smiled.

"Mary says being a mistake doesn't necessarily mean unwanted," I said, citing my only other source of information about these things.

"Mary's right about that, of course."

"Catholics say it's better to leave these things in God's hands."

"Well, that's one way to think about it. But rest assured, you were wanted. Definitely. And, I promise you, God had nothing whatever to do with it," Libby said, with a little smile.

When our talk was as finished as our banana split, we walked to our car and headed back to Goshen. As we neared our house on Guernsey Road with our loot in the back seat, a car passed us, going the other way.

It was the custom in Goshen to wave, even if we didn't recognize the driver. Libby half-raised her hand in a friendly gesture, then turned to look after they'd passed by. "Was that a Plymouth?"

I turned to look. "Yes, I think so. A forty-nine gray Plymouth."

"I thought so," Libby said, as her teeth caught the edge of her lip.

CHAPTER SIX

Mary brought Persian Pink lipstick and mascara with her to the sock hop. We stood side-by-side in our felt skirts, facing the mirror in the girls' restroom, applying the contraband to our virginal lips and eyelashes. Our mothers, so different in so many ways, agreed on this one thing—we were too young for makeup.

"Do I look cheap yet?" Mary asked me by way of the mirror.

"No, but less expensive than when we first came in here," I replied, struggling to keep the lipstick within the natural outlines of my lips.

"Very funny," Mary said, blotting her own lips on a piece of toilet paper.

"I look like a clown," I said, bending closer to the mirror for a better look at how I'd smudged the mascara until my eyes looked like dark, empty holes. We dabbed and swiped until we saw ourselves edging into floozy territory, then blotted and wiped with toilet paper and reapplied.

The school gym had been transformed. Only the day before, dressed in our embarrassing blue-bloomer gym uniforms, we'd done jumping jacks, tumbled somersaults, and dribbled basketballs here. For the dance, our blue plastic gymnast mats had been stacked, folding chairs were lined up along the walls, decorations taped up, and lights dimmed.

Two ninth-grade boys, radiating self-importance and wearing giant earphones, sat at a table under a basketball hoop, playing 45s through the school's public address system.

Mary and I presented our painted selves at the gym door, and each deposited a dollar bill into the shoe box provided. We took off our shoes, added them to the line of footwear along one wall and joined the others, sliding across the freshly waxed floor in our socks.

Mrs. Z., together with Mr. Bramhall and his wife, Eileen, stood just inside the door, as chaperones. Mr. Bramhall wore one of his tweed sports jackets and stood with his big, boney hands clasped behind him, shifting his weight, toe to heel, to the music.

We girls danced together in a tight circle to "Blueberry Hill." Between records, we sat in the chairs along the wall, wiggly and nervous, our felt skirts flaring and unruly. We practiced being wall flowers, waiting for the more adventurous boys, one by one, to work up their courage to ask us to dance.

I danced with Bill Duffy, Fred Crawford, and even did a ridiculous polka with Paul Colpitts. All the while, I watched and waited for John L. to appear.

The far corner of the gymnasium, where the shadow of the folded bleachers blocked light and the view of the chaperones, everyone called The Sandbox. There, couples who were "going together," plus the eager boys with the "fast girls," as Mary called them, were already locked together, barely moving to "Earth Angel," rocking together in place, stiff-legged as robots.

Still seated against the wall, I strained to see through the murk, hungry but also nervous, trying to educate myself in the ways of love.

My first glimpse of John L. was of his feet, large and stocking-clad in bleached white sports socks. He stood right in front of me, looking down, his dark eyes steady and solemn. He placed one hand flat against his stomach, the other behind his back, and did a stiff little bow.

In response to his mock chivalry, I stood up, murmured, "Thank you," and followed him like a puppy onto the gymnasium floor. He stepped inside the tip-off circle where, due to his height, he played center for the junior high basketball team. He pulled me in after him and put one arm around my back, enclosing my right hand in his large left one.

We danced to "Blue Velvet," "Only You" by the Platters, "Mr. Sandman" by the Chordettes—all music for slow dancing.

We drank punch that tasted like Jell-O from paper cups. "I hope somebody spiked this stuff," John L. said, grinning down at me from his height. I felt a new, warm sensation in my body, which I couldn't wait to discuss with Mary, when I caught him—staring, really—his dark eyes lingering, amused, contemplating me.

We joined the line dancing, including an infantile bunny hop, then danced some more, mostly uninterrupted by anything resembling conversation between us. Mary danced with Brendan Morrison and Bill Duffy, a boy with freckles, who could have played Huckleberry Finn in the movies.

Whenever my eyes met Mary's, she formed her lips into an "O" and nodded, as if she were egging me on, to what exactly, I wasn't sure.

"Who are you making eyes at? We're dancing here," John L. said, his eyes laughing.

"Just at Mary," I said, "so don't be jealous."

"She giving you tips on how to handle me?"

"Yes. She's my coach."

John L. chuckled and drew me in tighter. "Is it true your Mom teaches upstairs at the high school?"

"Yes, she teaches civics to sophomores," I said.

"Not sure what civics is exactly," John L. said. "We both have to take it, year after next."

"She says civics is about learning to be a citizen." I smiled up at him.

"I've heard the kids like her. They say she's…well, you know, kinda out there."

"Meaning what?" I asked.

"You know, radical. Far out politically. Kind of a left-winger."

"I guess so," I murmured.

"They say she's pretty, too."

"She *is* pretty," I said, feeling a ripple of familiar envy.

"You are too," he said, pulling me closer.

"Thank you. You're pretty…tall!"

Every fifteen minutes or so, the chaperones, who were huddled near the gymnasium door, dispatched an emissary to The Sandbox. Their job was to tap entwined couples on their shoulders until they loosened their grip. Sometimes, the seal was so tight between the "dancing" couples that they almost had to be pried apart. As soon as the chaperones left, bodies moved like magnets, back together.

By ten o'clock, John L. maneuvered me into The Sandbox. I resisted, but weakly. He arranged our arms as if we were mannequins, and soon we were rocking side to side, like the others, to the music that grew more sultry by the hour. John L. drew me close, and I let my head rest against his chest.

He smiled down at me, eyes half closed, and I could feel his heart beating. It felt good, and I wondered if Mary could see me.

This dreamy interval was short-lived because soon John L. leaned down to whisper in my ear. "Uh-oh. The dance police are coming!" He released me so suddenly, we both stumbled backwards a little.

Mr. Bramhall looked embarrassed as he stepped between us. "Sorry, folks, but I have to ask you two to please at least feign some semblance of dancing."

"Yes, sir," said John L., saluting.

Bramhall walked away and we rearranged ourselves, this time, closer still. John L. leaned down and, fumbling to find my lips, kissed me. It was quick and awkward, but it was a first.

"You like this, don't you?" John L. whispered.

And yes, I did like it. It felt soothing and safe, but also exhilarating. I couldn't tell him that, of course. The guilty pleasure of the wicked urges I felt in my body, although I barely acknowledged them to myself, were rivaled only by an awareness that John L. was excited, too.

Knowing that he might have to struggle to control himself confirmed a completely new sense of my power in the world.

It was bracing and, I thought, could easily become addictive.

CHAPTER SEVEN

First thing Monday morning, John L. was called out of homeroom to the principal's office. He returned fifteen minutes later with a hang-dog look and a warning glance. I was next.

I dawdled along the corridor, a hall-pass flapping in my hand like a paper bird's broken wing. I was a good student and well-behaved in school, except for sometimes talking too much in study hall with Mary. I hadn't been inside the principal's office since Libby had checked me in on my first day of school in Goshen.

"Come in, Sara. Sit down, please." Mr. Peel, with a thin line of moustache on his top lip, wore a corduroy jacket and one of his perky bow ties, which crowded his Adam's apple. A smelly rotating pipe stand, with two Meerschaums aboard, stood on his desk.

"Do you know why you're here, Sara?"

I avoided his stern look. My mind raced. It had to be about the dance, The Sandbox. "No," I said.

"You're a smart girl. You must have some idea of how irresponsible you were being."

I stole a look at him and saw he had no sense of humor at all about teenage experimentation, as Libby called it.

"I understand you were not alone, that you were egged-on."

"I guess so." I had to squelch a giggle as I pictured John L. in his giant white socks.

"I just want you to appreciate the seriousness of the situation," said Peele. "Your classmates, with very few exceptions, behaved in an appropriate manner."

I met his eyes in what I hoped he might consider a responsible manner, but I wasn't sorry. It had felt good to be so close to John L.

"I'm sure your classmates," Peel continued, "also found it uncomfortable to be folded into knots under their desks."

"Oh," I murmured, taken by surprise. My mind's eye had to shift from visions of The Sandbox to Bert the Turtle and mushroom clouds. The telephone on Peel's desk buzzed and he picked it up.

"Just give me a minute or so more. Then you can send her in," he said and hung up.

I relaxed, relieved to hear my interrogation wouldn't last much longer.

"Apparently," Peel went on, "one of the young men in your class was urging others on…." He trailed off, leaving space for me to fill in the blank—like, name John L., for example—which I wasn't going to do. If I had learned anything at Libby's knee, one of the worst things you could do was rat on people, name names and be a stool pigeon. My lips were sealed.

"Very well," Peel said to my silence. "If you prefer to take full responsibility, that's your choice. Just understand this may involve time in after-school detention." I nodded, consoling myself with the hope that detention might involve John L., while Peel nervously aligned and re-aligned a letter opener on his desk. Then he pointed it right at me. "I just want everything to be clear before your mother joins us."

My stomach dropped. Libby? Outside, gusts of wind swirled dry leaves around the playing fields where, except when snow was on the ground, we had Phys Ed, ate lunches from home, and some, who were "going together," met under the branches of the Burgoyne Elm at the far end of the teachers' parking lot.

The bell for first period rang, and Peel's office door swung open, and in swept Libby. She'd been summoned from upstairs, occupied by grades ten through twelve, Goshen's junior high being down on the first floor. Libby wore a long denim skirt, an aqua sweater, and those darn ropey espadrilles. A white, rayon scarf draped her neck.

Peel stood up and pointed to the chair next to me. Next to Libby's imperious beauty, he looked small and colorless, just the way I felt too.

She looked around the office. "What's this all about?" she demanded.

"I apologize for pulling you out of your class, Mrs. Green, but I need to inform you that Sara was one of a handful of students in the entire school, who was uncooperative and apparently unaware of the importance of the drill we had here last Friday. I don't believe you were on campus that day."

Libby cocked an eyebrow at me. "A fire drill?"

"No," said Peel, puffed up with self-importance. "A civil defense drill. Our first."

Libby settled back in her chair and began to tap the toe of her espadrille on the floor. "I see," she said evenly, "I was unaware there was such a drill."

"As you can imagine," said Peel, "we absolutely need the full cooperation of all the students and staff during such an important exercise. The safety and very survival of everyone could be at stake."

Libby's face looked blank, but I could see her cheeks starting to flush. "Since when have there been nuclear bomb drills here in the Goshen schools?" she asked. "I was under the impression the town was more…enlightened."

"Perhaps Sarah's flyer never made it home last spring?" Peele said.

"I never saw any flyers," said Libby, turning to me, then back to Peel. "I think my daughter uses her own judgment about what school literature to bring home and which to leave in the circular file."

Peel winced and gave me a questioning look. "We are one of the last school systems in the state to institute them." There was an awkward pause.

Then Libby leaned forward in her chair. "First," she said, "let me make it clear that if Sara *had* brought the flyers home, my husband and I would have had a discussion with her about why such drills are a poor idea."

Peel's eyes widened. "I'm surprised and frankly concerned to hear you say that, Mrs. Green. We need all our parents and, of course, our teachers to support our educating students about the seriousness of what we face at this time in our history."

"I assure you, my husband and I have educated Sara about the horrors of nuclear war. But air raid drills are bad policy because they promote the dangerous, irrational idea that nuclear war can be survived, and should therefore be contemplated and prepared for. Drills like these are part and parcel of the hysteria gripping our country, a symptom of 'The Red Scare.'"

Peel cleared his throat. "You are certainly entitled to your opinion, Mrs. Green, but I'm sure you would not begrudge your own child the preparation these drills provide. In the future I hope you will encourage Sara to, at the very least, comply and cooperate with mandated procedures."

Libby's chin rose that additional fraction of an inch I had learned to fear because of how it preceded an escalation of her stubborn determination. "I'm sorry," she said, not sounding a bit sorry, "we can't do that. What Sara herself chooses to do, or not do, is her own affair."

The principal sighed. "The school can't view it that way, of course. We must have consistency. Everyone must participate."

"In that case," Libby said, "if Sara decides not to participate, we will write you a note excusing her from any further participation. She can sit in the library for the duration of the…drill."

"That's simply not possible," said Peel. "Everyone must remain with his or her class. It's part of the drill protocol."

"Fine," said Libby, "the next time a drill is planned, whether or not it's a day I'm here on campus, I'll simply pick her up and take her home for the duration…and bring her back when it's time for her to return to academic learning."

Peel turned slowly toward his office window as if he expected to see a nuclear flash now. "Mrs. Green," he said to the window, "please understand. To have less than one hundred percent cooperation undermines the morale of the entire school. And, most importantly, it's not good for your daughter."

"An actual nuclear war would be a lot worse for her and for the other children *and* for morale, as you call it." Libby gripped the arms of the chair, and I could see her knuckles turning pale. "Goshen would do well to rescind this counter-productive policy. Are the students going to be wearing dog tags next?"

Peel caught his breath, turning to face her. "Some school systems have gone in that direction. We're giving it consideration."

He turned to me next. "Sara, you may go back to class now."

"I'll see you back at home, Sara," Libby said as we both stood up to leave.

"Mrs. Green, if you wouldn't mind staying for just a few minutes. I have another matter of importance to discuss with you."

Libby sat back down.

I left the two of them together. My last glimpse took in Libby's stony expression and the rope soles of her espadrilles planted firmly on Principal Peele's linoleum floor.

CHAPTER EIGHT

That evening, I stood over a big aluminum bowl, spooning kitchen grease out of the condensed orange juice cans Libby saved under the sink. This was a habit leftover from World War II, they explained, when leftover grease was donated to the army to make into explosives.

Hank sat at the table reading The Goshen Town Annual Report while he "sidewalk superintended" my preparation of a new, fall batch of suet, seeds, and peanut butter for the bird feeders. Libby swept into the kitchen with gale force and dropped her two canvas briefcases on top of the dryer, producing an ominous boom.

"Good day, Lib?" Hank asked warily. We could see she was in a state.

Libby glanced at the mess I was making on the table, opened the freezer compartment of the refrigerator, took out a block of frozen hamburger meat and began running water over it in the sink. "Did Sara tell you what went on in school today?"

"Nope," he said. "Tell me." Focusing on my task, I dug deeply into the next can of yellow grease.

"Tell him, Sara," Libby said.

"*You* tell him." I said.

Hank calmly turned a page on the town report. "Will *someone* please tell me what the heck is going on here?"

I peeled the tin foil cover off the last can of grease. Libby stood at the sink adjusting the temperature of the running water and gazing out the window. Hank watched her with the slightly love-sick expression he got whenever he looked at her, but there was concern, too. Obviously, something was up.

Eventually, Libby left her window and the defrosting meat and went to him for a kiss. After that, she kissed me lightly on the forehead. I felt her lips and smelled her lipstick. "Fine," she finally said to him, with a little toss of her head, "I was called out of my class to the principal's office this morning about *your* daughter."

"Oh, I see," Hank said. "So, Sara, what did you do to deserve this special attention?"

"I was slow to respond to an emergency," I said as I poured a package of sunflower seeds into the bowl with the grease.

"What emergency was that?"

Libby stepped back to the sink. "Mr. Peel was concerned that Sara didn't behave with the appropriate sense of urgency during the school air raid drill last Friday."

"I didn't get under my desk fast enough," I said.

Hank winced. "I thought we didn't have that nonsense in the Goshen schools."

"Apparently, we were mistaken," said Libby.

"Uh-oh. So, what did you tell him, mi pasionaria?"

"What do you think I told him?"

Suddenly, in his fake radio announcer voice, Hank began reading aloud from the Town Report: "One hundred twenty-five births. Forty-seven deaths. Two house break-ins…." He looked up from the page and smiled. "What I love about Goshen is how nothing ever happens."

"Trampling on a child's civil liberties isn't nothing," Libby said sharply.

"I'm not sure making students duck under their desks is exactly trampling on their civil rights," Hank said.

Libby's eyes narrowed. "I believe it is."

Nervous butterflies broke loose in my stomach. Libby being awakened was like waking Hank's pasionaria. Until today with Mr. Peel, I'd mostly only seen this in her when she suddenly sprang at Grandpa Joe.

"Sa—*ra*." Hank lowered his chin and waggled his eyebrows at me. The Groucho eyebrows were a high sign Hank had used with me ever since my parents first realized I might be paying attention to their conversations, whether I appeared to be interested or not. Those eyebrows meant they were about to have an adult discussion—a dialectic, as they called them—and I should go to my room.

Tensions might arise between them over something like a dumb air raid drill, but fundamentally they would always agree in the end. They were together, two peas in a pod. I gripped the sides of the bowl in silent protest. Why should *I* have to leave the room? I was too old to be dismissed like a child. As it was, I spent half my life in my room, lying on my bed, trying to hear their muffled conversations.

This was *my* business. It was my school and my life. I reached for the large jar of peanut butter and stayed put. Libby continued the story as if I had already left. Or maybe she didn't regard me as the delicate flower Hank seemed to think I was, believing I shouldn't witness even the mildest contention between them.

"I told Peel it would be Sara's choice whether or not to take part in the drills. That she could stay in the library during a drill. He didn't like that idea at all. Then I told him I would pick her up and take her home during a drill."

"What did he say to that?" Hank asked.

"He looked at me as if I were absolutely crazy and a bad mother to boot. How could I be so unconcerned for my own child's safety and welfare? I'm not sure he'll agree to any plan. He seems to want to make a federal case over it."

I scraped peanut butter into the bowl.

"Hopefully, he'll just calm down," Hank said.

"I seriously doubt that. He's bought the civil defense propaganda—hook, line, and sinker." Libby chewed her lip. "Looks like it's impossible to get away from the poisonous fear that's taken over this country." She sighed. "But we can't just let these things go unopposed."

"Okay, okay," Hank said. "Can we just take it easy here for a minute? Let's see what, if any, move he makes before we hit the streets, shall we?" My stomach eased because Hank's tongue was now in his cheek, where I counted on its being when it came to Libby. He would kid her out of whatever her fiery nature had in mind to do.

"Don't worry," Libby said, and shot him an unfriendly look. "I'm not planning on doing anything rash."

"Oh, I wasn't suggesting anything like *that*." Hank gave her a cockeyed smile.

"You know perfectly well that peace and quiet isn't always a good thing. We can't just let Sara be forced to go through the charade of preparing for a nuclear war." Libby gave him an impatient toss of her head. "I'm sure I can count on you to back me up," she added.

Hank patted the chartreuse table-top and turned to me. "Okay, Sara, *now* would be the perfect time for you to go to your room so your mother and I can…talk."

"You *are* talking," I protested. "I thought I'm supposed to be an equal around here."

"Sa-*ra*," Hank said, taking a tone he rarely used with me.

Libby rose from her chair, stepped to the over-the-sink window, and looked out into the dark. "It's probably best, Sara. We'll call you when supper's ready."

I made a pouty, foot-dragging exit and left the bird food project for them to deal with.

From my bedroom window, I watched my birdfeeders fading into the gathering dusk. Tensing was at the nearest one, working carefully through the little metal cage to get at the last dregs of the suet, which made me feel less alone.

I flopped down on my bed and glowered at the ceiling where the shadows cast there had lately been shifting from childhood's scary monsters to more worldly threats. Atomic bombs. Nuclear war. Non-existence. Orphanhood.

Spread-eagle on the bedspread, I thought, if I had a sister, or at least a brother, I'd have an ally, someone to talk to, to commiserate with about how *our* mother was so enthusiastic about everybody else's civil liberties and civil rights. And how *our* father always sided with her, and how neither of them really seemed to care about *our* rights or *our* peace of mind.

I switched my bedside radio from FM to AM and spun the dial to 1090. I stopped turning when I heard a low, smooth disc jockey voice saying: "This is ten-ninety on your AM dial, WILD broadcasting from studios in the heart of Roxbury. By FCC regulations, the station will sign off at sunset, which, today, will be 5:23. But, before we do, we have time for one more record. Badass, Big Mama Thornton," he said, "singing 'Hound Dog,' just released on Peacock Records, for your listening pleasure."

I lay back on my pillow, closed my eyes, and took in Mama's rhythmic growl, so low, it rumbled my bed springs. At first, I only barely grasped the idea that the hound dog was really a man who'd done the singer wrong, but slowly, gradually, the truth dawned. Libby and Hank and Goshen disappeared into the backbeat of drums and guitars, and I was transported by the casual disillusionment in Mama Thornton's voice to other worlds that

I, so far, hadn't imagined. "You ain't nothing but a hound dog, been snoopin' round the door...."

I awoke with a shudder to the Star-Spangled Banner, followed by a storm of static as the station went off the air. I switched back to the FM classical station, and left Mozart at medium volume for cover as I crept along the bedroom hall. I crossed the living room, past the hulking piano—destination, the dining room. I dropped down to all fours and army-crawled the rest of the way toward Hank and Libby's voices, drifting by way of the pass-through from the kitchen.

I positioned myself under the dining room table, on my back, legs crossed, inhaled the scent of the linseed oil Libby periodically rubbed into the teakwood, and listened.

"Have you forgotten we moved out here to Goshen so people would leave us alone, so we could keep making a living, so Sara wouldn't get picked on and called a Commie kid, or whatever, and we could all be closer to nature?"

Libby made a disparaging noise with her lips. I pictured her lips—tense, pursed—whenever she was feeling determined. "I didn't forget, but how can we stand by and watch and do nothing when things are so off, so wrong. I'm surprised you can."

"For Pete's sake, Lib," Hank said, "It's *me* you're talking to here. You don't have to preach to me. I *am* the choir. I'm simply asking you not to make a big deal about the drills, that's all. Sara understands they're ridiculous."

"Sometimes I feel like you forget what's important, and I have to jog your memory," Libby said.

"That's unfair. I've always been there, backing you up. And the whole point is, we just finished with the big to-do back in Mattapan. And, just like you say, things are still dangerous out there in America The Beautiful. The hysteria is far from over. They're looking for scape goats. We still need to keep our heads down and be cautious."

Somebody turned the water spigot on hard and then a pot came down hard on the stove. Under the dining room table, I held my breath through their silence. The refrigerator changed gears.

"Well, I'm getting tired of hiding," Libby said. "I'm fed up with government snoops lurking around. Going through our mail and our trash and garbage. It's outrageous they actually spoke to Sara. They have no right."

"Mutt and Jeff are clowns, I tell you," Hank said. "Government drones who don't have enough to do. And you're right, it's outrageous, but can we just take it easy? Call it a strategic retreat, if you want, but you and I agreed we'd lay low for a while for the sake of the family, for the sake of Sara. Maybe you can work out a compromise on the drills."

"People shouldn't have to choose between family and their principles. Whose future are we fighting for anyway, if not the children's?" Libby said.

"Sometimes you have to wait out a storm, In the meantime, you batten down the hatches. That's what we're doing. Eventually, this thing will blow over."

"I just can't leave attitudes like my father's unchallenged," said Libby.

"Come on," Hank said in a warning voice, "this isn't about your father."

"Maybe not, but I'm *glad* he's not coming out here anymore to try to make us feel guilty and afraid and wrong. He said they were going to burn crosses on our lawn, because we're Jewish and because, in his charming lingo, we were pinkos, remember?"

"He's the only one who's ever given us a moment's grief since we moved out here. How about we let it stay that way?" Hank said.

During the silence, I crept out from under the table and peeked through an empty knothole in the pine partition between the dining room and the kitchen. Hank was framed there, tall and dark, and slumped against the sink.

A chair scraped and Libby came into view. She walked around the table and reached up to play with Hank's hair, then ran her finger along the outside of his ear. I cringed but kept watching.

"You always say I can charm the birds out of the trees?" she whispered.

"It still works on me," he laughed. "But Peel may be a tougher customer. Let's give his better angels a chance to emerge, shall we?" He raised her chin with one hand, and they kissed again.

I'd seen enough. I retreated and took up my listening position under the table again.

"Mr. P's better angels have already deserted him," she said. "This morning, after Sara went back to class? He suddenly informs me I need to sign a loyalty oath."

"What the— You never said anything about a loyalty oath."

"I never heard anything about one either. Now, conveniently, he produces one."

Hank groaned. "Oh, brother!"

"They're so worried the innocent, untroubled little minds will be sullied by 'Communist' thinking, like share the wealth and….and don't discriminate against people whose skin's a different shade. What do they think might happen if the students brought some true Christian values home to their little white clapboard houses?"

"I have no idea," Hank said.

"Anyway, it's my business what my beliefs are and my associations and what organizations I belong to. And where my loyalties are."

"Lib, all you probably have to say is you're loyal to the Constitution and that you don't want to overthrow the government by force or violence… and that you aren't a card-carrying party member. You can say that, can't you?"

I cocked my head, like Nipper, the RCA dog, to be sure I heard her answer. "You know I'm not going to sign anything like that," Libby said in a calm voice. "Nobody should be able to make a person sign something about their beliefs in exchange for letting you keep a job."

"Right," Hank said, defeat in his voice.

"I can finish out the school year, but if I don't sign by January first, I won't be invited back next year."

"Invited? What a joke."

"And," Libby said, "if I lose my job and then you can't get government contracts anymore? Where will we be then?"

Hank didn't answer for a few moments; then he said, "Back where we started from. Which wasn't so bad, mi pasionaria."

I army-crawled back to my room and collapsed onto my bed. I covered my eyes and waited for my breath to calm down. I wished I hadn't heard this dialectic of theirs. Selfishly, as Mary would say, I'd be glad if Libby didn't teach anymore in my school.

What I was afraid of was that Libby's nuclear passions would be unleashed and there would to be consequences. For us. For me. I turned off the radio. I was exhausted and not hungry at all. My eyes closed.

* * *

Now I am younger, just a kid. I'm walking the two blocks to school in my old neighborhood. A nasty boy, a year or two older, with Hostess Cupcake crumbs and crème filling clinging to the corners of his mouth, blocks my way on the sidewalk. He sticks out his chest and bumps up hard against me.

My precious cowgirl lunchbox crashes to the sidewalk, sliding with a screech of metal on concrete. The cover pops open, and the tuna sandwich Hank has carefully wrapped in waxed paper, the sliced carrot sticks and a small box of raisins, sprawl out onto the pavement. The boy leans over to examine the downed contents of my lunch, then looks up at me and laughs.

"I just wanted to see if it's true you carry a picture of Stalin in your lunchbox. Guess your mother forgot to put it in there today."

I awoke with my heart racing. Hank was knocking at my bedroom door to tell me supper was ready.

CHAPTER NINE

The Wednesday before Thanksgiving, traditionally a half day off school, was the prelude to winter, a season devoted to liberating heavy sweaters from their mothballs, taking down screens and putting up storm windows. Birds that stayed on for the winter, the chickadees, nuthatches, and blue jays, were already gathering at the feeders I checked each day.

"What are you doing to that poor bird?" I asked Libby in the kitchen.

With a grimace, Libby plunged her hand deep into the body cavity of the raw turkey. Once this carcass had been a living, breathing bird. I cringed with her as she pulled out the neck and a little bag of gizzards and tossed them into the sink.

"Making Thanksgiving dinner. Maybe you'd like to help. Go put your books away and wash your hands."

I trudged to my room, took off my school clothes and put on dungarees and a sweatshirt. I chose the frilliest, most ridiculous-looking apron I could find to play sous-chef to Libby's reluctant chef.

Libby never seemed to like cooking that much, although, once in a great while, she would suddenly produce something fancy, using recipes she found in a cooking magazine. Or when she cooked Spanish food, like paella or, in the summer, gazpacho. Or even bananas flambé, which Hank loved and liked to make jokes about.

"Will you peel and cut me an onion in quarters, please?"

I took an onion from the refrigerator and a knife out of a drawer. "Are Grandma and Grandpa coming?" I asked.

Libby hesitated. "I don't think so. Your father invited them, but...." Libby cut up a lemon and an apple and tossed them into the turkey. We would make the stuffing tomorrow morning, stuff the poor turkey with it, and cook it all day.

"Why won't they come? It's not that far," I said.

"Your grandfather is hard to understand sometimes. And very stubborn." Libby pursed her lips. *Stubborn like you*, I thought. I dutifully peeled the onion, cut it into quarters, and did my crying for Grandpa and Grandma that way.

"But Thanksgiving's not like Christmas," I argued. "It's not a holiday just for Christians, is it?"

"No," she replied, tossing the onions into the turkey next. "Although it does sentimentalize the relationship between the Indians and the pilgrims. The Indians supposedly teaching the pilgrims to plant corn with a fish in the hole as fertilizer? That's probably a myth," Libby said. "Meanwhile, the Pilgrims gave them white man's smallpox. The point is, your grandfather and I have never agreed…on…things."

"He's a republican and we're democrats, right?"

"That's true," Libby said.

"But why won't they come tomorrow?"

Shaking her head silently, Libby sprinkled salt and pepper all over the turkey's skin, under the wings and legs, and began to wrap it in aluminum foil.

"Why won't you tell me things?" I asked.

"Tell you what things?" Libby looked up from the turkey, maybe surprised at my new penchant for asking questions.

"Like why he's mad at you."

"Your grandfather is hard-headed. He carries old world ideas about everything. He thinks we're supposed to respect what he says just because he's old." Libby stopped as if frustrated with herself. "I just don't think you're old enough to understand."

"I'm almost fifteen," I protested.

"I don't think you can understand how problems between parents and children can go on and on. You've been…protected. Your father and I have sheltered you. We listen to you. We let you have your own opinions. We don't try to mold you into images of ourselves."

This required my taking a deep breath. "But I think just what you think."

Libby looked annoyed. "But that's your choice, right?"

"And…you do keep secrets."

Libby shook her head. "What secrets?"

"That's what a secret is, isn't it?" I laughed. "If something's being kept from you, you can't know what it is, right?"

Libby, who looked as silly in her cooking apron as I did, put her hands on her hips. "Don't you practice Bramhall's debating tricks on *me*, young lady." She paused. "Anyway, secrets are burdens. Maybe we'll just have to figure a way for you to go see Grandma and Grandpa on your own. You can ask him your questions."

Thanksgiving Day came and went without Grandma and Grandpa. The stuffed turkey was a little overdone, and there were green beans with toasted onions and almonds. Hank and I made a pecan pie using maple syrup instead of Karo. Uncle Arthur and Aunt Dorothy brought sweet potatoes, topped with marshmallows. Libby said it was the way Grandma Rose used to make them, and I noticed she helped herself to seconds.

The Friday after Thanksgiving was a long, quiet, lonesome day. I missed Grandpa and Grandma and wondered if they had even had a Thanksgiving, since it was an American holiday and involved Indians whom Grandpa seemed to hold in low regard.

Just after a lunch of leftover turkey sandwiches, it began to snow. Hank announced he was going to brave the weather and go out to his back-room office to do some "figuring," which meant calculating from blueprints and specifications just how much a building project would cost to build, adding profit, which was never enough, before submitting a bid to try to win the job. This was the life of a small building contractor.

I stayed in my room doing homework most of the day, although mostly I gazed out the window. Birds came to my trays, but even they looked cold and aimless, like they had the blues. They picked up the seeds listlessly, one by one. I considered calling Mary, but then I thought about how lively and loud her house must be with all her brothers and Annie O. in the kitchen, whipping up some cookies probably. Thinking of the O'Reillys made me feel sadder and lonelier.

In the mid-afternoon, as I sat at my desk, gnawing down my pencil eraser and watching the snow, the piano bench in the living room scraped on the concrete floor. Random note combinations descended the keyboard. Libby must be cleaning the piano keys. Every so often, she embarked on a cleaning frenzy, vacuuming, scrubbing, dusting, cleaning windows. That sometimes included the piano.

She refused to have anyone come and clean for her. Hiring help to do your cleaning exploited poor women, she said, who had their own houses to clean and children to take care of. So she did the housework herself, but sporadically, when the spirit moved her, and with equally erratic help from me.

Now, as I stared out at the silent, falling snow, a cascade of scales, then arpeggios, perfectly articulated without a flub or a hesitation, filled the house. Libby was playing the piano! After this warm-up, she launched into a lilting, dance piece, probably Schumann, quick and light.

I sat listening. I watched the scene outside my window, its frosting of white, and imagined the piano notes accumulating, too, as Libby continued to play. The music rippled on. I was mesmerized. I didn't dare come out of my room to look because then she might stop.

She had moved on to Bach when there was a light knock on my bedroom door, and Hank, without waiting for me to answer, stuck his head in. Grinning conspiratorially, he beckoned me to follow him. Together, we crept along the bedroom hall, stood behind the blue granite interior wall that divided the entry from the living room and took turns gaping at Libby.

The piano lid was open like a seabird's wing and Libby, in profile against the picture windows, seemed lost in the music. Her eyes closed, her lips slightly parted, she looked transported, as if she might at any moment float right off the piano bench. Her brow was knit, and she swayed from side to side, as if to some counterpoint melody only she could hear.

"Bach," Hank, whispered, as if he were speaking the name of God.

We both crept back to my room and left the door open, so we could continue to listen. Hank sat at my desk, casually leafing through the clutter of papers and notebooks I had piled there. I sprawled on my bed against the pillows.

"I love to hear her," Hank whispered. "She's so obviously at peace when she plays. It gives her such pleasure."

"I wish she would be that way all the time," I said in a low voice. "She's so vehement and fanatical about everything."

"You've been studying your vocabulary words," Hank said. "'Vehement,' that's fancy. She's vehement because she's full of passion. She feels things deeply. I admire that."

"But she never considers how it is for us. She gets that look in her eyes."

"She can lose…perspective," he smiled. "That's where *I* come in. I'm here to lend perspective."

I prayed this was true.

As days grew shorter and Goshen geared up for winter, the tufted titmouse, the dark-eyed Junco, and even a cardinal, the Christmas bird, came to the feeders. The moment December began, festive wreaths of balsam fir materialized on every house and church door except ours. Christmas trees tied up with string appeared in the empty lot next to the fire station and then on the roofs of cars. Strings of lights looped along the eaves of the two blocks of stores that made up downtown Goshen.

Hank and Libby allowed me to have Santa Claus because, they said, he wasn't really religious. Though it was only the first week in December, I broke out my large wool stocking with my name knitted into it and thumbtacked it to the thick redwood plank of our mantelpiece. It dangled there, scrawny and empty, until Christmas morning when it would miraculously be full of oranges and apples and nuts and raisins, suggesting that Santa Claus was a bit of a health nut, like Libby.

Hank smiled at the stocking as he laid the season's first fire in the hearth. "Hope springs eternal," he said. "My only question to you is: Have you been good enough to still get presents from Santa?"

"Of course I'm good. What other choice do I have around here?"

"And what do you mean by that?"

"I have saints for parents," I said.

"Humph," Hank said in mock humility. "If that's what it takes to keep you on the straight and narrow."

Despite the exception for Santa Claus, the Christian holiday and the lead-up to it stirred shameful longings in me—to be like everybody else in Goshen—holiday lights, wreaths, and cookies but, above all, to have a Christmas tree.

"I think they should let you have one," Mary said. "It's just a tree. What's religious about a tree?"

"It's a symbol, they say, and as people of Jewish heritage, they say they have to draw the line somewhere. For them, not having a tree is their statement of not being Christian, thereby being Jewish, I guess."

"Wow, that's some fancy logic," Mary said. "I thought they weren't religious."

"I don't get it, either. It's a way of declaring what you're not and what you are at the same time, using the same symbol—the tree? Libby says there are hundreds of trees in the woods to enjoy without cutting them down. Maybe they're afraid Grandpa and Grandma will show up and see it."

"That makes sense," Mary granted.

"I just feel funny that our front door is the only one without a wreath on the most important Christian holiday."

"The most important except for Easter."

"We don't celebrate that one either," I said.

"Some Catholics believe the Jews were responsible for Jesus' crucifixion."

I swallowed hard. "Do you believe that?"

"Of course not. It's a bad rap," Mary said. "Father Gregory says the real history is much more complicated than that, and we should be nice to Jews *and* everyone else. Of course, Big Patrick says that Jesuits are so progressive, they're almost heretics."

Despite Mary's implanting new worries in me about Eastertime, which, thankfully was a long way off, it remained the birth of Jesus, not the death, that separated me and my family from the rest of Goshen.

Maybe to show they didn't harbor any hard feelings about the death of Christ, the O'Reillys invited me over to help decorate their Christmas tree.

"That's very kind of them," Libby said. "It's nice to see other people's tribal customs."

An O'Reilly Christmas was enough to shake the faith of even the most confirmed Jew or atheist. The moment their Thanksgiving leftovers were gobbled up by Mary's brothers, Annie O.'s preparations began, culminating in the ceremonial decorating of a massive tree in their high vaulted living room. A twelve-foot blue spruce—all the way from Canada—stood, for the moment, without ornaments, just strung with lights not yet plugged in but filling the room with evergreen smells.

"Oh, Sara, how darling of you to come and help us." Annie O'Reilly hugged me gingerly, as her hands were white with flour. "Christmas is such a lot of work. How are you at gingerbread men?"

I pretended to have more experience than I did. I had made shtrudl with Grandma Rose, but those days were long past. Libby never baked. Cookies came from Pepperidge Farm and coffee cake was Entemann's. Libby's idea of dessert was fruit or else something very fancy like crêpes suzettes, or flambé, which she'd made a couple of times and nearly set the house on fire. Combustibly delicious," Hank exclaimed, slurping up brandied orange sauce.

Annie O. pulled me into the kitchen, handed me an apron, and I took my place at Mary's side, wielding rolling pins and cookie cutters, flour and confectioner's sugar. Red and green sprinkles flew everywhere. Big Patrick appeared at the kitchen door, rolled up his sleeves and ran a finger through the gingerbread batter.

"Thank you, Sara, for coming to help us out," he said. "Does Mother make a to-do or what? I don't suppose your holiday, Cha-nukah, is anything like this." He pronounced the "Ch" as in "chunk."

"No, it isn't," I said, lowering my eyes.

"No, Daddy, it's *Ha*-nukkah," Mary said, performing the initial guttural perfectly, just the way I'd taught her, which I'd learned from Grandpa, who had coached me as a child until I finally mastered it.

"Yes, I know. Cha-nukah," Patrick repeated, precisely the way he'd said it the first time.

Mary's brothers, John, Kevin, and Patrick, Jr. arrived to attack the batter too, only to be run off by Big Patrick pretending to go for his belt. The gingerbread men were soon laid out in perfect rows to be decorated with white frosting and raisins for eyes.

Before the decoration of the tree, there was setting up the crêche, which made me think of a miniature doll house. With great ceremony, the figures of Mary and Joseph, baby Jesus, wise men, sheep and goats, and the three kings on camels bringing gifts of frankincense and myrrh, whatever they were, came out of the cupboard.

I was given the honor of placing baby Jesus in his tiny straw manger. "After all," Big Patrick said, "Jesus was born a Jew," which didn't make me feel any more comfortable about possibly being complicit in his cruel death.

Once the crêche was placed on the fireplace mantel between candles, Mary and I climbed up on stepladders next to the tree, as Big Patrick and one of Mary's brothers handed us ornaments, one at a time, from a big wooden box. The other brothers held the ladders for us so we wouldn't fall.

I concentrated hard on balancing and holding each ornament carefully by its little wire hook. There were ceramic angels, Santas, sleighs, felt elves with hats, and glass snowflakes. I took the responsibility of each delicate ornament very seriously, as one after another came out of the box. The heady fragrances of balsam candles and pitch from the spruce filled my head.

Mary's brother, Tim. reached up to hand me my next ornament. Made of glass and delicate, it represented a quarter moon with a cow jumping over it. I strained to reach an empty branch and then, dazzled by all the fragrances and candlelight, I dropped it. It landed on the floor and broke.

I looked down, humiliated, as Big Patrick bent to pick it up. "No harm done, Sara, dear. Every year at least one of them drops," he said.

I felt dizzy, looking down from what felt like a great altitude. Christmas candles seemed to rotate. I hung on tight to the ladder and hoped Kevin wouldn't let go.

"Well, will you look at this," Big Patrick said as he sat down on a nearby couch with the ornament's remains in his hands. "What's left of it reminds me of a crossed hammer and sickle. The Communist symbol, isn't it?"

I strained to see the remnant he was holding. It did resemble the hammer and sickle, a symbol I knew. The crossed tools represented the factory workers and farmers who used them, the hard-toiling people of the world who deserved respect, decent pay, and unions to represent them. I inhaled the sharp aromas of spruce and ginger and felt even more keenly like the alien I was.

"Sweet Jesus," Big Patrick chuckled, "we surely can't be hanging anything like that on a tree that's supposed to glorify the name of God, now can we?"

Was Big Patrick harping on the hammer and sickle because he'd heard something, something about Libby? Did he know something about Libby that I didn't know? And did it mean I'd never be asked back again to help with an O'Reilly Christmas?

Mary admonished her father, "I'm sure the blessed mother would want us to be especially open-minded at this time of year. The little Lord Jesus would be as sweet to communists as anyone else. Some people say Jesus would have been a Communist if he were alive today. He was poor and a carpenter, a working man."

Big Patrick put his head back on the couch and closed his eyes for a moment. "Oh, my dear Mary, where do you pick up the likes of that? As if

I didn't know. It's those Jesuits," he sighed. "What will they be telling you next? Just be careful, my fine girl," he said, "that you don't blaspheme the Lord by teasing your poor, uneducated father half to death."

"Sara Green," Mary ordered me from her ladder, looking concerned," you come right down off that ladder before you fall down."

The next day, with the fragrance of spruce resin still in my nose, and as soon as the coast was clear, I took Hank's hatchet from the tool wall in his back office. I marched out into the woods and cut down a perfect little pine tree I found poking out of the snow—about two feet tall. I brushed it off and carried it inside.

I filled a flowerpot with gravel, set the tree in it and set it up in my bathtub. Over the next two weeks, I watered it faithfully and decorated it with paper cut-outs and ribbon and yarn I found around the house.

CHAPTER TEN

Low-pitched knocking on a hollow tree down near the road disturbed my sleeping-in on Saturday with the covers over my head. Last winter, a snowplow, working all night so the school buses could get through so we'd never have a snow day off, had clipped the tree, disturbing the tree's bark and its roots. I crawled out of bed, put a parka on over my pajamas, slid barefoot into boots, and grabbed gloves and binoculars.

I brushed off the snow from a big flat rock outcropping, halfway down to the street, and sat still there to do my observations.

Halfway up the trunk of the dying tree was a large woodpecker. Word must have gone out because the other woodpeckers that had already discovered the tree's decrepit condition—sapsuckers, red-headed woodpeckers, flickers—who'd been working away, mining it for grubs and insects, were nowhere to be seen. They'd made way for my woodpecker because of his amazing size, the biggest land bird I'd ever seen.

His jaunty red crest made me think of the red hats of the French Revolution's vicious Jacobins, which we were studying in Mr. Bramhall's history class. White markings like lightning bolts streaked across the bird's dark, thick, feathered back. Propped by his stiff tail feathers, with his gnarled, clawed feet gripping the craggy bark as fulcrum, his neck, head, and beak, jackhammered away. It made my head ache just watching him work.

To me, all woodpeckers resembled a cross between bird and machine. They were like humans, too, the way they labor, stop to rest, and take time out to survey their progress, then go back to work with renewed energy. My woodpecker was like John Henry, the steel-drivin' man, his red crest undaunted by hours of violent head-banging, sometimes at twenty times a second, according to my bird books.

All woodpeckers, I knew, also from books, had these long, barbed sticky tongues that rolled out, to extract bugs from the deep holes they bored in dead trees.

The next day at the library, Mary and I lugged a large, bulky copy of Audubon's folios, *Birds of America,* a bound version, up onto our table. In a happy escape from homework, we turned the pages and sat, mesmerized by the colorful reproductions of Audubon's pictures and his word descriptions of the birds.

In winter, Mary and I went several days a week after school to the town library, where we encamped at an octagonal oak table that nearly filled the small reference alcove. Libby and Hank approved of the arrangement, so I wouldn't be alone at home for long stretches and probably so that Mary would exert her good influence on me. As for Mary said her parents were too worn out from having so many kids to have energy left over to closely monitor her.

Our paneled nook's stained-glass windows featured scenes from the Bible, including Moses carrying the tablets down from Mount Sinai. Waist-high bookshelves held atlases, sets of encyclopedias, and a dozen different dictionaries, including all ten volumes of the Oxford English Dictionary. We spread our green bookbags from school, our coats and our hats across the massive table to discourage anyone else from joining us.

We whispered, giggled softly, took lots of bathroom breaks, and, intermittently, did our homework. Aside from our wariness about Mrs. Osmond, the head librarian, and her hawk-eyed surveillance of the place, we felt free to roam and explore. The stacks were as open to us as freshly steamed clams.

"He was a bastard," Mary said quietly, looking up from a book about Audubon she'd found on the shelves.

"Oh?" I said, surprised to hear her use a flat-out curse word.

"His father wasn't married to his mother," Mary continued. "He was the illegitimate son of a French plantation owner in Santo Domingo. His creole mother was his father's servant and maybe a slave. His low beginnings were overcome when he was officially adopted by his father and his father's *actual* French wife, and then brought to France to be educated."

I wondered if Libby knew anything about this. It sounded as if Audubon's father might have taken advantage of a powerless person.

Mrs. Osmond sailed, almost danced, into our alcove—in a very good mood. She dropped two pair of white cotton gloves onto the illustration of two passenger pigeons in beautiful blues, their heads and necks gracefully intertwined. She instructed us to put on the gloves to protect the library's valuable folio from grease on our hands. We did, wiggling our fingers at one another, before returning to leafing through the pictures.

With my chin resting on my folded arms on the table, at times on the edge of sleep, I listened to Mary reading, in her lowered, library voice, from Audubon's descriptions of the birds. Audubon's self-imposed mission had been to paint every bird in North America. The Rathbone Warbler, the Swamp Sparrow, the White-eyed Vireo, the Great Horned Owl, and the amazing Passenger Pigeons that had once moved in endless sky-darkening flocks. Audubon would shoot his bird models dead, then manipulate them into poses with strings and wires like marionettes.

"He shot them?" I said.

"Yes, but he also calls the mating season the love season," Mary said with a mischievous look in her eye.

The portrait of the Ivory-billed Woodpecker and his drab mate showed them hard at work on a dead, white, moss-laced cypress branch. The text said the Ivory-billed lived in the southern hardwood forests. It was called "Lord God Bird," because people exclaimed "Lord God!" when they spotted one, they were so huge.

Although I doubted I would ever invoke "God" at the sight of a bird, the Ivory-billeds in the pictures and the descriptions *were* amazing. I was gradually becoming convinced that my woodpecker was one of them.

Mary returned from the bathroom, after what seemed like a long absence, slid back on the smooth seat of her oak chair, and folded her arms across her chest. "I saw them," she whispered, her nose crinkling.

"Saw who?"

"Those guys…the ones we saw that day on the road outside the college.

We crept to the edge of the alcove. Fear shot through me. There they were, in overcoats now, their hats sitting on top of the card catalogue while they fingered through cards in the drawers.

"What are they doing around here…back again?" I said.

"There's something so strange about them," Mary said.

"Hank wouldn't even let me call the gas station that time."

"What do you mean?" Mary asked.

"That day, you remember. Their car was out of gas? When I got back home and tried to call Tony's to help them out, Hank grabbed the phone out of my hand and hung it up. He wouldn't let me call. And he was mean about it."

"That is weird."

When we peeked out again at the two of them, they had their hats in their hands and were following Mrs. Osmond around, who appeared too busy to give them the "time of day" as Hank would have said.

Back in the alcove, distracted and shaken, I stared at the picture of the Ivory-billed couple, male and female, perched on the moss and lichen-covered branch. They mated for life, said the text. I thought of Hank and Libby. I thought of the Rosenbergs.

Should I tell my parents about seeing Mutt and Jeff in the library? I knew it would upset them, although I didn't understand why. They were creepy and mysterious, but there was no reason they shouldn't go into a public library.

I couldn't forget the haunted look on Hank's face when he so rudely stopped me from calling Tony's for them or on Libby's when we saw that gray Plymouth again. But I was afraid Libby and Hank might start making me stay closer to home, and I'd lose the little bit of freedom I had.

I decided the best thing was to keep the information to myself, to file it away with all the other things I didn't feel I could say or ask them about. They weren't forthcoming about a lot of stuff, and turnabout was fair play.

The next day, instead of heading to the library, Mary came home with me on the school bus. Hank and Libby weren't getting home until later. I wanted Mary to see the woodpecker, my magnificent Ivory-billed.

Grainy snow, like little hailstones, clattered down on our nylon parkas as we huddled together on the ledge outcropping, passing the binoculars back and forth.

"They don't get headaches, concussions, or brain damage from all the banging because they have double skulls and the impact is absorbed," I informed Mary.

"They're still bird brains," Mary said, "so not that much to protect. God thought up a lot of weird creatures with strange adaptations."

There! The brightness of his crest and dark wings folded over his shoulders, like a heavy cape, stood out against the snowy white landscape. I was sure he had to be appreciably longer than twenty inches, maybe more like twenty-five. He had the spooky, yellow-ringed eyes and the bright red crest jauntily rising from the top and back of his anvil-shaped head, just like in Audubon's painting. Though he was beautiful, my Ivory-billed was also fierce, brave, and pitiless in his assault on the dead tree.

The temperature was falling. My woodpecker, magnified in the binocular view, labored away, while Mary and I huddled closer together on the ledge for warmth, our nylon jackets rustling against one another, snow accumulating in the creases.

"So, tell me, are you still in love with John L.?" Mary asked.

"I'm *not* in love," I said. "I've spoken to him twice since the sock hop."

"You're kidding me," said Mary. "What's wrong with that boy?"

"His parents probably think my family are a bunch of pinkos."

"What difference does that make?" Mary asked. "You're not planning to get married to him, are you?"

"No," I said irritably.

"I have a crush on Robby," Mary said, leaning close. "One of my brother Kevin's friends."

"Which one is he? How old is he?" I asked.

"He's the redhead. He'll be sixteen in December."

"He's too old for you," I said, adjusting the focus on the binoculars.

"He is not. You sound like Annie O.," said Mary. "I think he maybe likes me, too."

The woodpecker had stopped drilling and was now delicately picking bugs out of the tree wood with the tip of his long beak. I pictured his long tongue carrying grubs like a conveyor belt down to his stomach. In profile and magnified, he looked even bigger and more magnificent as he clung to the vertical of the tree with his feet like a telephone repairman in spiked boots.

"He's an Ivory-billed, right?" I asked Mary.

"Of course he is," said Mary.

Any remaining doubt left me. Rare, I knew, believed by some to be extinct, but people claimed over years to have seen them, and now *I* had seen one. With Mary as my witness, I felt I'd seen something out of the ordinary, maybe even unique. I yearned for something amazing in my life, something to make me stand out. This, for the moment, seemed to be it.

It was getting too cold to be sitting outside. "We should call the Audubon Society," I said. "You can call them up and report sightings to them."

"Wait, I thought they're extinct." Mary said.

"*Nearly* extinct, I said. But there he is!"

"Lord God Bird!" Mary laughed. "Like the second coming of Christ, it sounds like."

"Well, seeing one would be sort of a miracle."

The woman who answered the phone at the New England office of the National Audubon Society sounded like she was in a rush. "We're about to close the office for the evening," she said, "but how can I help you?"

"My friend and I saw a…rare bird," I said.

"Yes, dear. Where did you see him? In the woods? In your back yard? What bird did you see?"

"An Ivory-billed Woodpecker," I said boldly, anticipating a dazzled response. Instead, there was silence on the other end of the line. Immediately, I felt on the spot and nervous, but Mary took it upon herself to urge me on, silently prancing around in front of me, head bobbing, thumbs-up, leaping into the air, making hand signals, as if she was conducting an orchestra or directing traffic.

"I see," said the woman on the phone, finally. "And where are you calling from, dear? Must be long distance. Somewhere down south, near the woods or swamps?" she guessed. "Louisiana, Arkansas, Alabama?"

"Eastern Massachusetts. In New England," I answered.

"And that's where you saw him?" she said, sounding dubious.

"Yes," I said, still excited, but with doubt edging in.

"Oh, my dear, have you seen a picture of this bird?"

"I've seen Audubon's prints in the library."

"How old are you, if I may ask?"

"Fourteen," I replied.

"I see," she woman sighed. "How large would you say this bird you saw is?"

"Probably twenty-five inches," I said.

"Wingspan and markings in flight? Did you see a wide, white trailing edge on the wings?"

"I've never really seen him fly," I said. "He's drilling in an old, dead tree down at the end of our driveway."

"Have you by any chance seen the female?"

"No, he's alone."

There was a long pause. "I don't want to disappoint you," the woman said, "but I'm sure you've heard—the Ivory-billed Woodpecker is believed to have been extinct for many years. And even when they were still occasionally spotted in the 1920s—rare, even then—they were only seen in the old growth hardwood forests of the southeastern United States. Places like Louisiana, Alabama, and Arkansas."

I fell silent as initial waves of humiliation rolled in. My Lord God Bird had not impressed.

"I think what you may have seen," said the lady, "is a Pileated Woodpecker. Very similar, but a good deal smaller."

"No," I protested. "He's very big."

"It's highly unlikely," said the woman.

"But he's so big…" I said, my voice fading.

Mary could see me sinking and she came up close to my face while I was trying desperately to get off the phone. She kept trying to make eye contact with me, which I refused, waving her away until she walked off in a huff.

"I'm very sorry, dear," said the Audubon lady. "We appreciate the call, though."

"What's wrong with you?" Mary demanded, once the phone was back on the hook.

"They're extinct."

"She *said* that? How does *she* know? She didn't see him. Anyway, so what if we made a mistake? It's not the end of the world. Everybody makes mistakes."

Mary was right, of course, but it didn't help me. I had made a big, embarrassing mistake. I'd been caught with my "bare face hanging out," as Hank would say. Shame and embarrassment *were* the end of the world.

CHAPTER ELEVEN

Wet snow slapped against the Heap's windshield, swept aside by the windshield wipers, forming two perfect fan shapes. The heater in The Heap was unreliable and, riding in the back seat, I pulled the collar of my parka and my scarf up around my face. Libby theorized the annual Goshen Town Meeting was scheduled in January so that not that many people would attend, due to the weather

An early January thaw had only been Nature's tease. Now the temperature had fallen again. The ground hog's verdict was far off and, whether he saw his shadow or not, there would remain endless weeks of winter on the long haul to April.

Libby had heard from Mr. Bramhall—certainly not from me—that we students could get extra credit in social studies class by attending a town meeting and writing a report on it. The same report could be entered into the Rotary Club's Democracy Essay Contest, and the winner would receive a hundred-dollar savings bond.

Libby became all enthused about the extra-credit and the contest and insisted that I come to the town meeting with them. I pleaded that I didn't need the extra credit or the money—there was nothing to buy in Goshen—but she wouldn't relent.

At least I could be pretty sure none of my classmates would be there to see me. I'd begged Mary to come along to keep me company, but she didn't even dare ask her parents. They would have thought it was a ridiculous idea. I did have fleeting, covetous thoughts about actually winning the hundred dollars.

Of course, I should want to write a good essay just for the sake of democracy, but I imagined how the US savings bond would look—lying, long and crisp in my jewelry drawer among the rings and pins Grandma Rose had handed down to me. The bond would lie there, earning interest, until the day I cashed it in and left home, although I couldn't imagine leaving home.

"You're going to see pure democracy in action, as opposed to representative government," Libby said. "Votes are decided by a show of hands. Children aren't allowed on the floor, but you'll sit in the balcony and be able to see and hear everything that goes on."

"Guess they're afraid someone might try to subvert democracy by having some babe-in-arms raise his little fist and be counted as a vote," Hank said.

"The building back in the 1700s was a congregational meeting house," he added, "one of the few original meeting houses left standing in New England. Back in the nineteenth century, they needed more space for a lot more people inside so—believe or not—they cut the darn thing in half, down the middle, moved one end out and added a sort of extender in the middle."

"You're making that up," I said from the back seat.

"I'll be happy to show you exactly where the walls were cut…good old New England ingenuity."

Snow swirled as Hank steered the Heap around the big stone First Parish Unitarian Church at the corner of the Post Road and Church Street, where bedraggled chrysanthemums from the fall remained in the Goshen Garden Club's flower pot. He worked the car into a line of traffic funneling toward the town hall.

"You can tell there's some hot stuff on the agenda tonight to bring all these folks out," Hank said. "Maybe an opening on the Trash Committee? Or the Cemetery Board?"

"Don't be funny," Libby said. "You know civil defense is on the agenda—after the break."

I gasped into my scarf. They'd neglected to mention this little detail to me—accidentally on purpose. Civil defense was obviously one of Libby's things, and lying by omission was one of their specialties.

"You know your boyfriend's father is chairing the meeting tonight, Sara," Hank said.

"He's not my boyfriend," I snapped, stung by another of their withheld surprises.

"Okay, okay." Hank said. "Your classmate, John L.'s father, then."

I slid low in my seat and pulled my parka tighter around me. "I don't care about the stupid Rotary contest," I sulked. "And I bet I won't see one other student up in the balcony."

"Too many people take their government for granted," Libby declared, like the civics teacher she was.

"I, for one, think it's a brilliant idea of your mother's," Hank said. "Just be sure you don't go casting any illegal votes from up there."

Hank began to sing to the beat of the windshield wipers: "Flat Foot Floogie with a floy, floy...." I, for one, was in no mood for his antics. But I could see Libby's head against the lit-up windshield, moving to the rhythm of his ditty.

I decided I hated them, although that word was forbidden in our house. They didn't understand me, or the way what they did, or made me do, affected me. I lived in Goshen, too. They were not on my side. They were only on one another's side.

We entered the old meeting house. They walked me up the stairs to the balcony, which stretched three quarters of the way around the hall and had, in addition to the pipe organ console, five or six rows of fold-down seats. Not another soul was up there. Just a lot of stored stuff—cardboard boxes, overpacked with dusty, faded old draperies—and the organ console with pipes rising to the ceiling. The only light came indirectly from the hall below, and from a red exit sign over the door at the head of the stairs behind me.

Hank pointed at where they'd cut the building in half to expand it. I thought I saw what he was talking about—like an old scar under coats and coats of white paint. Hank seemed to know everything about building construction. It was pure coincidence that he and grandpa had both grown up in the country and both knew about construction and chickens.

"Did you bring anything to take notes with?" Libby asked me.

Of course, I hadn't, and she pulled a small, spiral pad and ballpoint pen out of the pocket of her heavy coat and handed them to me.

Hank dusted off a balcony seat in the front row with his glove. "Mademoiselle, will this be acceptable? A lovely box seat?" He chucked me under the chin. "We'll see you at the break. Oh, look, even Mr. Tooey's here. See him down there? The grumpy-looking guy in the front row, last seat to the left."

I barely glanced where he was pointing, I felt so grumpy myself.

"Take good notes," Libby said, peering out over the balcony railing. "You might want to note that in colonial times, the balcony was where 'lower class' families, women and slaves sat?"

"Guess that makes me lower class," I said. "Or a slave, maybe?"

"I understand you didn't want to come," Libby kissed me on the cheek, and they turned to leave. Like a condemned prisoner, I watched them close the door with the red exit sign above it. From my seat, I could see over the gleaming oak banister and down into the main hall but hoped not to be visible from below.

Below, the glossy white of the walls and the pew dividers against the polished honey-colored wooden floors looked dazzling to the eye. The American flag and the gold-fringed flag of the Commonwealth of Massachusetts drooped from eagle-crowned poles on either side of a raised platform and long dead selectmen of the town glowered from oil portraits along the walls.

A low hum of conversation rose from the hall, punctuated by the snap-slap of wooden folding seats as more than a hundred people found places. Removing hats and scarves, the citizens of Goshen, hung their coats and jackets over the backs of their seats. I spotted Hank and Libby moving along an aisle near the front, where Mr. Bramhall and his wife, Amanda, had saved seats for them and were waving.

John L.'s father stood at the podium, pounding a gavel with one hand, drinking from a water glass with the other, and greeting people who stopped by to say hello. He looked nothing like John L. He was big in the chest, and on the shorter side, with half-glasses and receding hairline.

Mary's parents sat about halfway back on the far right. I could see Annie O'Reilly chatting with everybody, while Big Patrick, already looking bored, twiddled his thumbs on his belly that bulged over his infamous belt.

There was the Pledge of Allegiance to the flag, everybody with their hands on their hearts, and then Reverend Alcott of the First Parish Unitarian Church led everybody in the Lord's Prayer. My lips moved silently just as they did at school every day.

Another bang of the gavel. "The Goshen Annual Town Meeting will come to order," Mr. L. said. "Welcome, citizens. It's gratifying to see so many of you here tonight, especially given the sloppy weather."

It was odd to hear the amplified voice of Mr. L, whom Mary liked to refer to as my father-in-law, but whom I'd never met. He said: "Before we get started, I'm sorry to announce that Peter Vogt has suffered a heart attack and plans to resign from the school board, effective immediately. Our prayers go out to him and his family for a speedy recovery. We encourage you to think about who might fill the vacancy. We will schedule a special election in June."

Mr. L. next announced that the Selectmen had approved the budget item, recommended by the Public Safety Committee, for hiring an additional policeman. This was affirmed by an overwhelming voice vote from the floor. A roar of "Ayes." Then, "Nays?" Silence.

"New cop," I wrote in the notebook. "Goshen-safest place on earth," I added, together with a doodle of a policeman waving his baton. Then, I drew a tree with a heart carved in it, "John L., Jr. and Sara G," and a bird of no particular species perched on one of the branches.

Next up was the Traffic Committee. Libby had explained earlier that someone always wanted to widen North Avenue, but most Goshenites didn't want to make it easier for people from Concord and Lexington to cut through town just to get to their electronics jobs a few minutes faster. Hank and Libby were against the widening because they didn't want to help the companies on Route 128, many of which had government contracts connected to the military.

I wrote down the number of votes, for and against, and added, "No widening road for Raytheon."

It seemed like forever, but finally, Mr. L. announced a break for coffee and refreshments, supplied by the "kind ladies of the garden club," and then: "We will take up the important matters around civil defense listed on your agendas immediately after the break. So, enjoy coffee and cookies, and don't forget to come back promptly in fifteen minutes."

"Un-civil defense after break," I wrote in the notebook, together with a fulminating mushroom cloud.

"Everything copacetic up here?" Hank asked, as he and Libby both appeared behind me in the door to the balcony.

"I'm okay," I said.

Hank pulled out a stack of chocolate sandwich cookies from his shirt pocket and held them up for me to see.

"It's interesting to hear Robert's Rules of Order actually used, isn't it?" Libby asked, as she ran her hand across the silent organ keyboard.

"Kind of," I conceded, nibbling on a cookie.

"Ugh!" Libby cringed. "The fillings in those things are pure fat and sugar." She paced nervously at the balcony rail and looked down into the hall.

"I vote for the second half to be short and sweet," Hank said. "And all we have to do, my bride, is stay cool and collected."

"I wanna go wait in the car," I said with a distinct whine in my voice.

"Oh no, it's much too cold out there," Hank said. "Just eat your cookies and take your notes. It'll be over before you know it."

Downstairs, Mr. L. was already pounding the gavel.

As Hank and Libby's footsteps faded, I stepped up onto the organ bench and, double-checking that the switch was off, I sounded a grand, silent chord with both hands. I played the Bach Invention that had led to my probationary status with Libby. Unfazed by mistakes I couldn't hear, my fingers flew over the supple action of the keys.

I closed my eyes and swayed. I raised my hands dramatically and made fearless attacks. I played with confidence and verve, just like Muriel would have liked, three-octave arpeggios, two hands. I whipped off scales, eyes closed. I was Myra Hess. Wanda Landowska. Phantom applause pattered in my head, a non-existent audience charmed by my flawless performance. I bowed modestly, returned to my seat, and took up my notebook.

"I hope the refreshments met with your approval." Mr. L.'s voice boomed into the hall, punctuated by his gavel. "Let's settle down, please. Thank you." Bang, bang. "As some of you may know, the Commonwealth of Massachusetts has charged each city and town with developing 'a coordinated civil defense plan.' I'm glad to say, your selectmen have already been hard at work doing just that. We've instituted air raid drills in the schools, for example.

"Most recently, the state has, in addition, allocated matching funds to build underground command centers from which town operations could continue in the event of a nuclear attack, ensuring what the state calls 'continuity of government.' These would also serve as extra storage places for emergency supplies. We're recommending that the town avail itself of these funds and vote to go ahead with such a plan. When combined with local resources, we should be able to have an underground command post, second to none."

"N-u-c-l-e-a-r attack," I printed carefully in my notebook with a drawing of people and birds hiding under a rock.

"Such preparations," Mr. L. continued, "are especially important for us in light of the fact that Boston's latest civil defense plans call for evacuation of the city. As we are only twenty miles out of the city, we can expect hordes of evacuees to stream west through our little town. It's terrible to contemplate, but let's face it, they could easily decide to stop and help themselves to… what we have."

Outbreaks of voices rose like puffs of alarm from the hall.

"I'd like to entertain a motion," Mr. L. said, banging his gavel twice, "to establish a committee to study the feasibility of building such a secret command center right here under the town meeting hall."

I could only see their backs, but Hank and Libby appeared to be sitting very still and close together, united, I could almost feel it, in their immediate disapproval and exasperation. Hank slid his arm across Libby's shoulders. To hold her down, I thought.

Fear and anger welled up in me and the old doubt and confusion too. What was the right way to think about this? To prepare for the worst that human nature could deliver or keep faith and be blown to smithereens? And now, the new threat—the looting of every grain of rice by marauding hordes?

Someone seconded Mr. L.'s motion, then "discussion" was called for, along with an instruction. "Please, if you want to participate in the discussion, first state your name and address. Thank you."

The audience murmured.

Shaking off Hank's arm, Libby raised her hand.

The gavel sounded, and then, "The gentle lady in the fourth row, you are recognized."

Libby stood up slowly. Even from the back, anyone could see that Libby, tall and slim, looked beautiful. I slid far backwards in my seat, but I could hear her voice loud and clear rising from the hall.

"Libby Green, 52 Guernsey Road. I'd like it on the record that I oppose building such an underground command post. Call it what you like…."

The hall rustled and murmured, but Mr. L. quieted them with one sharp strike of the gavel. "Let her speak."

"Keeping the existence or location of these places secret," said Libby, "from evacuees from the city, from our neighbors driven from their homes by bombs and fall-out, or even those just fleeing imminent danger, is plainly immoral and wrong." Libby sat down.

A loud buzz of murmured conversation erupted in the hall. I opened my eyes and slid forward to look over the banister.

Mr. L. spoke in a slow, indulgent tone. "Thank you, Mrs. Green. I should point out that these people evacuating the city of Boston would *not* be our neighbors. They would be strangers." The hall buzzed.

"Would they be 'strangers' or 'neighbors' in the Christian sense?" A voice came from a white-haired man in a priest's collar, who stood at the side of the hall, and gestured with a white Meerschaum pipe. "And this would assume anyone at all would survive such a nuclear attack...."

Mr. L. smiled. "Father, with all due respect, most of us are familiar with the minority and misguided view that because of how dangerous and destructive nuclear war would be, we should not prepare for it." Mr. L. cleared his throat noisily and searched the audience for more hands.

As the citizens of Goshen chattered among themselves, I noticed standing next to the man Mr. L. had just called Father was a tall, slim man, also in a black cassock and collar. His blond hair shone in the bright lights of the hall. It was the same young man we'd seen in the woods, swimming in the pond. I felt a rise of excitement and couldn't wait to tell Mary.

"Alright," boomed Mr. L's voice. "If there's no more discussion, we'll go ahead and vote. Proposition: Should the town of Goshen proceed to plan and build a bunker for the purpose of protecting and sustaining the town government in the event of a nuclear attack?"

A chorus of "ayes" rumbled through the hall, followed by a few, scattered "nays," most of which came from the area where the Bramhalls and my parents were sitting. Relieved that my ordeal was over and done with, I slipped on my parka and prepared myself to be whisked away.

The gavel sounded again and Mr. L. said, "People, we're not quite finished."

Then he called my father's name, loud and clear, over the speaker. "Henry Green? Could you identify yourself, please?" Mr. L. peered down from the podium over his half-glasses.

Hank stood up and raised his hand. "Henry. *Hank* Green, I'm right here."

"Ah, yes, Mr. Green. There you are. Some of us were wondering," Mr. L's lips brushed the microphone, making a harsh noise, "if you would do us the favor of joining or perhaps consulting with our planning committee for the bunker. We understand you are an MIT graduate in engineering, so you would be well-qualified to advise us on structural issues that might arise from the fact that this meeting house is so old and is located on pastureland with an unstable water table."

My heart raced. Why on earth would they want Hank, who disagreed with them on everything, on their stupid committee? The audience began to buzz when Hank took a long time to answer, Mr. L chuckled into the microphone, "I understand you may need time to think it over. And maybe consult your wife?"

Bristling, Hank answered, "I can assure you that I make my own professional decisions. But the issue here has nothing to do with tensile strength of materials or snow loads. It's the ethics of the thing. I'm afraid my conscience makes it impossible for me to participate in this project." And Hank sat down.

I cowered in my seat, embarrassed for him.

"I'm sorry you feel that way," said Mr. L. "If you have a change of heart we would be glad to hear from you. Thank you, Mr. Green—*Hank*. Ladies and Gentlemen, unless someone has something else to add, the meeting is adjourned."

I sank lower in my seat as I waited for my parents to come get me.

Driving home, nobody spoke for a long time. It had turned colder, and the Heap had accumulated a three-inch coat of light, powdery snow on top of the layer of slush from before the meeting. I curled up in the back seat in my parka, shivering with cold and annoyance.

"You were quite restrained, mi Pantera," Hank said. "I'm proud of you."

"But *you* were a tiger," said Libby.

"I came *this* close to citing scripture to them." Hank held up his thumb and forefinger an inch apart for Libby and me to see. "Swords into plowshares and such."

Libby turned toward him, her silhouette outlined against the windshield. "And what do you know about scripture, sir?"

Hank began thundering at the windshield words he said were from Isaiah II in what he called his radio voice, which always sounded like God to me, that is, if God existed and had a voice. "They shall beat their swords into plowshares," he thundered, "and their spears into pruning-hooks. Nation shall not lift up sword against nation, neither shall they learn war anymore."

We were all silent for a moment.

"I wanted to tell them they were being un-Christian and immoral," Hank said.

"Why didn't you?" asked Libby.

"The usual reason. We have to *live* in this town." He leaned over the steering wheel and cleared away some condensation from the inside of the windshield.

"How does he know where you went to school?" Libby asked.

"I have no idea. Did *you* tell somebody, Sara?" Hank asked.

"No," I replied sharply, muffled by my parka and scarf.

"Anyway, I'm not about to help them fortify a place where they can have their meetings to strategize how to keep out the poor people who come stumbling out here from Boston after an attack...." Hank paused. "Although I sure could use the work."

He reached out and pulled Libby closer.

I recoiled from their blood-curdling display that just confirmed for me that my parents remained their contradictory, secretive, but always united selves, mocking and contemptuous of danger.

Maybe I was jealous and feeling left-out. Maybe I wanted to shake them out of their self-satisfaction. But, all at once, I emerged from my cocoon of parka and scarf just long enough to say, "Did I tell you Mary and I saw Mutt and Jeff in the library a few weeks ago?"

Libby and Hank moved apart, and Libby turned around to look at me. "Why didn't you tell us before?"

I shrugged back into my parka. "I don't know. I forgot. But, who are they, really?"

Libby looked back over at Hank, who nodded. "They work for the FBI. They're assigned to watch us," Libby answered.

"Why? What for?" I demanded

"Because they think our ideas are dangerous and they're afraid we might *infect* the rest of America," Libby said.

"*Infect* America? Like polio?" I asked.

"I guess so," Hank said.

"Is that a crime?" I asked.

"Apparently, some people think it is, but really it's free speech," said Hank. "We don't have anything to worry about."

CHAPTER TWELVE

Mary and I broke out of the woods into the cold sun, our white figure-skates dangling from our shoulders like pairs of shot white birds. We gazed from a height out across the college pond. Seven acres of ice, covered last night in several inches of new snow. After months of alternating sub-zero temperatures and short thaws, the ice must be five or six inches thick. People said you could drive a car out on ice that thick.

"Now you'll probably write the best essay." Mary said, as we looked out through our breath at the small figures down below, skating and plowing the snow aside. "But you never told me anything about the town meeting."

"Your folks were there. It was bo-ring. I had to sit in the organ balcony by myself the whole time and listen to Mr. L drone on and on. He was the moderator."

"Your father-in-law! So what did the town discuss?" Mary asked, her cheeks on fire from the cold.

"Stop calling him that!" I said. "There was the traffic committee report, the cemetery committee report, etc., etc., etc."

"Glad I wasn't there. It must have been boring."

"After boring snacks, they discussed civil defense. Libby, of course, had to stand and speak up."

"Uh-oh. So, what did she say?"

"She basically told them all off, said the plans they have for a bunker to hide the town government after a nuclear attack was immoral," I said in a monotone. "Because it made people think nuclear war was a possibility and could be survived."

"She's right, but it must have been…embarrassing for sure."

"I ducked down so nobody saw me up there, I hope. Then Mr. L asked

Hank to be on their committee to engineer the bunker."

"That's strange."

"Yes, since he already heard Libby say they disapproved of the bunker"

"Sounds like they were just trying to embarrass him."

"I think so," I said. I was beginning to know about embarrassment firsthand. A few days after the town meeting, someone had scotch-taped a sign on my school locker saying, "Better dead than Red?" My heart racing with fear, I ripped it down and worried about how many people had already seen it.

Against a backdrop of snow-frosted evergreen trees on the opposite hill, we watched priests in black wool caps, their cassocks swinging like long, black bells, use wooden hand plows and brooms to clear snow off paths for skating and even for hockey rinks. Skate blades flashed as more and more people in brightly colored parkas, scarves, and hats began gliding over new sections of cleared ice. Hockey players and figure skaters appeared as the sun climbed higher, and children who were small enough to ride, four at a time, in the big, flat-bottomed snow scoopers, begged the priests to push them and twirl them on the ice.

We clambered down the hill toward the warming shack.

"You on or off with John L.?"

"Off. For sure now. Why would he want a subversive as a girlfriend?"

"But, you're not a subversive."

I shrugged. "Not exactly."

"That would be guilt by association."

"I guess so, " I said, although it had never occurred to me that I could be seen as separate from my parents on these matters.

The warming hut was a large ice-fishing shack permanently pulled up onto the bank, just off the ice. Once inside, which was dark except for yellowish light from two small, dirty windows, Mary and I sat on wooden benches within the circle of heat from a woodstove in the middle. Lost socks and gloves hung on benches, and snow boots were lined up against the walls.

On the other side of the stove, three white-haired priests sat together, close to the fire, talking, laughing, and lacing up their skates. Mary whispered to me that the one smoking a pipe was Father Gregory, who taught her Catechism class.

My eyes teared from the smoke as I peered through the gloom at the three shepherds of Mary's faith, in gloves and jackets, chatting and smiling like regular people. Though I was raised as an atheist, I invariably felt awe when I came face to face with the Catholic clergy. Maybe it was their dramatic regalia. I'd seen nuns in Boston, walking in twos, floating along in their flowing, black habits and starched white headgear like giant tufts up top, like enormous ruffed grouse.

Even now that I'd seen one of the purveyors of "opiate of the people" naked through binoculars, priests didn't seem any less mysterious or marvelous to me. Father Gregory smiled between puffs from his pipe and pointed its curved stem, across the wood stove, straight at Mary.

Mary whispered, "My parents will kill me if I don't go over there and say hello." She wrinkled her nose at me the way she did when she was having wayward thoughts, and wobbled on her skates over to where the priests were sitting.

"Good morning, Father." Mary's voice was high and clear above the fire's roar. Mary knew her manners and how to speak to grown-ups. Even though Big Patrick made jokes about the priests behind their backs, he expected her and her brothers to treat them with absolute respect.

In my house, where grownups and children were supposedly equal, there was no difference between just ordinary talking and polite exchanges with older or revered people. Formal phrases like "Good morning," "Good afternoon," and "Good evening," were only familiar to me from the nineteenth century novels we had to read for school.

Father Gregory stood up, tall and a little unsteady on his skates. "Hello, Mary. I wasn't sure I recognized you at first. These ancient eyes, you know. And who's your friend?" he asked, jutting his chin toward me.

"That's my friend Sara, Father."

From those same novels, I knew I was supposed to stand up now, make my way over there, and try to say something polite and, if possible, charming. I stood and made my wobbly way over on the rutted wooden floor, around the stove in their direction. "How do you do?" I murmured stiffly.

"Ah, Sara, a lovely Old Testament name," Father Gregory said.

"But with the Spanish spelling," Mary volunteered.

In his flowing cassock and heavy sweater, Father Gregory's bulk blocked out most of the light from the window. His eyebrows stood out white and tangled like barbed wire. His black knit watch cap perched on neatly combed white hair. "And do ya' have a last name, Sara?"

"Sara Green, sir," I croaked, focused on keeping my balance on my skates.

He looked hard at me and I was sure he could see right into my godless soul. He must be able to tell, just by looking, that I was not Catholic. Could he tell I was an atheist or Jewish? Maybe he could tell by the olive skin inherited from Hank's side of the family, or the hint of my grandmother's nose, or from the tell-tale absence of even a tiny cross on a chain around my neck.

"Well," said Father Gregory, his study of me apparently complete, "I'm pleased to meet you, Sara, and to see you young ladies out in the fresh air. This weather's sure to put roses in your cheeks."

"Yes, Father, it's very cold," Mary said.

"So, ladies," Father Gregory said, hugging himself, "I guess there's no more putting off the inevitable. I'll see you out on the ice."

Sun glistened blindingly from piles of cleared snow. The sky was cloudless, a searing blue. Mary and I teetered hand in hand, along the wooden planks laid out to bridge the chopped-up mixture of slushy ice and mud at the pond's edge. We stepped carefully out onto the cleared ice. Inching forward, we held our arms out as we got back our skating legs.

Soon we were gliding, pumping, and edging into the flow of skaters that moved in a counterclockwise direction in a long oval on the newly cleared ice. Some boys from our class raced by on tube skates, waving hockey sticks in pursuit of hockey pucks, yelling at us as they passed. An older couple, on a patch of cleared ice in the center of the oval, were having their first tentative ice dance of the year. At first, they looked as if they were just holding one another up, but soon they got their old rhythm back and began to waltz, rotating slowly.

As Mary and I glided along in the outside ring of skaters, a shadow appeared in my peripheral vision, skating very fast, wearing black corduroy trousers, dark sweater, a black cap. He shot by us, arms pumping, clouds of condensation streaming from his lips. When he reached the far end of the pond, he sat back, legs flexed, and, without losing momentum, crossed one skate over the other, carving a wide, graceful turn.

Mary jabbed my arm and whispered, "It's him."

"Who?"

"Our seminarian," she hissed. "The one we saw in the woods, swimming." Mary giggled into her gloves and broke out of the revolving circle of skaters, pulling me with her. We fell, sprawled at the edge of the ice together into a pile of plowed-off snow.

"It can't be the same one," I said, laughing and helping her up, but falling back down again. We slithered around like lizards at the edge of the ice and pretended to get our skates and legs tangled.

"He skates like an angel," Mary said as she lay back on the ice, skates wide apart, brushing her arms up and down, trying to make a snow angel.

"How do *you* know how an angel skates?" I demanded.

"A cherub, then," Mary's smile had a little twist at the edge the way it did when she was thinking impure thoughts, like naked cherubs in the cold.

We rejoined the flow of skaters, holding hands, and gliding slowly along with the rest, waiting for our priest to come around again. Soon, there he was, moving so fast, his outline was blurred, but this time I had a glimpse of his yellow hair, sprouting from under his black cap.

Mary was right. It was our towheaded, naked angel.

We became more excited and a little nervous. We convinced ourselves that he would recognize us if he saw us. By the time he came around for the third time, crouched fiercely, legs driving, we were laughing uncontrollably.

Our fingers and toes were numb and our cheeks were so cold they felt hot by the time we headed back to the warming hut. Father Gregory was standing at the edge of the ice, still on his skates, smoking his pipe and barring our way to the plank path to the hut. He appeared to be waiting for us. Surely there was no way he could know we were being lewd and gross about one of his priests in training.

As we came near, he pushed off and took a long glide in our direction and did a smart hockey stop right in front of us. In the bright sunlight, I could see the creases at the corners of his eyes were as deep as Grandpa Joe's. Thin red veins meandered across his nose and the smoke from his pipe filtered through his eyebrows before it dissipated into the air.

"So, my new fine young friend Sara—Sara Green. I've been thinking. Could Libby Green be your mother?"

Fear seized me. My gaze shifted to the landscape behind him, and to the chapel and bell tower on the hill. "Yes, sir," I said. "She's my mother."

"And she is the same person who thinks we shouldn't have bomb shelters or air raid drills in the schools?"

I took a small step backwards and my skates slid out from under me. I sat down hard on the slushy ice and I felt the cold water begin to soak through my overalls. Father Gregory glided forward, reached down for my hand and, with Mary helping from behind, pulled me back up onto my skates.

"Thank you," I said, nodding. "That's what she thinks."

Father Gregory pointed at me with his pipe stem. "Well, Sara Green, I say good for her. I agree with her. I've always said that when the ladies enter the public square, the world would be a more peaceful place. Only God can protect us from ourselves, certainly not drills and shelters. Don't you agree, Sara?"

I nodded again, my teeth beginning to chatter.

"Of course," Father Gregory said, "some people are so scared these days that they can't see what's right and wrong or that we are all neighbors."

Now I was sure. Father Gregory was the same priest who'd spoken up at the town meeting, echoing Libby's sentiments, with our blond priest by his side. He pulled a tobacco pouch from his jacket pocket, re-filled his pipe, pressing the flakes in with stained fingertips, and lit it with a wooden match.

He gazed at me through match flame, then through smoke. "It's an honor and pleasure to meet you, Sara. Ah, but you girls look cold. You'd better go in and warm up. And as for you, Miss Mary O'Reilly, I trust I'll see you tomorrow at Catechism and Mass."

CHAPTER THIRTEEN

Libby barged into my bedroom, no knock, no warning.

I sat cross-legged on my bed, bent over my geometry book, chewing on my eraser. I saw my closet half open and debated whether to jump up and casually close it. Too late. Libby crossed the room. Instead of closing the closet door, as she ordinarily might have, she pulled it wide open.

I watched, heart thumping, as she parted the clothes hangers and bent over for a closer look. She turned slowly, shaking her head at me in disbelief. "You've been hiding that thing here all this time?"

It was the Philco. I was caught red-handed.

"I haven't been using it," I said. "All you can get on it is snow."

"I see," Libby said and looked out my window as if appealing for help with the sheer difficulty of me.

"Oh, wow," Hank said, after she'd lugged it out and placed it on top of the washing machine in the kitchen for display. 'Where did *that* come from? Did the trash people reject it?"

I leaned against the doorframe, watching them.

"I can't believe your daughter would be so sneaky."

"Yes, Sara, sneakiness is not cool," Hank said. "We just need to decide what to do with it now, since Sara seems so…attached to it."

Libby shook her head in frustration. "I guess I'll have to take it to the dump myself to make sure it stays gone."

Hank scratched his head, as if deep in thought. "But, Lib, why punish the TV? In the marketplace of ideas, how are we going to compete if we don't know what the opposition is saying?"

"What's upsetting is that Sara purposely thwarted our attempts to protect her from corrosive commercial forces."

"She has a rebellious streak," he shrugged. "A chip off the old block. Probably hereditary. Maybe we should show mercy, chalk it up to her being fourteen, and banish the Philco to my backroom office. Then, when spring comes, we can all watch baseball!"

Libby hesitated, in a rare moment of doubt. "There is always baseball…." she said, trailing off.

"And if we let the monster stay, then by reverse psychology, she'll soon feel like tossing it out the window herself," added Hank.

"Reverse psychology?" I said. "Like when Brer Rabbit begs Brer Fox to throw him into the Briar patch?"

"Exactly," Libby said. "How do you know that story?"

"Fourth grade," I said.

"Those Uncle Remus stories are racist, you know. That dialect is a grown white man's fantasy from being read stories as a boy by his Black nanny."

"So you're treating me like I'm Pavlov's dog."

"I don't think it's a conditioned response we're looking for here. It's for you to learn for yourself," Libby said.

So, just like that, the Philco could stay. It was a miracle. Libby had actually changed her mind. Hank and I carried the little TV across the breezeway, to his backroom office, set it up on a cardboard box and dragged a webbed plastic garden chaise in from the back lawn.

"One of these days, we'll get an aerial for it, so we can actually see something," Hank said. Once, Hank had worked for Grandpa Joe in his construction company, until their arrangement ended because Grandpa was "too much of a roughneck," Hank said.

After that, Hank started his own company. He bid on small, what he called "odd-ball" government jobs. Short bridges that had to be built overnight, repair work on aging WPA projects from the 1930s, Navy practice sites in the middle of Boston Harbor. The government might be clunky and slow, he said, but eventually you did get paid.

Hank used the large barely insulated room attached to the back of the garage as his office. He had a cranky space heater, bins for his plans and blueprints and a drafting table with two, tall goose-necked lamps that looked like a pair of egrets performing a mating dance. His old mandolin hung on a nail on the wall.

When the cold weather came, and frozen ground shut down outdoor construction, he moved his operation inside to the dining room table, along with all his pencils, T-squares, gum erasers. There he estimated and bid on jobs that hopefully would begin when spring came.

As soon as the earth began to thaw, Hank left the house more often to check on his jobs as they came back to life, and I resumed duties as his part-time after-school secretary.

On days Mary and I didn't go to the library, the school bus dropped me off near my house and I picked up the mail from the RFD mailbox at the foot of the driveway—mostly bills. Then I went to the back room office to check for messages on the Gizmo.

What we called the Gizmo was the first automatic telephone answering machine, rented from the telephone company. It was a contraption of gray metal and plastic, the size of a small suitcase which sat on top of a filing cabinet. It "answered" the phone and recorded incoming messages on electromagnetic tape.

Hank's message said: "You have reached the Hank Green Corporation and my new futuristic answering machine. Don't be afraid of it. After the tone, just speak slowly and clearly into the phone with your message, and I'll give you a call back as soon as I can."

My job was to be there when he called in from a pay phone at 3:30 to re-play any new messages directly into the mouthpiece for him to hear.

One day in March, John L. rode his bicycle across town to my house. After an hour of homework at the kitchen table, we went out to the office to watch some television. The little Philco sat on a cardboard box across from a webbed plastic love seat draped with two thread-bare army surplus blankets.

Cold dust spiced the air. Foil-wrapped insulation puffed out between the studs of the unfinished walls. Cardboard boxes, full of never-unpacked engineering books, were everywhere, and rolled-up drafting paper and blueprints pointed out from Hank's bins like canons.

John L. stood warily in the doorway, while I got down on my knees among cobwebs and dust, and struggled to light up the space heater. "This is where you watch television?"

"Come in and close the door," I told him. "It's cold in here."

"Wow, I love your family," said John L., closing the door behind him. "They're so…different."

"Weird, you mean?"

"That's not what I said. What time do your parents get home?"

"Around 6:00, usually."

"Both of them? Can I help you with that?"

"No, I better do it."

John L. swung his book bag from his shoulder to the floor and went to Hank's drafting table. "Look at this," he said, pointing to an architectural drawing of a little bridge, complete with bushes and trees sketched in. "My dad's a boring old lawyer," John said. "Your dad's different, he's kind of like an artist."

"My dad is pretty cool, sometimes," I said, still on my knees on the floor.

"And your mother is pretty…um, pretty," John L. said.

"Yes. I know, my mother's pretty." I struck a match, while holding in the button for the space heater's pilot light, half expecting it to ignite and blow the roof off. Thankfully, it caught fire with a soft, breathy sound.

"And—she's got some pretty wild ideas," John L. said.

"Is that what your father says?" I asked.

"Yeah, kind of," he replied.

"I was there at the town meeting your dad chaired."

"I thought kids aren't allowed."

"My parents made me go. I had to sit in the balcony… by myself."

"So, you heard everything?"

"What did you hear about the meeting?" I asked.

"Well, not a whole lot. We don't discuss that stuff at the dinner table."

I found myself wondering what John L.'s family *did* discuss at dinner. "Come on, what did your dad say?"

"That your mom and dad don't believe in civil defense."

"Well, kind of. Everybody must think it's weird that I leave school for air raid drills."

John L. shrugged. "Maybe they just don't understand."

"Do you?"

"Kind of. Not really."

"It's because they think the drills lull people into thinking nuclear war is a realistic option."

"Guess that sort of makes sense."

We sat, side by side, on the plastic-webbed chaise. We wrapped ourselves in the army blankets, and turned on the television and found a daytime western

John said he liked. The screen filled with snowy pictures of horses and men, yelling over foreboding music, the hollow wooden soundstages resounding.

"You're definitely going to need an aerial," said John L. He stood up, opened his blanket, and wrapped me, my blanket, and himself up into one olive drab bundle. With the feeble contribution of the space heater, things began to heat up.

The effect of John L.'s hands moving, exploring, darting, and touching—at first with a layer of clothing separating our skin, then not—became thrilling. I was acutely aware of the recent amplification and enlivenment of what Libby's book called "secondary sex characteristics," and I never wanted him to stop.

Meanwhile, some part of me that wasn't melting in his hands, observed as if from above, part voyeur, part nervous frontier guard, enforcer of the hazy line between exploratory and dangerous, holding out against incursions that I now knew could land me in one of those maternity homes.

The black telephone on top of one of the filing cabinets began to ring. I struggled to free myself from the blankets and scuttled across the cold room, fumbling to rebutton my blouse. I gave John the shush sign and picked up the receiver.

"Hey, Sara. You busy?" came Hank's invariably cheerful voice from a payphone somewhere. He always sounded as if the most extraordinary thing had just happened to him and he couldn't wait to tell me all about it. "D'ya have a few minutes to get the messages off the tape machine for your old dad?"

"Sure," I said, shaken by the coincidence of his call and our using his office for what Mary would call carnal purposes.

I could hear the roar of a milkshake machine over the phone. I loved to catch him in the act of stopping in for the afternoon chocolate frappe. He supposedly drank it to soothe his stomach ulcer. "Are you at Brigham's or Schrafft's?"

"What kind of a question is that? Where do you think I am?"

"Brigham's," I said.

"Good guess," Hank said.

"I'll have those messages for you right away, sir." I put the phone down. With John L. watching closely, I switched the Gizmo to rewind. The tape squealed and whirred, rewinding. I pressed the "playback" button and I held the phone receiver against the machine's speaker so Hank could hear as it played back the new messages.

"Hey, Hank," said the first recorded voice, "my children are starving. Cut me a check, will you? This is Jeff."

There was an electronic buzz and then, the next message: "For the love of Mike, Hank, send me money. Kids need milk money. We need to pay the electric bill. This is Patrick." The third: "For God's sake, Hank, senda cash money. This is Tulio. The wife is making my life miserable."

The fourth and last message was from Mr. Lake, whom I'd met once, a man so pale, his skin had a blue tinge. "Mistah Green," his voice came out of the machine flat, with the drawn-out vowels of New England. "Sorry to tell yah, that dredgin' job I just finished for you down at the hahbah." His voice cracked. "Chain snapped on the barge, and everything we took out of there's back down on the bottom again. I'll go back to work soon as I get her fixed, but…I'm gonna need some money for that and to tide me over."

"That's the last message," I said into the phone.

"Okay, Sara, thanks a lot," said Hank, sounding less cheerful than he had before. "I'll take care of everything as soon as possible. I feel bad. But the building business is a daisy chain. The government is slow. I can't pay the subs until I get paid. Okay, bye, Sara." With the frappe machine still loud in the background, he hung up.

I walked slowly back to where John, shivering, opened the blankets and wrapped us up. "Who *were* those guys?" John L. asked, looking troubled.

"They're the 'subs,'" I murmured, bringing the blanket up around my face. "The subcontractors who work on his jobs."

"It sounded like they were really desperate," said John L. "They were begging. Why doesn't he pay them?"

"He has to wait for the government to pay him. He has deep respect for the workers." I tried to give the word the noble, uplifting feel it had when Libby or Hank said it, but it felt a little flat on my tongue. "They're the salt of the earth. The folks that make the world go 'round," I added.

"And get paid late," John L. chuckled, as he worked to unbutton my blouse again.

"He does the best he can," I said, pushing his hand away. "My father respects people who work with their hands and sweat through their clothes. The guys who dig the trenches, carry cement in bags on their shoulders and lug the wheelbarrows full of sand and gravel."

"My goodness," said John L. "You really sound like you believe all that… Commie stuff."

"It's not Commie stuff," I said, "but I guess I do believe it."

No sooner did we settle back to kissing, with John's hands finding their way back into my blouse, than the Gizmo clicked to life with another incoming call. I had forgotten to turn down the volume, and an unfamiliar loud voice began to speak.

"Mr. Green, you don't know me, but it's come to the attention of some of us that your wife, Libby Green, née Cohen, is trying to stand in the way of Goshen developing a safe and sane plan for Civil Defense in and outside of the schools."

John L.'s eyes went wide. "Who's that?" he asked.

The speaker on the phone cleared his throat. "With full disclosure, Mr. Green, you should know that we know all about your wife's subversive past, ever since her mention in Agent Herbert Philbrick's memoir, and I'm sure you wouldn't want such damaging information to become widespread knowledge around town where you and your family have chosen to live. A word to the wise should be sufficient." Click, whir. Rewind.

Wrapped in the blankets, I suddenly felt very cold. A cold sweat broke out from every nook and cranny of my body.

John drew his hands back to himself. "What does he mean about your Mom's past?" he asked.

"I'm not really sure," I said.

John L. slowly, but deliberately, untangled himself from the blankets and stood up. "I guess I'd better get going," he said, looking confused. He watched me as I stood up too and folded up the blankets, laying them carefully back on the chaise.

"I guess I'll…see you…back at school." John L. said and gave me a kiss on the top of my head and opened the door to leave. A blast of cold air blew in as he went out and, with it, came a sense of confusion, and loneliness, and of danger.

One thing was clear to me. If Libby heard that message, she would get her back up and do something—what, I couldn't imagine—but something to make things worse. I couldn't let that happen. I had to take care of this myself.

I went to the Gizmo, pressed the button to rewind the message tape, which set it so that when the next message came in, the machine would record right over the previous ones, sending the offending message to oblivion.

CHAPTER FOURTEEN

The anonymous message on the Gizmo haunted me, but, when I told Mary about it, she soon had us both laughing. "Don't you get it?" she said. "That message saved your virginity and therefore your future!"

After a week or two, John L. resurfaced at school, walking me to class, his hesitancies about me and my family's peculiarities apparently dissipated. Then he started begging me to take him to the college. I thought of the college as Mary's place, hers and mine, but when I asked her, she said, "It's fine. Just don't do anything I wouldn't do."

It was Saturday. John L. was on his way, peddling to my house. Hank and Libby had gone off to the lumber yard to buy some knotty pine to finally panel over the insulation in the backroom office, to "warm it up a bit." They'd left their bedroom door ajar.

Their double bed, with its Mondrian style bedspread and its plain blond wood headboard, plus the rag rug on the floor, was visible from the hall. I wasn't expressly forbidden to go in there. I had my own self-imposed rules concerning their privacy. I very rarely went in their room by myself and, then only if I had to get something in particular. I would *never* set foot in their bathroom. I was too squeamish about what I might find there, things related to the creepy idea that they might have sex sometimes.

Still, since the town meeting and the Gizmo message, I had a vague sense of the necessity of stepping up my surveillance of them—to know more. There were still secrets, especially about the past, being withheld from me. It wasn't right. I was old enough to know family secrets, but they preferred to leave me ignorant, helpless, and defenseless.

Having no idea what I might be looking for, and listening hard in case they might come home sooner than I calculated, I crossed the threshold into their bedroom. I looked out their window, across the lawn and the badminton court, and was startled to see Mr. Tooey, in his felt hat and overalls, coming over the wall with his bucket of corn for the pheasants.

The bed hadn't been made, and the boldly-colored bedspread had slid onto the floor, which made it feel even more wrong to have come in. Although their bedroom was modern, uncluttered and spare, a dressing table from Libby's bedroom, growing-up as a girl, stood against one wall. Unlike nearly everything else in the house, it was old, made of some kind of burlwood, had an upholstered, needle-point seat, and an elaborately-carved, three-faceted mirror, which seemed to watch me as I slowly passed the array of powders, atomizers, and cologne bottles.

Fresh bookmarks sprouted from the pages of new books, piled on top of the bookshelves that ran under the window looking out on the lawn, the badminton court clearing, and the pine woods. Someone had been to the bookstore—*The Adventures of Augie March* by Saul Bellow, *The Crucible* by Arthur Miller, *Go Tell It On The Mountain* by James Baldwin, *Fahrenheit 451* by Ray Bradbury, and *Too Late the Phalarope* by Alan Paton. What on earth was a phalarope?

Other books filled the lower shelves which, in the past, I'd only glanced at. Now these books held a certain allure, because, I thought for the first time, if they kept a book there in their bedroom, instead of on bookshelves in other "public" parts of the house, it might mean they didn't especially want anyone to know they had them.

I scanned the bindings: *The Communist Manifesto, Das Kapital, On the Jewish Question, Homage to Catalonia, For Whom the Bell Tolls*. And then, there it was. Without fanfare and, seeing it for the very first time, here was "the book." Herbert Philbrick's book—much ridiculed in our house—with the title, *I Led Three Lives,* right there on the binding. As Hank said, Philbrick must have had a multiple personality problem.

I don't know what I expected. Maybe pictures of Libby when she was young? I flipped the pages. There was only one photo—of Herbert Philbrick as a boy scout in short pants. Then I noticed a string used as a bookmark further on in the book. I scanned both facing pages, and there it was. In the text that even I could see was maybe fifth grade level, was: "Our Communist Club met often at Hank and Libby Green's apartment in Somerville. She often had snacks for us. Crackers and cheese, sometimes fruit, in the summer."

The book suddenly felt physically hot and dangerous in my hands. With a shudder, I slid it back into its space on the bookshelf. Herb Philbrick, I had to remember, was an unreliable stool pigeon who wasn't to be believed.

Edging back toward the door, I saw, tucked between two perfume bottles, an official looking envelope, the flap opened. Even without touching it, I could see it carried the return address and the pine cone seal of the Goshen Public Schools. I opened the envelope, unfolded the letter, and read. "Enclosed find the loyalty oath to sign before March 1, 1954. Yours truly, Thomas Peele, Principal."

The second page was the oath itself.

> I,_____, do hereby swear that I will support and defend the Constitutions of the United States and of the Commonwealth of Massachusetts against all enemies foreign and domestic, and will faithfully fulfill the part-time position of civics teacher at the Goshen Public Schools to the best of my ability, so help me God.

It continued:

> I have hereby listed below all my memberships and associations, past and present, that may hold principles and intention that may indicate questionable loyalty to the government of the U.S.A.
>
> Signed, and sworn this _____ day of _____ month _____ year
>
> Name _____
>
> Witnessed by _____

Questionable loyalty? Libby? Seeing that written on a document, was strange and scary. I didn't like Libby working in the same building where I was trying to go to school and be a normal kid. Nor did I look forward to having to take her required class in a couple of years. But I also knew she loved teaching civics and she was in love with the Constitution and all those darn Amendments.

"Hel-lo!" Hank called. He and Libby were back from the lumberyard. "We're home."

I tucked the letter back between the bottles and slipped out of their room, went to my own bedroom, and shut the door moments before they came down the bedroom hallway.

Shortly afterward, John L. arrived wearing a heavy red checkered lumber jacket and carrying a blanket rolled tight like a cowboy bedroll. Hank looked up at the two of us from where he sat, drafting and figuring on the dining room table, his eyes mischievous. "How's it going, John? Great day for a little birdwatching and—" He eyed the blanket: "A picnic, it looks like?"

John L. smiled at me. "Sara knows an awful lot about birds."

"That she does," Hank said. "Isn't it a little cold still for birdwatching— or picnicking for that matter?" He gave the blanket another skeptical look. "How many birds are you really going to see?"

"It's just above freezing." I said. "Lots of birds stay in the winter. Mourning doves, woodpeckers, blue jays, chickadees, the tufted titmouse, nuthatches, cardinals, rose-breasted grosbeaks, and dark-eyed juncos. You know them from the birdfeeders."

"Wow, you did that all in a single breath." Hank said, feigning shock and surprise. "I just had no idea there were so many. But a tufted titmice?"

"Yes," I said with authority. "The tufted titmouse."

John L. and I stepped over the chain onto the college land. Our breath sent contrails of condensation into the air. Despite the cold, you could feel spring was in the air and in the ground. John L. reached for my mittened hand and held it as we walked. "I never asked you what *you* did over the holidays."

"Not much, "I said. "I'm allowed to have a stocking and Santa, sort of. I half-celebrated Christmas on my own. I cut my own miniature Christmas tree, one I found in the woods."

John L. gave a little laugh. "Half-celebrate sounds real good to me. I barely survived ours. My mom makes too much of a fuss."

"Do you know that in New England, they didn't even celebrate Christmas til the early 1800s. The Puritans didn't approve of it."

"How do you know this stuff? Anyway, they had the right idea. I've helped my mother bake the cookies every Christmas since I was a little kid. By now,

I must have baked a million cookies."

"I am a student of history, and I spend a lot of time in the library," I smiled.

"Oh, yeah, with Mary, right?"

He kept hold of my hand as we went deeper into the woods along the paths the Jesuits kept open all winter by walking and praying. I liked that John L. was impressed by my knowledge, so I recited everything I'd learned, so far, about the college from Mary, including the existence of the pig farm. And stuff about the birds—how the large birds of the open country, like grouse and pheasants and partridges and bobwhites, ran smoothly along the ground as if riding a gyroscope. How the small brown birds of the forest floor tended to hop, because that was the most efficient way to move from branch to branch or along the ground in search of bugs, grubs, and seeds.

"I've always taken birds for granted…before," he grinned down at me.

We passed a small pond and the shack with a porch overhanging the water. I was pretty sure this was the same one where Mary and I had seen our priest swimming. A thin, transparent layer of ice covered its surface. John L., in a sudden inspiration, led me around the pond on a juniper-bordered path to the shack's front door.

"Where are we going?" I asked. We went up two steps, both creaking with ice and laced with lichen. The dark, rotten timbers and floor joists groaned under our weight as we stepped inside. John L. unrolled the blanket, doubled it over and laid it on the floor with his jacket at one end—as a pillow. With a shy, eager look, he gestured for us to lie down.

"Hopefully, we won't be interrupted by any strange telephone messages out here," he said.

I lay down like an over-stuffed doll in my quilted parka, and he lay down beside me. I focused on the timbers above, unsure about what exactly John had in mind. The bright sunlight came in from one of the windows where the glass was broken out. I savored the delicious feeling of his gaze on me. He leaned over and kissed me.

"Your lips are cold," I said, although it felt good. Very good.

"Maybe we can warm us up a little?" Slowly, tentatively, watching for my reaction, John L. unzipped my parka and began working his hands through the layers of sweaters and jerseys I'd bundled on against the cold.

His breath came out in a cloud. "It's actually quite balmy. Thirty-five degrees."

As soon as his hand found my breast, the cold stopped mattering. I closed my eyes and enjoyed the meeting of cold and warm, and the insistent current surging through my body.

A low hiss, like the leaking of a valve, came from above. I opened my eyes, feeling we were being observed. Anxiety seized me but, as I focused, I saw eyes set in a pale, downy, heart-shaped face. A Barn Owl. He—or she—perched just under the roof of the shack, probably hungry and waiting impatiently for darkness and the hunt.

I pushed John L.'s hand away, and pulled down the layers of clothes I had on under my parka.

"What's wrong?" John L. asked.

I pointed at the Barn Owl.

John L. laughed, and lay back, groaning. "Who's *he* gonna tell?"

As if we'd disturbed its nap, the owl took time to mobilize but after a few minutes, he flew right out the window.

"I always feel like someone's watching. Must be Jewish guilt."

"Are you Jewish?" John L. asked.

"Yes. My whole family is."

"Is Jewish guilt different from regular guilt? Aren't Jewish people allowed to…you know…kiss and stuff?"

"We're not *that* weird," I said.

John L. raised himself on one elbow. "But are you really Jewish? I've never met a Jewish person before…you."

"Do you think I'd make that up?"

"I guess not," he said, and began another excavation through my layers of clothing.

It was ridiculous, but now that we'd disturbed the owl, I felt like he had flown off to spread the word. His face had been so pale, so sad and mournful, so disappointed and, though I knew this was his natural face, I felt responsible.

I thought of Mary's caveat and felt the full weight of the threat all of us girls were under. To flirt with getting pregnant before marriage was to risk the worst fate possible. I pushed John L.'s hand away. "I…we shouldn't"

"Why not," he said. "I can control myself if you can."

"Sorry," I said, rearranging my sweaters with regret.

Looking disappointed, John L. gathered his long, lanky limbs under him and stood up. He walked out onto the porch that reached out over the water.

The whole cabin and porch trembled and creaked under his weight. I closed my eyes, half expecting the whole structure to collapse into the pond.

There was a crack and a splash followed by a hoarse scream. I jumped up and ran out onto the porch where John L.'s clothes lay in a heap. He'd stripped to his underwear and jumped into the partially frozen pond. Huffing, puffing, and gasping, he clambered out, pulled on his clothes, layer by layer, right over his wet skin.

"Just needed a cold shower," he said, grinning through chattering teeth.

"You're crazy," I said. "We need to get you home. Come on. Let's run back."

As he buttoned up his jacket, I tried to drape the blanket around his shoulders. "I have a better idea," he said. He pulled me in and wrapped both of us in the blanket. "Please," he said.

We sat on the floor, wrapped in the blanket, limbs intertwined. He slipped his freezing, shaking hands back under my sweaters, this time for the sake of survival. I watched frost form on his wet hair, felt him shivering violently.

"You're crazy. You're going to get pneumonia and die, and your parents are going to blame me."

He didn't speak, just buried his wet head against my chest. It took twenty minutes for him to stop trembling.

CHAPTER FIFTEEN

A phalarope, it turned out, was a bird, a shore bird, related to a sandpiper, with a straight pointy beak. Its range is Western Canada, the western U.S., and the western edge of South America. It loves salt marshes and sometimes shows up at the great Salt Lake in Utah.

The female phalarope's plumage is more colorful than the male's, she's bigger and more aggressive than the male. And she's polyandrous, which means she has more than one mate at a time. She'll abandon the male as soon as eggs are laid to go find another one—leaving the first "husband" to take care of the eggs.

In ponds, phalaropes swam in circles using their lobate feet, with toes like little paddles, to create whirlpools that stir up morsels to eat. Great migrators, some Canadian phalaropes wintered in South Africa, which was why Allan Paton, the famous South African writer who'd written that book, *Too Late the Phalarope*, knew about them.

Mrs. Osmond kept the library thermostat up around 85 degrees. Mary and I joked about her possibly being cold-blooded like a reptile because of it, but with Mary beside me and our books and papers intermingled on the table in our alcove, it felt like our separate little world. I felt warm and safe and drowsy.

"This may be my last day here," Mary said.

"Oh, no. Why?"

"Spring is almost here," Mary said. "Plus, my parents say enough is enough."

"What's that supposed to mean?"

Mary shrugged. "Suddenly they don't trust me. They say I'm getting boy crazy."

"Well, there aren't any boys here in the library."

"Unfortunately, no," she said, then added. "What happened with John L.?"

"Well, things got kind of hot and heavy."

"Really? How hot, how heavy?"

I whispered: "He touched my breast."

"Ah, second base," Mary nodded. "It feels good, right? How many times?"

"Why are you asking how many times?"

"That's what the priests always want to know. How many times?"

"Yes, it felt good," I admitted, glancing up at the stained-glass window with Moses, the lawgiver hovering overhead. "But I don't understand. Why are your parents saying that now? *Are* you boy crazy?"

"Maybe a little," Mary shrugged. "Aren't we all?"

"But what does that have to do with the library? Don't they trust me?"

"No, silly."

My mind jumped to a balcony-view of Big Patrick at the Town Meeting—which was the last time I'd seen him—with his hands folded over his belly and his eyes closed. His ears, though, must have been open. He had been listening. Of course, he'd heard what Libby had said.

"Did your parents ever say anything after the Town Meeting?" I asked

"Big Patrick just sleeps through those meetings," Mary scoffed. "Annie O. says he can fall asleep anywhere and that he likes to leave the politics to the women."

"Did she say anything about the meeting? About Libby?"

"She said your mother's beautiful," Mary shrugged. "And really smart. Must have gone to college and all that. She said something about the civil defense plans, right?"

"So, she *did* say something. Now they probably think Libby's a subversive, a left-winger, un-American, who wants to overthrow the government and," I added, anxiety seizing me, "that maybe I am, too."

"Why are you always so worried about what other people think?" Mary asked.

"Because now everyone is going to hate us. Maybe even your parents will hate us. Maybe even you."

"That's the most ridiculous thing I ever heard." Mary looked peeved, her voice rising. "That's paranoid. Nobody hates you. Certainly not me. Did you forget we're best friends?"

Beyond the low hubbub of the library, there was the intermittent thump of Mrs. Osmond's date stamp.

Mary closed her book on her pencil, saving her place. "Your mother doesn't really want to overthrow the government, does she?"

"Who said that?" I asked.

"Nobody. It's just what Communists want to do, isn't it?"

"I don't know what she wants to do," I said, my throat tightening.

"How can you not know something like that? You live in the same house with her!" Mary sounded almost irritated with me.

"I've never heard her say anything like that. Is *that* what your parents think? Do they think she's a Communist?"

"Well, they wonder, that's all. Is she?"

"I told you. I don't know."

"How could you not know? Haven't you ever asked her?"

"I'm afraid to."

"What are you afraid of?"

"I'm afraid to find out."

"Well. It doesn't matter what she is. You'll always be my best friend."

The world outside took on the color of medium amber maple syrup, seen through the stained-glass windows of our niche. A bearded Moses was still bringing those Ten Commandments down from the mountain and across the parted red sea. I shivered, in spite of the smothering heat in the alcove.

Maybe the world did have some order to it. Maybe someone up there was really in charge. If there really were rules, we all better watch our step and obey them, right?

"Ladies, ladies!" Mrs. Osmond appeared. She leaned on the table and drummed her fingers on the wood. "I can hear you jabbering, all the way over at the circulation desk."

By some trick of acoustics, our whispering often escaped the alcove, ricocheting off the high oak domed ceiling of the main reading room, and coming down right into Mrs. O's ears. And now, here she was in her untucked blouse and plaid skirt that came down well below the knee, come to pay us one of her "little visits."

"Okay, we need to separate you two. Sara, pick up your things and follow me, please. Then I can get something done and both of you can finish your homework, which, I'm sure is why your parents let you spend so much time here at the library after school."

I looked back at Moses lugging his tablets of laws and wondered if the commandment, "Thou shalt not whisper in libraries," was among them. In no hurry, I collected my things and prepared to follow Mrs. Osmond into the stacks for my exile.

"Now, Sara," Mary whispered, doing Mrs. O. as I was leaving, "try to use your time wisely."

"And don't you forget to come visit me on your way to the ladies' room," I retorted under my breath. Holding my books and folders in a disheveled stack under my chin, a miscreant for all to see, I followed Mrs. O across the nearly empty central reading room, through the periodical section where one old lady sat reading a newspaper on a bamboo stick, then past the children's corner where two little kids were reading with their mother.

Mrs. O parked me deep in the stacks, beyond the ladies' rest room, in a section where back issues of periodicals were kept. She told me to make myself comfortable at a small desk under a window. I let my notebooks, books, pencils, loose papers, and a ballpoint pen slide noisily onto the desktop, my puny little protest.

"And don't manhandle the periodicals, please. Some are very fragile." She put a cautionary finger to her lips and left me there.

A late snow drifted down slowly, accumulated at the outside corners of the windowpane, and whitened the branches of a little spruce standing alone outside near my window.

Occasionally, there were the sounds of the toilet flushing, doors opening and closing and, as always, Mrs. O's date stamp. In my little Siberia, I felt a niggling sense of injustice. Why was I always the one sent away?

The stacks were eerily quiet, as the snow, accumulating on everything I could see from my little window, seemed to muffle sound inside as well as outside. Listless, I opened my social studies book to the chapter on The Emancipation Proclamation, which Mr. Bramhall had just assigned. My head swam over its gothic lettering—all the whereases and therefores and henceforths. Boredom and drowsiness kept drawing my attention away from my textbook to the scene out the window, and finally back to the shelves with the old magazines.

I rose from my desk and slipped a somewhat tattered *Life* magazine off the top of one of the piles. On the cover was a handsome man, wearing a uniform hat and a leather jacket with a fleece collar. Beside him stood a pretty woman in a blue nurse's uniform. It was an issue of *Life* from 1942.

Published before I was born, this magazine and the pile it was in had an instant attraction for me, that familiar, yet strange allure I felt about all things before my existence. These two could have been my parents, ten years ago. I carried the full stack of magazines, each with the large white letters *Life* against an oblong red field, to my window desk, pushing my schoolbooks aside to make space for them.

I felt pleasantly rebellious, not only because Mrs. O would object, but also because *Life* magazine had never, and likely would never, cross our doorstep at home. Henry Luce, the publisher, was a rabid, anti-Communist right-winger that my parents periodically demonized in our house.

I opened the magazine and turned the pages, slowly and carefully, since Mrs. O regarded them as so delicate. Little by little, the black and white photographs drew me deeper into a faraway, pre-Sara-Green world—Hank and Libby's world—before me.

Here was one from 1939. The women are wearing dresses with large pockets on their chests. The ends of their shoulder-length hair are rolled up the way Libby's hair does in the old, framed photos on the walls at Grandma and Grandpa's house.

In the Great Depression, men in hats and long, droopy coats stand in line for bread or soup. There are Hoovervilles, which is what they called the shanty towns built by people without homes. Hobos sleep under bridges and ride the rails. Not everybody is poor. There are movie stars in furs, smiling and climbing in and out of limousines.

There are Franco's Guardia Civil wearing funny, funereal-looking, three-cornered hats of polished black leather. Franco and his fascists are the bad guys in the Spanish Civil War, the ones trying to overthrow the democratic government of Spain. People my parents know fought in that war and some even died. Given my parents' aversion to war, I had never understood why some wars are noble while others were not.

Like some zombie salt-miner, I trudged back and forth, carrying pile after pile of magazines back from my desk, exchanging them for a new batch. I came upon the "sneak attack" on Pearl Harbor, the start of the Second World War for the United States.

I'd seen photos of Hank in uniform. He'd taught basic flying to young guys, who eventually went off to drop bombs from B-29s and, for many, to get themselves killed. Libby had worked for the Red Cross. She'd worn a light blue uniform in which she "looked pretty darn good," Hank had told me.

The *Life* photos show patriotic activities on the "home front," bandage-rolling, blood donations, the saving of grease, which Libby still does in gross little condensed orange juice cans she keeps under the kitchen sink. There are pictures of Adolf Hitler, the man with the strange little mustache that Hank joked he'd painted on with Shinola shoe polish. I look into Hitler's dark, beady eyes and shiver.

The clock in the main reading room startled me, striking four. Hank would be by in an hour to pick me up. But where was Mary? She must have forgotten about me.

In one issue, a map with directional arrows across Austria and Poland points toward Germany, showing where "our boys" swept east. As they go, in a race against the Russians coming from the other direction, they liberate what the captions say are prisoner-of-war camps they came to along their way.

The 101st Airborne Parachute Division, its enlisted men and their officers—majors, even generals, many of them in leather jackets with sheepskin collars—pose for photos at the gates of fenced, barbed-wire enclosures. These have been thrown open, with stark rows upon rows of low wooden barracks eerily visible in the background.

Prisoners appear in the camera frames. Their heads are shaved to control lice, the captions say, and they wear striped prisoners' outfits, some with matching hats I'd only seen in jail cartoons. Their bones and skulls push out of their skin. Some wear barely any clothes at all, even though there are patches of snow still on the ground.

My stomach felt strange, as if I needed to throw up. I brace for what the next turn of the page might bring but can't stop. The air pressure in my corner of the library has changed, blocking my ears and making my head feel like it's floating. I'm afraid to see any more, but I can't stop turning the pages.

Some of the prisoners turn their backs to the camera, others stare straight, defiantly, accusingly, into the lens. Their eyes look unnaturally large.

Gasping for air, I look up from the magazine to watch the silent snow falling peacefully beyond my window. It does not quiet the horror unfolding in *Life*. It just blends with it.

I forge on, turning the pages, looking for something to explain what I'm seeing and feeling. I stare at pictures of what the captions say are dead naked bodies, stacked like firewood. My mouth is dry, my stomach hollow. I've seen enough. I can't look anymore. Hank and Libby never read *Life*. Do they know about all this?

Of course, they must know. It must be just another thing they've been withholding from me. Protecting me.

"Hi!" There was Mary, standing right behind me.

I closed the magazine.

"Sorry I couldn't come before," she said. "Mrs. O. was watching me like a hawk. "What're we looking at here?"

"Just some old *Life* magazines."

"Let me see." Mary reached in front of me and reopened the issue I had just closed.

Mary looked hard, squinting at an emaciated man wearing the striped pajamas and a single boot, no laces, smiling without teeth for the camera. "What is this? Who are these people?"

"Prisoners-of-war," I informed her.

Mary frowned and flipped more pages, then ran her finger along the lines of a long caption under a picture of a woman, standing with her back to the camera, covering herself with rags as best she could. Mary read the caption in a low voice. "Thousands of prisoners; gypsies, Poles, homosexuals, who were required to wear pink triangles pinned to their prison uniforms, and Jews with yellow stars, were found in terrible condition."

She glanced at me. "Did you see this?"

"I stopped reading the captions." I leaned over to look at the sentence she'd just read, the categories of victims, with Jews as an afterthought.

I read out loud: "When the G.I.'s arrived, smoke was still rising from the chimneys of the crematoria. The smell of burnt almonds in the air was found to be Zyklon B, an I.B. Farben pesticide that had been used to exterminate prisoners."

There were no pictures of chimneys. I was left to imagine the sight of the smoke and the smell. I stared at the snow outside, which was coming down more heavily now. Mary's being nearby didn't feel as comforting as it usually did. I longed for Hank to come pick me up.

The shadow of Mrs. O. fell on us. "You know the rules, ladies. No visiting."

Mrs. O. tapped her foot with impatience.

"We're…studying…history," Mary said.

"Students need permission to handle these periodicals," reminded Mrs. O., still tapping.

I looked up into Mrs. O.'s stern, fleshy face, and suddenly saw the oppressor, someone who was imposing arbitrary rules on me, on us, for no good reason, trying to suppress a natural curiosity and my right to know.

"I have a right to read whatever I want," I said breathlessly in a Libby-like eruption. "Isn't this a public library?"

Mrs. O. stuck out her bosom and her chin. "Someone has been misinforming you. There are always rules, including in libraries, and everyone must follow them." She paused to gather herself. "Your father should be here in a few minutes, so put your things together so you'll be ready when he arrives."

Then she carefully closed the issue of *Life* we'd been looking at and carried my latest pile back to its place on the shelf.

"My father would agree with me," I announced.

"Well, young lady, I can't account for what your father would say. All I ask is that you follow the library rules."

I swallowed hard and silently gathered my things. Mary followed quietly along, and we soon settled back into the alcove where God was forever parting the waters for Moses, until our fathers came.

CHAPTER SIXTEEN

I tried everything to keep the starved people with the big eyes and striped pajamas out of my dreams. Some nights I would try not to think of them before falling asleep. On other nights, I thought about them hard before dropping off to sleep. Neither method worked. Maybe because they had no place else to go, these people and the stacked dead bodies clouded and moved through my dreams like a flock of starlings.

I became obsessed with executions. During our last days at the library together, I caught Mary looking over at me with concern, as I read everything I could get my hands on about death. Ordinary natural death, even violent or accidental death didn't interest me. I was fascinated by official, legally sanctioned death, that is, executions, but also unlawful executions like lynching. Drawing and quartering, crucifixion, hanging, beheading, guillotining, and eventually—inevitably—I circled back to electrocution.

I read about the dentist from Buffalo who became inspired when he saw a hobo stumble into an electrical transformer. He experimented on stray animals, then lobbied the New York legislature to adopt his method for human executions. In 1890, New York state "fried" its first condemned criminal. Sixty-two years, eleven months, and sixteen days after that, it was the Rosenbergs.

"Sara, you're so quiet," said Hank on a Sunday morning. "I think it's a perfect day for you to have your first driving lesson. And I think it should be at the dump because it has lots of nice flat dirt spaces between the piles of trash and the puddles. And there's a bunch of stuff Libby wants taken to the dump. She's been cleaning out her files."

"Do I have to?" I moaned. "I'm not interested in driving. I can't get a learner's permit for a year and a half."

"I'm surprised," said Hank. "I thought driving a car represented freedom to the American teenager."

"Not to me," I said sulkily.

"Come on. So what if it's years before you can perform for an inspector of the Department of Motor Vehicles? This way you'll be a virtuoso by that time."

"Oh, go ahead," Libby chimed in. "Keep your father company."

"Yeah. Come on. It'll be fun. An adventure," Hank insisted. "Maybe it'll even cheer you up. You seem a little down in the dumps lately."

"That's not funny," I said.

"And just maybe we'll have time for a pit stop at the Frosty Freeze."

A half-hour later, we were at the dump, sitting side by side on the cracked leather seat of the Heap, with me at the wheel, both of us catching our breath after my first embarrassing attempt to get the jalopy moving forward in first gear. Several large grocery bags full of Libby's "stuff" were jammed into the rumble seat behind us.

Smoke from smoldering fires, set each week by members of the Goshen Refuse Committee, wafted across the landfill. The air stank of burnt aluminum foil and oranges. You could taste it, and I was already feeling sick. The smoke and the smell made me think again of what I'd seen in *Life Magazine*.

Blackened orange and grapefruit halves lay around like scorched-out rubber balls. Bottles and cans and stacks of newspapers tied up in twine stood around unburnt, like beehives or gravestones. Mice and rats mostly stayed out of sight during the day, but I knew they were there. Boys I knew from school came here for target practice and loved to describe in gross detail how rat bodies exploded when they were "nailed" with a .22.

Hank reached over and jiggled the knob of the gear shift that rose out of the Heap's floor like an insect antenna. "Okay," he said, "you're in neutral. You can go ahead and turn on the ignition."

I did, and the Heap coughed back to life. I pressed the clutch pedal to the floor, which involved a full-body stretch, and wrestled the magic wand of the gear shift into first gear.

"Okay, so far, so good." said Hank. "Now, breathe and keep your left foot on the clutch. Now give 'er some gas with your right foot…gradually, gently, and let up on the clutch at the same time."

I arched my right foot and stepped on the accelerator. The engine raced wildly, I recoiled, let up too quickly on the clutch, and the Heap stalled with another lurch.

"Why does the lesson have to be here?" I whined. "This place is so creepy… and it smells."

"It's your first time, Sara. Here you can't destroy anything with the car," Hank said brightly. "We're going to have the place all to ourselves today. Nobody's gonna see you, if that's what you're worried about. Everybody else is in church." Hank grinned at me as if being the only Jews in Goshen was a good thing.

"What is all that stuff in the back?"

"Just old letters, magazines, newspapers—that kind of thing."

"Why doesn't she just burn it in the fireplace?"

He shrugged. "Oh, there's too much of it for that. We don't want any chimney fires. She just wants to get it out of the house and be sure it actually gets burned up." Hank jiggled the gear shift again to make sure we were in neutral.

"Did you know it takes fifty years for a pile of newspapers to decompose?" I asked, stalling for time by parroting a random fact from Miss Marble's science class.

"And did you know books burn at a temperature of 451 degrees Fahrenheit?" Hank countered.

"No," I groaned.

"You really should read *Fahrenheit 451*. You're just the right age for it. Okay Sara, let's take it from the top. Clutch, then give 'er some gas, nice and smooth."

I depressed the clutch, then slowly let up on it, and began to give 'er gas. The Heap lurched forward a few yards before, panicking with all that power under my foot, I took my foot off the gas pedal. We shuddered to another standstill.

"Okay, that was better," Hank said while the springs were still jouncing. "This time, let up on the clutch real slow and give 'er the gas slowly. One pedal moves up as the other moves down. It's like walking and chewing gum at the same time. I know you can do it."

"I can't," I whimpered.

"I believe you can."

A station wagon with wood-paneled doors passed slowly behind us. Hank followed it in our rear view mirror until it disappeared behind some piles of rubbish, some of which were ten feet high.

"I thought we were going to be alone today," I said.

"Guess I was wrong," Hank shrugged.

"So, can we leave now?" I begged.

"Okay, sure. Let me just drop off this stuff first."

He got out of the car, lifted the bags out of the rumble seat, and emptied them, one by one, onto the nearest trash pile. He wadded up some paper, held it near some smoldering trash to light it, and ignited Libby's papers with it. He stood watching the flames for a long time. Then, taking his time, he came back to the car.

"Okay," he said, wiggling the gear shift, "while it's burning, let's try this one last time. Okay?"

"Do we have to?"

Determined to make this my last try, I depressed the clutch and stepped firmly on the gas. Miraculously, the Heap moved forward. Then it was moving faster and frictionless, and then, it almost felt out of control. I kept my foot on the gas, though, managing to maneuver between the piles of trash, almost enjoying the speed.

Beside me, Hank yipped, yodeled, and bellowed. "Hi-ho, Silver! Away!" His feet came up off the floor, exaggerating the effect of the wild ride. I finally hit the brake, the car bucked, skidded to a stop, and stalled.

"A perfect dead stick landing," crowed Hank, his arms braced against the dashboard. "That wasn't half bad. Maybe I should teach you to fly next."

"No, thank you!" I shuddered, my grumpiness extended.

He laughed and slapped the seat between us. "Okay, let's quit while we're ahead and go get that Frosty Freeze." We switched places, and he took the wheel and drove back to the pile where Libby's stuff was burning. As we watched it through the windshield, the same woody station wagon reappeared and pulled up beside us. There were two people in the car, but I couldn't really see them. At first, they just sat there.

"What are they doing?" I asked Hank.

"I don't know," he said.

"I think it's Mutt and Jeff," I said.

"Could be," Hank said. He turned to watch them, squinting. "Different car, though."

The two FBI guys climbed out of their car at the same moment. Sliding on gloves, they approached our trash pile.

Hank jumped out of the car and ran over to stand between them and the burning trash. He raised both hands with his palms open like a cop directing traffic. "Hang on, boys, slow down. Don't you guys ever take a day off? Even the Lord takes a day of rest."

Neither of them paid any attention to Hank or cracked a smile. They just kept trying to walk around him to get to the trash pile. He blocked them, fending them off like he was playing keep-away, without ever touching them. The short one got around Hank and stepped up onto the burning pile.

My heart pounding, I sat frozen to the seat, watching and listening intently.

"Why don't you leave us alone?" Hank shouted at them. "You're on a fool's errand. You don't even know what you're looking for, do you? You spend your Sundays ruining your nice shoes for a bunch of old love letters?"

"Sure," said Mutt, "if they're signed, 'Comrade.'"

Hank smiled and shook his head. He turned toward the fire that was flaring all around Libby's papers and turning them into black ash. "Looks like the newly elected Goshen Refuse Committee has done its job well," Hank said to Mutt and Jeff, as he climbed slowly back into the Heap.

"Why are they here?" I whispered.

Hank shook his head. "They're just persistent. They have no idea what they're looking for. They're just fishing. They're just surveilling us. Let them collect the ashes, if that's what they're interested in." Hank gunned it, and we skidded out of there.

The Frosty Freeze was a white cube of a concrete building out on North Avenue in the middle of a dirt and gravel parking lot. It was where the older high school kids, especially the ones with cars, gathered after school and on Saturdays. On its roof stood the giant figure of "Frosty," a waffle cone with eyes, topped by a rising swirl of airy ice cream that resembled the pompadour hair styles the tough boys wore.

We leaned on the Heap's fender, licking carefully to get our cones under control. "Why do they follow us around?"

"They're supposedly collecting information, documents and such for a file the FBI keeps on us."

"What for?"

"It's what they do. The country is in a panic about what they call subversives, people who have progressive ways of thinking. There's just a lot of fear."

"They're afraid of *us?*"

"Well, they're afraid of the Soviet Union, but they're also afraid of ideas… like ours. Progressive ideas. Change, I guess."

"That's creepy," I said.

"I know, but there's nothing we can really do about it. The government is powerful, if misdirected. They're just following orders."

"But why do they pick on us?"

"I'm not sure. Maybe because your mother is so outspoken."

My problem with her, exactly, I thought.

When the cones were half-eaten and more or less under control, we got back into the car and headed home. Hank looked over at me. "Is there something wrong, Sara? Even before Mutt and Jeff, you've seemed kind of blue." We crossed the little bridge that arched the Boston and Main tracks, sending my already queasy stomach into weightlessness.

"I'm just tired," I said.

"And what do you have to be tired about, young lady?"

"Couldn't sleep."

"How come?"

"Bad dreams," I said.

"What about? It's an outrage that anything should disturb my little girl's rest." He grinned and his teeth gleamed.

I took an extra gulp of air. "Prisoner-of-war camps."

Hank looked over at me, and the Heap swerved slightly. "Hey, you're supposed to keep your eyes on the road," I said.

"What about prisoners-of-war?" he asked.

"Nothing. I mean what does it mean exactly?"

He did one of his loose-limbed shrugs. "POWs are soldiers who've been captured by the other side in a war and kept in prison camps until a war is over. Then they're repatriated back to their own countries."

"I saw pictures in old *Life* magazines. The people looked starved, and they had been kept behind barbed wire."

Hank tightened his grip at the top of the steering wheel, his hands close together. "Don't let your mother hear you've been reading *Life Magazine* on the sly." He frowned. "Is this for history class or something? The war in Korea, did you say?"

"World War II," I said. "Mrs. O. exiled me to the stacks where they keep the back issues."

"And why did Mrs. O'Crotchety send you there?"

"Mary and I talk too much," I sighed. "She's always separating us. Well, separating me."

Hank made a clucking noise with his tongue. "You shouldn't be driving Mrs. O crazy. You and Mary are in the library to study. If you can't manage to do your homework while you're there together, we may not be able to continue that arrangement next year, and I may just have to install you as my full-time, all-weather, all year 'round, secretary and take the automatic answering gizmo back to the phone company."

"No, no, I'll be good," I said.

"Ah, I see the way to whip you into shape is to threaten you with a real job."

"They were starving," I said so softly I was surprised that he heard me at all. "The dead ones were naked and piled in trenches in the ground."

"Aw, sweetie, why do you look at that stuff if it upsets you?" Hank rubbed his scratchy chin. "What years are we talking about here?"

"1945. In Germany, Austria, and Poland," I said. I stared into the depths of my cone where the ice cream was gone.

"Well, that war was hell, just like any other," Hank sighed. "Millions of innocent people suffered and died. Every day during the War, I woke up and thanked God I wasn't one of the ones doing the actual fighting."

"But you *were* in the war," I protested.

"In a war, everyone has a job. Mine was to teach young men to fly, as I've told you. They were the ones who went overseas and a lot of them got killed."

"But you could have gotten killed, too."

"Not likely. The only real danger for me was maybe falling out of one of our open-cockpit trainers and ending up having to walk back to the base carrying my deployed parachute." He shrugged. "Anyway, I'm glad I stayed stateside because I happen to enjoy very much being your father." He glanced at me and continued. "The infantry and the airborne did the actual fighting. They were the ones who liberated the concentration camps."

Here was a new term that hadn't appeared in the magazines. Concentration camps. The words coursed through me, leaving an awful, bad feeling. I could tell from the way Hank's voice dropped and his eyes narrowed, that it referred to some indescribable horror he didn't want me to know about. But it was too late.

"I thought Libby gave you Anne Frank's diary to read," he said.

"Yes, in the fifth grade."

"What do you remember?"

"She was Dutch. Her family was Jewish so they had to hide from the Nazis, and they couldn't turn on lights at night and had to be very quiet during the day because they didn't want to be heard by the factory workers downstairs."

"Do you remember how it ends?"

"It just…ends. The foreword said she died of typhus in a place called Bergen something. And her sister, too."

Hank sighed. "After the family was discovered, they were taken to a concentration camp. They were horrible, inhumane places run by the Nazis. They worked people to death, and starved them. And they killed them."

"Jews?" I said.

"Yes, many were Jews."

"But, why?"

"Why?" Hank sighed. "Because Hitler was insane. A monster. He thought Jews, also gypsies and communists, were a plague on society. Inhuman. So, he decided to exterminate them. Us."

Hank wanted to pick up the Sunday papers, so we headed for Eaton's drugstore. Families just let out of church streamed across the street in their Sunday clothes, faces scrubbed, dressed in ties, jackets, dresses and gloves, a scene created, as Libby would say, by Norman Rockwell. But as we slowed down to let them cross, the naked, starved people of my nightmares, their striped clothing hanging off them, their eyes large, mingled like phantoms with the well-nourished citizens of Goshen.

I closed my eyes hard to squeeze them out of my head.

Hank pulled up into the diagonal parking in front of the drug store grinned at me. "Coming in?"

"I'll wait here," I said. Through the drugstore window, I could see him, smiling, joking with Mr. Eaton, who handed him the newspapers across the soda fountain. On the way home, we discussed the Red Sox Opening Day coming up in April, and all the games we would watch on the little Philco that spring and summer and, hopefully, way into October.

CHAPTER SEVENTEEN

With the first crocuses, Libby deputized Hank to arrange a cease-fire with Grandpa and arrange an overnight for me. This caught me completely by surprise, but I was glad.

Maybe Libby felt guilty about my not seeing them. Or maybe—the chilling thought crossed my mind—she wanted to make sure they would be there for me if anything ever happened to her and Hank.

Hank gladly stepped in as her peace negotiator. If Grandpa and Grandma wouldn't come to Goshen, then I, like the mountain, would go to them. The logistics were simple. I would attend my piano lesson and then go on to meet Grandpa his job site. He and his crew were redoing the leaking roof of the synagogue he had built twenty-five years before, and the synagogue was a straight shot on the Mattapan streetcar line from Muriel's.

I looked forward to being fawned over and spoiled once again and maybe fed strudel with raisins.

The night before, Hank got his mandolin down from its hook and sat down to play, which he hadn't done for quite a long time. After a little warm-up, he said, "This is dedicated to your Grandpa, since he's mending a roof and we're mending our bridges. 'An Arkansas Traveler' seems just the right song. Lib, want to accompany me on the piano?"

Libby smiled but shook her head, no. "But I'll sing," she said.

Hank started playing and tapping his foot, and Libby sang, "Oh once upon a time in Arkansas, an old man sat in his little cabin door…" while clapping the time and laughing with him at the punch line about an old fiddler who wasn't bothered by his leaky roof.

* * *

"Think you're strong enough to stand up to Grandpa's propaganda?" Libby asked, as she dropped me off at Eaton's, with my little suitcase, to catch the bus.

"I'm gonna try," I said. "Why did you decide it was alright for me to visit now?"

"He's a tough old coot, but you're older now," Libby said. "You can give him a run for his money." She kissed me on the cheek, which felt nice.

With my sheet music and small suitcase by my side and a quarter readied in my pocket for my little man under the marquee, I settled in behind Mac. As the miles passed, my nervousness grew. Despite my promises to Muriel, I hadn't cleaned up my act at all over the year. Far from it, and both of us knew it. I remained a committed non-practitioner. My "Graduation" by Muriel was a foregone conclusion.

I dawdled on my way toward the Fenway Theater, determined to do right by my troll, who demanded a toll. Maybe I'd buy two pencils. But the pencil man was not in his place against the ticket booth. I fingered the quarter in my pocket and scanned the dark inside corners of the plaza for signs of him, but there were none.

There had to be somebody who brought him here. He certainly didn't get here by himself. My mind rushed through the possibilities. Had his ride failed him? Had there been an accident? It struck me that he was like one of the starved ones, just in different clothing, but also on the edge of desperation, someone who needed others to do something to help.

I felt ashamed of being so repelled at first by his existence and his simple attempt to survive. Now he was gone.

Muriel had already changed the slipcovers on her sofa and chairs for spring. From the moment she opened the front door for me, her lady-like fragrance enveloped me in what felt like a sad aura of missed opportunities. Fresh white tulips, beautiful, but mournful, stood in a glass vase, their long stems crisscrossed in the water.

She sat very still in her chair by the piano bench in a beige sweater and pearls and waited for me to begin a Mendelssohn caprice. All I had to do was practice it up to the double bar.

"Andante con moto. Cantabile," Muriel instructed, closing her eyes.

"Make it sing."

The notes of the piece, which I'd attempted only a few times, danced before my eyes. They scampered around the clefs, hung upside down like imps, the stems the wrong way up from the staff lines. Crescendo and decrescendo marks and phrasing lines swooped and swirled before my eyes, as if to purposely confuse me.

Once I'd struggled through it, Muriel sat back slowly in her chair. "Oh, Sara," she said with a sad smile, "I had hoped our little joke about graduation would motivate you. I hoped this lovely piece would inspire you. I'm afraid we have to face the fact that you and I have been going through the motions, somehow," she shrugged. "Maybe to please your mother. I think everybody would be happier if we just say it's been an interesting experiment."

Here it was. The promised "Graduation." I could hardly believe it. "When?" I whispered.

"I think we should call this our last lesson. What do you think?" She smiled at me, but looked truly sorry.

"But what am I going to tell Libby?" I asked, with a touch of fear and shame..

"Don't worry," said Muriel. "I'll call her. She'll understand. At some point she quit the piano, too, remember."

"I could never play like her, even if I practiced twelve hours a day."

"Well, we don't know that, now do we? Your strengths are probably in other things."

Beyond the lace-covered windows, Commonwealth Avenue clanged with trolleys. I sat, unsure of what to do now. I had a floating sensation as if I were being carried away in a hot air balloon, mistakenly let loose from its moorings. One of my sources of information about Libby was flying away with it.

"When did she stop playing the piano?" I asked.

Muriel's hands were crossed on her lap, perfectly still. "In college, as I recall."

"Why did she quit?"

Muriel's palms turned helplessly upward. "She just became interested in… other things."

"What other things?" I asked, sounding rude and demanding even to myself.

Muriel carefully replaced the cover of the metronome and secured it with the little hook. "I guess you'd have to say…politics. She became interested in politics. It was the Depression. Our fathers had no jobs. People had to line up to get free bread and soup. People were desperately looking for answers to why what your mother would call the Capitalist system wasn't working for most people."

"She's still interested in politics," I said.

Muriel smiled. "I'm not surprised."

"She's fighting now about some books they banned from the Goshen libraries. She wants them returned to the library. She's always fighting."

"Sounds like Libby," Muriel said.

I took a breath. "Do you know if she's a Communist?"

Obviously startled, Muriel looked at the clock. "Why do you ask that?"

"Some people in Goshen—like my boyfriend's father—think she might be."

Muriel got up from her chair and walked to the far end of the piano. She regarded me under the open lid. "I didn't know you had a boyfriend, Sara. That's nice," she said, lowering her eyes. "But you can't imagine how it was. We were all immigrant's children. My father was a house painter and there was no work. He stayed home all day listening to the radio and staring at the wall. When I got home from school, he'd beg me to play the piano for him. He said it was the only thing that made him happy. People were desperately looking for answers to why The American Dream had eluded them." She ran her fingers along the smooth wood of the piano case. "But, as to your question about your mother, I truly don't know. As you know, we lost touch over the years."

"Were you political, too?"

"Me? Oh, no. I was much too timid for that. Too selfish, I suppose." Muriel got one of those faraway looks that adults get when their minds are going into the past. "I did go to a political meeting or two with her. They talked about things I didn't understand," she continued. "It's where she met your father, I think."

Muriel returned to her chair beside me, smiled, and patted my arm. "All I've ever managed to do was play the piano. Your mother was always different. She didn't hide from the world. She always wanted to change things, make them better."

* * *

Newly graduated, I caught the Blue Hill Avenue trolley for Mattapan, got off at Fessenden Street, crossed the trolley tracks, and the synagogue was right there. The streetcar clanged and screeched, metal on metal, and rolled off down the rails.

Grandpa, in one of his dark striped, vested suits, was halfway up a ladder, propped against the side of the brick synagogue with its Moorish windows and domed roof. He was yelling orders to the workmen, who were lugging rolls of tar paper on their shoulders up adjacent ladders.

"If you men don't hurry up," Grandpa Joe railed at them, "the Torahs are gonna get wet and God will be angry." He shook his fist at them and at the raw, darkening sky.

Libby said Grandpa liked going up on ladders, although he didn't have to anymore. She said he enjoyed being up higher than his laborers, while they sweated and dug trenches, laid out sewer pipes, swung pickaxes, pushed wheelbarrows, schlepped dirt, gravel, and bags of cement. These were the workers—Irish, Italian, even Negroes, who, Hank said, had learned to do cement-finishing when they served in the Seabees during the war, and so were allowed to work, even though they couldn't get into the construction unions.

In Libby's opinion, working people needed their conditions and pay improved, and Grandpa Joe was too old to be going up on ladders in his suit.

When he saw I'd arrived, Grandpa backed slowly down the ladder. Just as he reached the ground, it started to rain. "Come here, Sara," he said, opening the trunk of the Nash. He yelled at the workmen in a gruff voice, "Come get your pay so we can all go home." I stood with him under the open door of the trunk as he handed the men their pay in little yellow envelopes.

"She's making gefilte fish special for you," Grandpa said as we drove home. "It's been swimming in the bathtub since yesterday. And the capon has to be the freshest. She would get 'im alive, if she could, and let 'im walk home himself."

He pulled out his pipe and filled it from a pouch while he drove. I held on for dear life to the soft plush arm rest.

"I'm glad to be back visiting you, Grandpa. It's been a long time," surprised to hear myself knowing how to talk politely to a grownup.

"Rosie likes to have someone to cook for. But, remember, I'm the one who knows about chickens," Grandpa said. "When I was a kid in the old country, my job was to crawl under the hen house for the eggs. I got stuck one time. They left me there for a half a day to teach me a lesson. I was the bum in the family, you know."

Just hearing once more what Libby called Grandpa's warhorses, the stories he repeated, over and over again, made me feel warm and safe.

"What happened to the Philco I got for you?"

"It's in Hank's back office."

"So," said Grandpa, "she sent it to Siberia."

Their dining room, with its heavy draperies and oriental rugs, was suffused with smells of schmalz, Grandpa's cherry-flavored pipe tobacco, and his Havanas, all mixed together. Like at Muriel's, crystal tinkled everywhere, from the breakfront cabinet to the chandelier.

"Sara, you're old enough to have a little wine. Give 'er some, Rosie."

Grandma took the stopper out of the crystal decanter and poured me an inch and a half of the dark maroon, sweet wine. I took a tentative sip.

She lit two candles, then did her sabbath hocus pocus, waving her arms as if to bring the flame and light toward her and saying words in Hebrew I'd heard a hundred times when I was younger, but still didn't know the meaning of. After the gefilte fish, she filled my china dinner plate—rimmed with gold and a tiny rose pattern—with a drumstick from the capon, two slices of brisket, and over-cooked string beans. "Eat," she commanded.

I eagerly gobbled the food, which I found delicious, no matter how overcooked, or how much fat or sugar was involved. My plate and my glass were soon empty, and my mind floated with the wine. My cheeks burned, and my eyes threatened to close.

In the reflections of light in the crystal glasses, I could almost see the muddy little shtetl and Grandpa Joe as a skinny kid with a warm hen's egg in each hand, being scolded by his father, my great-grandfather, the sage-looking man with the long split-beard, looking down on us from the sepia photo on the dining room wall.

I imagined Libby as a girl in this house, too—in this dining room, eating this food, drinking this wine, and seated in this chair at the table. If my grandparents longed for the original, it was impossible to tell. Photos of Libby around their house seemed to stop with high school. I reminded myself of the precariousness of my position. At any time, I could find myself on Grandpa's bad side, cut off from Grandma's food and from the frayed anchor-line to the family past.

Grandpa was about to pour more wine into my glass, but Grandma wrestled the decanter away from him and, clutching it to her bosom, took it off into the kitchen. "Enough, Joe. She's had enough."

"Your mother is afraid of me, so she sends you all alone?" Grandpa said suddenly.

"She's not afraid of you, Grandpa," I said.

"Then why does she send you here by yourself?"

"She thinks I'm old enough to...."

"To what?" Grandpa scowled. "To argue with me?"

The room swayed with his harshness and the wine. "Why are you so angry with Libby?" And there it was, the old, suppressed, fundamental question, loosened by Manischewitz wine.

Grandpa coughed and cigar smoke spewed from his mouth. "In this house," he scolded, "you will call her by her right name, young lady, which is 'Mother.'"

Already I'd offended him. "Okay," I said. "Why are you so angry with Mother?"

In one swallow, Grandpa downed the remaining inch of Slivovitz plum brandy from his shot glass. "She's a black goat, your mother." A smile formed around his pipe stem. "Just like I was."

"I think you mean a black sheep, Grandpa."

"A goat, a sheep. What's the difference? She did wrong."

"What did she do?"

"You ask too many questions. Maybe you're gonna come out like her."

I checked Grandpa's face for how serious he was. I wasn't ready to give up being his "best girl."

Grandma, back from the kitchen, leaned across the table and pinched my arm. "Shah, Joe. This is a beautiful, good girl. You leave 'er alone now."

Grandpa brought his thick hand down on the lace tablecloth, ignoring her and glaring at me. "Your mother has a hard head. Smart, always smart, but no respect. What good is all that school for a girl?"

"Just because you were not a studier," Grandma said, as she began to clear the table. I jumped up to help her.

"Sara, you stay here and listen," Grandpa ordered. "Too much school makes a person not want to be Jewish anymore. And not keep kosher. Like your mother and father."

Slowly, obediently, I sat back down. "We're Jews, too, Grandpa. We're secular Jews."

"This is what she tells you?" Grandpa said. "What does it mean—secular?"

"According to Jewish law, she's Jewish because Grandma's Jewish," I explained the matrilineal inheritance of Judaism as it had been explained to me. "And I'm Jewish because she's Jewish. We just don't agree with all the rules and rituals. And beliefs."

"Okay, maybe she's Jewish," Grandpa said grudgingly, "but she's not loyal…to her own country. America."

Hearing him say this gave me a chill. Could this be true?

Grandpa watched smoke from his cigar thread up among the dangling crystals of the chandelier. "This country saved my life," he said.

"Yah, you would be in the Russian Army in Siberia," Grandma agreed.

"So," said Grandpa, "this country saved your mother's life, too, but she doesn't see that…and yours…."

"I understand," I said. "If *your* life wasn't saved, then she wouldn't be here and I wouldn't either."

"You see, you're smarter than she is already."

"Libby…my mother…wants to make America even better than it is."

"But she has no respect," Grandpa fumed, and then he grew dreamy, lost in Slivovitz and time. "So, we left Russia, me and my brother. We didn't want to go to the army. We didn't say goodbye. Nobody cried. We left my papa, my mama, and my two sisters who always took care of me. We left them…alone. They wrote letters and we wrote letters. Then the letters stopped."

Grandma eyed him warily. "Joe, don't talk about it. She's only a child."

"Elka and Esther, my schöne sisters…" Here, Grandpa let out one solitary shaking sob that sounded almost like a laugh. "Slaughtered like animals in the muddy snow." He put down his pipe. "I dream it every night."

"Joe," scolded Grandma.

I sat very still in my high-backed chair, bleak snowy scenes forming in my head with murky dark, unspeakable things happening in shadows against the white.

"So," Grandpa growled, anger bubbling up. "You ask a lot of questions,

Sara, just like your mother. I have a question for you….What do you secular Jews have to say about God, Sara?"

I looked down at the little roses around the rim of my plate while I tried to think up the best answer.

Grandpa shook his head. "Your mother thinks she's smarter than everybody else because she went to college, which I paid good money for, by the way. She doesn't believe in God. She says there's no proof. No proof? Look at all the terrible things that happen in the world. Pogroms, killing, concentration camps, atom bombs. No God? Of course, there's God, but he's no mensch. He's a schmendrik, a fool, who lets people do terrible things."

"Joe!" Grandma covered her face with her hands.

I sat back in my chair, shocked by Grandpa's vehemence.

I could see that the same hot blood that flowed in Libby's veins flowed in Grandpa's and maybe in mine.

CHAPTER EIGHTEEN

The lion-lamb arrival of spring in Goshen gave way to "mud season." Moisture trapped and frozen in the ground all winter melted and super-saturated the soil, turning our driveway to slithery quicksand. The air still felt cold, but promising currents of warmth infiltrated its chill. Libby announced she was going to make my favorite food—a casserole that Hank had dubbed "Armageddon," because if Grandpa and Grandma ever discovered us eating it, it would cause the final, catastrophic battle between them and Libby and us.

The recipe for Armageddon had come from a babysitter who'd stayed with me for a week while I was in the fifth grade. Libby and Hank had gone to Mexico for a conference and a little vacation, on their own. At the time, we still lived in Mattapan across the street from Grandma and Grandma, but Libby made it clear to them that they would only be serving as back up while she and Hank were away. She didn't want me to become "too much" for them.

Mrs. Rebecca May, a tall, slim, rather solemn Negro lady, who volunteered with Libby at the NAACP, was left in charge of me, although Grandma and Grandpa checked in every day. I was to call her Miss Rebecca.

Miss Rebecca asked a lot of questions. The first night as I helped her with supper, as I had been instructed, she asked, "So, young lady, tell me what you are learning in the fifth grade these days?"

"Oh, we have math and English and social studies."

"And what, may I ask, do social studies consist of?" She continued making hamburger patties while I set the table.

"It's geography, history, and current events."

"Wow," said Miss Rebecca, "that's quite the hodgepodge."

"What's that," I asked.

"It's kind of a mixture of ingredients—like a stew. Sounds like your social studies is a little bit of everything. So, tell me what you've learned about lynching."

I swallowed hard. "I…ah think it's when they used to kill…." I stammered, then stalled.

She turned to look straight at me. "You're almost there. It's the extra-judicial execution of usually Black men, mostly in the south, but not only. And it's not only *used* to. There have been several known ones in the last few years. But let's not talk about that, when it's nearly dinner time, okay?"

Miss Rebecca went back to cooking and she began to hum. I busied myself with finishing the table setting, but the tune soon came clear to me. It was "Strange Fruit," the song about lynching from Hank's Billy Holiday album. Miss Rebecca taught me two Negro spirituals, too, that week, accompanying herself on the piano. She sang "Joshua Fit the Battle of Jericho" and "Go Down, Moses," both Old Testament stories, maybe because of our being Jewish.

Miss Rebecca broke out the recipe for the Armageddon casserole on her very last night with me, when Hank and Libby were due back the next day and after Grandma and Grandpa had already dropped in for their evening check-up. The recipe called for macaroni, cheese, a heavy cream sauce, small cubes of ham, and butter, lots of it. Every ingredient was forbidden, alone or in combination, by the Jewish dietary law, or by Libby's own ideas of what was edible as food.

"We can't let my Grandma and Grandpa see this because of the ham," I told Miss Rebecca as I helped her grate the cheese.

"I understand," she nodded with a conspiratorial look. "We'll clean up good and air things out by tomorrow."

In the weeks after Miss Rebecca left, I begged so pitifully for the Armageddon that Libby finally gave in and called her up for the recipe. Since then, Libby had made it once a year for my birthday. Why she would make it for supper today was a mystery.

Libby dug deep into the Armageddon with a large, slotted spoon and placed a molten, steaming helping onto my plate, then Hank's, and then a small amount on her own. The savory aromas of ham and cheese entered my nostrils. The creamy, buttery sauce flowed, the macaroni slithered, while the pieces of forbidden ham lurked in cheesy crevasses. I inhaled its ambrosia-essence, convinced that the world was good.

"I hope you enjoy...Armageddon," Libby smiled.

"It's great as always," said Hank.

"And," Libby continued, "I have some good news for a change. Your father already knows."

"Good news?" I said with my mouth full.

"Yes," Hank said, "good news."

"Today," Libby said, "the Supreme Court handed down a decision in a case called *Brown vs. the Board of Education of Topeka, Kansas*. The justices said that racial segregation of children in public schools is *un*constitutional. Isn't that wonderful?"

I stared a bit stupidly at her. I surely knew that Negro children in the South had to attend separate, segregated schools, and that their schools were not up to par. But this news didn't hit me with anywhere near the impact that Libby seemed to expect. The South seemed far away, like a foreign country, and, of course, there were no Negro children in my school.

Hank explained, "The Court said that separate public education for Negro children is inherently *un*equal, and the Fourteenth Amendment to the Constitution says everyone is entitled to 'equal protection under the law.' They threw out the idea of 'separate but equal.'"

"Psychologists found out that little Negro children, when they're segregated in public schools, even if they had the same books, the same facilities, et cetera. still feel inferior," Libby added.

"Oh," was all I said.

"Now," Libby said after offering us seconds, which both Hank and I accepted, "I need to tell you something else, so you won't be taken by surprise."

I waited, feeling nervous.

"You complain we don't tell you anything, Sara, so I'm telling you now that I am not going to sign the loyalty oath the school is requiring for me to keep my job next year at GHS."

"So, you won't be teaching civics anymore?" I asked, masking the fact that I'd actually seen the letter from the school.

"That's what it amounts to, I'm afraid," she said.

"I thought you liked your job," I said.

"I do. Very much," Libby sighed. "But, the oath they want me to sign is a clear violation of my right to free speech and association. It's un-American.

An American citizen should not—*cannot*—be compelled to sign an oath of loyalty in order to keep a job."

"Your mother feels very strongly about this," Hank added.

I could see how much the situation upset her, but, selfishly, I was glad. It might mean she wouldn't be around the school—my school—next year. I wouldn't run into her in the halls and be forced to acknowledge her, and even introduce her to my classmates. Maybe best of all, I wouldn't have to take civics from her in two years.

We'd almost finished off the Armageddon. Libby started pushing salad on us, as an antidote. Salad in the winter consisted of shrunken iceberg lettuce, usually chopped up, some cucumbers, and hard, half-ripened tomatoes, all topped with Steakhouse dressing. We crunched in unenthusiastic silence.

"I hate to lose those classes," Libby frowned, then brightened, "but, they can't get rid of me that easily. I've decided to run for the open seat on the school committee next month. Ted Bramhall said he would help me."

Hank's head turned slowly, and I could see that Libby's latest news was new to him, too, not just to me.

"But why…why would you do a thing like that?" Hank looked crushed.

"I doubt I can win," Libby went on, oblivious to his reaction. "My platform will simply be to reinstate the banned books removed from the school libraries. I hope you'll be on board," she said, looking at Hank.

I put down my fork and stared at her.

Hank played dismally with his half-eaten salad.

Libby rose from the table and glanced out her over-the-sink window. "I know you both would probably prefer that I do nothing at all…in public. But I can't let these things just slide. When things are not right, we have to register our protest."

Libby sat down again and helped herself to a second plateful of salad. "Maybe you can help me with flyers and whatnot."

It was unbelievable. Didn't she listen to me at all? Or Hank? To me, Libby's little announcement spelled doom, and it wasn't fair. Any chance we had left of keeping a low profile in Goshen would be gone. Did she consider, even for one minute, how what she said or what she did affected me? Did she really think she could bribe me with food?

"Please," I said, the words sputtering out of me, "don't run for anything."

"Why not?" Libby said. "I'm a citizen. I can participate in local government.

And, if we succeed, it will help you with your book reports," she smiled.

"I don't care about the book reports," I said sourly. "I have to live and go to high school in this town."

Libby looked at me like I was a cuckoo chick hatched illegitimately in the family nest. I fought hard to keep my anger from turning to tears.

Hank raised one eyebrow that said, *don't make things worse than they already are, Sara. Let me handle this.*

CHAPTER NINETEEN

"You have to go with me to the college for a little while," Mary whispered over the phone. "I have to get out of my house."

"Me, too," I said. "Why are you whispering?"

"Will you come?"

"I can be there in fifteen minutes. I have stuff to tell you, too."

I grabbed the binoculars from their hook on my way out the door. "I'm meeting Mary," I yelled to Hank and Libby, who were standing in the driveway circle, fretting over an ailing rhododendron.

Mary and I met and then walked to go sit on a rock ledge next to a little spring flowing out of a hillside. She seemed pensive. I told her about my weekend with Grandma and Grandpa and my graduation from piano lessons.

"How did it go with the Pencil Man?"

"He was gone," I said. "Just when I stopped being afraid of him."

She smiled. "He was your bogeyman."

"I wonder where he went," I said. "If he's okay."

"Whoever brings him there must be taking care of him, right?"

"I guess."

We trailed our hands in the water, which was ice cold.

"Libby is refusing to sign the loyalty oath, so she's not coming back to school next year."

"You must be glad about that, right?"

"But now she's going to run for school committee."

"What's wrong with that?"

"She'll just call attention to herself…and us…and me."

"Sara, you've got to stop worrying so much about what your mother does and what other people think about it."

"You're probably right, but I can't...."

Mary poked with a stick at some lichen on our rock. "I did it with Robby."

My chin dropped. "You did it? You mean you had...sex?"

"Yes," she said, lowering her eyes.

I couldn't help staring at her, looking for how she had changed, as if she should look like an entirely different person, so stark was the difference in our minds between the two states of being female—virgin and not. But no, she still looked like Mary.

"You didn't call me," I murmured.

"I can't get near the phone in my house."

"What...what was it like?"

Mary locked eyes with me, then dropped her head so that I was looking directly at her reddish blonde hair, perfectly-parted for braids. "First, it was exciting," she said, "and then it hurt, and then I was scared."

"It hurt?"

"Yes...down there."

"Ooh, sorry," I winced.

"What are *you* sorry about? It was my stupidity," Mary said sharply.

"Do you have to tell it in confession?"

Mary shook her head. "I just won't take communion. Then I won't have to go to confession."

"Wouldn't the priest automatically forgive you?"

"Probably, with a few penances, but then he would know."

"I thought the priest can't see who it is."

"But he would just know in a parish this small." Mary looked sad. I squinted at her in the sharp afternoon sun slicing through the trees. I'd never seen Mary like this, with the spunkiness drained out of her. It made me feel badly for her and scared for myself.

"I know what let's do," she said, brightening, "let's go find the pig farm."

"Why now, all of a sudden?" I asked.

"I don't know," she shrugged and wouldn't meet my eyes. "Just something to do."

"Sure, okay."

"Come on," Mary said, getting up to walk, "let's go before it gets too late." I followed her along the path we'd taken into the woods.

I know," I said, "you thought of finding the pigs because we're reading *The*

Odyssey. Because Circe turns his sailors into pigs? Because they're trayf."

"Tell me again what trayf means," Mary said.

"Forbidden. Unclean. Poison."

"Oh right, against the dietary laws." Mary tapped her forehead with her fingers. "As for *The Odyssey*, I haven't gotten that far yet. What book are you on?"

"Just finished Book Ten," I said, savoring being ahead of her for once in something.

Mary hesitated at a branching of the path. "I have no idea where this pig farm place is. Or even *if* it exists anymore."

"You told me Big Patrick says the priests have to have their Easter hams."

"He says that, but it could just be some of his malarkey. Parents don't necessarily tell you the truth all the time, you know. The priests could just get their ham and bacon from the grocery store like everybody else."

The ground was moist, muddy in spots, and pungent aroma of spring came up from the earth. In one place, where the path sloped down into a gulley, there were still some patches of shriveled snow shaded by the trees. Somewhere a hermit thrush and his possible mate were singing back and forth to one another.

"Never been down this way," Mary said, pausing at the next crossroads.

"Let's try it," I said.

"Why don't you lead today," Mary said, stepping aside, "since I don't know where we're going either?" For Mary to shy away from taking the lead, or for her to walk behind me, felt odd, but it also made me feel accomplished, adventuresome, fearless, pushing ahead into the unknown.

The path was bordered on the left by a grove of thin white birches, still bare from the winter, with star moss forming a carpet beneath them. With Mary following close behind me, I led the way through a grove of maples and oaks, tinged now with green, as small, curled leaves were about to burst into life. The woods were alive and noisy with birds singing and squawking, their minds on mating and nest-building.

We crossed a field of long pale grass, then found the path again and re-entered the woods. We went down a muddy incline, then up and across another open pasture, past a collapsed barn. Beyond that, in a clearing of rutted dirt and mud without a blade of grass, was the ruin of a low wooden structure, bare of paint, all enclosed by a dark, broken-down split rail fence.

A steady breeze kept the grasses behind us stirring.

Silent, walking carefully, we drew closer to the remnants of two wooden sheds. "This has to be it," Mary said. "The pig farm. The remains, anyway."

A huge brown and black sow, indistinguishable at first from the dirt and mud, came slowly to her feet. As she began to move, her young, still attached to her teats, dropped off one by one into the mud. As we stared, a hairy boar, small compared to the sow, but with large, overgrown tusks and tired, angry eyes, rushed forward, stepping nimbly across the fallen fence rails. He trotted straight toward us until he was no more than ten feet away. There he stopped and glared at us.

Terrified, we turned to one another and ran back across the field as fast as we could, only stopping when we reached the edge of the field and carefully made our way across the rusted barbed wire lacing the stone wall. We crouched behind the wall and looked back.

The boar moved more slowly now but was still coming towards us with a strange delicacy, placing each cloven foot carefully, like a woman in high heels. His small, dull eyes on either side of a flat, scooped-out face and enormous tusked snout, seemed unable to focus on us.

"He is ugly," Mary said.

"Butt ugly," I agreed.

Our pounding hearts slowed, we laughed, and it was good—as if Grandpa's terrible memories, Libby's iron will, and even the painful aspects of a future lived as a woman, evaporated in the air. Mary gave me a conspiratorial look and, for the first time all day, I felt free and exhilarated—also subversive—because Mary and I remained a team, and now we'd found the secret source of the priests' Christmas hams.

CHAPTER TWENTY

"Maybe this is the year we break The Curse, right, ladies?" Hank said. Mary and I followed Hank's tall, loping figure through a dank stadium tunnel that led toward the light coming from an arch of bright green opening onto Fenway Park. These murky passageways still creeped me out as they had when I was a little girl.

"Let's hope," Mary said, giving a little skip. "Maybe I should confess now that Big Patrick and my brothers are Braves fans."

"That's okay," Hank said. "We like you anyway."

Baseball games were my special time with Hank. Even though baseball was "the people's game," Libby showed little interest. Anyway, she was out canvassing for a seat on the school committee. And now with Mary along, it promised to be a perfect day.

Maybe this year there *was* a chance of breaking The Curse of the Bambino. The Curse had befallen the Red Sox just after they won the 1918 World Series against the Chicago Cubs, and they made the fateful error of trading Babe Ruth to the Yankees. Since then, the Red Sox hadn't won a world series—for thirty-six years.

The bright, true colors of Fenway Park—the green of the grass and the white of the Red Sox uniforms—shone bright as we emerged from the tunnel. Over the early spring, watching the games on black and white TV, my mind's picture of Fenway had been drained of liveliness. But here again was the color, the crowd yelling, the droning of the electric organ, and the boom and echo of the announcer's voice. It confirmed for me that I was still Hank's little girl and that the world was good, beautiful and, for the most part, safe.

We made our way around to our bleacher seats, right next to the Green

Monster, the thirty-seven-foot-high wall in left field. Hank liked to sit where the working people could afford to buy a ticket, in the sun. From there we'd have an amazing, close view of Boston slugger and outfielder Ted Williams, number 39.

Hank pulled me by the hand, and I pulled Mary, through the tide of fans, mostly men, rushing in all directions. When we were almost to our seats, we had to stop in our tracks because the organ began to play "The Star-Spangled Banner." The crowd stopped yelling. People stood absolutely still, facing the flag, and while people sang their hearts out, we sang along. Hank held his hat patriotically over his heart and stared toward right field, brows knit, at the billowing American flag.

As soon as we were seated, Hank caught the eye of the peanut man, who threw us a big bag. Hank rubbed two quarters on his sleeve and tossed them back to the guy, who caught them behind his back.

By the fifth inning, the game was bogged down at two to one, with Washington Senators ahead. Nobody was hitting. The sun was already on its long, slow, blinding descent that would end with its sudden drop behind the right field stands. Lengthening shadows shot out from the feet of the players and umpires.

The bored crowd started booing Ted Williams each time he came up to bat. He was a WWII flying ace and homerun hitter, but after his second strike-out, as far as the impatient crowd was concerned, he was just a bum in a slump.

Hank leaned back, covered his face with his hat and said, "If Teddy boy doesn't produce something pretty soon, we're going to need helmets to protect ourselves from the flying coca cola bottles. How about some hot dogs, girls?"

"Sure, we'll go and get them. What do you want?" I volunteered.

"By yourselves?" Hank looked skeptical but reached into his pocket for money.

"I survived Mass Avenue every week, alone. Mary and I can go together to buy a couple of hot dogs."

"Okay, you're right. You have some street smarts. Just don't take any wooden nickels. I'll have a hot dog with mustard and lots of relish."

I slipped the money into my dungaree pocket, and Mary and I descended the concrete steps, walked around the concourse to the first hot dog stand and joined the line. We were still three people away from the refreshment counter when a deafening roar of cheering and whistling and cowbells rose from the crowd. We didn't move. We didn't want to lose our place in line.

"Captain Ted Williams of the United States Marine Corps may have flown thirty-nine missions against the Commies in Korea," came a man's voice right behind us, almost in my ear. "But he's sure letting his fans down today, eh?"

I kept looking straight ahead. So did Mary.

"Looks like the Boston fans aren't that in love with him," a second man chuckled. "So, young ladies, you must be Boston fans? Not doing so hot this year…again."

Mary frowned at me with a look that said, don't talk to strangers. But Hank wasn't that far away, and I didn't like my team being insulted.

"I'm a loyal Red Sox fan," I said, half turning toward them. "No matter how they do."

Even though they both wore Washington Senators caps with big W's, I recognized them. Gone were the suits and the felt hats: Mutt and Jeff.

Mutt took his cap off and pointed emphatically to the "W" embroidered on it. "As you can see, we're from out of town. Senators' fans, you know. Washington, DC. But you've got the right idea. Loyalty's the most important thing."

My heart beat fast and hard. Steadying myself, I managed to buy the three hotdogs wrapped in paper and three sweating bottles of root beer. We turned to go.

Mutt and Jeff were right there in front of us, blocking the way back to Hank. "Some interesting mail your mother saved," sneered Mutt.

"It all burned up," I snapped back at him.

"Not all of it," Jeff said in a singsong voice. "I bet no one ever told you the communists practice free love."

"That's stupid," I blurted, confused.

"Why don't you mind your own business and leave us alone?" Mary chimed in.

"Well, it's been nice talking to you. May the best team win," the short one said, and they both walked off together.

"Oh, go fly a kite," Mary called after them. "Are those the same guys?" she whispered.

"They're my family's FBI tail," I said, beginning to shake.

"What do they want from you?"

"I don't know. They have something against Libby." My legs were shaky, but fear propelled me quickly back up to our seats. I handed Hank his hotdog and drink.

"Thanks, ladies." Hank took a large bite of his hotdog, about half of it gone. In a daze, I nibbled at mine as I sat there beside him. Mary just sat, looking away from her food. "Sorry, I don't think I can eat this."

Just then, Ted Williams came up to bat and, just like that, on the first pitch, hit a home run right over our heads, clearing the Green Monster and dropping somewhere unseen, probably into Kenmore Square. The Red Sox fans went crazy. Hank stood up and yelled, "Take that, you damn Senators!" Then he laughed and apologized to me and Mary for his language.

A guy behind us, who was smoking a cigar, made a disgusted noise and yelled, "I don't care. He's still a bum. Sit down, will ya,' fella?"

Hank sat, but with a smug look, like a little kid. I looked back down toward the refreshment concourse to see if I could spot Mutt and Jeff.

Hank questioned Mary, "You all right, sweetie? You don't look so well."

Mary shook her head. She did look miserable.

"Mutt and Jeff," I said quietly to Hank. "They were at the hotdog stand."

Hank leaned closer to hear me over the crowd noise. "Who? You did? Where?" Hank took the binoculars out of my hands and trained them on the concourse below. "Did they bother you? I shouldn't have let you go alone. What did they do? What did they say to upset you?"

"They're Senators fans," I said weakly.

Surrounded by the crowd going wild over the home run and the Red Sox pulling ahead, Hank got up again on his feet. "I'm going down there. I won't be long," he said, taking the stairs two at a time.

"Don't…!" I called after him.

When Mary couldn't wait any longer, I went with her to the ladies' room. She disappeared into one of the stalls and latched the door after her. She flushed the toilet, but I could hear a gagging sound and vomiting. She flushed again.

Had seeing Mutt and Jeff scared her? That didn't seem like her. Maybe the frankfurters at Fenway were as bad as Libby said they were, full of chemicals and "fillers," although she said it was probably okay if you only ate a few per year.

By the time we returned to our seats, the sun had dropped behind the right field stands. There were pink streaks in the clouds, and a chill in the air. Hank came back, huffing and puffing from climbing the steps. He dropped into his seat next to me. He wiped sweat from his face.

"Did you see them?" I asked.

"Naw, must have gone back to their seats or else they're long gone."

"What do they care about our garbage at the dump or whether we go to baseball games?"

Hank sighed. "They're looking for anything they can find, or trip over, to show we're guilty of 'suspicious' activity, or we have left wing associations or tendencies, or just to show the government they're doing their job."

He looked over at Mary with concern. "Is Mary okay?" he asked.

"I don't know," I replied. Mary did look paler than usual.

"Hope she's okay," said Hank. "Why didn't you tell me about them before?"

"We didn't want you to worry." Hank shelled a peanut with one hand and ate it, crushing the empty shell in his fist and dropping it onto the pile accumulating at our feet. "We hoped you would never have to know. We figured they would get their info and call it a day. But that's not how they work. They want to intimidate us."

There was a loud crack of a bat. Ted Williams, up to bat again, had smacked one into short left field for a base hit. All was right with the world again.

The left fielder picked up his grounder and threw it to second base to stop Williams, already on his way to second. Williams spun around and tried to go back to first. He was caught. The first and second basemen threw the ball back and forth, like in a game of keep-away, until Williams put his head down and tried to slide to safety at first. The first baseman caught the ball and gently laid it with his glove on the war hero's back. "Out!" yelled the umpire.

Mayhem broke out. All around us the Boston fans were infuriated. I moved closer to Hank, and then noticed that Mary's eyes were closed, and I suddenly felt the need for protection. I moved closer to Hank.

As the crowd quieted, the big arc-lights of the stadium snapped on with a loud, electrical zing that felt like it was going right through me. Without intending to, I grasped Hank's sleeve.

"You okay, sweetie?"

"Are they going to electrocute her someday?" I blurted, suddenly.

Hank's body jumped as if his finger was in an electric socket. "Wait. What? What are you asking?"

"You know, Libby…like…the Rosenbergs," I said.

"Oh, my god. Sweet Pea." He hugged me so hard, it hurt, and his weekend beard scratched. "Nothing like that is ever going to happen to her. Or any of us. I'm so, so sorry you've been worrying. Come on, let's get out of here. Mary doesn't look so good. I just hope she doesn't have food poisoning."

CHAPTER TWENTY-ONE

"I'm going to ride my bike over to John's house."

"Will his parents be home?" Libby asked.

"They're going to be nearby, having lunch at the golf club."

"Ah, that's interesting," Hank said, sitting back in his chair at the kitchen table and doing Groucho with his best nasal twang, flicking a non-existent cigar with his fourth finger. "I don't care to belong to a club that would have *me* as a member."

The ghost of a smile crossed Libby's face. "It's fine. Let her go. Maybe it's fun to chase a little, dimpled ball around, in and out of holes in the ground, like a gopher."

"Just remember," Hank said, "golf is the ultimate bourgeois sport, played by people in bright-colored slacks and white shoes with leather flaps to keep their laces dry."

John's family house overlooked the Goshen Country Club golf course. I knew country clubs were bastions of class privilege that only accepted people of a certain sort and that, although I might be welcomed as John L.'s guest, people like me, *my* people, as in Jews, were not acceptable as actual members.

Getting there involved three miles of hard pedaling, while thoughts of John and where he might touch me providing extra energy for the journey. I rode in through the open gate with its initials GCC worked into the wrought iron filigree, then over a short bridge arching a stream that meandered through the golf course, and finally, across a gauntlet of flying golf balls that John L. had warned me about. The family house was a sprawling white cape cod with two wrap-around, screened porches, overlooking the ninth hole.

From a distance, I saw John L sitting on a porch swing, waiting for me. He jumped up when he saw me, waved, and then met me at the front door of the house. "You're on time for your golf lesson," he said.

John's mother had put out tea sandwiches for us, before she and Mr. L had gone out. "Hope you're not too hungry," John L. said. "My mother makes these silly little sandwiches which aren't enough for even one small child." They consisted of crustless white bread, filled with delicate tuna salad, cucumbers, or olive spread. I found them utterly delicious, as I took in the utter good taste that pervaded the L's home.

My promised golf lesson took place on the L's front lawn. which blended almost imperceptibly into the rough of the ninth fairway. John L demonstrated the basic golf swing by standing behind me, adjusting my hands on the grip and guiding my attempts to turn, twist, and swing the club at the same time.

As much as I enjoyed trying, inside I believed that I was incapable of learning to play such a bourgeois sport. I stared down at the gleaming, pockmarked white ball, trying to concentrate, while John L., stood up against me, jiggling and adjusting, helping me to get the feel. "You just have to relax," he said.

Like me, John L. had more on his mind than helping me find my swing. He'd borrowed a golf cart, which he'd parked at the back door of the house. We drove off across another fairway, then down into a little vale of birches and daffodils. There, we lay in the grass. John L, completely relaxed on his own turf, sprawled out his long lankiness, while I worried that at any minute a flock of golf carts, filled with offended, brightly plumed club members, would come over the rise behind us. We moved closer to one another, kissed, and he began to run his hands over the regulation collared golf shirt he'd lent me to wear on the course. Soon his hands found their way under the shirt. Little moans from both of us floated on the spring breezes and dissipated into the dewy air.

Deep down, I was worried. The threat of the worst thing that could happen to a girl felt awfully close—pregnancy—all wrapped up in a beguiling package of pleasure. I wanted it to go on forever.

John's parents were waiting for us on one of the wicker-furnished porches, each with a drink in their hands. A bowl of salted nuts stood on the glass table between them.

Mr. L stood up when we came in and extended his hand to me. I shook it, unsure of how hard to squeeze. Mrs. L smiled from a flowered wicker couch. "This must be Sara. How do you do?"

"Yes, I'm Sara," I said.

Mr. L, whom I recognized from the town meeting, turned to John. "Where the heck have you been with that cart? Ernie's been looking for it. He wants it back pronto."

John L. gave me his uh-oh look. "I just wanted to show Sara the birch meadow."

"It's certainly a lovely place." Mr. L harrumphed and sank back into the sofa, his highball glass deep in his lap. "Don't you think so, Sara."

"Oh, yes. It's beautiful."

"Johnny, darling, you shouldn't cause Ernie any more worry," said Mrs. L. "He works so hard. Why not run the cart back now?"

I got up to go with him, but Mrs. L said to him, "Why not let Sara stay here so we can get to know her a bit?"

John turned to me uncertainly. "You'll be alright? It'll just take me a few minutes."

As it looked like I had no choice but to stay behind with his parents, I nodded. "Sure."

"Don't worry, we'll take good care of her. Sara, how about a ginger ale?"

As soon as the back door closed, Mr. L. added, "So, Sara, it's good to finally meet you."

"Yes...," I answered, making a calculated decision not to add "sir."

"John tells me you're a fine young lady."

"Thank you," I said.

Mrs. L went to the far end of the porch and let down some Venetian blinds to block the afternoon rays. Mr. L brought me a ginger ale from the paneled bar, then returned to refill his own glass. "John says you're a good student, too...."

"My parents want me to do well." I said and studied the fizzing of my ginger ale.

"Yes," said Mr. L, "I know people of your faith value education a great deal. Of course, we want our John to do well, too. He sometimes seems to be a bit casual about his studies." He smiled. "Maybe you can be a good influence on him—in that regard."

By now, Mrs. L had settled herself at the far end of the flowered canvas couch where I was sitting. She glanced in the direction of the door that John had taken to go out. "You know, dear," she said, "puppy love, at your age, can sometimes interfere with serious concentration on studies. It might be a good thing to—well, go easy," she smiled. "In the romance department. Boys have trouble controlling all of that, but we—well, we girls are somewhat better at it, if you know what I mean."

A spasm of terror seized me. Did she know what we'd been doing? I nodded vaguely, giving her leeway to interpret things as she wished.

"And, while we're at it," Mr. L interjected hurriedly, "although I believe in leaving matters of the heart to my wife, the body politic is my domain."

I must have looked confused or possibly terrified, but he smiled benignly at me and went on.

"I know your family holds some rather unconventional—well, *radical* ideas in the political arena. But I'm sure you're not letting those views interfere with your good citizenship at school. John tells me you're an independent thinker. Sometimes, you know, children need to make their own minds up about things. Take John, for instance. His views are a far cry from mine—from *ours*. He goes his own way, and I know he highly respects what you think...."

I nodded, at a loss for which of his statements I was supposed to respond to.

"And, Sara, if I may give my own opinion, it's probably for the best that your mother won't be teaching civics when John—and you—move upstairs to official high school. I hear she's been introducing controversial subjects that tenth graders just aren't mature enough to understand. Japanese internment. Emmett Till. *Brown v. Board of Education,* and the like."

Mr. L got up to refill his glass while I tried to use my mind to suppress the cold sweat breaking out all over my body.

"You know," he continued, adding ice cubes with silver tongs, one by one, from a silver bucket, "ninth grade is when grades and performance in school really begins to count—you know—for college."

It shouldn't have surprised me. Mr. L knew all about Libby—the loyalty oath and all. The whole town probably knew by now. The afternoon sun was finding its way through the closed shutters, blinding me as I sat, distracted by a buzzing in my ears.

"Well, "I said, swallowing my fear, "I'll miss having her for civics. I've heard the kids really like her as a teacher."

"Kids often don't know what's good for them," said Mr. L. "That's why we have school committees, I suppose."

I winced. Surely he couldn't know yet that Libby had plans to run for school board? At last, we heard the side door open and close. The knot that had formed in my stomach loosened slightly. John was back.

"We've really enjoyed talking to Sara," Mr. L announced as soon as John appeared on the porch, sweaty and breathless. He must have run all the way back. He scanned each of our faces in turn. "What did I miss?" he asked.

"We got a chance to get to know Sara a little," Mrs. L smiled.

"Oh, that's good," said John L, looking at me for confirmation.

Later, outside, like the gentleman he was raised to be, John L. saw me off on my bicycle. "What did you really talk about while I was gone?"

"Oh, not much. Your dad seems to know quite a lot about Libby."

"Really?" said John L., seemingly with genuine surprise. "How come I don't?""

"Maybe because we don't talk that much," I teased.

"True," he answered with a smile. "We have more important things to do."

I took my bike from where it was leaning on a tree and snatched a last, greedy look at him. I hoped it would last me for the long ride home.

"But you must have talked about something," John L. frowned.

"They said they hoped I was going to be a good influence on you," I said.

"Oh, boy." John L. looked warily back toward the house, then kissed me on the cheek. "Well, so far, you *have* been," he laughed and gave my bike a little push, sending me on my way.

CHAPTER TWENTY-TWO

"Those are the four thousand registered voters in Goshen, in alphabetical order, by street address," Libby said, indicating the many pages of the dog-eared list I held on my lap.

"Four *thousand*," I groaned, picturing endless days of going door-to-door as her sidekick.

We were in the Heap on our way to go canvassing.

"Ninety per cent of the voters in Goshen are registered republicans," Libby said cheerfully, "but that doesn't matter. The school board election is non-partisan."

Just as I'd feared, Libby had gone ahead and registered to run for the open seat on the school board—the one seat left vacant by the man who'd had the heart attack last winter. The election would be in early June. Libby's campaign platform was short—just returning the banned books to the school libraries and discontinuing school air raid drills.

I'd done my best to wriggle out of this, but Hank had to stay at home, waiting for one of his subs to call. After that, he said he'd try to come to relieve me. Mr. Bramhall was unsure, but also said he'd catch up with her later if he could. So, for now, I was the one at her side as we approached the first unsuspecting citizens of Goshen.

"Isn't this exciting?" Libby had a faraway smile on her face as she drove towards the north side of town. "The last time I did any canvassing was in 1948 for Henry Wallace's campaign for President."

"Never heard of him," I grumbled.

"He was Roosevelt's vice president for his third term," Libby said brightly, as if unaware of my reluctance. "He was too progressive, though, and so the democrats nominated Truman instead, and Wallace decided to run for president with the progressive party. Roosevelt won, of course, and Truman became president when Roosevelt died in 1945."

I prayed that the Colpitts clan would be somewhere else today. They had been plumbers in Goshen for three generations. They'd lived down a narrow, bumpy old road at the north edge of town for so long, the town had named the road for them. Paul was the youngest of three sons, and he had a bunch of cousins who also lived on the same road, and I "helped" him with his math in homeroom each morning,

"We'll just ring each doorbell, see if anybody's home. If they are, we'll talk to them. If not, we'll just leave them flyers and go on down the road."

A cardboard box full of mimeographed campaign flyers with Libby's picture slid around on the back seat of the car as we turned off North Avenue. A group of RFD mailboxes had "Colpitts" written on every one of them. We bounced along the dirt road, gritty with rocks, interspersed with islands of mud, and crisscrossed with exposed tree roots.

Concentrating, Libby clamped part of her lower lip in her teeth and held tightly to the juddering steering wheel. She was going too fast for this road. Even with my driving limited to the town dump, I could see that. She could be a lackadaisical driver when her mind was elsewhere, which it was a lot of the time.

I gripped the sides of my seat and wondered what she was thinking right now, although I knew that a person's inner thoughts were supposed to be private, if they wanted it that way.

We jounced along past a rusted farm tractor and an old refrigerator with the door hanging open, until we came up to the first Colpitts' house, which looked pretty run down.

Libby shook her head. "These people go to work every day, get their hands dirty, fix our leaks, snake our drains, make the town run, and they don't make enough money to get their road paved or get their trash hauled away."

"They're not so good at math, either," I said, attempting to make a joke.

"What do you mean?" Libby's face registered disbelief and disapproval.

"It's just that I have to do Paul Colpitt's math every day in home room."

"You *have* to?" Libby said.

"Well, by now he expects me to."

"That's very charitable of you," Libby said, "but maybe if the school did a better job of teaching him, he wouldn't need your charity."

I saw too late that I'd stepped right into one of Libby's ideological boobytraps. Charity wasn't always a good thing. Sometimes it demeaned people and made them feel inferior. In a well-designed society, charity wouldn't be necessary because everyone would have enough of whatever they needed.

"Didn't Marx say, 'From each according to his abilities, to each according to his needs?' Isn't that what I'm doing with Paul Colpitts each morning?"

"Oh, Sara," Libby said.

I riffled through the pages of the voter list and tried to calculate how many hours I'd have to be in involuntary servitude to Libby. I prayed for Hank to get his darn phone call over with and come rescue me like he said he might.

The first Colpitts' house stood high on its foundation in a clearing in the pines. There was a backyard incinerator, an airstream trailer up on blocks, and a propane tank beyond the clotheslines. Between the house and the road, an old Chevy pickup truck was up on jacks, and a pair of large boots I recognized stuck out from under the car.

Hearing the Heap, Paul Colpitts worked his way out from under the truck and sat up, blinking in the sunlight. He stood up, next, and tucked in the shirt he wore under his torn-up, greasy parka and waved at me. "Hi, Sara."

"Hi," I answered.

Libby surged forward, extending her hand, which Paul hesitantly shook with his greasy one. "I don't think I've ever met you, Paul, but it's very nice to meet you now. Are your parents at home?" Libby asked.

"No, sorry," Paul replied, "they've gone to visit my grandma. She's in a home now."

"Okay. We'll come back another day," said Libby and added, "I hear you and Sara are in the same home room in school."

"Yeah," he smiled shyly, "Sara's one of the smart ones."

"We're proud of Sara's academic abilities," Libby said, "but you know, young people develop in different ways." She pointed to the jacked-up truck. "I wish I knew more about the workings of a car. It's impressive that you do."

Paul swept his greasy hair back from his face. "Yeah, well, I get to drive it as soon as I turn sixteen."

"That's great," Libby said, and she seemed to mean it.

"Guess so."

I couldn't help noticing Paul was talking more to Libby than he ever did with me at school, even though I was the one who did his geometry. He sneaked looks at her, too. I inwardly cursed her for having this effect even on boys my age and not even noticing it.

"I'll come back next weekend to speak with them personally," Libby announced. "Maybe you'd be kind enough to mention that we came by?"

At an indication from her, I handed him a flyer, and she went on: "What I hope to do, if I'm elected, is reinstate some classic books that have been removed from the libraries. We want to bring back the right to freedom of speech…you may remember that from your social studies class with Mr. Bramhall." She flashed him one of her devastating smiles and started back toward the car with me close behind.

Paul followed us, holding the flier out in his hand. "It's probably better if I just give it back to you now," he said. "No offense, but I heard them say they wouldn't vote for you…because, they say, well, you're a… Communist."

Libby went a little pale as she took the flier back. "Of course, Paul, it's not fair to you. Don't worry, I'll talk to them myself—another time. We'll just continue on down the road."

"All my uncles and aunts have gone to see granny, too, so they're not home either."

"Okay, another day, then," Libby said, looking deflated.

We bounced back out Colpitts Road, past all the rusting, crumbling evidence of society's unfairness. As we neared the north highway end of the road, a car coming the other way had to pull over to the side. It was Mr. Bramhall in his black Chevrolet. He came to a stop and he and Libby spoke, their driver's side windows open, no more than a foot apart.

I was tired and always a little embarrassed to see Mr. Bramhall outside of school. I closed my eyes and leaned back against the seat, listening.

"I thought I'd better come personally to see how you're doing and get a raincheck on canvassing for the day," Bramhall said.

"Well, since it's not raining, I'm not sure I should give you a pass," Libby said.

"Well, I have a very good alibi," he answered.

"And what is that?"

I didn't hear exactly what he said next, but, as I listened, something tugged at me. There was something odd in his voice and something flirty and playful in Libby's. She often kidded with Hank, but with other men she was usually no-nonsense. The words of Mutt, the short one, suddenly resounded in my ears. "You know, Commies believe in free love."

When they were finished with their little conversation and were rolling past one another, Bramhall called out to me, "Hey, Sara, I saw you submitted an essay for the contest. Good for you."

This embarrassed me more and I didn't like the conspiratorial little smile they exchanged, even if it was only about my being coerced into writing that stupid essay.

After three more grueling hours of canvassing on the north side of town, where most people weren't home, we drove out to the town's north highway, waiting for a break in the cars whizzing by in both directions.

"Why did we *ever* move here?" I asked.

"What do you mean? We've told you so many times." Libby shrugged impatiently. "We wanted you to grow up in a healthy place, where you could breathe. Away from the crowding that breeds polio. We wanted to build our own house."

The answers were so familiar, but so tired and hollow by now, given that we'd ended up as Commie pinko Jews in a town of republican Christians. I studied Libby's face in profile against the car window as she watched for a gap between the cars.

"Grandpa says everybody out here hates us," I said.

"Your grandfather is wrong," Libby said impatiently. "Nobody hates us. When your grandfather was growing up in Europe, there was a lot of anti-Semitism."

"Is that why they put us Jews in concentration camps?"

Libby missed the next, perfectly good opportunity to pull out onto the highway. She sat gripping the wheel, eyes lowered. "Those were the Nazis. Where did you hear about that?"

"Magazines in the library. I saw pictures."

"Yes, your father said you asked him about it." Libby let out a world-weary sigh. "The Nazis put communists, Gypsies, homosexuals—and Jews—in concentration camps."

My heart began beating as crazily as when I had first seen those pictures—wanting to know, not wanting to know.

"What does it mean, 'concentration?'"

"People were crowded into them," Libby said, her eyes narrowing. "With no regard for their being human beings. Not enough space, not enough food, inhuman. They used people for slave labor. The rest they just…killed."

More cars passed on the highway.

"But why, *why* did they do all that?"

Libby let more cars go by. She stared out through the windshield the way she looked out the kitchen window sometimes, eyes distant, mouth a little crooked. "Nobody understands it, really. When a group of people is seen as sub-human, they can become scapegoats. When the masses are kept down and uneducated, their dignity and sense of purpose usurped, they'll believe anybody who appeals to them with messages of hate." She shrugged and readjusted her fingers, tapped her rings on the steering wheel. "Human beings have a tremendous capacity for good. They are also capable of doing terrible things to one another. That's why we need good government to make sure people do the right thing."

Libby obviously just wanted me to accept her explanations for things. She didn't really want me to push. But, poised there with her on the verge of the highway, I couldn't help it. "Why did we move to Goshen—*really*?" I asked.

"I guess you don't believe the reasons we've explained."

"I don't know," I said.

"Maybe you don't remember," Libby said, her eyes steely on the passing traffic. "You were being harassed at school in Mattapan. Maybe you've blocked that out. The kids were calling you names. You cried and, afterwards, we found you crying a lot."

"What names?" I asked.

"Red, Commie, atheist, spy, traitor."

"I was too shy is all," I said, looking down at my lap. "The kids didn't like me."

"It was hard to tell which came first, the teasing or the shyness." Libby's eyes remained on the road and her foot found the clutch. "But I'm afraid it was my fault."

"Your fault?"

"People thought I was a Communist. Some kids heard talk, and they decided to…punish you."

"*Were* you? A Communist?"

Libby paused as if the answer to this required deep, concentrated thought. "No, I wasn't," she said, turning to glance at me. Libby pulled jerkily out onto the highway. A car, moving east, slammed on its brakes and swerved to avoid us. The driver shook his fist and yelled out the window, "Woman drivers!"

I was relieved for the moment, but I agreed with him. Communist or not, Libby *was* reckless. She could get us all killed.

CHAPTER TWENTY-THREE

Twice a week, on the Tuesdays and Thursdays that Libby taught her civics classes, I rode home with her instead of taking the school bus. One Tuesday, she told me she had to drop off a bunch of winter sweaters at the dry cleaners and stop for gas. She pulled into a diagonal parking space in front of Eaton's, handed me money, and said I should go in and get myself an ice cream cone, even though summer was still weeks away.

She would walk down to Puritan Cleaners, and we'd meet afterwards, across the street at the post office. She needed stamps.

Despite longer days and intensifying sun, shrunken patches of snow, laced with black still lay here and there, in downtown Goshen. Birds were becoming very noisy, especially in the early morning and right before sundown. According to my bird books, the males, triggered by the angle of the sun and the temperature, were tuning up to attract mates.

I had pulled open the front door of Eaton's, when I saw them, standing partway down the block, looking in the window of the Five and Dime. The overcoats from their library appearance were gone. Their fedoras were back, replacing baseball caps. Libby would have to go right by them with her arms full of the sweaters.

They turned from the window as she approached, watching her.

My heart began to gallop. As Libby got nearer, they removed their hats. I couldn't see clearly, but I could picture the smug, phony-polite curl of their lips, saying, "Good afternoon, Mrs. Green."

Libby, who had plenty of experience handling rude men—the wolves, as Hank called them, as if all were members of the same pack—tried to walk around the two men. They blocked her way. She hugged the sweaters to her chest as if for protection.

Letting the door to Eaton's fall shut, I walked slowly down the block in their direction. Even at this distance, I could see Mutt and Jeff were calm, while Libby's movements were jerky, short and quick. They didn't notice me coming, so intent were they on whatever they were doing. I walked up and stood silently, a little behind Libby. I gave each of them, Mutt and Jeff, my dirtiest look, but they only had eyes for her.

Sensing me behind her, Libby shifted the sweaters into one hand and said, "Oh, do you need more money, sweetheart?" She reached into her purse and pressed a five-dollar bill into my hand. "I have some business to discuss with these gentlemen," she said in a low voice. "Go ahead and get that chocolate ice cream you wanted. Then take the change to the post office and buy me those stamps. I'll meet you back at the car."

She was dismissing me, I knew, but I obeyed and walked deliberately, eyes front, back up the block to Eaton's. By the time I turned to look, it appeared that Libby had brushed the two of them off and was continuing on to Puritan's. I breathed easier.

But they were moving with her, hats in hand, one on either side. She looked straight ahead and walked briskly into the cleaners. They lingered outside.

Would they actually hurt her? I thought for a moment of going in and telling Mr. Eaton. But then I'd have to explain something he wouldn't understand and that I didn't entirely understand either. The policeman, Officer Eddie, whom I'd seen ogling Libby plenty of times, was right across the street, sitting in a chair propped against the wall of the fire station, catching the sun. I couldn't imagine how I could explain the problem to him either.

When Libby came out of the cleaners, I could tell she was angry. She would be telling them off now, I told myself. But whatever she said to them appeared to amuse, rather than put them off. They adjusted the creases in their hats, put them on and went off down the street.

She stood there for only a moment before she started marching back to the Heap.

I ducked into Eaton's, bought the ice cream—strawberry, not chocolate, my new favorite. With the ice cream cone dripping down toward my hand, and after checking that the coast was clear, I crossed the street to the post office.

Mutt and Jeff were waiting for me along the dirt path to the post office where several old colonial relics were displayed: a granite millstone, a plow, antique wooden stocks with holes for where the criminal's legs went, and a pillory, with holes for the hands and the head. I tried to go around the two men.

"Hey, Sara, you know what this is?" Jeff jerked his thumb toward the pillory.

I stared at the contraption. I knew from a field trip the year before that they were for punishment and shaming in the colonial days. Horrified then at hearing how they were used, now I felt I couldn't breathe. I could almost feel the heavy wood weighing down on my neck. I veered wide around them and ran up the post office steps.

With hands shaking, I bought a sheet of three-cent stamps from the post office lady and came back outside. They were still there, standing on either side of the path. I dashed between them, and Jeff, the tall one, said: "Don't forget, Sara, the post office is government property. No sabotage or espionage allowed, or we might have to let you cool off for a night in the stocks."

I kept walking back in the direction of Eaton's, shaking with fear and anger. They followed with long strides.

"Come on," said Jeff, coming alongside me, after we were past Officer Eddie, who never even opened his eyes. "We know Sara's a good girl."

"It's nice your parents taught you not to talk to strangers," Mutt said, "but we're really not strangers anymore, are we?"

"Right," Jeff chimed in, "We know more about your mother and your whole family than you do, I bet."

Seething, I spun around. "You leave my mother alone," I squeaked, using every bit of available breath.

They smiled at me, as if I were just some kind of ineffectual little child.

I shook my fist in their faces. "Do you hear me? Leave us alone!"

They kept on a quiet laughing, shaking their heads. "Look, lovely Sara, don't get yourself all bent out of shape," said one "It's just about over."

"We've got about all the information we need now."

"We may even get reassigned,"

"Parting is going to be such sweet sorrow."

I darted across the street without looking, to where Libby was sitting in the car, her eyes blazing. "Get in," she ordered. She started the car and backed out, headed for Tony's. "What did they say to you?"

"What do they want?" I asked.

"Who really knows," she said, with disgust, her hands shaking as she gripped the steering wheel. "They're on one long fishing expedition. They know all about me already. It's just to intimidate us."

"They said they had all the information they needed, that parting was going to be sweet sorrow. Maybe they'll leave us alone now."

Libby bit her lip. "They said that?"

"Yes. I told them to get lost," I said. "To leave us alone." I looked over at her, hoping to see some recognition that I'd been a worthy chip off the old block—standing up to the FBI, being defiant and brave.

Instead there was something else there on her beautiful face, something I'd rarely, if ever, seen there before. It was uncertainty. It was fear.

CHAPTER TWENTY-FOUR

I was in the house alone when the doorbell rang. A pale man with thin blond hair and wearing a brown corduroy jacket stood on the other side of the screen door. Mr. Washington, our mailman, waved at me as he drove back down our driveway, leaving the guy standing there on our welcome mat. He had apparently gotten lost trying to find our house. Luckily for him, anyway, he'd run into Mr. Washington, who'd apparently given him an escort straight to our address.

The man said to me: "Does Elizabeth C. Green live here? Are you thirteen years of age or older?" Nodding yes to both, I signed and took the envelope he handed me.

He went straight to his car and climbed in. "I'm almost fifteen," I murmured when he was just out of earshot.

The return address on the envelope was: "US House of Representatives, Congressional Office building, Division 40, Washington, District of Columbia." I held the envelope gingerly, away from my body, as if it were a hot potato or something contaminated. I didn't know what it was, but it had something to do with the government, and that couldn't be good.

I brought the envelope into the kitchen and put it on top of the clothes dryer, where we always put our mail. It lay there with the rest, unexploded.

A half hour later, Hank walked in. He picked through the mail and found the envelope addressed to Libby. "Oh, boy," he said and sat down hard in a chair. "Who brought this?"

"Some guy. He made me sign for it. What is it?"

Hank wiped his face with his palm. "I'm not sure, but we'll let her open it herself."

The envelope lay on the dryer untouched, while I went through the motions of telling Hank about my day. I gave him a doggedly sequential rundown—we'd just learned the term in Bramhall's English class—of events at school, but both of our minds were on the envelope from the government.

Around six, Libby arrived. She gave each of us a perfunctory kiss and went to the stove to make herself a cup of tea. When she'd sat down with the tea, Hank picked up the envelope and slid it across the table to her.

Her eyes went big for a moment. Then slowly, carefully, she opened it, using a table knife. She unfolded two thick white pages and after reading a moment, said. "What an honor. The Honorable Francis Walter, himself, the newest chairman of HUAC is requesting a private talk with me on May 15th at 10:30 in the morning."

"Oh, great," Hank groaned. "Where?"

"Right here in Boston. The Old Federal Courthouse downtown in Patrick Henry Square," she said. "That's where HUAC does its dog and pony show when they come to town."

Hank sighed and closed his eyes. Libby, expressionless, got up, moved to her window, looked out into the darkness that reflected back the lights of the kitchen. Hank got up and went to her and began rubbing her back in gentle circles. She closed her eyes.

Hearing that Libby had to go to the Committee and "answer some questions" scared me. I'd heard about HUAC for years, how they were illegitimate, that they were not truly investigating, that they badgered people, trampled on their civil liberties, as Libby called them, and ruined their lives. Like a lot of things I'd heard my parents talk about, I didn't fully understand the implications, but the grim mood that descended in our kitchen now was unmistakable.

The hum of the refrigerator motor was the loudest noise. Somewhere outdoors, a bird, probably a thrush, maybe confused about the hour, began to sing loud and extravagantly, angling for a mate in the dark, and providing me with a distraction from the awful tension here inside our home. "I don't understand.," I said. "What's happening?"

I must have looked as pathetic as I felt, because Hank, who never stopped rubbing Libby's back, tried hard to explain:

"What just came is an invitation to appear and answer questions. You get one of these, and you go, because if you don't, the next thing is an actual subpoena, a court order to appear. HUAC is a bunch of old men, congressmen, legislators, who make the laws and have the right to investigate, or to do research on a subject. But these guys have taken to going on the road, like in a musical comedy or the Marx brothers or the Andrews Sisters, all in the hunt for Commies."

"What do they want to know?" I asked.

"They want to know what your mother thinks," Hank said. "They seem to think that what people think is what makes them dangerous or not. Probably the clubs she's belonged to. They're probably afraid she's poisoning her students' minds, when, really, she just wants to enlighten them. Our progressive ideas are not very popular right now. They may ask her to give them the names of people who were in the clubs and organizations with her."

"Which I won't do," Libby said.

"It isn't fair, and it isn't right." Hank said. "But, Lib, they do have the power. We need to find you a lawyer to go with you for your little talk with Chairman Walter."

"A lawyer?" Libby said. "What for? I've done nothing wrong. I shouldn't talk to him at all."

Hank rubbed his forehead then, as if to wipe away his own feelings so he could deal with her.

Libby glared at each of us, in turn, as she poured herself more tea and put more sugar in her cup than I'd ever seen her do. Any fear she might feel was covered by outrage, even with the awesome power of the United States government staring her in the face. Her jaw re-set into that steeliness I so admired in her—and feared.

"Everyone says it's good to have a lawyer with you," Hank said. "Just to protect yourself."

She turned to him sharply. "No lawyers. I don't need one. It's just a discussion. I'm good at discussions."

Hank scrubbed at his jaw. "You're not planning to cooperate, are you?"

"Of course not," Libby said. "I'll just tell him the truth. I'm not going to answer his questions because of my constitutional right to speak—or not speak."

"But.... He could make you testify publicly."

"If I have to, I will."

That night, I lay stiff and still in my bed to avoid rustling the sheets that might interfere with my listening. An old hand at surveillance, I could ordinarily pick up something—a key word or two—from the music of their conversation coming from their bedroom across the hall. Libby's voice would rise and fall. Hank's voice was low, steady, a soothing rumble.

But tonight, the music didn't flow. It fluttered, then would glide noiselessly for long periods, then resume, hushed and unintelligible, even to my practiced ear. To make matters worse, my attempts to hear kept being interrupted by the insistent, "whoo-whoo," of a great horned owl that lived in a big pine next to the badminton court.

CHAPTER TWENTY-FIVE

May 15th arrived. At breakfast, all three of us were bleary-eyed from being awake most of the night. Hank, in his bathrobe, clutched his coffee. "Ready to face the old fart?" he asked Libby.

Libby had gotten up early and dressed as if she were going fancy clothes shopping. She wore the dark green suit she had saved for funerals. She did *not* wear her espadrilles, but a pair of brown pumps she always said were very uncomfortable. She told us she'd be gone all day.

"I'm perfectly capable of driving myself," she said, brushing off Hank's offer to drive her. "I'm better off on my own."

"You mean in the absence of your doting husband, you'll be better able to charm that old bird out of his tree?"

Libby frowned at Hank. "I doubt that, but we'll see. Anyway, it's not about charm, it's about what's right."

"I could just cool my heels in the Public Gardens while you talk to them," Hank insisted.

"Yes," I chimed in, "And I can ride the swan boats…."

"You, young lady, *you* will be in school. The swan boats will always be there," Libby said. "Let me handle this."

"But Sara and I will be worried about you," said Hank.

"Don't worry about me," she answered.

She left even before my school bus came, tossing the bags she used for school into her car, and waved matter-of-factly as she drove off.

In school that day, instead of paying attention, I gazed out the window at the Burgoyne Elm. I was in a trance, picturing Libby in a basket, being dunked in water after each question, like the Salem witches.

When I got back from school, her car was still gone. Hank was sitting at his drafting table, doodling with his 4B pencil on onion skin, drawing little trees, some with small birds and even nests in the branches.

"Not home yet?" I asked. Would they keep her there, not let her come home?

"I'm sure your mother is just busy giving them a piece of her mind."

Yes, I thought, her mind—a dangerous thing.

Mary called soon afterwards, saying she had to talk to me and would meet me at the college. "I can't be gone long,…I have to be here when Libby gets back," I told her.

"That's okay. It won't take long."

The woods was a riot of bird noises, a mix of twitters, trills, squawks, hoots, and cackles, like an orchestra tuning up. Mary didn't say much as we jumped the chain and started down the college path.

"Where is your mother?" she finally asked.

"She had to go talk to some guy from the committee."

"What committee?"

"Somebody from the government in Washington. It's called HUAC. Listen," I said, to distract myself. "You can hear the cardinal, the bluebirds. The females sing, too. Listen, you can hear them answering the male, but they sound far away because they're hiding, deeper in the woods. Did you know they alter their songs to conform to the male's?"

"Females are always doing whatever males want," said Mary, in a bitter tone, which was not like Mary.

"But, not all birds sing," I rattled on. "The ones that do have special places in their brains for it. It helps them mate for life."

"That's…great," Mary said, sounding unimpressed with my newest tidbit of bird knowledge.

"Don't tell anyone, please, about Libby."

"I won't tell," Mary said. "I promise."

We sat by one of the little streams that trickled out of the ground, one of many that brought melted snow out of the hills and fed the big pond that was as full as I'd ever seen it. We made ourselves "fishing" sticks from thick, budding forsythia stems about to burst with yellow flowers, and poked at the ice-cold water.

"HUAC is investigating subversive education," I said, with as much authority as I could muster. "They're worried about kids being brain-washed.

They think Communists know how to wipe people's minds clean and plant their own ideas there."

"Big Patrick says that's what the Chinese communists did to American soldiers they captured in the Korean war. They erased their brains and then infected them with Commie ideas. Is that really possible?"

"Libby says if people are tortured, they can be made to believe anything."

Mary visibly cringed and, hugging herself, said softly, "Sara, I'm in trouble…. Real trouble."

I wasn't sure I'd heard her right at first because of the rushing water and the birds. She spoke so softly. I leaned closer. "What do you mean? Grades? Violin? What?"

"No…in *trouble*," she repeated and began to hug and rock her body back and forth as she looked up into the trees.

"What kind of trouble?" I demanded, annoyed at her for not just coming out with it.

"I'm pregnant," she said.

My mind swam. I couldn't take in the idea. "What? How?"

"The usual way," Mary said mildly.

Finally, it hit me, like a roll of thunder following a lightning flash. *Pregnant*. "Really? How is that possible? How do you know?"

"I've missed two periods."

It upset me to think that, despite my synchronicity with Mary, my own period had come and gone like messy clockwork during these last two months, and I hadn't felt a thing. I knew full well the implications of "the curse" not appearing on schedule. It was dire. "Does your mother know?"

"She knows now." Mary's face contorted with anguish.

"Who is…you know…the father?"

"Robby. I had sex with him…once."

"Does he know?"

Mary closed her eyes and shook her head slowly. "I don't want him to know."

"What are you going to do?"

"There's only one thing I *can* do…."

"What?"

"I have to have it—the baby," Mary shrugged and closed her eyes in misery..

I stared at her freckled, young face and at her hair she always put in braids for our rambles in the woods. "But you're still…a kid."

"I'll have to go away for a while…."

"Go where?"

"Some place in Brookline. It's a…home."

"When? For how long?" I asked in a rasp of a whisper. Annie O. says, before I begin to 'show.'"

"What about school?"

"School…?" she repeated dreamily.

"You *have* to go to school!"

"They have school there," Mary said.

"But, not real school," I said. "You won't be with me." She didn't seem to hear me. "I'll have it, then I'll give it up to be adopted by a couple who really wants a baby and can't have one."

It was obvious Mary was channeling someone else's words, and I felt her moving away from me, being swept into an unplanned, separate future from me. "I'll come visit you," I said.

"You don't have to," Mary said. "You can't anyway. They don't allow visitors. Only family. Parents."

"You can say I'm your sister."

"I can't lie to the nuns."

"What am I going to tell them at school?"

"We're going to say I have a bad case of mono." Her eyes glistened. She was refusing to cry. I reached across the little stream to hug her. She let me, but she didn't really hug me back. She collapsed, cringing into herself.

I felt sick to my stomach, on the verge of crying, too. I walked her all the way home, but she barely said goodbye, as she turned to go into her house.

I came home quietly, in a sort of daze, and sat on the Moroccan hassock by the fireplace. Libby had already kicked off her shoes, plunked herself down on the marshmallow couch, apparently getting ready to give Hank her report.

"Good, you're here, Sara," Libby said to me. "You should hear this, too. Her cheeks were touched with color, from the exhilaration of a fight, I decided.

I had a faint sense of pride in being the daughter of my gallant mother, but my mind kept returning to Mary. I imagined her belly swelling and how big it would have to be, before she would have to leave school and go away…to

Brookline and the "home."

"So," Libby said, "I met alone with Chairman Walter, democrat of Pennsylvania. They say he's a farm boy and you can almost believe it. He's *so* polite. He must have called me, 'Mrs. Green,' fifty times in less than an hour. He said I'd been mentioned by Herb Philbrick—'Herbert,'" he called him—in his book. That's what put me on their radar. I said, 'So you know all you need to know about me already.'

"'But we want to hear it directly from you,' he said, 'what you believe, not just hearsay. We want to give you the opportunity to defend yourself, to rehabilitate yourself, and to help us out and help your country, Mrs. Green.'"

"They're such hypocrites! They eat hearsay for breakfast," Libby continued. "I told him I had nothing to defend, and that the committee had no right to ask me questions about what I believed, what organizations I belonged to, now or back whenever, or who I had associated with. He must have jumped a foot when I said I refused to be a 'stool pigeon' like Herbie Philbrick and that I wouldn't name names.

"He claimed there was no better way to determine if a subversive had sincerely renounced communism than to invite him or her to name his former compatriots in public."

Hank was listening intently and studying her, like a boxer looking for an opening, as he would say. I was getting impatient. I wanted to escape to my room to worry about my life, and about Mary. I was tired of worrying about *her* problems, problems that Libby had created for herself.

"I told him, 'You're trying to use the power of this committee to persecute me, deny me a livelihood, shame and punish my family, and deny me my constitutional right to free speech.' 'No, Mrs. Green,'" he told me, 'You're wrong. We are gathering information for the good of the country and to help us formulate new laws that will protect us from the menace of communism.' I told him under no circumstances would I name names, or answer questions related to my free speech rights.

"You should have seen his face. The farm boy evaporated and the Red Baiter rose up. He said, 'There is no absolute right to free speech. You should know that, Mrs. Green, in your line of work. The Supreme Court in *Dennis vs. US* recently upheld the convictions of leaders of the Communist party of the United States, on the grounds that communists, by definition, intend to overthrow the government by force and violence and so are not protected by the First Amendment. We are at war with Communist countries. Forty thousand Americans died in Korea.'

"When I pointed out that the Chinese and North Koreans lost a million men, he said, 'Shows we're better fighters than they are, right? In any event, Mrs. Green, you had better prepare yourself to give public testimony…and you better bring a lawyer this time.' Then he handed me the subpoena."

Libby rummaged in her canvas bag and laid a document out on the Noguchi coffee table for us to see.

"What's a stool pigeon?" I asked.

"Ah, so there's a bird you don't know," Hank said. "A stool pigeon was a sort of decoy they used long ago, to entrap other birds. These days, it means a spy or informer for the police or, in this case, the government."

Libby said, "I don't need a lawyer. All I need is the First Amendment," and then she rattled it off, more familiar to her than the Pledge of Allegiance: "Congress shall make no law respecting an establishment of religion, or prohibiting the free exercise thereof; or abridging the freedom of speech, or of the press; or the right of the people peaceably to assemble, and to petition the Government for a redress of grievances."

"But, Lib, why tempt them to throw the book at you?" said Hank. "They're going to try to lure you into contempt or perjury. That's their game."

"I refuse to bow down to them," Libby said. "He said I was officially an 'unfriendly witness.'"

"Unfriendly. That's quite the understatement." Hank's expression, as he looked at her, was a mix of pride and fear.

Libby pointed to the crucial line on the subpoena. "I'm ordered to appear at a public hearing of the full committee next week."

CHAPTER TWENTY-SIX

Hank found a place to park along one of the cobblestone streets that ran up from the waterfront and smelled like fish. He held Libby and me both by our arms as we wobbled across the cobblestones. On our way to the New Federal building, which, unlike the rest of brick and brownstone Boston, was a thin art deco monolith of gray and green marble. It shot straight up into the sky.

Libby wore a suit I'd never seen before, high heels, and a hat—a strange patch of black felt with a little netted veil across the top. Hank wore a jacket and tie and dark slacks he never wore in the daytime. I wore a school skirt and sweater set and carried a small leather purse with nothing in it but an old handkerchief of Libby's and a Chapstick. There was no question about it—we looked like we were going to a funeral.

We walked by historic Faneuil Hall, and Libby, mimicking a tour guide, said in a sing-song voice, "The so-called 'Cradle of Liberty' was built by a slave trader. Slave auctions were held just around the corner."

In the crowded lobby, photographers from The *Boston Globe* and the *Herald* held their big accordion press cameras above their heads as they made their way through. Hank located the hearing room and held the big wooden door open so our trio could troop in.

A man I didn't recognize came up to us just as we entered. Libby nodded to him, then submitted to a kiss from Hank and planted one on my forehead, before following the stranger to the front row where other witnesses sat, with their lawyers. The man, Hank explained, had attended law school, although he didn't practice, and was familiar with the ways of HUAC. He would sit with her and help her with the questions she was asked.

I followed Hank to one of the visitors' rows and slid in next to Aunt

Dorothy and Uncle Arthur. To my astonishment, next to them on the other side, sat Grandma, fidgety and uncomfortable in her summer fur, and Grandpa with his arms folded angrily across his chest. Beyond them, sat Mr. Bramhall with his wife, Evelyn.

Surprised, I nudged Hank. "Grandma and Grandpa are here!"

"Yes," he whispered. "I guess Arthur must have convinced them to come and lend moral support, finally…to their own daughter."

"Why is Mr. Bramhall here?"

"Just…for support, too," Hank said. "There are people who very much admire your mother for standing up for important American principles."

I got Grandma's attention by waving across Uncle Arthur and Aunt Dorothy, and she gave me a shy nervous smile. Grandpa acted like he didn't see me. Then I saw, in the row behind us, Muriel, my piano teacher, looking prim and serious. Beside her was a large man, with a kind face and slightly disheveled hair; he resembled a bear.

"And Muriel's here!" I said to Hank.

"Yes, quite the reunion. People really want to support your mother."

Hank touched my arm and pointed up to where the Committee was sitting, facing us, and the witnesses, with their backs to us. "Wait till you get a load of the first guy. Your mother says he was a teaching assistant when she was in college."

Chairman Walter sat dead center at a long table with six of his colleagues, all of them smoking, which created a white haze concentrated near the ceiling. The Chairman began banging his gavel like a kid with a hammer and peg toy. With the other hand, he stubbed out his cigarette. "Come to order, please. Order…!"

"The House Committee on Un-American Activities will hold three days of investigations into subversive activities here in Boston, especially in the areas of education and union activities," Walter began. "Our witnesses today are individuals we have reason to believe have information that could be helpful to the committee in rooting out communism and Communist influence in our education system. Is there anything further my colleagues would like to say at the outset?"

Walter looked up and down the row of six dark-suited men. Silence. "Apparently not. Then, the committee calls Mr. Anthony Carmelo."

Someone placed a glass of water and an ashtray near the witness microphone. A man seated in the witness row, stood up, dressed in a gray knitted beanie, thick, square glasses without frames, and with thick trousers tucked into heavy boots. He carried a canvas bag over his shoulder.

Hank whispered to me: "Looks like he came straight up from the docks, doesn't he?"

Mr. Carmelo went to the witness chair and sat down. As soon as he was sworn in, he pulled out of the bag what appeared to be a partly knit dark green sweater, dangling with stitch holders, which he draped across his lap. He set a large ball of green yarn in the glass ashtray on the witness table in front of him and proceeded to knit, fast and expertly, the needles clicking softly.

Hank leaned towards me. "I told you this one's a character, right?"

I nodded, yes. Hank was trying to lighten things up, as usual, but I felt nervous. The soft tick-tick of Carmelo's knitting needles made me think of Madame Defarge and the guillotine, and then Mary. And then Mary and the problem growing in her belly. I missed her and wished she were here, or that I was wherever Mary was.

I could only see the back of Libby's head and shoulders, as she sat in the witness row with perfect posture next to her non-practicing lawyer. The funny black hat flattened her hair and, with the little net veil sticking up, suggested a bird's nest on top of her head.

"State your name, please, and your profession."

"Anthony Carmelo. Stevedore," he said loud and clear into the microphone, while continuing to knit.

"Are you a member of the International Longshoremen's Union?"

Carmelo looked up from his knitting. "Do you mean the International Longshoreman's Association?"

"I'm sure you know the terminology better than I do, Mr. Carmelo. Are you a member of that…association?"

"Yes."

"Is it true that you were at one time a college professor?"

"Yes."

"And what did you teach?"

"I taught United States history to freshmen."

"And why did you leave that teaching position?"

"My university began to try to intrude into the content of my teaching and to pry into my associations."

"Were you fired from your faculty position at Harvard, Mr. Carmelo?"

"No, I left of my own volition."

"And you became a dock worker?"

"A stevedore, yes."

"Mr. Carmelo, are you now or have you ever been a member of the Communist party?"

Carmelo leaned closer to the microphone to speak, but never stopped knitting. "I refuse to answer on the grounds of my right not to bear witness against myself…against self-incrimination afforded me by the Fifth Amendment of the United States Constitution."

"Are you represented by counsel, Mr. Carmelo?"

"No, but I have consulted a lawyer."

"So, you are refusing to answer the question so as not to incriminate yourself."

"Is that a question?"

"Yes, it is a question, Mr. Carmelo."

"I refuse to answer *that* question under my Fifth Amendment rights."

"Then we would be correct to infer from your response that you have done something against the law in the area of that question, such that you do not wish to reveal?"

"I refuse to answer—"

"—Do you understand, Mr. Carmelo," the chairman interrupted, "that you are under subpoena and under oath to testify wholly and truthfully before this committee?"

"I do. And have *been* testifying truthfully to this committee for nearly fifteen minutes already." Carmelo examined his knitting, then appeared to be counting rows. "I've done twenty rows while I've been testifying, so I know how long it's been."

The room rumbled with low laughter.

"Order." A single bang of the gavel. "You realize, Mr. Carmelo, that since you are under subpoena that you can be held in contempt of Congress for refusing to cooperate?"

"I do."

"Well, you're not helping yourself by knitting or whatever that is you're doing during this hearing. I believe this is a not-so-subtle form of contempt."

"Is that a question, Mr. Chairman?"

"Very well," Walter said, obviously annoyed. "I'll get to the point. Are you now or have you ever been a member of an organization that advocates the overthrow of the government of the United States?"

"I refuse to answer the question on the basis of my Fifth Amendment rights."

"Are you now or have you ever been a member of the Communist party?"

"I refuse to answer…."

Chairman Walter leaned over to whisper to the congressman next to him. "Perhaps you've heard the expression 'Fifth Amendment Communist,' Mr. Carmelo."

"I have," said Carmelo.

"Let me tell you what it means, in case you or anyone in the public doesn't know. The committee has found that there are many subversives and communists who use the Fifth Amendment to hide behind in hearings like these. They are not truly afraid of incriminating themselves, since they believe they have done nothing wrong. They simply don't care to testify wholly and truthfully before this committee or share valuable information about other subversives. I suspect you are one of those, Mr. Carmelo."

Chairman Walter glared at the silent, knitting Carmelo for a long moment, then consulted in whispers with his nearby colleagues. "No further questions. You are dismissed, Mr. Carmelo, but don't be surprised if, in the near future, you hear from the Department of Justice."

Carmelo gathered up his knitting and strode out of the hearing room. The big oak doors closed behind him.

A break was called for, and a roar of conversation filled the chamber. Hank stood up to stretch his legs. "He was something, right?" he said to me, then stepped over to speak to Mr. Bramhall. I stayed seated, feeling numb and wanting to hide, until Grandma patted the bench beside her. I slid over next to her.

She looked as nervous as I felt, but she smiled and gave me a kiss, enveloping me in her powdery smells. She took both of my hands in hers. "Your hands are ice," she said and held them against her bosom.

Grandpa didn't move or unfold his arms. He looked like he had swallowed a volcano and was barely managing to keep it from erupting inside him.

Muriel, smiling, slid forward on her bench and tapped me on the shoulder. She pointed to the man sitting beside her and whispered. "Sara. I want you to meet Ralph. He's my…boyfriend." Ralph, who looked nothing at all like a boy, nodded at me and patted Muriel's hand.

After the break, Libby Green's name was called. She stepped tall and proud to the witness chair with that bird's nest of a hat perched jauntily on her hair. She stated her name, loud and clear and raised her right hand.

"Do you swear that the testimony you are about to give before this committee will be the truth, the whole truth, and nothing but the truth, so help you God?"

"I do."

"Please state your full name," said Chairman Walter.

"Elizabeth Cohen Green," Libby leaned forward to speak into the microphone. Her voice was clear and steady.

"Mrs. Green, are you familiar with a book by Herbert Philbrick entitled *I Led Three Lives: Citizen, Communist, and Counterspy?*"

"Yes."

"Are you aware that you are named in that book as a person who attended and hosted the Communist cell meetings that the author also attended, when he was working undercover for the FBI?"

"I've heard that, yes."

"Mrs. Green, have you read the book?"

"I refuse to answer the question."

Congressman Walter scowled. "Why would you refuse to answer a straightforward question like that?"

"Because what I read is none of the government's business. Although I will tell you that I tend not to read trash of that kind."

The visitor's section around me rumbled with amusement as Walter and the congressman next to him put their heads together to consult.

"Order," said Walter, again banging his gavel.

"Mrs. Green, are you presently employed?"

"Yes, I'm a part-time teacher in a public high school."

"And where is that public high school?"

"Goshen, Massachusetts."

"What subject do you teach there?"

"I teach civics to tenth graders."

"Can you tell us in short what the study of civics consists of for high school students?"

"Civics includes the study of how the United States government works, and of the rights and duties of citizenship, including voting and other participation in the governing of the United States."

"How long have you been teaching in Goshen?"

"Two years."

"Is it true, Mrs. Green, that you have been fired from your job for teaching certain historical subjects with a subversive slant?"

"No. I have been informed that unless I sign the Massachusetts loyalty oath that my teaching contract will not be renewed."

"And do you plan to sign the oath, Mrs. Green?"

"No, I don't."

Walter shook his head and rolled his eyes. "And what's the basis of your refusal?"

"The government has no right to make my employment contingent upon swearing an oath of loyalty."

"Mrs. Green, let me cut to the chase here—are you now or have your ever been a member of the Communist party?"

"I refuse to answer the question."

"Because you might incriminate yourself?"

"I refuse to answer the question."

The man sitting beside Libby whispered in her ear.

"I refuse to answer the question as per my rights under the United States Constitution," she added.

Congressman Walter leaned into his microphone. "I assume you're referring to the *Fifth* Amendment against self-incrimination?"

"No, Congressman, I'm referring to the First Amendment. My right to free speech and freedom of thought."

There was a buzzing of voices in the hearing room. I could see Grandpa seething, and Grandma trying to calm him.

"What's going on?" I whispered to Hank.

Hank put his finger to his lips, shushing me. "Just listen for a moment. I'll explain it later."

"Far be it from me to question a scholar of the US Constitution," Walter said, his voice heavy with sarcasm, "a ninth-grade *civics* teacher, no less. But let me inform you that the First Amendment does not protect you from your obligation, under subpoena, to testify fully and truthfully to a committee of the United States Congress."

Libby remained silent. I couldn't see her face, but I knew she was staring coolly, defiantly, back at Congressman Walter.

"Do you understand what I'm telling you, Mrs. Green?"

"I understand, but I don't agree," Libby said.

"Mrs. Green, what did you do before you took the teaching job at the Goshen Public Schools?"

"I was a housewife."

"And before that?"

"A college student."

"Did you participate in extra-curricular activities?"

"I refuse to answer under my First Amendment rights."

"Isn't it true, Mrs. Green, that you served as the chairman of the Young Communist League organization associated with your university for two years during your time there?"

"I refuse to answer the question."

"Mrs. Green, are you a member of the Veterans of the Lincoln Brigade, which is on the Attorney General's list of subversive organizations?"

"I refuse to answer," Libby said.

"Isn't it true that you dropped out of your senior year of college to travel to Spain, despite the US stance of neutrality and against the Congressionally-enforced embargo, to fight in the Spanish Civil War with the so-called Lincoln Brigade?"

"I refuse to answer the question. My associations are my own business."

"Mrs. Green," the Chairman leaned closer to the microphones in frustration, "do you understand that you are under subpoena and under oath?"

"I do. I wouldn't be here otherwise. I am not here voluntarily."

"So, the term 'unfriendly witness' would apply to you?"

"My degree of friendliness would be in the eye of the beholder, Mr. Chairman." Again, there was a wave of laughter in the room. Next to me, Hank closed his eyes and let air escape slowly from his lips.

"Mrs. Green, the purpose of these committee hearings is to root out Communist influence in our education system, where subversives have easy access to innocent young minds, ripe for brainwashing. The moral fate of the country depends on teachers being pure of heart and understanding the danger of certain ideas. Would you please tell us who else was in the YCL Club with you?"

"I refuse to answer the question on the basis—"

"—Alright, Mrs. Green." Walter impatiently slapped some papers from one pile to another. "There's no need for you to waste any more of our time…or yours, as you insist upon making this hearing into a charade. As far as I'm concerned, you, as a witness, are beyond unfriendly. In fact, you are contemptuous and, more precisely, in my opinion, *in* contempt, literally and legally, of this committee and of the Congress of the United States that empowers us. You are dismissed."

Walter banged his gavel. "We are in recess for the day."

Hank grabbed my hand in his sweaty one, and we moved forward, toward the front of the hearing room and toward Libby, against the flow of people leaving. I saw Grandpa, pulling Grandma in the other direction toward the exit.

As we surged forward, I realized Grandma was right there behind me. She'd separated from Grandpa, and was fighting her way against the current of people, using the arm-and-elbow technique I'd seen her use to maneuver in lines at meat and bread counters on Blue Hill Avenue.

She managed to reach Libby first and, clutching at her sleeves, on tiptoes, put her mouth to Libby's ear. The ghost of a smile crossed Libby's face. She took Grandma's face in her hands and awkwardly kissed her.

Hank's expression was grim as he pulled Libby, me, and Grandma toward the front exit door where Grandpa, in a fury, was still waiting.

In the car on the way home, Libby sat silent and ramrod straight in the front seat.

"What did Grandma say to you?" I asked her, breaking the silence.

"Bleyb shtark," Libby said, without turning around.

"What does it mean?"

"It means 'Stay strong,'" Libby said.

CHAPTER TWENTY-SEVEN

The tree we called the Burgoyne Elm stood next to the school parking lot. It had supposedly survived Dutch Elm disease in the 1930s, but long before that, during the Revolution, it had served as a sleepover site for British General John Burgoyne. He and thousands of his troops were on their way to Saratoga, New York, to surrender to the patriots. A bronze plaque embedded in its bark commemorated all this,

The newly sprouted spring leaves arched protectively over couples in love during Goshen High's lunchtime. "Sara, we need to talk," John said, as he met me under the canopy of green, without touching me, though. "I don't think we can do this anymore."

"Can't do what?"

"This!" John waved his hands, gesturing up at the tree and the sky and at the oblivious couples gathered on the grass under its branches. I was taken by surprise, although I probably shouldn't have been.

"My parents say I'm not concentrating enough on school. That I need to focus."

"And I'm supposed to be the cause of that?" I demanded.

"Well, one of the causes." John L. looked down the considerable distance to his shoes.

"What are the other causes?"

"That I'm a lazy bum?" John L. shrugged. "Anyway, they say if I don't shape up, they're going to send me away to boarding school."

"Send you away…?" I said, devastated. Mary was leaving me, too. "Well, the obvious solution is for us to spend more time together so that I can tutor you."

John L. hung his head. "I don't think it's that simple. My parents don't want me to hang out with you anymore."

I couldn't believe it. John L. and I had settled into a semi-chaste routine, meeting around the demands of homework and basketball and, I thought, parental scrutiny. We were both keeping up our grades. I was, at least.

We kept the above-the-belt petting under control, taking as much pleasure as we could. I strictly policed the border line between second and third base, especially since the revelation of Mary's situation.

"Do they know about our…fooling around?"

"I don't know…they probably just assume it."

I pictured the not-that-long-ago scene of John and me driving a golf cart through an emerald field of daffodils. Then, it struck me. Libby. By now, word of her uncooperative performance at the Boston Committee, had to be all over town. If there was anybody who hadn't heard rumors about Libby before, by now they had to know. It had even been in the papers.

I glared up at John. "This is so unfair," burst suddenly from me. "Just because my mother has crazy ideas, how did that make me guilty or dangerous? Your parents just don't like me."

"That's ridiculous," he said. "They like you. In fact, they admire you…."

"Admire me? Maybe as some clever alien—"

"Come on, Sara. You know that's not what they think." He looked down at me like I was crazy.

"How would I know what they think?" I said, the hurt still rising. "Do they think I'm some sort of Commie-pinko just because people think Libby is."

John L.'s shoulders rose and fell in a helpless shrug. "I don't want to break up," he said. "But I can't go against them. They *will* send me away. My father went to boarding school. He doesn't think of it as some terrible punishment. He says it's an opportunity. And my mother, she would never go against him on something like that."

I stood with him under the protective branches and felt exposed and vulnerable, as if we were naked like Adam and Eve about to be thrown out of our little paradise. "I think it's guilt by association."

"What do you mean?"

"I mean, it's been in the newspapers about my mother having to testify at the committee."

He shook his head as if I were all wrong. "They already knew all about your mother."

"They did?" The possibility rolled over me. Everybody knew about Libby, even if I didn't. "Anyway, maybe it's the best idea," I said in an attempt to salvage some pride, "under the circumstances."

"Really?" He looked down at me, obviously hurt.

"Did you expect me to cry," I said, "when you're just doing what your parents want you to do?"

"Well, *I* cried." He turned his head, so I couldn't see his eyes.

"Well, I'll do mine in private, too, thank you." I turned and walked off, fighting tears and clinging desperately to self-control and whatever shred of dignity I had left.

I wished I had something—a ring or a letter sweater that I could pull off and throw back at him, but there was nothing like that.

CHAPTER TWENTY-EIGHT

Mad, mostly sad, over John L., I lay awake, still under the covers, indulging in self-pity and waves of tears, when Libby, after a soft knock, let herself into my bedroom.

"What's going on in here?" She threw the curtains open, letting in too much sun.

"Nothing," I said, wiping my eyes with the sheet.

She wore an apron, had the sleeves of one of Hank's work shirts rolled up, her hair wrapped in a red paisley bandana. She looked like just like Rosey the Riveter on the poster Hank had taped up on his office wall.

"No moping allowed over misguided men. Come on. Get up and come give me a hand."

"With what?" I slurred my words, pretending to be groggier than I was. The last thing I wanted was for Libby to see me whimpering over John L.

"We're spring cleaning the back office," she said.

"What for?" I said from underneath the tented, sun-illuminated bedsheet.

"Because it's dusty and the spiders are swinging from the cobwebs. I need your help," she said and quickly left my room, leaving the door open.

I dragged myself out of bed, closed the door, put on clothes, and stuck my head out into the breezeway. The roar of the vacuum cleaner was already coming from the back office, where Libby almost never went and certainly never cleaned.

I ventured closer and stood in the doorway. The windows of the office were cranked wide open, and the place smelled like Lysol, a toxic chemical Libby abhorred. An old feather duster sprouted from Libby's back dungaree pocket, as she dragged our ancient Electrolux around by the hose. It scraped over the concrete floor like a sled over rocks.

When she noticed me in the doorway, she beckoned me in. There seemed no choice but to join her in this unexplained housekeeping fury.

"Why, all of a sudden, are you doing this?" I asked, over the vacuum's roar.

"Stop asking so many questions and just help me."

Soon I was attacking a winter's worth of cobwebs collected during the cold spell when Hank used the dining room for his drafting and figuring. Together we raised enough dust to kick off my allergies on top of my hay fever, already well underway. Libby tossed me a spare kerchief to tie over my nose and mouth for the dust, which gave me an outlaw aspect I liked.

We wiped off the drafting table, the filing cabinets, the Gizmo, the Philco, and the space heater. When Libby deemed the place clean, she unplugged the vacuum cleaner, wrapped up the cord, and we returned the woven plastic love seat to its usual position opposite the television that now sat on top of a tall, corrugated box.

Together we carried the old army blanket out to the back lawn, shook it out, setting off more attacks of sneezing from me, and back inside, folded it carefully across the webbed love seat. We both collapsed onto it and stared, exhausted, in the general direction of the cold gray Philco screen. Libby unwrapped her red paisley kerchief from her hair, I untied the mask over my nose and mouth, and we sat close, mopping sweat from our faces.

"Okay," I said, "so why are we doing this?"

"Okay. After those goons showed up at Fenway, we decided it would be best if you and Hank could watch baseball in the comfort and safety of our own home."

Hank popped his head in just then. "Look what I have!" he said, lugging in a large TV roof aerial with its wires hanging down, to show us.

I couldn't believe my eyes. It was the unsightly aerial that Grandpa had envisioned. It was a dream come true.

"See you ladies later," Hank said. "Anyone needs me, I'm up on the roof trying to hook this thing up. Turn on the TV, so you can tell me if and when it starts to work."

Without a hint of the revulsion I would have expected, Libby switched on the Philco. What could have been a mid-winter blizzard filled the screen. She turned down the sound and both of us sat mesmerized by the "snow." Soon, there was the crunch of Hank's footsteps overhead on the roof.

"Still sad about John L.?" Libby asked, looking furtively up at the ceiling as if Hank might fall through at any moment.

"Still angry," I said, determined not to let her see the actual effect on me of John's betrayal.

"It's hard, first love," she said.

"It wasn't love," I insisted.

"I'm glad you recognize that."

"Did you have boyfriends before Hank?"

"A few, sure," she said.

"Did you think it was love, each time?" I asked.

She smiled. "I suppose I did. I can't really remember." She turned to look out one of the newly cleaned windows.

"John L. told me his parents are threatening to send him away to prep school."

"All of a sudden?" Libby glanced at me curiously.

"They say he's not focusing on his studies."

"So, they think he's focusing too much on you?"

I shrugged. "I guess so."

"But you're not letting *your* studies go, are you?" Libby said and began chewing at her bottom lip.

"No, and I don't think he was either."

"How were they when you went over there?"

"They were friendly enough." I hesitated. "His dad did say something about how 'your people' value education…."

"Your people? Was that all?"

"Well, he knew about you not coming back to teach next year."

"And now he must know about my appearance at the Committee. I wonder whether all this could have anything to do with that."

"Maybe." It annoyed me how naturally everything seemed to come back to her. And I was angry at the idea that John L. and his parents might be punishing me for Libby's actions. It wasn't my fault that Libby was my mother. A tightness in my throat threatened to burst with outrage.

"I'm sorry," Libby said. "It isn't fair…if that's what's *really* happening."

"What else can it be, unless he just doesn't like me anymore?"

"I just wonder if it could have anything to with…our being a different religion…being Jewish," she said.

"That would be guilt by association, too."

Libby smiled. "Yes, it would be."

Hank appeared, sweaty and dusty from climbing on the roof. "Can you see anything yet?" He glowered at the Philco. "You'll come out and tell me if anything shows up, right?"

"We will," Libby and I said in chorus.

As soon as he was gone, I said, "Mary's in trouble."

Libby took her eyes off the TV and leaned towards me. "What kind of trouble are you talking about?"

"She's pregnant," I said in a low voice, with a glance at the door where Hank could reappear at any time.

Her lips opened and her eyes went larger. "Oh, no. What could she have been thinking…or not thinking?"

"I don't know."

"What a terrible thing for her," Libby said, looking stricken. "Her education…what an awful thing."

"I know," I said.

"It's an abomination that our system provides no rational way of dealing with this." Libby jumped to her feet, paced the concrete floors of the now pristine back room, fuming. But her voice was restrained when she added, "No legal birth control, no *real* sex education, and abortion illegal. Poor thing."

"She has to go to a 'maternity' home."

"What about school?"

"So far, they're saying she's got a bad case of mononucleosis."

Libby covered her face with her kerchief and made a little noise of disgust. "Oh," she said. "That poor child. As if it's still Dickens' time. We are so unbelievably backward. When will we wake up?"

"She's going to give the baby up for adoption. I'm not allowed to visit."

"Then you'll write her lots of letters," Libby said.

"I do. But I really want to go see her…."

"You just said you're not allowed to."

"Every day the nuns come and talk to her and the other inmates."

"Inmates?" Libby said in disbelief.

"That's what she calls herself and the other 'fallen women.' They're told every day about how they've disappointed God, that they're unworthy of being mothers, and they can only be redeemed by giving the baby up for adoption, even though she already told them she would. It's like they're afraid she'll change her mind."

"You have to go see her," Libby said.

"I'm not allowed."

"Well, then you'll need a very clever plan," said Libby.

We sat silently staring into the snow on the television screen, when it suddenly cleared and a test pattern for ABC came on the screen, clear as a bell.

CHAPTER TWENTY-NINE

Mary was going to have her baby at Carney Hospital around Christmastime. Until then, she would be what she herself called an "inmate" of the maternity home run by the Sisters of St. Joseph in a big two-story brick house, complete with portico and pillars. From the street the place looked like the other grand old houses in that section of Brookline.

Out back, there was a scraggly garden with roses, a large expanse of grass and, toward the back of the property, a derelict greenhouse where I was supposed to meet Mary.

At five past 2:00, Libby and I parked behind a flat-bed truck on the street outside the big back gate, which was left unlocked for a couple of hours on Saturdays, Mary had written in her latest letter, while the gardeners brought out a large grass mower.

"Good luck," Libby said to me. "I'll wait for you right here in the car. I brought a play to read." She smiled and held it up to show me. It was a thin little paperback, with a picture of a cartoon penguin near the bottom and the title—*The Crucible*.

"What's it about?" I asked, although my mind was busy with finding Mary.

"I've heard it's basically about suspicions of witchcraft, a time like our time, but in the 1600s." At that moment, the big lawnmower coughed to life, then set up a continuous, snarling drone. Leaving Libby in mid-sentence, I jumped out of the car and slipped in through the open gate.

Mary had given me careful instructions in her letter. I had from that moment until the mowing was finished to be on the grounds. I'd have to rush back out the gate before the mower exited and the gate was closed and locked behind it.

Once inside, I proceeded, according to Mary's instructions and a hand-drawn map. Just as she had described it, the greenhouse was broken down and neglected, the door hanging open. I stepped inside, into the hot, muggy atmosphere. Mary was already there, sitting on a bench among the flowerpots.

My heart leapt. We hadn't seen one another for three weeks. She stood up from the bench and we hugged. She already felt changed, the baby creating a space between us. We sat down on the bench together. She swung her legs forward and back like a little kid, and in the close, unearthly light and thick air of the greenhouse, I could see Mary was definitely "showing."

She wore a kind of linen smock that to my mind emphasized, rather than hid, her expanding belly. Still, I told myself, she was the same. She was still my Mary, the strawberry blonde kid, her blue eyes alight in the morning sun.

"You look…good," I said, speaking over the drone of the mower.

"Yes," said Mary, flouncing in her smock, "like Botticelli's Venus. Right?"

"Kind of. How many more months?" I asked, though we both knew. Her due date was the week of Christmas.

"They're already starting to put the pressure on. They have tag-teams, a different sister each time. Sometimes a real priest from the archbishop's office comes. They tell you about the heartbreak of these young couples, who can't have babies and want them more than anything…and how your baby will be so much better off with them.

"They come around to prepare you for signing on the dotted line, to give away the baby right after you give birth. They even showed us the document and the exact spot where we'll be signing. They say it's best not to even see the baby, although supposedly we have the choice."

It was impossible for me to conjure up a picture of Mary giving birth at all, even less of her giving away an actual baby to some "deserving couple," sight-unseen.

"Have your parents been to see you?"

"Annie O. comes." Mary ran both hands over the curve of her belly and half closed her eyes as if she were caressing the baby itself.

"And Big Patrick?"

"He's pretty silent these days. He calls me on Sundays, I think, to check that I've been to Mass." Mary jumped up and went, with a hint of a pregnant lady's waddle, across the greenhouse. She stepped up on a bench and motioned me to follow.

In a corner of the structure, where the glass ceiling and the metal frame met, was a messy-looking nest made up of short, broken twigs. Nestled inside were four smooth, white, elongated eggs. The nest, which she said belonged to a pair of chimney swifts, was glued together with saliva and perched on top of a metal box that enclosed a non-working fan.

"How do they get in?" I asked.

Mary pointed to some broken out glass near the peak of the roof.

"Wow," I said, and the four white eggs did seem especially miraculous, given Mary's situation. "It won't be that long before you're back in school," I said.

"First I have to give birth." Mary touched one of the eggs gently with her finger. "My parents think I should go to a different school…afterwards. Maybe a Catholic school."

"No! Why?" I said in sudden panic. We climbed down and settled back on the bench.

"So I won't have to go back where everybody knows me and…the situation. The comments. The questions, all that. People might say stuff to me. My parents think the permissive attitude of the public school somehow led to my problem. And even though they have classes for us here, I'll be behind." Mary gave a sad little shrug.

"No," I said, "you *have* to come back to GHS. Don't worry, I'll stand up for you. I'll protect you. And next time I come here, I'll bring you the homework so you can keep up."

"Thanks," Mary said, "but it doesn't matter what school I go to. What am I gonna miss, really?"

"But *I'd* miss *you*."

"And I'd miss you terribly." Mary gave me a hesitant look, then changed the subject. "And what about John L.?"

"He broke up with me."

"Really? Why?"

"His parents are threatening to send him to boarding school because he's not focusing in school."

"And they think you're contributing to that?"

"I guess. Do you think maybe they don't like me because of Libby and the HUAC thing?"

The question appeared to stump Mary or maybe she was trying to spare my feelings. She looked at me and then back toward the nest. "I have no idea."

"Do you think it's because I'm…we're Jewish?"

"Well, if that's true, you don't want to have anything to do with him," said Mary.

Outside, the sound of the mower suddenly went quiet. At the same moment, a bell from the clock tower bell of the old mansion rang down four deafening clangs on top of us. We put our fingers in our ears and giggled together. Mary had to be back for vespers, and I had to get outside the gate before they closed it.

CHAPTER THIRTY

There *was* an unmentioned, ulterior motive for Libby's feverish spring cleaning of Hank's backroom office and the new aerial. It was not only so Hank and I could watch baseball safely at home. It was because the Army-McCarthy hearings were being broadcast live and during the day on ABC. Hank and Libby were eager to see these hearings, though I didn't understand why, at least at first.

On the first day of the hearings, Libby rushed to school to teach her civics class, then hurried home to watch the hearings. She'd flatly rejected Peele's offer of a substitute to fill in for her until the school year ended. She still had her job until June, she said. It was her "last hurrah" with the kids, she said.

"Hopefully, by the end of the school year," Libby said, "I'll be able to tell my students that Joseph McCarthy has finally succeeded in shooting himself in the foot." What Libby and Hank found so riveting, week after week, looked completely boring to me—more old men in dark suits talking endlessly, with microphones in front of them and smoking, lots of smoking. Photographers crouched nearby like dark frogs at a pond.

With only a week left of school, I came home on the bus to find them both—Hank and Libby—sitting on the plastic-webbed love seat, their eyes glued to the Philco's small screen. She sat with hands folded primly in her lap, as if she were about to play a recital. Hank sat forward, his long legs bent at the knee, feet planted on the concrete floor, chin in hand, glaring at the screen as if about to spring forward like a football player.

I lingered for a moment at the office door.

"Come on in, Sara. Bring in a chair and watch it with us," Hank said without taking his eyes off the screen.

"I have a lot of homework," I said and moved to go.

"Come on," Hank crowed in his sports announcer voice to lure me in. "This is the World Heavyweight Championship fight between Senator Joe McCarthy of Wisconsin and the United States Army,"

"If you come in, I'll give it to you, play by play, punch by punch," Hank said, raising clenched fists in front of his face, like a boxer. "In the black trunks, Senator Joseph R. McCarthy, the mean-looking guy with dark eyebrows and the all-day five o'clock shadow. He's a republican from Wisconsin and chairman of the Senate's version of HUAC.

"He's been running around the country with his Senate Permanent Subcommittee on Investigations, holding hearings to expose and smear suspected subversives, always claiming he has lists of communists. And in the far corner, in red, white, and blue trunks and fruit salad, we have the US Army."

"Secretary of the Army Stevens is the one in the white summer suit with the generals sitting behind him with all the fruit salad," Libby added.

"What fruit salad?" I asked, taking a tentative step into the office.

"It's what they call all the medals on those dress military uniforms."

"Why fruit salad?"

"Because the medals are so colorful. You can't see them on a black and white set."

"Maybe we should watch them on Grandpa and Grandpa's new color television set."

"I doubt they'd be interested," Libby said. "Either that or they'd be rooting for the wrong team."

"Okay," Hank said quickly, side-stepping the grandparent subject, "here's what's happening: McCarthy accuses the US Army of sheltering and being soft on Communists. He claims there are subversives in the Army Signal Corps, the communications branch of the Army, at Fort Monmouth in New Jersey, where the Rosenbergs worked.

"Then the Army turns around and accuses McCarthy of trying to get special treatment for a private in the Army, a guy who used to work for the Committee. So, now the Army brass and Joe McCarthy, are duking it out on national television."

As I stood undecided in the doorway, something someone said on the TV made the somber crowd of old men laugh. I stepped inside. I sat down. It would be the first time all three of us had watched television together since we used to congregate on Sunday nights at Grandma and Grandpa's for the Jack Benny Show.

Libby pointed. "That's Joseph Welch. He's serving as special counsel to the Army. He's a partner in an old Boston, white shoe, fancy and expensive, law firm."

As the hearings dragged on, day after day, I guess you could say I surrendered. After school, I began bringing my homework into the back office, set myself up on Hank's drafting table, and watched with them. It felt good, just the three of us.

After weeks of hearings, which I alternately found confusing and boring, the same Joseph Welch, a small man who looked like a Christmas elf in a three-piece suit, bluntly challenged McCarthy and Roy Cohn, his sidekick, to produce the names of the one hundred fifty people they claimed were communists working in the defense plants.

McCarthy seemed thrown off guard and replied that if Mr. Welch was truly concerned about people aiding and abetting communists, he should consider "a young lawyer in your own law firm who's been a member of The Lawyers' Guild, a known Communist-front organization." Hank and Libby both caught their breath.

Welch responded in words that brought a hush to the hearing room: "Until this moment, Senator, I think I have never really gauged your cruelty or your recklessness. Fred Fisher is a young man who went to the Harvard Law School and came into my firm and is starting what looks to be a brilliant career with us.

"Little did I dream you could be so reckless and so cruel as to do an injury to that lad. It is true he is still with Hale and Dorr. It is true that he will continue to be with Hale and Dorr. It is, I regret to say, equally true that I fear he shall always bear a scar needlessly inflicted by you. If it were in my power to forgive you for your reckless cruelty, I would do so. I like to think I am a gentleman, but your forgiveness will have to come from someone other than me."

Seeming oblivious, McCarthy continued his attack in his usual monotone. Welch interrupted him again. "Senator, may we not drop this? Let us not assassinate this lad further, Senator. You've done enough. Have you no sense of decency, sir? At long last, have you left no sense of decency?"

The television cameras showed people in the visitors' seats applauding at that. Hank and Libby both came to their feet simultaneously, right there in the back office and began to clap slowly, too, very slowly.

"We knew Fred Fisher," Hank told me quietly, "in the old days."

I stayed seated. As with so many things having to do with my parents, and as much as I tried, I still didn't fully understand. Yet, I felt something, something profound that connected me to them. The spectacle on the small screen referred to times before me, times that remained out of focus, but I knew were important. Something had happened there before my eyes. I'd witnessed some kind of ritual skirmish in which a small, eloquent David had struck a crucial blow against a cruel, bullying Goliath. I could feel a swell of pride—a small victory for what I knew was our side.

Libby drove me back to Mary's maternity home. She'd brought another book and would wait in the car.

The inside of the greenhouse was warmer and more humid than when we'd met before. Mary sat on the bench in her smock, waiting for me. This time, she looked so different, I almost missed my step into the greenhouse. Her beachball of a stomach threatened to crowd her chin. She looked older, as if I was seeing her years from now, no longer a girl. There was no mistaking it. She was a woman now.

From being inside so much, her complexion looked even more pale, although her freckles were still in place. Her hair was a darker orange, longer and thicker. "Look," she smiled, holding up her fingernails to show me. "They grow so fast, and I've stopped biting them!"

"Your hair is really long, too," I said. "And your stomach…is it hard to walk?"

"Yes," she said and sounded exhausted.

We sat together in the heavy humidity, and I felt an awkwardness that came from our three weeks' separation. She'd changed so much. There was no getting around it—Mary was not only a woman but—it felt real now—she would soon be a mother. It all seemed crazy.

"How are the swallows doing?" I asked, glancing up to the corner of the greenhouse where the nest was.

"I think they're okay. I can't climb up there anymore."

"I'll go see," I said.

"Sara," Mary whispered and put her hand on my arm, "I'm going to keep it...I'm going to keep the baby."

"How?" I sat back down.

Mary looked furtively around the green house. "When the time comes, and they put the papers in front of me, I just don't sign."

"You can do that?"

"A baby comes from your body, so it's yours unless you say otherwise," she said.

"But then what? Your Mom's okay with it?"

Mary looked down to where her lap used to be. "I wouldn't say she's okay with it. She went to see Father Gregory about it."

"Really? What did he say?"

"I guess, he said it was okay, given the circumstances," Mary said, running one hand over her swollen belly. "He said not to tell anyone she'd spoken to him."

"What will you...tell people?"

"We're going to tell them it's my new baby brother...or sister," she shrugged with a smile. "But really, it'll be *my* baby, my mother says. Some people will believe it's hers, but plenty of people will figure it out."

"You'll have to be... so strong," I said, surveying the array of neglected, struggling potted plants all around us. "Are you afraid...of the birth...you know...of the pain?"

"Yes!" Mary said. "Annie O. says it's nature's way, and you forget the pain. The priests say labor pains are punishment for original sin."

"Poppycock and balderdash," I said. Two of Mr. Bramhall's favorite expressions. Mary laughed.

"Do you care if it's a boy or a girl?" I asked, veering away from the pain question.

"It has to be a boy." As if she were issuing orders to it, Mary looked again at her belly. "I don't want my child to have to go through anything like this."

Slowly and carefully, I climbed up to look in the nest, knocking an empty flower pot down in the process. Two small downy creatures with scary-looking eyes and wide-open beaks looked back at me. Next to them sat one egg, unhatched. I got down quickly, before they mistook me for their parents and expected me to feed them.

"They're okay, but hungry," I reported to Mary, and took up my place on the bench beside her.

"Well. Now neither of us are virgins," she said, surprising me.

"I still am," I said, hesitating.

"But you're not the same. You've been done wrong by a boy like I have."

We heard a rustling outside the greenhouse, then saw the top of someone's head, ducking up and down to see inside the windows partially blocked by overgrown plants. We scrambled off the bench and crouched low. Then Mary motioned me toward an upended wheelbarrow, and I moved to hide myself behind it. Mary eased back up onto the bench.

The door to the greenhouse squeaked and scraped open. "Oh, it's you, Mary. I see you've found a quiet place to contemplate things, away from the lawnmowers and the prattle of young girls."

"Yes, Sister," I heard Mary say in a low voice.

"That's a good thing because there must be so much to contemplate and seek forgiveness for. Even though you've sinned against God, pray that he gives you a healthy baby and that someone worthy will be able to instill good values in the child growing up."

"The good values will have to come from my family."

"What do you mean, child?" The nun came closer.

"Annie O. and I are going to raise the baby ourselves."

"But, but…surely you intend, and your parents have advised you, that it's best for all to give the baby up immediately after its birth."

"I've been advised. The baby is mine until or unless I sign him away."

"But that would not be wise. And it couldn't be God's will. You came out of that same family. They couldn't have taught you very well."

I could feel the heat of Mary's anger in the silence that followed.

"Is there someone else here?" the Sister asked. "Whoever it is, come out from behind there. I see you."

I emerged from behind the wheelbarrow, and it fell over loudly against the nearby bench.

"What on earth!?" The Sister stared at me in shock.

"That's my friend, Sara," said Mary.

"Well, you know perfectly well no visitors other than family are allowed to visit. In the future, you will keep to that rule and inform your friends."

My heart pounded. My mouth felt dry. "Sorry. I'll write to you," I said to

Mary and hurried out of the greenhouse.

Libby sat with the ignition key in her hand and listened to my tale, her head bowed.

"The arrogance. The hypocrisy." Libby shook her head. "That's pretty courageous of both of them, Mary and Annie O.," she said softly as if exhausted from outrage. Libby looked tired, and I thought of her and me and Grandma Rose and whoever had come before her, links in a chain of women, like Mary, Annie O., and now the baby Mary hoped wasn't a daughter.

"Did it hurt a lot...when you had me?" I asked without planning to.

Libby looked surprised. "You know, I've kind of forgotten. I assume it hurt. It's a herculean task to get a baby out through such a small...opening." She smiled and turned the key in the ignition. "But I can tell you it was well worth it."

CHAPTER THIRTY-ONE

"Ah, a little billet doux from our government," Libby said when she saw the envelope lying on top of the clothes dryer. She knew. The letter was from the US Department of Justice—a citation for contempt of Congress.

"I'm not going to fight it," she said, chin raised, before she had even opened it. "I refuse to spend one cent of our hard-earned money on lawyers.

"You can't just ignore it." Hank watched her intently.

"Well, I *do* hold the Committee in contempt. They use their power illegitimately, they create an atmosphere of intimidation all over this country, and they cause innocent people to lose their jobs and livelihoods."

Hank tried his best to convince her to at least consult a lawyer, but she refused. I watched as the stubbornness, which she obviously genetically shared with Grandpa, visibly hardened like molten chocolate on a marble surface.

Without any legal defense, there was no delay. Libby was ordered to report to the federal prison in Danbury, Connecticut, on the first of July, to serve a six-month sentence. She would get out about the same time Mary was due to give birth.

I couldn't sleep or eat. During the last week of school, my stomach hurt all day. I felt shaky inside. Now she'd done it, hadn't she? She'd given the middle finger to those men in the black suits, and to Mutt and Jeff, and now she was in for it. *We* were in for it. She was leaving us, Hank and me, without even putting up a fight.

"It's only for six months," Libby said, nibbling at her lip. "And I won't be that far away. Just down in Connecticut. Danbury is a minimum security Federal Correctional Institution. The prisoners are non-violent, held for financial crimes, tax evasion, conscientious objectors, and a few other people who've challenged the Senate committees. We know people who've been in there—they say it's pretty civilized."

I felt like I was about to vomit. "Why do you know people who've been in prison?" I demanded angrily.

"Look, Sarah," Hank said, "let me explain. The people we know who've gone to prison have gone because of their principles. Like your mother. The people in Danbury are what they call white-collar criminals. It's kind of interesting when you think about it. They put the worst capitalists and the most outspoken progressives in there together? Must be some volatile stew," he chuckled.

I saw nothing amusing or "interesting" in any of this. I looked for fear, embarrassment, or anything that made sense, on Libby's face. I was trying to understand, but I was looking for something that showed *she* understood that what was happening was a bad thing, and that she was going to miss us—Hank and me.

Instead, as the three of us sat in our webbed chairs on the carved-out-of-the-wilderness lawn the Saturday before she had to report to prison, Libby had a glow that only enhanced her beauty. It reminded me of the radiance in the faces of the religious martyrs I'd seen in my history books. I despised that look, that upward gaze, as if someone up in the sky was going to save them or her.

As much as Hank tried to keep things light, he looked pretty gloomy. Was he actually, finally, angry with her, too?

Late that afternoon, Libby went quietly into the living room and sat down at the piano, apparently not caring, for once, whether or not she was alone in the house. She stayed silent for a long time, then slowly raised her hands to the keyboard and began to play—a Bach invention. The house filled with a rush of sound, note perfect and up to tempo. I slipped into the front hallway to listen and watch.

When she was finished with the Bach, she lowered her hands onto her thighs and sat in silence again, looking out at the woodland scene beyond the windows. After a minute or so, she played another invention, lowered her hands and gazed out the window, seemingly at peace. Watching her, I half expected—it seemed like the perfect moment—for a bird to fly into the window and break its neck.

She packed the stiff little duffel bag I used for overnight stays with Grandpa and Grandma and, until recently, overnights with Mary. I stood in their bedroom doorway, bursting with the indigestible mixture of admiration and outrage Libby stirred in me.

"Come in," she said. "I'm only allowed to bring a few things. Underwear, talcum powder, a toothbrush, a washcloth."

I stepped into the bedroom and sat at the corner of their bed. "Are you scared?"

She took her time answering, as she inspected, then rejected, items from her drawers, and I thought I saw her glance with longing at her dressing table, with its little jars, cotton puffs, secret potions, tweezers and eyebrow pencils. "A little nervous, maybe." Libby smiled and shrugged. "As Hank says, they're white-collar criminals and they're women. Tax dodgers. Forgers. Other contemptuous people, I guess."

I tried to smile, but my face felt stiff as if covered with a mask made up of the jumble of emotions inside. "How long will it take to get down there? To the jail?" I asked.

"It's a prison, being federal. It's about three hours away." Libby smiled reassuringly, then suddenly she added, "Next Tuesday is the school committee election. It's too late to take my name off the ballot. Maybe I'll still get a few votes."

It was mean and evil of me to take satisfaction from the fact that she was going to lose the election badly, but I did.

Hank and Libby waited with the motor running while I climbed into the back seat of the Heap. I was starkly aware today of being the "caboose," as Hank had called me ever since I'd graduated from the middle of the front seat, squashed between them, with my short legs sticking straight out, to the back seat all by myself.

With a wave of sadness and fear, I was reminded I would be riding in the front passenger seat next to Hank on the way back. "Hey, Sara," Hank said, as we passed the dead tree at the bottom of the driveway, "isn't that a yellow-bellied sapsucker?"

"It's a flicker," I corrected him curtly, fed up with his good cheer.

"Okay, you're the boss," he said, pulling out onto the road. "We're off. We just follow the Boston Post Road, direction New York City. At Hartford, we hook a left and follow the Connecticut River, then hang a right at the Housatonic at New Haven, and we're there."

"It is a beautiful day," Libby said, gazing out her side window.

I couldn't actually see it, but I knew they were holding hands on the seat between them, while Hank drove with his left hand. In a lot of ways, it was like a Sunday drive through the countryside in late summer. Except Libby wouldn't be coming back with us.

"When will you call us on the phone?" I asked.

"Every Sunday," Hank said cheerfully, answering so Libby wouldn't have to.

As we drove, they took turns feeding me Pablum answers to my nervous questions. What will you do in there? What's the food like?

"There's a library right there inside the prison. According to the scuttlebutt, the food isn't too bad, although there's a lot of starch and fried food. I'm allowed two phone calls out, every Sunday. Visitors are allowed after the first three weeks of what they call 'orientation.'"

The real, aching question remained unasked and unanswered. How were we going to get along without her? Why did you do this, Libby? To yourself? To us?

"Robert Lowell served time in Danbury during the war as a conscientious objector," Libby said.

"Who's he?" I asked, annoyed by what sounded like prison who-do-you-know?

"A poet from Boston."

"And Ring Lardner was in there for nine months," Hank said. "He was a Hollywood writer, one of the Hollywood ten," he explained, turning halfway around so I could hear from the back seat. "Lardner was famous for telling HUAC Chairman J. Parnell Thomas, back in '47, that he'd love to answer the Committee's questions, but if he did, he'd hate himself in the morning."

I didn't really get the joke, but I saw the edges of Libby's sly smile.

"Such distinguished alumni," Hank chuckled.

I still didn't see anything funny about any of it. She was leaving us for six months. At least that's what they were saying. What if something changed to make the time longer, or worse, that if they weren't telling me the whole truth at all?

The Rosenbergs, in those black and white pictures from the newspapers, kept coming to mind. Had the Rosenberg kids known, when they last visited their parents, that it would be their last time? I curled into myself in the back seat and dozed in and out, the rest of the way.

The long, low concrete federal prison building, with narrow, vertical slits for windows, looked bleak and frightening. We stood close to Libby as she was checked in at a booth with armored windows and Hank set up an account for her so she could buy what she needed while she was inside.

Our goodbyes took place in a reception area with a grim-faced matron standing by, averting her eyes. Libby squeezed me in a tight embrace and, in spite of myself, I hugged her back hard. To keep from crying, I occupied myself with staring down the matron, while Hank and Libby clung to one another for a long time.

Libby turned then and followed the woman through a heavy door with a small window crisscrossed with security wire. We stood, Hank and I, and watched as the door shut and the lock clicked loudly.

Walking back to the car, I crumpled up my copy of a pamphlet we'd each been given, "Information for Families of Federal Prisoners," and tossed it into a nearby trashcan.

CHAPTER THIRTY-TWO

Letters from Libby appeared in our mailbox every day. Some were addressed to me, some to Hank, and others to both Hank and me. Each handwritten letter, white and enticing inside the mailbox, or deposited carefully on top of the dryer, was cause for great excitement.

The ones addressed just to me, I squirreled away to some secluded place to read. I read each one slowly, carefully, hungrily, but then increasingly with boredom as the letters went on describing vividly her limited days. She got up early, fought for space and privacy in the bathroom, went to KP—kitchen patrol like in the army, she said—which meant a lot of potato peeling. Her visits to the deficient library granted her relative peace and quiet.

She wrote about the terrible food, although, once in a while, there was a gross-sounding dessert she said she enjoyed. With so much about food in her letters, I worried she might not be getting enough to eat. Meanwhile, it was obvious, it was the people in there that made her days. She was making friends and wrote about them by name.

On little waves of jealousy, I waited impatiently for her letters to come to an end, where she would finally say she loved me, something I didn't hear that much out loud from her in person. To see it written, finally, filled me with longing and sadness and a certain comfort, too.

My letters to her always began, "Dear Libby," although I had the silly urge to write "Mother." I filled them with birds I'd spotted and newsy updates on Mary and on us—our reduced household. "Mary says she isn't nauseous anymore. Hank and I are learning to cook and do laundry," side-stepping the fact that I flatly refused to iron. I ended each letter, "Love, Sara," with a bunch of childish loops, swoops and flairs, showing off my best, fancy handwriting, and adding a very small, cramped drawing of a heart.

The summer days were long and lonesome without Libby, without Mary, and without John L., who, I kept having to remind myself, was no longer my boyfriend and shouldn't matter anymore. I took myself on solo bird walks. I did Hank's very short payroll. My main job for the summer was to hang on, be a good sport and brave, until Libby came home.

She was always brave or maybe stubbornly hard-headed, as Grandpa thought. As her daughter, I had to at least pretend to be valiant and undaunted. I forced myself to visit the library, face Mrs. O, make appearances at Eaton's Drugstore for ice cream or the newspaper, and to say *yes*. rather than my instinctual no, whenever Hank invited me to come along with him to the lumber yard or the hardware store.

With Libby in prison and no opportunity to go back to see Mary, I wrote to Mary too, nearly every day. I put leaves and sometimes feathers in her envelopes, thinking she must miss our rambles in the woods. I certainly did.

In her letters, Mary said her body didn't feel like her own anymore. She said she whispered to the baby at night and sometimes sang to him.

Libby's empty chair at the kitchen table reminded us of her absence every time we put food in our mouths. At breakfast, like every morning, Hank looked tired from staying up late, writing to her. As he leafed through the news, the corner of the last page of his paper flopped down, without his noticing, into his coffee.

I watched the brown stain creep up and saturate the page, the way Libby's absence permeated everything else in our lives. I bet with myself about how long it would take until he noticed the paper's flop.

"Wooah…," Hank exclaimed. "Why didn't you tell me?"

"What were you thinking about?" I asked.

Hank sighed as he carried the newspaper to the sink to wring it out. "Mostly I think about your mother."

Reluctantly, I took on some of the woman-of-the-house duties, doing the laundry, for example, since I did know how to operate the washing machine. I folded the laundry and piled it on top of the dryer, where Hank picked up his stuff and glumly carried it to their bedroom. Because I drew the line at ironing, Hank, who liked to wear a "decent" shirt every day, unfolded the ironing board and plugged in the iron. Every Sunday night, he made a great show of testing its heat with a drop of water and ironed a shirt for each day of his work week.

He ironed very slowly, giving himself plenty of time to let his mind wander and dream, probably of Libby. "Your mother always said she did her best thinking while ironing. I understand that now. Kind of hypnotic—and inspiring."

We made one tense visit to Grandpa and Grandma early on a Sunday. We scrupulously avoided talk about Libby beyond giving a report on her health, and we kept an eye on the clock, because we had to be back for her phone call at five o'clock.

"Pop, how about those Red Sox?" Hank said.

"Who cares?" Grandpa sputtered around his cigar. "Baseball is a game for the goyim."

"But, what about Greenberg? He came *that* close to breaking Ruth's record!" Hank said, holding up a space between his thumb and forefinger.

"Yeah, he said every homerun was a hit against Hitler. But then they took him into the army, so he wouldn't break the record," Grandpa said, as if the government had conspired to deprive a Sabbath-observing Jew of breaking a baseball record.

After a couple of hours of narrowly avoiding conflict and arguments, we hurried home to wait for Libby's long-distance reverse-the-charges call. There was a lot of noise on the line, and Libby seemed to be yelling into the phone over static and women's voices.

"How are you doing, Sara? How is Mary?" When I was on by myself for a few moments, she added, "How do you think your father is doing?"

These questions overwhelmed me, although I forced myself to answer with lies of omission, soft-pedaling notes of hopelessness and resignation that filled the house. What was the true answer to how we were doing? Did doing well when someone was forcibly absent mean you didn't miss them, didn't love them?

Hank took the phone, and I went into the next room, pretended to read, but actually listened intently. I cringed through his whispered endearments, especially when he said "Dar-ling," which he never said in my presence, with all the missing and the edge of desperation in his voice. Hearing him made me feel excluded and alone, and angry.

She'd done this to us. She'd done it to herself. She could have avoided the whole thing if she'd wanted to. I'd seen it myself, how the guys in the suits had been so polite to her, calling her Mrs. Green every five minutes, asking her what seemed to me such easy questions. She had disrespected them, so they had "thrown the book at her."

The Saturday before the Sunday we were first allowed to go visit Libby, Hank paced the house like a locked-up lion. He ironed an extra shirt but said very little to me all day. He sat at his drafting table, staring off into space.

I woke up Sunday morning at 5:30, feeling sluggish and resistant. I should want to see her, and maybe I did, but I also wished the months would just pass without the ache of seeing her there in the prison, then having to leave her there, when it was time to go home.

While I lay in bed without moving, watching the sun gradually illuminate my bedroom ceiling, Hank was already making noise in the kitchen.

At 6:30, when I didn't appear, he came into my room to wake me up. He wanted to get an early start, he reiterated. He had ants in his pants, the way he would say it. "Come on, Sara, get up, please. Now you have a half hour to get ready, okay?"

His nervous impatience made me more obstinate. I pulled the sheet over my head. "You never said what time we were leaving," I whined into my pillow.

"Of course, I did," he said, throwing open my curtains. "I said seven o'clock. We don't want to miss any of the visiting hours."

"You didn't say exactly," I argued from under the sheet. I was possessed by some force pushing me back from where he wanted—and even I really wanted—to go.

"I don't get it," Hank said from my doorway. "Do you need an engraved invitation to go visit your mother, whom you haven't seen for almost a month? Sara, I don't understand you."

"That's for sure," I snapped.

"I try, but you make it hard sometimes. Let's just get ready and go, okay?"

"Fine. You go," I said. "I'll stay here…and 'hold the fort.'" I pouted, purposely using one of his own jaunty expressions.

"Jeezus," he said, turning away from my bedroom door. Five minutes later he was back. "No," he said, "You can't stay here by yourself. You have to come. Come on. Get up."

"Are you going to loosen your belt and threaten me?"

"I have no idea what you're talking about, young lady."

"Don't I have any say about anything in this house?"

"Jeezus," he said again and marched away down the hall. I heard the front door slam.

I couldn't believe it! I leapt out of bed and ran out the front door in my pajamas. He was gone.

I stayed in bed all morning, feeling bad, sad, mad, blaming Hank, but knowing it was me, something within me.

Around eleven, I got up and got dressed. I skittered down through the trees to the little stream that meandered between our land and Mr. Tooey's property beyond. I sat on a moss-covered rock with my knees drawn up like an over-sized frog, and I sulked.

I was angry at Hank, who didn't understand me. I was angry at Libby for not being there, at John L., for being his disloyal, chicken-livered self, and at Mary for letting a boy lead her astray.

While I brooded, a small nest floated by. It must have fallen out of a tree and landed in the stream. Intricately woven, the nest held three speckled eggs inside, one cracked and with wet feathers sticking out, and no movement. Abandoned, I decided, convinced of a scenario that formed in my head: the mother bird had neglected, then abandoned the nest and, unprotected, it had plunged to earth, killing her hatchlings.

I trudged back up the hill to bury the nest, eggs and all, in my bird cemetery.

"Your mother missed seeing you very much," Hank said when he dragged himself in just after dark. "She was very disappointed."

By then, I was already drowning in regret and guilt. I'd behaved like a rotten, ungrateful child.

"On the other hand," Hank said, "she actually said it might be better that you don't come." He opened the liquor cabinet I thought of as Grandpa's for the schnapps we kept there, and Hank poured himself a glass of whiskey.

"Why did she say that?" I croaked, flooded with anxiety, hoping he'd kept the truth of my evil temper tantrum from Libby and dreamed up some plausible excuse for my absence.

"She says they can make her undergo a strip search after she has visitors."

"You mean she has to take off her clothes?" I asked, my stomach turning.

"Well, yes," he said. "Supposedly to make sure she doesn't receive contraband. That her visitors aren't bringing anything in against regulations."

I felt a chill. "That's not fair."

"No, it's not. But they have the right. When you're in prison, you don't have many rights. She says they're not that bad, the searches—but she's afraid they might make you do it if you came to the prison. Maybe to get back at her for her…disloyalty. She told me, even there in prison, some of the inmates and the guards tell her she's a traitor to the country."

The next day, probably to cheer us both up, Hank suggested we go get a Frosty Freeze. It was our shared place of guilty pleasure since Libby would never go there. The ice cream was all puffed up with air and probably made of some sort of plastic, according to her.

I recognized the pimply-faced kid in the white paper hat, who worked alone there on Sunday afternoons. He was an eleventh-grader I knew only by sight. His name tag read "Mike." He served up our cones, then took his time dropping the money, coin by coin, into the cash register drawer. Following me down the length of the counter, he waited until Hank, meandered out the door ahead of me, and then said in a loud whisper, "I hear your mom's a jailbird now. Serves her right for being a Commie red traitor."

Shocked and stung, I kept walking and caught up with Hank in the parking lot.

"Did that boy just say something to you?" Hank asked as we approached the car.

"No," I said, although he could see I was shaking.

"Are you sure?" Hank said. "I thought I heard him say something." Hank squinted up into the sharp, angled setting sun as he climbed in.

"He's just a fresh, stupid kid," I said, once safely back in the car, regaining my voice. "He said, 'Your mother's in jail and deserves it for being a Commie.'"

"Damn. People are so ignorant." Hank pushed the door open and started to get back out of the car. "I'm going to give him a piece of my mind."

"No, no," I said, grabbing his arm, "don't go back in there."

"Why not?" Hank demanded.

"I'm afraid."

"Of what?" he said.

"Of what happens when I get back to school. You'd just stir up more of a hornet's nest."

He shook his head. "You mean, I'm not allowed to defend my own daughter?"

"Please, just don't," I begged.

We drove home in silence, his hands clenched on the wheel.

That night, I lay awake, seeing that ugly face with the paper hat, spewing hateful cracks I could now expect would be popping up anywhere I went. Replaying the nasty tone and the sneer that went with it, I felt weak and defenseless. We would be permanent pariahs now—in Goshen, the place that was supposedly our haven and respite. Libby had fouled her own nest, which was our nest, and all of us were going to keep on paying for it.

Gross images of my strip search followed. Visualizing how it would feel made me glad I hadn't gone to see her. At the same I flagellated myself for being a daughter who didn't love her mother enough, and who was a coward on top of it.

CHAPTER THIRTY-THREE

"A hurricane's on its way up the coast," Hank announced at breakfast, "and her name is Carol."

"It has a name?"

"Yes, *she* has a name. They think she's going to make it all the way up here. She's already deviated from the usual path these tropical Caribbean storms take. They usually spin up the coast and peter out on the shoals of Cape Hatteras. This one's further out at sea, has avoided North Carolina, and now looks like she'll make landfall on Long Island before continuing on north and east to us."

Hank snapped on the radio, pulled out the atlas, and opened it on the kitchen table to show me the route. "They're predicting one as big as the one in '38. Back then, of course, there was no hurricane tracking. And almost no warning except a sudden dark sky. I remember '38. It was the biggest hurricane anyone alive could remember, and 'way before they'd thought of giving them names."

He chuckled. "Your Grandpa knew because he got a long-distance call from his brother in Florida. He immediately started buying up all the plywood he could find, by the board foot to sell, installed, to shop owners to protect their plate glass windows. Can you picture him staggering down the street in an eighty mile an hour wind—a short, round guy with a giant piece of plywood?"

I could, and it made me smile. There was Grandpa, complete with his three-piece suit, gold watch and chain, wrestling with a huge piece of plywood that had caught the wind and threatened to sail him away.

"I was courting your mother then, so I tried to give Grandpa a hand, but, let me tell you, it was scary out there. It felt like, any minute, the wind would just carry you off like a squirrel in a hawk's talons.

Hurricane Carol arrived a few nights later like a freight train. I lay in bed awake, listening to the roar and whistle of the wind and, every once in a while, the ominous crack of a tree trunk. I wondered where birds went during a hurricane and wished Libby were here and safe with us. I imagined the prison without lights, no heat, no food, and all the prisoners cowering in the darkness.

The wind, rain, and noise were disturbing, but they also reflected the chaotic weather inside me, raging in disappointment against everybody and everything. Around three in the morning, I awoke, heart pounding, to an especially wild burst of wind and rain.

I climbed out of bed and, like a zombie, went barefoot down the hall and stood outside the door to Hank and Libby's bedroom. The door was open a crack and moved with the shifts in air pressure. I pushed it open with a squeak. Hank didn't stir. He lay hunched up on his half of the bed, snoring peacefully.

I made my way to Libby's side, by the window, and carefully climbed up onto it, drawing the extra blanket up over me. The crack of another tree breaking outside made me pull the blanket over my head. Hank didn't move, but his sheer bulk in the bed was comforting, and after a while, my heart stopped pounding. When no tree fell through the roof to crush both of us, I felt embarrassed for being a little scaredy-cat, running to my parents.

Hank turned over onto his back. "Sweetheart, is that you? Trouble sleeping?" He listened for a moment. "I think the wind is letting up some."

I began climbing off the bed to go back to my room.

"It's okay. You can stay," he said, patting the covers and moving even further to his side. "It's lonely without her, right?"

I pulled the blanket back up. "Yes. I'm worried about her."

"So am I. I worry she's not telling us the truth, that she's trying not to worry us."

"I wonder what she's doing right now."

Hank forced a laugh. "Well, right this minute, I'm sure she's doing the same thing we're doing," and his voice broke a little, "hiding under the covers."

"Do you think she misses us?"

"I know she does." He reached over and patted my hand.

We lost several big trees that night and had no electricity for the next two weeks. We cooked outside on the barbeque instead of on the now useless electric stove. Hank tried to make it all into some kind of pioneer adventure, until Sunday when it turned out that phone calls couldn't be put through to Libby and she couldn't make calls out.

Then Hank's worry about her and my fears went through the ceiling. Once we got our electricity back, we finally got a call from Libby. She said she was okay. Someone on the inside had given her the news that the hurricane had toppled the steeple of the Old North Church in Boston. That's where the lantern that signaled Paul Revere's freedom ride had been hung. "How's that for symbolism? Paul Revere's steeple goes down."

Hank planned another visit to Libby for the day before Labor Day. He assumed I wasn't going, and so did I. The threat of strip searches loomed in my mind. "But, I might want to come this time," I said, my voice unsteady, my will wavering. "I haven't seen her for so long."

"I know you must miss her terribly," Hank said, "but I really think it's better if you can just hold on a little longer. I don't want you to go through anything like a strip search."

"Just wake me up in the morning, please. I'll decide then, okay?" But I didn't sleep. All night, it seemed, I listened to two lonely barred owls calling endlessly to one another until it was almost dawn. They must have gotten together because they finally stopped all the fuss.

As daylight filled my bedroom, I thought about Mary and how sad it was that anybody would want her and the baby to be separated. By the time Hank knocked on my door, I had decided to go see Libby.

The prison loomed in the shimmering heat of that muggy August day, as we drove the long road into the sparsely-filled parking lot. And then, much as I'd played it in my head, I was hurriedly separated from Hank and taken, by the matron I recognized from the first day. She didn't seem to recognize me.

"Come with me, please." She led me to a bare room with two metal folding chairs. A chill ran through me as she closed the door. "We have to be sure inmates don't receive contraband from outside," the woman said in a monotone. "Take your clothes off. Everything. Please."

She sat down on one of the chairs and stared at the opposite wall. Obviously, I was supposed to take my clothes off and place them on the second chair. My hands shook so much, I had trouble unbuttoning buttons. I became very cold as, one by one, I took off my blouse, my skirt, my socks and shoes, and stood next to the chair, shivering in my camisole and panties.

The matron emitted a low groan of impatience. "Just do it. We don't have all day."

I took a breath. I told myself it was the only way I was going to see Libby. But, I couldn't do it. As much as I longed to get this over and done with and back into my clothes, I couldn't move.

"Look, kid," the matron said, "let's just say we'll forget the cavity search since it isn't your fault your mother's a Commie traitor and a security risk. But let's get on with it, okay?"

I peeled off the rest of my clothes, as the little room grew colder and smaller. Once the matron had palpated my clothes piled on the chair, she said to get dressed again, and we walked out into a hallway where I was reunited with a pacing Hank.

"You alright?" he asked, scrutinizing me closely.

"Yes, fine!" I said sharply, shutting down any further questioning.

We sat with Libby in a family visiting room where several little kids were acting up, sabotaging the visits with their imprisoned loved ones. I saw myself in their flushed, sweaty little faces.

Libby, who looked thin and pale, sat, mostly silent, looking back and forth between Hank and me. She seemed to be taking us in like bread and water, in preparation for the next long haul before she'd see us again. Even in her drab prison uniform, Libby looked beautiful, her hair pulled back and tied loosely in a scarf. At times, she'd favor us with a smile, which seemed to require all the energy of this paler, more serene version of herself.

"Are they treating you okay?" I asked.

"They're doing the best they can," Libby answered, and I took this cryptic statement to mean "no," and my worry for her just dove deeper.

"I hope they didn't make you take off your clothes," Libby said without quite looking at me.

I caught my breath. "No, she just patted me down," I said.

CHAPTER THIRTY-FOUR

Without Libby at home to remind us of its true meaning, Labor Day was just like it was for regular kids, just an extra day off before school started again. There were no lectures over meals about the importance of collective bargaining, or the history of the eight-hour workday, or child labor, or the Triangle Shirtwaist Factory Fire. I missed Libby's lectures.

Hank and I spent most of the day trading out screens for storm windows and cleaning up the bird feeders. I silently dreaded my first day back at school.

That Tuesday, the halls of GHS clanged with metal lockers opening and closing and the roar of high-spirited voices. The surge and jumble of the faces overwhelmed me. It was like I'd lost the ability to read faces over the summer. Familiar faces, friendly faces or faces trying to appear friendly, faces that looked away, on purpose and pointedly, or maybe just worried about stumbling into saying the wrong thing.

I couldn't tell the difference anymore. I kept my eyes lowered and said and did only what seemed absolutely necessary. The first thing I had to do in homeroom was pledge allegiance to the flag. We all clattered to our feet.

I stood, arms by my side, neither hand placed anywhere near my heart, and moved my lips. When it came to "one nation, under God," which they'd added to the pledge over the summer, I just couldn't. My lips stopped moving completely, and when it was over, I felt proud that I'd promised nothing, and nobody seemed to have noticed.

Mr. Bramhall, his long, boney face tanned from his family's summer in Maine, stopped me in the teeming hallway between classes and welcomed me back. He said that if I ever wanted to come talk to him in his counseling office, his door was always open. "And I'm so sorry about your mother. Has she been writing to you? Is she doing alright?"

"She gets out in December. Only three more months," I told him, though he probably knew it already.

"That's good," he said, stroking his chin. "It was very wrong what happened to her."

I ate my lunch under the tamarack tree by myself, something I'd thrown together and packed in a brown paper bag. A peanut butter and jelly sandwich—childish but comforting—and a little box of raisins.

The warning bell for the end of lunch sounded, and I drifted back to my first afternoon class by way of the Burgoyne Elm. And there, like in my nightmares, was John L. with a blonde girl. They were hanging onto one another, their eyes closed. She must have moved into town during the summer. I'd never seen her before.

Maybe by some telepathy we still had, John L. opened his eyes for a moment and saw me. His eyes went large, then he closed them again. I turned and walked back to class humiliated—and seething.

Later, on the staircase between classes, John L. passed by me in the line flowing upstairs while I was going down. He stepped out of line and pulled me to the banister. "Look, Sara I'm truly sorry about what happened…to your mother."

I felt my face turn red as I struggled to keep down the turbulence of colliding feelings—anger, jealousy, humiliation—in an attempt to think straight. "Thanks," I said. "Looks like you didn't get shipped off to private school after all."

He smiled and looked at his feet. "No, luckily."

"Probably luck had nothing to do with it," I said. "Sellout," I added.

John L. needed a moment to take this in. "Okay, Sara, see ya around," he finally said, shaking his head and stepping back into the upstairs flow.

Still shaken, I walked into my first personal-use typing class. "Personal-use" distinguished this class from the secretarial or business course typing classes. It was a touch-typing course designed and required for "college-bound" students in the ninth grade. The class was taught by Mrs. Z., the business and secretarial teacher, who'd been my homeroom teacher the year before and had witnessed my eruption of Libby-like behavior during the air raid drill.

Mrs. Z. stood in the doorway to the typewriting room in a gray shantung suit, greeting each of us with a "business-like" handshake. "I'm glad to see you back, Sara. I know you've probably not had the easiest summer."

I mumbled a thank you. Her handshake was so firm, it hurt. How quickly news traveled.

I took a seat in the third row in front of a typewriter that came up to my chin, leaving lots of space between me and John L. who was already in the last row in the seat nearest the door.

First thing, Mrs. Z. called our attention to a bar graph on the wall. It displayed the typing speeds, words per minute, achieved by the business-secretarial students, which ranged from fifty to seventy words per minute, or wpm. She informed us that by the end of the course, the best any of *us* could possibly hope to achieve would be in the vicinity of forty wpm.

We would be learning touch-typing versus the hunt-and-peck method we would be relegated to if we failed to practice every day. The first step was to memorize the keyboard. "ASDF" on the left hand and "JKL Semi-colon," on the right.

Soon, we were practicing "The quick brown fox jumped over the lazy dogs," a sentence which, Mrs. Z. pointed out, used every letter of the alphabet.

"That's us, the lazy brown dogs," John L. piped up from his seat behind me, near the door.

Mrs. Z. chose to ignore this remark and continued pacing, chicken-walking, up and down the rows of desks, on her three-inch patent leather heels, making sure we didn't sneak glances down at our keyboards or at one another. Clack-clack, went the typewriter keys landing on the paper, click-click went Mrs. Z.'s heels on the asphalt tile floor.

Throughout this exercise, John L. was outside my field of vision, but never out of my thoughts. That was when I vowed I would be, by Thanksgiving, the fastest personal-use typist in the class. Whatever it took, I was going to beat John L.

With a dedication I'd never applied to the piano, I practiced at home constantly, on any surface available. I practiced at the table and on my knees during meals. Hank occasionally noticed and asked me about it. At first I told him it was just a nervous tic, but later divulged my secret, "I'm going to beat that guy."

"What guy are you talking about?" he asked.

"John L. He has another girlfriend."

"Oh, that must be hard."

On my way to sleep each night, I practiced touch-typing on my stomach. By Halloween, my bar on Mrs. Z.'s personal-use-typing graph stretched the furthest, all the way out to twenty-five wpm, further than most of the class, including John L., who was, I hoped, stalled out at a pathetic sixteen wpm.

Libby was scheduled to leave prison on a Sunday, a week after Mary's due date. Two days before that, Annie O. called to say that Mary had given birth a little early to a baby girl. Mother and baby were doing fine. They would be coming home in a few days.

"So, Sara, dear, please come by the house for a wee get-together to welcome them home."

She'd said *them*, hadn't she? It was stunning. They'd actually done it. Mary had given birth to a baby and was taking it home to Annie O. An actual baby. Mary was a mother.

A few days later, Annie O. led me through her living room toward what the O'Reillys called the "parlor," a room that didn't exist in our house. I had no idea what to expect there. A relieved, flat-stomached friend is what I imagined. And the baby was a girl!

We passed a darkened room where I could just make out Big Patrick's profile. The light from a television set flickered on his face with the sounds of a baseball crowd. "Pa-trick," warbled Annie O., as we passed, "we have a visitor. It's Sara!"

He didn't seem to hear her. I appeared to be the only guest. But here was Mary sitting on a little couch next to the baby, who lay gurgling on a cushion beside her, swaddled in a receiving blanket.

"Hi, Sara." Mary gave me a shy smile. "Meet Annie-Marie." The baby had a wrinkled little pink face, sparse orange hair and was using her bowed, skinny little legs and wrinkled feet to kick free of the blanket decorated with flying-lambs and clouds.

Annie O. picked up Annie-Marie and expertly unwrapped and rewrapped the blanket, and then held the baby up like a package for me to see. The baby settled her wobbly gaze somewhere in the vicinity of my face, all the while dazzled by the light coming into the sunny parlor.

"She's so little. And she has red hair," I said.

"Yes," was all Mary said.

Annie O. sat down in a chair with an exhausted smile and her hair coming loose from its bun. She was dandling the baby on her knee, while the blanket unraveled again and trailed down.

"It's so darling of you to come, Sara."

A telephone rang in the hall. Annie O. pressed the baby into Mary's arms and went to answer it. Mary held the baby stiffly, like a football player who's surprised to have made a catch and is afraid of dropping it. "Do you want to hold her?" she asked me.

The last thing I wanted to do was hold a newborn baby. I couldn't remember ever seeing one so young. "Okay. But give her to me carefully." I held out my hands to take her. "I don't have any experience."

Mary handed the baby over, saying, "Mind the head. She can't hold it up yet."

I took Annie-Marie under the arms, somehow managing to keep her little head up with my fingers. I brought her toward me and let her rest against my chest and shoulder. The feel of her compact little body was surprising. I couldn't recall feeling anything quite like it before. She was an alive package, so small, and yet so solid and flexible.

I worked her down into my lap, so we were both facing Mary, who sat on the sofa, watching both of us intently. "Big Patrick wants us to give her back," Mary said quietly. "He won't even look at her."

"Oh, no," I said.

"He says it's not right—pretending the baby's someone she's not—that she's *their* daughter and my baby sister. He says it's not right to lie to cover up for my—shame and the family's shame."

I cringed, seeing Mary shrink under this awful weight of guilt and humiliation. It wasn't fair.

"You can just give her back?" I asked.

"The adoption agency says it will gladly take her anytime," Mary answered.

"But she's so…sweet," I said, touching a tiny toe that was already outside the blanket.

"You're so good at holding her. I don't seem to be able to get the knack of it." Mary's eyes were fixed on Annie-Marie who "sat" peacefully in my lap.

"You're probably just tired out from giving birth," I said.

"Maybe. But after the first labor pains I never felt anything. They gave me something, and I slept all the way through it. When I woke up, there she was—a baby. I don't remember anything. She doesn't feel like mine, Sara. Or that she's even real. She felt more real to me when she was in my stomach."

"Well, she's obviously real and she *is* yours," I said. "Look at her hair." The resemblance to Mary was obvious—but also to the unnamed, red-headed father.

Big Patrick appeared in the parlor doorway, surveying the three of us. "So sorry, Sara, to be rude. I was holed up in the dark with the wretched TV, feeling sorry for myself. The Braves are losing."

Big Patrick stepped closer behind me and looked down at the baby. "Dear Heart, thank you for coming to see Mary."

Mary looked down into her lap.

"The baby's beautiful," I said.

"That she is," he said.

"Then why don't you want to keep her… sir?" Mary looked up at me with shock. I was equally shocked at my own audacity. A hush fell on the room.

"Oh, dear," Big Patrick said from behind me, "it's not that we don't want her. We're just afraid she'll interfere with Mary's education. And the kids in school will not go easy on her."

"You don't have to worry about that," I said. "I plan to protect her."

"And how do ya propose to do that, may I ask?"

"We're going to stick together and stand up to unfair name-calling," I said. "We have to resist being shamed."

Big Patrick stroked his chin. "Well, that's a brave plan, Sara, but has it occurred to you that shame might be justified since the rules of chastity have been broken? The sin of fornication has been committed."

I looked with horror at Mary. Her head was bowed, and I couldn't see her eyes. This theological argument caught me completely off guard. Panic rose in my throat. I was beyond my depth in debates involving the fine points of religion. Yet argument was in my blood, and a rebuttal flowed out of me like water from a spring:

"But should one mistake be punished with unhappiness for everyone?"

Big Patrick, who had moved to a chair diagonal to the couch, studied Mary, then me. "Well," he finally said, "if this is an example of your ability to defend your friend here, maybe we can trust it will happen."

The baby had completely freed her legs from the receiving blanket. "Here," Big Patrick said, suddenly stretching out his arms, "let's take a good look at this wee angel. Not sure if I remember how, but give her to me for a minute, why don'tcha?"

I glanced at Mary who gave unspoken permission for the baby's transfer.

Carefully, I placed Annie-Marie in Big Patrick's big, outstretched hands. He surveyed the baby at arm's length and then, very slowly, brought her to his chest. "Thank you for being such a loyal friend to Mary."

Big Patrick looked over the baby's head. "So, tell me, how is your mother?" he said, looking relieved to be able to change the subject.

"She's coming home next Sunday."

"Good. You must have missed her terribly."

"Yes."

Annie O., back from the phone, stared when she saw her husband holding the baby. "Well, Annie O.," said Big Patrick, "if it doesn't feel as good as it ever did. A brand new soul so recently sent by God for her little perambulation on His good, green earth."

Annie O. exchanged a glance with Mary, who came close to smiling. "Didn't I tell you, Patrick, a baby is a baby," she said, collapsing into a chair and closing her eyes.

Conceding nothing, Big Patrick handed the baby back to Mary and headed out of the room. "Better get back to my game. The Braves need all the help they can get."

With Annie-Marie back in Mary's arms and soon asleep, she whispered, "That's the first I time he's touched her. First time he even *looked* at her. I can't believe you talked to him like that."

"I can't either," I answered.

Annie-Marie let out a gurgle, and Mary leaned over and kissed her on her nose. "Can you believe it, Pumpkin? I think he's going to let you stay."

Libby's release date arrived. I was excited to be picking her up, but nervous too, because something could still keep her release from happening. We could get there, and they could just say she wasn't free to leave. This seemed almost logical. The government was so powerful, it could say she had to go *into* prison, so what could stop them from saying she couldn't leave? Hank seemed nervous, too, which was obvious because he hummed and drummed his fingers annoyingly on the steering wheel all the way to Danbury. As we approached the prison, dull gray against white snow, we broke into "Joe Hill," the famous union song, doing all four verses. We were letter-perfect, lusty and loud, until finally we were yelling, with Hank slapping time to the music on the seat between us.

> *I dreamed I saw Joe Hill last night,*
> *Alive as you and me.*
> *Says I, "But Joe, you're ten years dead"*
> *"I never died," said he,*
> *"I never died," said he.*

We found Libby, sitting on a bench in the discharge area, waiting for us. She wore the same clothes she'd worn the day she went in—slacks, a green sweater, and the espadrilles. The duffle bag lay on the floor next to her feet. When she first saw us, a gentle, subdued smile crossed her face, first at Hank, then at me, and something inside me that had been tight and clenched for all these months, finally let go.

She hugged each of us. It felt very good to hug her, although she felt thin—kind of boney in her back—and it occurred to me that I must have grown over the time because I felt closer in height to her than before. I buried my face in her hair. She was still beautiful, of course, but, especially in her own clothes now, her skin looked pale, translucent, washed-out, a diminished version of the woman we'd left here six months before.

Hank grabbed the duffle, took Libby by the waist, and we, all three, exited Danbury Federal Prison.

Once we were out on a smooth, open road, Libby moved over to the middle of the front seat and laid her head on Hank's shoulder. Seeing this, an irresistible drowsiness overtook me. Probably it was the relief that we were again the perennial threesome—also exhaustion from the summer without her and anticipating what it might mean to have her home. I sprawled across the back seat and quickly fell asleep with my wadded-up jacket as a pillow.

I came to with the wonderful, groggy-dazed feeling of having been to oblivion and back in the middle of the day. My eyes were still closed when

I heard Hank's voice: "Is our little birdwatcher still asleep?" I squeezed my eyes shut tighter and listened harder.

"Yes, looks like she is," Libby said. There was a long silence, as we ate up the miles between prison and home.

"So, you never really told me what went on with that crazy matron."

I opened my eyes, saw the tops of trees whizzing by, and quickly closed them again.

"Almost right away," Libby said in a low, slow voice, "it became obvious she had a thing about communism. She decided I was a Communist, and she started baiting me."

"Oh, Lib, that's terrible. You didn't say anything…."

Libby's voice faltered. "They read our outgoing letters, and the visiting room was bugged. Anyway, it wasn't exactly a B movie about women-in-prison, or anything like that…but…."

"It's okay. You can tell me now."

"It's embarrassing," Libby said, almost too softly for me to hear.

"Don't worry. Sara's sound asleep."

"She just tried to make life tougher for me whatever way she could. She intercepted my incoming mail, probably read it, and delayed giving it to me. Somehow, I was always drawing toilet-cleaning duty. Latrine duty, she called it. She'd say, "Green, this way you can get a taste of what real working people do. Or, if it was the kitchen, it was always the onions. At least that gave me an excuse for a good cry."

"She knew what you were in there for?" Hank asked.

"Oh, yes. Everybody knows what everybody's in for. She'd been an army nurse in Korea and hated communists. She spoke for a lot of people in there, inmates and guards, too. I guess when it comes to the red-baiting, everybody thought being a Communist was worse than anything they'd done to get themselves incarcerated. In prison, there are no secrets. It's like a small town. The yard is the town square. Strip searches are the stocks and pillories."

"I'm so sorry, Lib."

"She especially got a kick out of intercepting my laundry," Libby continued, "even the old lady underwear I wore in there. One time they came back from the laundry dyed bright red."

"That was subtle," Hank said. "She must have had a thing for you."

"Maybe, I don't know. Whatever it was, she'd pop up everywhere and manage to find things I did wrong, and the punishment was always strip searches. Anything to humiliate me."

"Oh, Lib."

"It's okay," Libby said. "It's over now."

From where I lay in the back seat, I pictured Libby peeling potatoes and cutting onions, which, I could see was probably the only thing that could make her cry. She hated complaining, especially about superficial things, like underwear. I imagined her enduring the strip searches, shivering and cowering. Libby was proud of her stalwart nature, of her imperviousness to ordinary insults and pain, but prison had worn her down.

I lay there with my eyes closed, feeling awful for her and for myself. Without the benefit of onions, tears formed, and I blotted them with my sweater.

"And did you maybe undertake a little re-education of the inmates while you were in there, mi pasionaria?" Hank asked.

I held my breath, smiling through my tears, waiting to hear if Libby's weakness for Hank's kidding still held.

She hesitated. "Well, maybe, a little. Not much."

"That's my girl...."

CHAPTER THIRTY-FIVE

Libby wasn't herself. She moved around the house in slow-motion, as if afraid to lift her feet too far off the floor or make any noise. Being in prison had turned the rolling boil temperature in her blood down to barely a simmer.

Even her old nervous habits had faded—like the way she used to worry her lower lip with her teeth. She didn't spend time gazing out the kitchen window anymore. I missed these signs of Libby's being on the verge of action, even though I always worried about what she might be about to do.

She didn't come back to school to teach her civics classes anymore, of course—she hadn't been "invited back." But neither did she go back to the NAACP. She barely left home at all. She floated aimlessly around the house, straightening things here and there, moving just for the sake of moving, it seemed. Sometimes, she took a dust rag and swiped at surfaces she'd just been over minutes before.

Then, suddenly, she would go out. She'd just climb into the car, sometimes still in her bedroom slippers, and drive off without saying anything to anybody about where she was going or why. It hurt to see her this way. It worried me, upsetting me even more than when she wasn't there at all, far away in prison.

I felt a strange hollowness in my chest whenever I saw her engaged in one of her inexplicable, futile activities—as if something was threatening to cut off my oxygen. If Libby was different, the whole world was different, no longer on the way to being improved.

The fog she was in seemed to be creeping into my own being. I sat in the back of the school bus near the exit door, where I felt every rut, crack, and wash-out in the road. I hugged my lunch, with my jacket and scarf up around my face, my knitted hat half-covering my eyes. The fog felt protective somehow.

My highest hopes were abysmally low. I considered it a good day if I didn't overhear a remark about Libby or about me or about reds or pinkos. I barely did my homework, except for typing practice. I brought Mary's homework to her every other day and longed for her to come back to school.

As far as the school and the larger world of Goshen were concerned, Annie O. had been blessed with a surprise, late summer, baby. The plan was for Mary to return to school with her parents attesting to her bad case of mononucleosis, starting in August.

Supposedly, no one knew Mary'd been pregnant at all, even her brother's red-headed friend, Robby, the actual father of the baby. Although he must have suspected. We did it only once, Mary had said.

"I can't wait for you to get back to school," I whispered to Mary over the phone. "I need reinforcements."

"Do you think anyone suspects?" Mary sounded nervous.

"I don't think so," I said. "I haven't heard anything. People do ask about you, though."

"My stomach has to be perfectly flat," Mary said.

"Are you doing your sit-ups?"

"I'm trying to be good. I hope people buy the fairy tale." Mary stopped talking for a few moments while somebody passed through the O'Reilly parlor, where the phone was.

"How is school?" Mary asked when the coast was clear. "Have they been bothering you? You know—about your mother?"

"Not that much. But I just feel like everybody's looking at me."

"I hope your mom is okay now," Mary said.

"She doesn't seem okay."

"What's wrong?"

"She's not herself. She mopes around the house and takes drives while she's still in her bedroom slippers."

"Oh, no. I'm sorry," Mary sighed. "What's wrong with her, do you think?"

"I think it's because of being in prison."

"That's terrible. Does she say what happened in there?"

"She's pretty cagey about it, but I think it was slow torture."

"Mary was silent for a long time on the phone. She changed the subject.

"Did John L. come back to school?"

"He's back, alright. He found another girlfriend over the summer."

"That's convenient."

"Isn't it? He told me he was sorry about my mother, though."

"That was nice of him, I guess."

"He was just trying to cover up his obvious betrayal. Boys are fools," I said.

"So are girls." Mary gave a nervous laugh. "We'll soon find out who exactly people can be meaner about—loose out-of-wedlock teen mothers—"

"—or anti-American pinkos," I said, finishing the thought.

"We can 'compare and contrast' the two categories as threats to our civilization," Mary said. "Mr. Bramhall will be proud of our research."

I breathed a sigh of relief and thanked whoever it was that atheists thanked for goodness in the world. Mary was back and she was feisty.

The air at school had changed over the summer, although it may have been my own paranoia that made it seem that way. Some days it was just a feeling. Other times it was a sidelong glance, or indecipherable words whispered among some of the high school kids from upstairs.

Or there would be a conversation between two teachers that stopped suddenly when I walked by, followed by a guilty-looking smile of reassurance from one or both of them. Even on good days, school felt like mined territory. Everybody must know about Libby by now. Anybody who read the newspapers would know that she'd been called to the committee at least.

They might even know she'd defied HUAC, and was probably a Communist, and that was why she'd gone to prison.

That's what I was thinking that day, as I came up to our house from the school bus. Hank poked his head out of the breezeway and signaled me to come into his office. He settled on his drafting chair and I sat down on one on the webbed chaise loungers. He said he just wanted to know how my day had gone.

I told him it was fine, which wasn't true.

First thing that morning, I'd found another note taped to my locker. It was not the first. Mr. Bramhall, who happened to be walking by, saw me rip it off and stuff it in my school bag. "Sara, I think I'd better take a look at that, don't you? Are students harassing you?"

"It's alright," I said, holding my school bag behind my back. "I'll show it to...my parents."

"Well, be sure you do that, Sara," he said. "And remember, my door is always open." He meant unlocked, I guess, because whenever I walked by his office, the door was closed and on the pebbled glass, it read: Mr. Bramhall, Dean of Students. Please knock."

I hadn't shown Hank or Libby any of the previous notes. Why? Because the Greens didn't complain. We Greens were progressive, even radical thinkers, but we were also stoics. It was part of what was expected of me as Libby's daughter.

More important: I didn't want them to worry, any more than they already were—or worse, *do* anything.

That day, instead of my ripping the note into a hundred illegible little pieces—illegible even to FBI snoops—and then tossing the bits in the school trash can, as I usually did, I'd brought the note home in one piece. I took the crushed piece of paper out of my book bag and I dropped it onto Hank's drafting table like a crumpled paper airplane. I didn't say a word.

He opened the crumpled note slowly and carefully, then read it aloud: "Dear fellow traveler, why don't you pack your bags and take a long hike. We don't want your kind in Goshen."

He squinted at me. "That doesn't sound like a kid."

"I have no idea who it was," I shrugged. "I don't care who it is. I don't really even understand it. What's a fellow traveler?"

Hank rubbed his chin. "Fellow traveler. That's an insulting term Commie-haters use for a person who, even if not a Communist themselves, subscribes to Communist ideas and supports so-called subversives."

"I guess that would be me."

"It's not fair. You're a kid. I'm so sorry, Sara. That's awful." Hank closed his eyes and rubbed them. He crumpled the note back up again and reached out to pat my hair.

I stepped out of reach. I was afraid if I let him soothe me, I might cry in front of him. Also, because I was angry at him—as well as Libby.

"Mr. Bramhall wanted to see it," I said. "But I told him I'd bring it home to show you. He doesn't really know what's going on."

"And what *is* going on, Sara? Tell me."

"It's not a lot and it's not every day...it just gives me the creeps that everyone knows about Libby now. Sometimes I think they say things, just out of earshot."

"Like what things?"

"Obnoxious things about Libby, about me being a Commie-pinko, too."

"That's ridiculous." Hank rubbed his eyes some more.

"Maybe we shouldn't show the note to Libby," I said. "It'll will just upset her…more."

"It will upset her for sure. But I have to discuss it with her. She needs to know how all this is affecting you."

"Most people at school are cool," I said, hedging. "They don't participate in any of…this kind of thing."

"I'm glad to hear that," Hank said.

I looked up at Hank's poster of Rosie the Riveter, her muscular arms and her healthy, pink cheeks, gazing out boldly. "What's wrong with Libby," I asked.

Hank followed my gaze. "Old Rosie, she's a good, strong woman, right?" Then he grimaced and rubbed his forehead. "I'm no doctor," he said, "but, to me it looks like Libby has shell shock, battle fatigue, or something like that."

"What is that—shell shock?"

"It's what they used to call the mental problems soldiers got from being in combat. They used to think it was because of the shells exploding—the noise, the concussion," he said. "Later they changed the diagnosis to 'combat fatigue,' when they realized it was the stress and horror of war that made people crazy, having flashbacks and such. It's as if Libby's been in combat. Prison did something to her."

So, Libby was wounded. The idea that there might actually be something wrong with her, something permanent, scared me. There was her time in prison, plus, I couldn't help thinking, there was my cowardice in not going to visit her every time I had the chance.

"'Slightly worse for wear,' is what she says about herself," Hank added. "Says she has the blues."

"The blues?"

"Well, you know, in music, it's the blue notes," he smiled. "If you flatten the third and the seventh in a major chord, it changes the mood immediately to sad or suspenseful, right?"

"Sort of…," I said. Blue notes were not something Muriel had ever explained to me, so something was sorely missing from my music education.

"Come inside for a minute. Let me show you." Hank led the way to the living room and sat down at the piano. He played a C-major chord, C, E, G, and C again. He moved his second finger down from E to E-flat and his fourth finger from B to B-flat and played it again. He looked at me.

I did hear it, like the air changing in a moment, from normal and happy, to distant, foreboding, and haunting. It did sound like the way Libby was now, mournful and sad, the world having changed. We both wanted her back, Hank and I, each in our own way, back in a major key again. I wanted my beautiful, impossible Libby—my mother—back again.

Hank grinned reassuringly. "I worry, too, but soon, somehow, she'll get back her old gumption and everything will be copacetic again, okay?"

"Okay," I said under my breath. I desperately wanted it to be true. Also, I wished I could get back the feeling I used to have when I was near Hank—of being small, and safe. That was impossible now. He couldn't protect me now. He couldn't make things right for Libby or me anymore.

On Sunday Grandma and Grandpa came out for the first time since Libby had gotten home from prison. Libby and I broke out the only fancy lace and embroidered tablecloth we owned and set the table as close as we could to the way Grandma did it. Libby, I think, wanted to please her. I certainly did.

I pared the carrots and potatoes and cut the onions to spare Libby reminders of prison. As if no time had passed and nothing had changed, Grandpa emerged from their big celery-green Nash, dressed in a suit, sweating and grumbling at being directed by Grandma. His hands were protected by large, silly-looking potholders, as he lifted Grandma's roasted capon in its blue-speckled enamel roaster and carried it inside.

I had a long hug with Grandma. Then I took her fall fur coat to the hall closet, taking the opportunity to rub it against my cheek and inhale her aroma before I went to the kitchen.

During the fuss of getting the bird safely to the top of the stove, I watched closely for any signs of Grandpa softening toward Libby after her ordeal. Did they both enjoy battling that much?

Grandpa Joe patted me on the head, but then was unusually silent. He made no interior decorating comments, and there was no acknowledgment from either of them that they hadn't seen Libby in more than six months.

Grandpa demanded whiskey, and Hank dug up a bottle from the little used cabinet next to the fireplace. He dusted the bottle off and poured Grandpa a shot glass full, and also one for himself, taking a quick swallow even before he replaced the stopper.

"You're too thin," Grandma Rose informed Libby, as soon as we were all sitting at the table. "You don't eat."

"Shah, Rosie. What do you think—they give them fancy food in…inside *there*?" Grandpa grumbled.

"Look at her," Grandma insisted. "Her arms are like bones. No color in her sheyna punim." She reached over to take Libby's chin in her hands, as if she were a child.

Libby recoiled and held both hands up. "I'm alright, Ma. I've been eating much better since I got home. Hank and Sara have become excellent cooks since I was away."

"They should feed them good in jail. We pay for it with the taxes," Grandpa said.

"Eat, eat," said Grandma, her hands shaking and nervous.

I scrutinized Libby carefully for signs of the thinness Grandma was so worried about and thought I saw it in a darkening below her eyes. I saw it in her shoulders, which were stooped forward in a sort of permanent cringe. I remembered feeling the bones in her back when I hugged her the day she came out of prison. Maybe Grandma was right. Maybe the problem involved Libby's not eating.

After taking a few mouthfuls, Grandpa put down his fork. "So, what are you gonna do now?"

"What do you mean, Pop?" Hank asked before Libby could answer.

"I mean, what are you going to *do*? Everybody knows about you now."

"There's nothing we *can* do about it now—"

"—I told you before. This place is no good for you," Grandpa interrupted. "A Jew hiding with the goyim, it's a chicken hiding in the fox's house. A red hiding in a republican town! I worry all the time."

"Pop," Hank said, joshing him, "I've told you a hundred times you don't have to worry. The house isn't going to fall down. I learned from the best how to build a house." It was unclear whether by "the best," Hank meant Grandpa or M.I.T. Probably both, I decided.

"Not *fall* down," Grandpa insisted. "I worry somebody's gonna push it down or burn it down. You have to go live someplace else."

"Thanks for your concern, Pop," said Hank as Libby looked down into her plate. "But we're not going anywhere."

"You can't stay here," Grandpa repeated.

Libby woke up now from what had seemed some trance she'd been in. "Maybe you've forgotten? You don't tell us what to do anymore. We make our own decisions now."

"Certainly, we decide where we're going to live," Hank agreed.

"You don't know how to step inside from the rain," Grandpa snapped. "How can you decide where to live?"

I studied their faces—Hank's, Libby's, and Grandpa's—all crouched for the fight, the same old battle that had begun a long time before I was born.

Grandpa shook his fork at Libby. "You gotta go where nobody knows you. You shoulda taken my advice a long time ago. I know about hiding."

"We *haven't* been hiding," Libby said through tight lips.

"Hiding in plain sight," I said quietly.

Hank looked over at me. "Yeah. Maybe that's what we've been doing. Hiding in plain sight."

"*This* is not hiding," Grandpa scoffed, sweeping his hand toward the picture windows. "We don't have to hide in this country. But if someone attacks you, you can't just hold a white flag up."

From my place at the table, I could see across the living room, under the open piano lid, and beyond out the picture windows. The woods were still littered with downed branches from fall storms, including a medium size pine that had broken right off, leaving a high, jagged stump with the bark peeling. A group of downy woodpeckers was already hard at work on it.

"When came the pogroms," Grandpa said abruptly, as if he were continuing an interrupted story, "I was seven years. Izzy was five. We hid under the chicken coop. Our father told us to go there, to put our fingers in our ears and close our eyes." As he said this, Grandpa looked at me with a severity that made me squirm.

"So we wouldn't hear the screams," he finished.

"Who was screaming, Grandpa?" I asked, my heart pounding.

"Pop!" Libby warned him.

Grandma mouthed his name, "Joe."

Ignoring them both, Grandpa kept peering at me through his glasses. "Yah, my sisters were just about your age," he said. "And my mother...? They beat up our father. They kicked him in the head with their boots." Grandpa's hands were trembling.

"Joe, please," Hank said quietly.

"I told my father to leave that place…*before*. And I told him to leave *after*. But did he listen to me? *Nah*. Nobody listens to me. After my bar mitzvah came, I took my brother and we left for America."

Grandpa took off his glasses and scrubbed at them with his handkerchief, so hard I thought he would break them. "Twenty years after that, the Nazis came to finish the job. I wasn't there to protect them. I was here in America—four thousand miles away."

Silent tears ran down Grandma's cheeks, making paths in her face powder.

Grandpa took a fresh cigar from an inner pocket of his suit jacket and clipped off the tip with the miniature guillotine he carried around in his pocket. He lit it up and began puffing with fury, nearly disappearing in the smoke that was filtering upward through the chandelier.

"You have to leave this place…*now*," Grandpa said in a gravelly whisper.

"But, Grandpa, this isn't Poland. This is our home," I said.

Grandpa didn't look at me, just mumbled something under his breath. I took comfort in Grandma's tears. *Some*one saw how sad Grandpa's story was. How sad that his family was defenseless in the snow, which I imagined had smears of red blood painted in.

The thought of leaving Goshen was frightening and formed an empty, hollow place in my stomach, a place without people, barren and silent, and even farther away from Grandma and Grandpa than Goshen. It would be a place without Mary, my only true friend. And without Tensing, my intrepid tuxedo-clad chickadee and the other birds I knew.

Goshen was my home. I could picture roots reaching down from my feet, making their way into Goshen's soil that Grandpa always said was infertile. My root tendrils wound down into rich layers of leaves and loam. "We don't *have* to leave," I explained to Grandpa, attempting to sound calm and reasonable. "We can stay right here. We can stand up for ourselves, fight for our American rights."

I felt myself sitting up very straight at my full seated height at the table, bolstered by my confidence that Hank and Libby would never take Grandpa's advice on anything.

Both Libby and Hank turned to look at me as if I were an alien creature rising out of the primordial ooze—the soupy substance from which Miss Marble said all life had emerged.

Grandpa glared at me. "See, Sara, now you're talking crazy, too." Then he turned accusingly to Libby. "She got infected from you."

Hank jumped in, "Okay, how about we all just calm down? Libby and I are competent adults. We'll make the right decisions for our little family."

I looked down into my lap. None of them, it seemed, were particularly interested in *my* opinion or my First Amendment right to free speech.

Before dessert could be served, which was a honey cake with pecans, Grandma's specialty, Grandpa announced he had no appetite. He didn't feel well and wanted to go home. He stood up slowly from the table as if every bone in his body hurt and headed for the door.

Grandma gave us quick hugs and kisses and followed him out. Soon, their upside-down green bathtub of a car was inching down the rutted driveway and away.

"Well, that was quite the Irish goodbye," Hank said as we stood in the driveway and watched the car disappear up Guernsey Road.

"Why does he say that stuff?" I asked.

"Because he's a contentious old coot," Libby said, coming up behind us.

"And because it's what he feels," Hank shrugged. "He worries about us, but don't you worry. We make our own decisions around here. Let's get to bed now. Okay? Your mother is exhausted."

CHAPTER THIRTY-SIX

Under the covers, I felt lonely and angry with Grandpa for the first time ever. He'd hurt Libby. He'd disrespected Hank—and me. Meanwhile, the story he'd told—or half-told—haunted me the way a dimly-remembered bad dream does. Something terrible had happened in the "old country," although the details were blurred by that fog or snow curtain that divided the early times of our family history from mine.

The screen, which Hank and Libby, and even Grandpa in his clumsy way, had maintained to protect me, just provided places for past horrors and future threats to lie half-hidden. Images from the same murk consolidated now into a moving van, an orange U-Haul, and an over-packed Heap. An update on the past? A premonition? Did it mean Hank and Libby might actually listen to Grandpa and move away?

Either way, past or future, I hadn't, and never would have anything to say about it. They were the parents, and I was the child. That much was clear.

There I was waving tearful goodbyes to Mary with little Annie-Marie in her arms and to Tensing and the other birds. There were empty suet and seed feeders, my untended bird graveyard, and our empty, unfinished dream house.

That Sunday, Libby took me by surprise by asking if we could go together to the college woods where, as far as I knew, she'd never been since we'd moved to Goshen.

"Are you interested in birds now?" I asked, worried this meant we would be moving for sure.

"I have always been interested," she shrugged. "I just never found the time."

"I know you're a city girl," I said, using the banter I'd heard for years, "and Hank is the country boy. A farm boy. New Jersey when it was rural and all that."

"All true," Libby smiled, as far as I knew for the first time since she'd gotten home.

A tightness somewhere inside me let up just a little. I welcomed the idea of a ramble in the woods with Libby. I wanted to cheer her up, which was part of my job as her daughter, as an only child, and as a partner in the father-daughter team with Hank to keep things copacetic.

Maybe a dose of nature would help cure her shell shock and bring back some of her old spark. Plus, I just wanted to be near her.

Hank had recently moved from the dining room table to his back-room office, which he did in early spring, and I went there to tell him where Libby and I were going and ask if he wanted to come along.

"I have a bunch of stuff to do," he said, waving at his cluttered drafting table. "Someone's got to bring home the bacon," he winked, then lowered his voice. "But what a terrific idea. It'll be good for the two of you to spend time together." He pumped his fist, cheering me on.

"It was her idea."

"Even better," he said.

With Libby close behind me, I stepped over the chain across the entrance path to the college woods. I wondered if she would hesitate at the "No Trespassing" sign because she'd just been so severely punished for breaking the rules. But no, she climbed right over. As 'Libby' as she ever was, she followed me into the woods. "It's so beautiful," she said, as we tramped along. "I don't know why I've never come out here with you before."

Because you were always too busy, I thought. But, had I ever invited her? Not really. The college woods had been Mary's and my place.

Remaining patches of snow lay here and there on the ground, laced with black at the edges like barbed wire. Libby wore one of Hank's lumberjack shirts over several layers, making us slightly mismatched twins.

"In prison," Libby said, looking up into the stark, bare trees, "on weekends, they took us jail birds out for an airing. You could even call them hikes. Danbury is famous for its prison, but it also has some lovely, wooded parks. I lived for those days," she sighed. "I felt free. Otherwise, there was only the racket of the common room with the television yammering all day long. I'd escape to the library where it was quiet, at least. We weren't allowed to stay in our cells during the day."

I pictured Libby in a bird cage and felt an ache in my stomach, imagining her still a cooped-up inmate being let out into nature for one day a week. Libby had always been mildly curious to hear what Mary and I saw in the woods. Now she relished the forest, the dappled light on the forest floor, the accumulation of leaves from the deciduous trees, the rust-colored pine needle carpet.

I told her some of the tales Mary had told me, including about the pig farm. Libby laughed out loud when I quoted Mary saying, "The priests could just get their ham and bacon from the grocery store like everybody else."

I pointed out the birds, mostly dull-colored ground feeders, wrens and thrushes, half-hidden as they tossed up leaves, foraging for bugs and worms. "You know, Alger Hiss was a dedicated birdwatcher," she said wistfully. "He watched them from the window of his cell."

"Tell me again who he was."

"*Is,*" Libby said. "Alger worked for the State Department and was falsely accused of passing secret documents to the Soviets. He was sentenced to five years for perjury but is serving seventeen months. He's getting out soon."

"Was he in Danbury, too?"

"No, Lewisburg. In Pennsylvania. His favorite bird was a rose-breasted grosbeak that would come to his cell window every day."

"Do you know him," I asked, worried I might sound like HUAC, asking so many questions.

"No," Libby smiled. "They say he wrote about it in his letters to his son."

"I've never seen a rose-breasted grosbeak," I confessed as we turned down the path leading to the big pond.

"Birds never came to our windows in Danbury," Libby said.

A brown bird, probably a thrush, rustled as he hopped from bush to bush, off to the left of the path. "Was jail really…awful?" I asked hesitantly, afraid to really find out.

"It wasn't fun, no, definitely not." Libby's head was down now, her body bent forward, maybe afraid of tripping on tree roots across the path, but I saw that cringe she'd come home with from prison. "First of all," she continued, "it was noisy and deadly dull, except for the people, that is."

"What was your roommate like?" We'd reached an elevated, wooded spit of land overlooking the big pond.

Libby gazed out across the water. She straightened up, and her large, beautiful eyes gleamed. "Well, my cellmate—Betty—was an embezzler. She stole money from the government agency she worked for. Everybody called her Betty the Bezzler. The guards gave her that nickname. They thought it was hilarious."

"Were you…friends?"

"You could say we were friends, yes. In prison, you learn to have one another's back."

"You mean, it was dangerous?"

"Sometimes people got rough. They were so cooped up, some of them for a long time. When they got to feeling desperate, they sometimes got physical. My roommate knew the ropes, like what and who to avoid, and when."

"Sounds scary."

"Yes, but I learned things in there."

"Like what did you learn?"

"Patience, I think, mostly," Libby sighed. "And tolerance. Embezzling is wrong, of course, especially from a program that's supposed to help people, like the poor. But Betty had a good heart, and she was expert at getting us extra snacks sometimes. She'd already been in for three years. She still had—has—a year to go."

Libby kept her eyes on the water. I was probably asking too many questions, but the window was open and I needed to know more.

"Did anybody hurt you while you were in there?"

Libby's gaze remained on the water, but in that moment, I wondered if she might have realized I'd been eavesdropping on the drive back from Danbury. "Not…physically, as I told your father," she said pointedly, "but some people there harbor deep anger at being treated unjustly, probably the same anger that made them commit crimes in the first place. Lots of the inmates thought being a Communist or a subversive was worse than anything they'd done. Maybe it helped them feel less guilty." She paused. "And, well, you know about the strip searches."

"How did you survive?" I asked, with a shiver.

"I just thought of all the work left to be done." Libby buttoned Hank's wool shirt up to her chin. "And I thought of you."

I could feel a blush coloring my face. "We missed you, a lot" I said softly, unaccustomed to expressing tender sentiments out loud or hearing them very much either. It was so much easier in letters.

"And I missed *you*," Libby said, looking straight at me for a moment, before her gaze darted back to the pond. "I missed you terribly." Her eyes looked as if they might overflow, although the glimmer effect might have been due to the wind and the angled late afternoon sun reflecting sharply off the pond's surface.

Libby lifted the tail of her shirt and blotted her eyes. I felt the tears coming, too then. I let them come, and they felt warm on my cheeks.

It was getting colder. A breeze ruffled the water. Red-wing blackbirds rode swaying cattails rising at the edges of the water, and reeds and gold and gray grasses bent in the wind. Swallows swooped over the water, changing course in the blink of an eye, on the hunt for bugs.

A flock of Canada Geese gathered on the water framed by the stand of reeds. They're easy to identify by their size, their proud black heads and necks, and their white cheeks or "chin straps," as the bird guides say. Hank said they looked like their jaws and ears were bandaged up from a barfight, but their movements on the water were smooth as swans.

Libby stood silently and raised the binoculars. "What are they doing here at this time of year?" she asked as she brought the geese into focus.

"Getting a late start maybe," I said.

"How far south do they go?"

"Florida, South America…or maybe just New Jersey."

Libby chuckled. "You're a kidder…like your Dad."

"I try," I said, pleased with the notion, although I couldn't help noticing how each of them, Hank and Libby, tended to say I was like the other parent. "Canadas were nearly hunted out of existence for a couple of centuries, but they've been coming back."

The geese milled randomly like bumper cars, closely packed, then drifting apart on the pond currents. They paddled against the wind to stay close together. One individual swam off to one side, squawking at the rest, as if scolding to get their attention.

"That one must be the leader," I said.

"I see that," Libby said. "Good luck to her."

I smiled to myself. Libby had just made what we called in my house "a crack," but what Mr. Bramhall in English class called "irony." Maybe it was a good sign.

Gradually, the geese organized themselves into what was unmistakably a V-formation on the water. The rippling current kept pushing them out of the line, but each bird paddled vigorously to maintain their position. Then, the leader at the apex of the V took off, flapping her huge wings, her webbed feet "walking" on the surface of the water until airborne, she tucked them in. One by one, the group rose in flight, each flying a little lower than the one ahead of them. The V flew off to the west, straight into the glare of the setting sun.

We watched for several minutes until the leader veered right, followed by the others, and still in tight formation, they made a wide U-turn back to the pond. Landing, one by one, skidding on their heels, each settled down to bob on the water.

Now, a second group repeated this routine, while the members of the first V went back to foraging, dipping their bills for food that lay beneath the water's darkening surface. After a while, the second group took off, made the turn and came back.

"They look as if they're practicing," Libby said.

"Yeah, maybe it's just a drill."

"Mr. Peele would approve then," Libby smiled. "I'm glad they decided to rehearse today so we could see." She lowered the binoculars but continued to watch the geese, then said, without taking her eyes off them, "Sara, I know you were upset the other night when Grandpa and Grandma came over."

"It was what Grandpa said about moving away."

"Yes, I know." The natural glow in the sky darkened as the sun sank lower. "You *do* understand that your father and I are the ones who have to decide."

"That's what you said."

She handed the binoculars to me then. "Well, we did discuss it, all of it. Everything that's happened. And, um—we've decided Grandpa may have a point."

Panic took me by the throat. The idea that they, and especially Libby, would allow themselves to be guided by Grandpa on anything, especially where we would live!

"But, why? What makes you think he's right?" I tried to sound grown-up, suppressing, as best I could, a little-kid whine in my tone.

"It must be obvious to you that we've worn out our welcome in Goshen," Libby said.

"What do you mean?" I asked, pretending ignorance.

"We're kind of like visitors here. It's like they're sick of us now that they know who we really are."

I took a step backward and leaned against the rough bark of a large pine. The pond wavered and blurred. I closed my eyes, waiting to feel steady again. "Not everyone is sick of us," I protested. "And I'm not a visitor. This is my home."

"I know, and that's what makes it so hard," Libby said, bowing her head. "But, anonymous phone messages, nasty notes on your locker, calling a child a red and a traitor? That's not enough to make it clear how people feel?"

"But starting all over again!" I said, ignoring that she'd just called me a child. "Is that a good idea? It seems a little…crazy! Why would we do that?" I felt frantic; my words tumbled over one another.

"For you," Libby answered, matter-of-factly. "We would do it for you."

"How is it for me?" I demanded.

Libby frowned. "It's always been for you, Sara. You don't believe that, but it's always been to protect you. To keep you from having to hear the taunts and insults and harassment."

"I don't need protection," I said, quiet and grim. "I'm almost grown."

On the pond, the geese floated peacefully, at leisure dipping their bills, then drifting apart again, some out of sight among the reeds.

"I'm not questioning your maturity." Libby's forehead wrinkled. "But everyone knows about me now. And most of the town is against us. Your father isn't getting jobs or even opportunities to bid on them. He may already have been blacklisted for government jobs. He's depended on those. And I'm sure I can't get work…probably anywhere. Like Grandpa says, you can't just hold a white flag up. You have to do *something*. I don't want you to have to hear one more hateful comment because of me."

"But what if it happens again in the next town? Moving away is like surrendering," I said.

"Let's call it a strategic retreat,"

I took the binoculars back from her, and pronounced, "Mary is coming back to school soon, and I have to be there."

"No chance her parents will send her off to Catholic school?"

"No," I said firmly, although some doubt flickered. "She's definitely coming back to Goshen High School. They're going to say she had mono, and the baby is Annie O.'s."

"Really? That's really brave—or foolish, I don't know which." Libby's teeth found her lower lip.

"They want to keep the baby in the family."

"That's noble. Under the circumstances. But it's absolutely outrageous that a girl so young has to bear a child that's…unplanned. I'm not sure you understand what's at stake for her—and for you and for us—continuing to live here in Goshen."

"I know some people aren't going to be nice," I said. "They're going to harass us—me, anyway—unless people put two and two together about Mary. Anyway, I promised. Mary and I are going to have each other's backs."

Libby sighed, and her shoulders sagged. "You're a loyal person, Sara. That's admirable. But can you understand that I don't want you to suffer…for my decisions?"

"Isn't that a child's job?"

"It shouldn't be. Is that the way you feel it's been?"

"Sometimes, yes." I stole a wary glance at her.

"I know I can be a bit headstrong sometimes. I find it difficult to live in a world where so many things are wrong. I had to try. I feel terrible if you've come to think your job is to suffer for my actions."

"I know it's not true—"

"—I was just living my life, following my nose and maybe a childish sense of justice."

"Why is a child's sense of fairness unreasonable?"

"It isn't. Not really. It's probably the purest form. The unadulterated, uncorrupted, pure culture of fairness."

"Bramhall says 'adult' and 'adulterated' come from different Latin sources, unrelated. Otherwise 'adulterated' would mean grown-up…and 'adulthood' would be a corrupted loss of innocence."

"He said that?" she smiled. "I don't want adulthood to corrupt me, I guess. But part of the result of my naïve philosophy is *you've* had to suffer for it." Was she saying that being progressive was naïve, or did she possibly mean communism?

Darkness was coming quickly. The sky above the horizon was still lit and streaked with blue and pink and gray clouds. It hadn't been predicted, but a light snow began to fall. Libby smiled and held out her glove and watched the flakes land, then she touched my shoulder. "It's getting dark. We should go."

We started back through the woods, the sound of our footsteps already muffled by the dusting of snow. I buttoned Hank's shirt I had borrowed all the way up. "Did you *really* go fight in the Spanish Civil War?" I asked.

"Only for a few weeks," Libby replied over the brush-brush of our footsteps on the path. "I wanted to drive an ambulance."

"Why only a few weeks?"

"I got sick, and they sent me home," Libby sighed.

"Sick? What kind of sick?"

"It was dysentery. It was very embarrassing."

"But why did you go in the first place?"

"It was pretty simple. A new, progressive and democratic government had been elected in Spain. And the old guard, Generalissimo Franco and the Catholic church, was trying to overthrow it. Hitler sent air and armored units to Franco, so the civil war became a dress-rehearsal for WWII.

"We went over there to defend democracy against the fascists. We knew nothing about fighting. We were pacifists. President Roosevelt and most of this country wanted the US to remain neutral. He ordered an embargo and American citizens were forbidden from going there to fight. We were just crazy kids, I guess."

I glanced at her in the waning light and the falling snow. Her profile looked proud against the remaining light. No denying it: Libby the rebel was beautiful. She hugged herself against the cold.

"So *are* you a Communist?" I asked, shivering.

"I haven't been a Communist since 1939, my senior year in college."

I could see my own breath from a long, slow sigh of relief I didn't know I needed. "But why did you become one to begin with?"

"The Communists seemed like the good guys. They believed in peace. They saw that Negroes were oppressed. They knew about lynching in the South and other places and weren't afraid to talk about it. They recognized unfairness and brutality and understood the power relationship between the poor and the rich. I was young and idealistic and, frankly, uneasy with my folks for being so comfortable during the Depression, when so many people were broke. I wanted to fix the world."

"Then why did you quit…being a Communist?"

Libby sighed. Whether she was exhausted by my questions or just world-weary, I couldn't tell. But, it didn't matter. I needed answers, and I needed to hear them from her.

"The party was becoming authoritarian and dogmatic, and, more and more, it seemed it was being run from Moscow. Then in 1939 the Soviets signed a non-aggression pact with Nazi Germany and that was it for me."

"What was it?"

"Hitler was evil. He was also clever. He offered Stalin an agreement that neither country would fight each other for ten years. Stalin took the deal. They called it a non-aggression pact, but it was Hitler's ploy to keep the Soviet Union from opposing him while he invaded Poland, which he did a week later. Right after that Hitler dreamed up the 'final solution.'"

"The final solution…to what?" I asked.

"I don't think they teach this in school. His 'solution' to the Jewish problem. *We* were the problem. Hitler thought Jews were a plague on society. He despised Jews, thought they were sub-human, along with dissident Poles, gypsies, and homosexuals. He wanted them—*us*—gone. Nazis rounded up Jews in Poland and the Ukraine, where Grandpa's from, killing them outright, or putting them on trains to labor and extermination camps. That's when lots of us got off the Soviet train. The pact gave the Nazis a green light to conquer Europe and spread their hate."

We were coming to where the path emerged onto Merriam Street. The chain and its No Trespassing sign were already laced with snow.

"I wish you'd told me this stuff. I've heard about Nazis, but the concentration camps—"

"—We didn't want you to have to think about that. We wanted you to grow up thinking the world is a good place," Libby said, stepping over the chain.

"Isn't it?"

Libby paused to think hard about the question. "It can use a lot of improvement." We walked singe file along the side of the road against traffic.

I wasn't finished. "But why did you refuse to answer the Committee, if you weren't a Communist anymore and didn't believe in it anymore. They already knew all about you."

"It was the principle of the thing," she said, her chin rising. "The Constitution says we have freedom of speech. You can think and say anything you want, except, as you told your grandfather, you can't yell fire in a crowded theater. You can belong to whatever group you want. And once you're attached to a cause, an ideal, even after you stop believing in it completely, it becomes something hard to let go of. Like a spiritual lifeline. It's hard to explain, but to abandon it feels like betraying yourself. Can you understand that?"

I nodded. "Do you regret your decisions?" I had to step up beside her to hear her answer as a car passed us, headed in the direction of Goshen Centre.

"Which ones do you mean? Which decisions?"

"Like joining the Communist party."

"No," Libby said in a half whisper. "No regrets."

We crossed the railroad tracks and trudged onto Mr. Tooey's land. I took a halting breath. "Well, the cause, the ideal of the thing is why I can't move away now. I can't run away. I have to be here when Mary comes back to school. If, or when, they find out about the baby, they're going to call Mary hateful names, too. They're going to persecute her, too. I can't leave. I can't abandon her."

"I understand completely, but we—your father and I—must be the ones to decide. Our job is to protect you."

"But isn't it the same thing, the reason you always fight with Grandpa?"

"I don't fight with *him*." Libby laughed. "He fights with *me*."

I said. "You fight with one another."

Libby paused. "I think I'm always trying to change his mind."

"He's not going to go from being Atilla the Hun to—"

"—I don't expect that. I guess I just want him to think of the world as a good place, a safe place, or at least one that can be improved. I've completely failed at that."

"He loves America."

"Yes, he does, but for him America is the exception. Underneath that, he believes the world is not good, that people are not good. He saw too much when he was young and made up the rest."

We climbed up the incline and over the stone wall to our backyard, barely beating out the darkness descending on the woods. I wondered if Libby could see she was failing to convince me. With my innocence lifting like a ground fog, I was beginning to see the world more the way he did *and* the way she did—in need of much improvement.

CHAPTER THIRTY-SEVEN

I stepped off the school bus and marched straight to Hank's back office, where I found him hunched over his drafting table, doodling on a sheet of onionskin.

"What are you doing?" I asked him.

"Not a whole lot, to be honest. Not much business lately." He straightened up and shrugged. "I'm sure things'll pick up."

"Do you think they will, really?"

"I just have to cast a wider net to find work." He twiddled his compasses, then drew several perfect, intersecting circles.

It hadn't been a great day for me either. At lunch, Nancy, one of the popular girls, had picked up her cafeteria tray from the table where I'd just sat down and moved to another table, followed by those Mary used to call Nancy's acolytes. "Your mom hates this country," Nancy said as she stalked off.

As I contemplated whether to tell Hank about this, I noticed the Gyzmo's green light was out. "Is something wrong with the Gyzmo?"

"I, ah…unplugged it."

"Why?"

"I was getting some peculiar messages."

"Peculiar?"

"Well, unpleasant. Nasty."

"About Libby?"

He nodded.

"But how will people get in touch with you for jobs?"

"It'll be harder," he said with a faint smile.

Seeing his face so sad and stoic, I let myself feel badly for him. I'd spare him an update on what he would call the ignorance of the young these days. Then a ruthless streak rushed in to protect my stance. "We can't leave Goshen," I said.

"Yes, your mother mentioned your, um, recalcitrance."

Just when things were toughest for them, the little satellite—me, who had always rotated around the twin suns of them—I was suddenly carving her own reckless orbit. I was a clumsy nestling flopped to the edge of the nest, contemplating a leap into the void—assuming flying would somehow come naturally.

"She says you don't seem to grasp the seriousness of the situation we're in."

"But I do."

"You want to be loyal to Mary. We both admire that. But have you considered her parents might pull her out of public school and put her in a Catholic school? To protect *her*? There you'll be, on your own, defending yourself—alone."

"Mary wouldn't. She won't desert me. We're doing this together."

"What exactly is 'this,' may I ask?"

"*This* is standing up for ourselves, fighting unjust, mean, and wrong ideas about who we are."

"And what are these wrong ideas?"

"That I'm a junior Commie who's disloyal and hates my country, and when people find out about the baby, then Mary is a cheap little tramp without any morals."

Hank closed his eyes.

"That's why we need to stay and not let them drive us out."

"Well, they're not exactly driving us out—"

"—No. They're trying to intimidate and humiliate us, so we *want* to leave."

Hank began scratching down some numbers, added them up, and then quickly added a grove of little trees surrounding them. He looked up. "Of course, it will take a while to build another house."

"You're going to build *another* house?" I said, aghast at the idea.

"That would be the plan, yes," Hank said. "Wherever we decide to go. It took me two years and some to build this one. From the time your mother became 'famous,' because of the book, to the day we moved in."

"This house isn't even finished yet."

"I know...."

"Sorry, I shouldn't have said that."

"I'm not offended," Hank said, almost cheerfully. "A house you build yourself is never finished."

"It's nice, this house. It's our home," I said, glancing around at the rock wool insulation between the bare studs of his office. Hank looked at me long and hard, and as much as I wanted to look away, I held his gaze. He climbed down from his stool, crossed the room, and turned down the heater.

"Okay, Sara. Let me talk to Libby some more." He took a deep breath to signal the end of our little talk. "So…tell me what you have on tap for this afternoon, young lady?"

I wanted so much to believe him, to believe in them. But the way he phrased it—*let* me talk to her—didn't give me confidence. Really had I ever kept them from talking? They talked and talked. I was always the one listening, whether I was right there at the no-such-color-in-nature chartreuse table, or on my back under the dining room table, eavesdropping.

I gave an empty reply to his empty question. "Nothing important. Homework. Refilling the birdfeeders. Although, really what's the point if we're going to move away?"

"The birds still need food."

I left the office in a huff. Hank followed right behind me. I made a beeline for the kitchen. I ducked under the sink where Libby kept the cans of cooking grease.

"Let me help you with that, Sara."

Silent, I spread newspaper on the kitchen table and retrieved the bags of seed from the pantry closet. I took out a large bowl and a slotted spoon. Hank hovered, ostensibly helping. But he was there to cool me down. "You probably think I always back her up."

"You don't?" I snapped, unable to hide my bitterness.

Hank peeled back the greasy foil covers from the orange juice cans. "Not always. I just don't think it's advisable to take a Custer's Last Stand approach to this situation."

"The Indians won that one. Did you know Sitting Bull had visions of Calvary soldiers falling like grasshoppers before the battle?" This information was from Bramhall's social studies class.

"Well, we can't predict the future." Hank scooped suet out of a can with a putty knife and scraped it into the bowl. "You know, Sara, leaving Goshen wasn't your mother's idea."

"Whose was it then, Grandpa's?" I hoisted a five-pound bag of sunflower seeds and set it loudly on the table.

"It was mine," he said.

"Yours?"

"Yes, it's my job to protect you…and your mother," Hank said as he pulled the opening string from the bag of seeds.

"Where are these Victorian ideas coming from?"

"Victorian?" Hank laughed. "Not quite, but yes, she needs protection."

"From herself, maybe."

"Come on, Sara. Maybe you do, too."

"I told you," I grunted. "I want to stay here for Mary. We'll stand up to them. We'll be pariahs together. It's a matter of principle."

"You sound just like your mother."

I peered into the chaotic mixture in the bowl, a riot of seeds and grease. "That's a good thing, right?"

Hank shook his head. "How in heck did I ever end up in the middle, between two of the most powerful, opinionated females in existence?"

Well past the time they'd assume I was asleep, I was back at my post under the dining room table, inhaling linseed oil fumes.

"What if we put off the decision until the end of the school year?" Hank's voice trailed from the pass-through to the kitchen.

"What are you talking about? It's the rest of this school year I'm concerned about. Principal Peel certainly isn't going to protect her."

"Sara says she wants to face the music herself."

"How can you expect her to buck the ugly mood of the whole country by herself? She's a child."

"But, Lib, she wants to feel capable and independent and protective of her friend. She wants to stand up for herself. Anyway, where can we go? It'll take me time to find land and build a house."

"My parents will let us stay with them 'til we find a place."

"Your parents?"

"Don't look so shocked. It's better than leaving Sara dangling, a perfect target for the casual cruelty of children. Just until we find a place to lay low."

"Lay low? Not sure you're capable of that, mi pasionaria."

"Hank, stop!" Someone, probably Libby, plunked the kettle down on the stove.

"She can't go back to that school in Mattapan," said Hank.

"She'd be in high school this time around," Libby said. "We can't make a living here now."

"Do I also go back to work for your father?"

"No, that's out."

I could almost see her—Libby—with her arms folded in front of her, absolutely firm in her conviction, all the while looking beautiful.

"Libby, listen, please. Think of it this way. Sara's an innocent. She learned at our knee that the world was good. We took her where *we* wanted to go. We made our bed, and she had no choice but to lie in it. Shouldn't she have the right to play out the hand we gave her, now that she's coming of age? She's put down roots here, maybe more so than we have. And she's right that it could happen all over again someplace else." Hank paused. "The Senate did censure McCarthy in February. Maybe we're at the tail end of this thing."

Libby sighed. "Are you saying you've changed your mind about leaving Goshen?"

"I just think maybe we have to let her grow up and cope with the real world. We can't protect her forever."

"Maybe I don't want her to grow up. The real world is not so good."

There was a long silence during which I strained to hear what would come next.

Finally Libby said, "I'm not sure I could stand to live with my parents again. I don't know about you. So maybe we have no choice. Maybe we have to stick it out here….at least for a while. Nothing's forever, right? There's always Mexico. Decisions can be unmade."

"Sure," Hank said.

A chair scraped on the linoleum floor. The refrigerator shifted gears.

"Come here, Lib. How about we go to bed now."

"Yes," she said softly. "We might be able to improve some on the real world."

I cringed at this and was about to abandon my listening post, but Hank had something more to say. "I meant to tell you. An odd thing happened today. I saw Mr. Tooey. He came up to scatter his corn for the pheasants.

Usually, I just wave to him, and he doesn't wave back. But today he goes out of his way to come up and speak to me.

"He's looking pretty old and decrepit, I have to say. So, he says to me, 'How're you doin' Mr. Green? How's the buildin' business?' I told him business was kind of slow. Then he gives me this long look and says, 'I wonder maybe I could help out with that.'"

"That's odd," said Libby.

"Yes, it was. Then he says, 'You know I'm land rich and cash poor these days. I'm going to have to do something with the land back there pretty soon. I have about twelve acres.'"

"I told him, 'I'd love to buy some of it from you, but I don't have any money.' I felt like I should turn my pockets inside out to prove it to him. Then he gives me another strange look and says, 'Maybe you could build some houses for me back there. They say there're a lot of people who want to move out here to the sticks these days.'"

The kettle whistled. Either Hank or Libby got up from their chair.

"Do you think he was kidding you?"

"I have no idea."

CHAPTER THIRTY-EIGHT

To my great relief, Mary finally came back to school, and soon we were eating our bagged lunches under the Tamarack tree, on the opposite side of the parking lot from the Burgoyne Elm. Like the two of us, the Tamarack is an oddball, a conifer with cones and needles that turned bright yellow in the fall and then dropped off, like a deciduous tree. We lay on our backs and looked up at the bare branches that would soon be green again.

"Do you know Tamarack means wood-used-to-make-snowshoes in Algonquin?" I asked Mary.

"You speak Algonquin now?"

"Didn't I tell you?"

"The things you learned in nine months while I was 'expecting!'" Mary said, gazing up into the tree.

"We both learned different things."

"Now I know where babies come from," Mary said.

"I know the difference between jail and prison," I said.

"Which is…?"

"Jail is local. Prison is state or federal."

"You could probably teach civics now," Mary said.

"Thanks, but no thank you."

Mary sat up suddenly and curled toward me in a confidential pose.

"I think people know," she said.

"How could they?"

"This morning, Georgie F. said, 'A bad case of mono, eh,' with that nasty laugh of his."

"Probably it's just his usual mean self."

"Hopefully," she said and sighed.

"Are you ever going to tell Robby that he's the father?" I half-whispered.

"I don't know. What if I tell him and he wants to *be* the father? That doesn't go with the fairy tale we've decided on."

"Your brothers must know."

"They've been sworn to secrecy."

"They knew you were…away."

Mary shrugged. "It's very weird at my house. I take care of the baby before I leave for school, then Annie O. takes over, then I'm mom again when I get back home."

"Do think it's weird for Annie-Marie?"

"I hope not."

The warning bell for the end of lunch sounded. "I've been meaning to tell you," Mary said. "You remember the novitiate we saw skinny dipping in the woods and then skating?"

"Oh, yeah."

"Turns out he graduated from Goshen high school a few years ago, then went on to the Seminary. Now he's quit the priesthood!"

"How do you know that?"

"The maternity home has its gossip network. In one of his classes, he apparently said something like 'Jesus would be a Communist if he were alive today.' The priest teaching the class told him to take it back, but he refused. They put a lot of pressure on him to recant until, finally, he just quit."

"Then, he really was a Christmas angel," I smiled, propped on an elbow, watching Mary's face. Then I said, "Hank and Libby have been thinking of moving away from Goshen."

Mary sat up straight and stiff. "What are you talking about? Why? That would be awful." Tears welled in her eyes. "What would I do without you?"

"I know. Me, too. They say they're worried about me. But Hank's having trouble getting jobs to bid. And of course, Libby has no work. I've been trying to talk them out of it."

"I can't believe they'd listen to you. It's not that way at my house." Mary flopped back on the yellow grass and closed her eyes.

"I'm not sure they do. But I think they've decided against it…at least for now."

"I can't do this without you," Mary said.

"Yes, we have to stick together."

Just then Nancy, the queen bee, walked by, swishing her latest felt skirt. She appeared not to see us at first, then turned around, glaring, and said: "Nobody believes that cockamamie story about mono and your mother having a baby. Everyone knows you just got knocked up."

There it was. I had to do something—but what? I hadn't rehearsed my promised, heroic defense of my friend, or of both of us, in the name of justice.

I stood up and roughly brushed off the grass. I put my hands on my hips rather than make them into fists, like the good pacifist I'd been raised to be. I glared into Nancy's flushed, triumphant face. "You don't know that. Why would you spread rumors like that about my friend? What do you gain from that?"

She laughed in my face. "I'm just telling the truth, and you know it. And *you're* a great one to defend her. The red traitor defends her friend the slut. It's almost funny."

I took a deep breath. "Gratuitous meanness is what that is."

"Haven't you done enough? Have you no sense of decency?"

"Don't throw those stupid vocabulary words at me," she said, chin up, as she stalked off toward the main school building.

"She's just ignorant," I told Mary, who sat cowering and shaking. I sat back down next to her. This was how it was going to be.

CHAPTER THIRTY-NINE

Weekends, Hank worked on cleaning up winter's downed branches, burning them with fallen leaves in little bonfires on the driveway. Sometimes I went out there, too, both of us leaning on our rakes and squinting into the smoke. He made lots of visits to the hardware store and the lumber yard too, and put finishing touches on the house—a roof patch on the garage, paint for the exterior wood trim, sealer for the redwood siding, a new cedar post for the mailbox.

Libby began going into Boston again to her volunteer job at the NAACP. She started looking better. Healthier. She was eating more, getting better, Hank and I decided. One early evening, she returned from Boston and took sheet music out of one of her canvas briefcases. She announced she'd gone to Schirmer's music store for the first time in years.

She plunked Schumann's *Scenes from Childhood*, for piano, four hands down on the piano's music stand. "You should practice the Primo part," she said casually to me. "I'll take the Secondo. One of these days, maybe we'll play it together."

"Looks like recovery to me," Hank whispered to me when Libby had left the living room. And although her duet proposal presented old piano-practice problems for me, could it also mean Libby was really resolved to stay in Goshen and fight?

Early Saturday morning, I was the only one home when the wall phone in the kitchen rang. Hank and Libby had gone to the lumber yard. It was Uncle Izzy, whose telephone voice I'd never heard before, but I recognized his gruff accent almost identical to Grandpa's. He hesitated when he heard my voice. "Where is your mother?"

"They're both out. I can give them a message."

"You're still a kid."

"I'm almost grown up—"

"Tell'em Joe's dead. He was in shul. God struck him down on the bimah."

I was stunned. Grandpa had died while he was arguing with God at Friday night services, in the synagogue he'd built and always kept in good repair.

Sunday morning, the O'Reillys and the Bramhalls sent flowers to our house, which Hank and Libby said Jews don't do when someone dies, but it was very thoughtful.

Two hours before the funeral, a long, black Cadillac sedan struggled up the graveled ruts of our driveway. Half-dressed, Libby dashed into my bedroom to peer out the window. "What is *that*?"

"Looks like a limousine!" Hank chuckled. "The funeral home must have sold Rosey a bill of goods."

"I won't ride in that," Libby said firmly.

"Come on, Lib, let your mother have her day."

We all climbed into the vehicle, including Libby with a sour look on her face like the thing was contaminated. We rode the forty-five minutes to make a stop in Mattapan to pick up Grandma. She came out of her house on the chauffeur's arm and climbed in, sad and nervous, but looking like the grand lady she always dreamed of being. We drove to the Jewish cemetery in silence.

Grandpa's traditional, plain, knotty-pine coffin—no nails, no metal screws—was poised at ground level above the hole dug for it, while four brawny workmen stood holding it in place with straps that passed underneath it. The dirt they'd taken from the grave stood in a pile nearby.

Libby, Hank, I, and Grandma sat close together on spindly folding chairs under a canopy, holding hands in a tense chain.

Grandma gripped my hand so tight I thought the circulation would be cut off. Libby was stone-faced next to Grandma. Hank sat to my left. Uncle Izzy was next to him. A rabbi, wrapped in a prayer shawl embroidered with what looked like tiny gold birds, chanted in Hebrew, of which I understood not a word.

I couldn't believe Grandpa Joe was dead, that he was gone. Before the service, lots of people touched my face or pinched my cheek before they said they were so sorry—but what a long, full life he'd lived. Still, I expected him to surprise us all by showing up late to his own funeral in one of his pin-striped suits, looking impatient, checking his watch, and complaining about how slowly the event was moving along.

It was comforting to know that behind us, balanced on their spindly chairs, were Muriel and Ralph, Arthur and Dorothy, the ladies that played cards with Grandma, and some of the old men who prayed with Grandpa in the synagogue. Mary was there, too, with Annie O. and so was Libby's friend, Miss Rebecca May, the bringer of the Armageddon casserole.

When the rabbi finished his "boobitzing," which was Hank's made-up word for Hebrew chanting, the rabbi nodded to the cemetery men, and they lowered Grandpa into the ground. With a tightness in my throat, I watched the casket, which looked too long for my short, round Grandpa, go down, down. Then it was time for each of us to throw some stones and dirt on him to keep him from flying back up.

Being Grandpa's grandchild and Hank's daughter, I knew how to handle a shovel. When my turn came, I took a large shovel-full and stepped to the grave. I held the shovel above the casket, and stared down into the hole, its sides resembling cross-sections of layer cake. He was going to be down there for so long. The sense of endless time without God boggled my attention and I stood, shovel poised, head swimming, unable to take the next step.

A tense, silent moment of immovability was broken by swifts darting above the grass, gorging on invisible insects. Then, Libby was there beside me, smiling, with tears in her eyes. Taking hold of the shovel with me, she helped me turn it until the dirt and stones thundered with finality down onto Grandpa's plain pine box.

The rasp of the Electrolux yanked me from sleep. From the hallway, I saw that the piano lid was wide open like a one-winged bird and Libby was running the little round vacuum brush inside it, over the strings and the gold-painted harp that held them taut. She switched off the vacuum, opened the keyboard cover, and went to work with dreamy intensity and a soft rag on the white keys, using milk and vinegar. Then she did the black keys.

Methodically, she lined up the bottles of vinegar and milk on the floor next to the piano bench, and sat down to play. It was a slow, sad movement of a Beethoven sonata. And there it was—the beautiful legato Muriel had always been trying to get from me. It flowed from Libby like a natural spring. It was note perfect, worked into her muscle memory a long time ago and emerging now unscathed. When she finished, she sat with her hands resting lightly on her thighs, the way Muriel had taught me. The music in her had obviously survived the onion and potato peeling, the toilet cleaning, the strip searches.

When Libby sensed I was there behind her, she turned and beckoned me. She slid to the left-hand end of the bench and patted the other end for me to come sit down beside her. With trepidation and heart pounding, I did. And so, we sat, shoulder to shoulder, hip to hip, together on the bench.

She opened the book of Schumann duets to the first pages with the Primo and Secondo parts on opposite pages. "You see?" she said. "This first one's called 'From Foreign Lands and People.' Don't look so scared. We can do this. It's slow and lilting and swingy—a dance, really. Legato. Only one sharp. You have mostly just one hand, *but* you have the melody. I play the accompaniment and I follow you."

She pointed with a long, graceful finger at the double-bar, repeat. "Just repeat twice and we're done. Don't be afraid."

I hadn't agreed to this, but there I was, waiting as she counted out a couple of measures to set the tempo. One, two, and we were off. She was right. We stayed together, Libby following me, because I was the primo.

When I slipped-up, which I did a few times, even missing a sharp, she waited for me and eased us back into synch. With the second repeat, it came easier, and I loosened up. By the third time around, we were having fun, swaying a little, our bodies moving with the lilting melody, dancing together.

Finished, we sat breathing hard and laughing, as if we'd done something wonderful. We both turned in unison to gaze toward the windows, toward the woodland scene outside. I thought of the birds, and of the geese on the pond, and felt Libby's being close, next to me. The pines stood, unobtrusive and protective, and I pictured my chickadee, Tensing, flying nearby, free and confident that I would always feed him.

I thought of Grandpa, who wasn't in the earth in Goshen proper, where my family and Mary and I would be sticking it out for now and fighting the good fight. But he wouldn't be that far away. It was the same ground, the same earth, the same dirt, and it was all part of America, which he loved, and we all loved, each in our own way. All kinds of birds flew back and forth across the land, ignoring the boundaries drawn by people.

ACKNOWLEDGMENTS

Profound thanks to my incomparable writers' group: Dora Levy Mossanen, Leslie Monsour, Joan Goldsmith Gurfield and, in memory, Paula Shtrum, without whose love, fine eye for the written word, and support, I would never have endured.

To the legendary John Rechy, my first and only writing teacher.

To my beautiful adult children, Liz Kivowitz Boatright-Simon, Leigh Spencer, and Cliff Spencer, who urged me on and read the manuscript and gave thumbs up.

To my husband, Charlie Kivowitz, who always wondered what I was doing tippy-typing away, but who supported me on faith alone.

To my sister, Linda Corman Rock, my dear friend in writing and so much else.

And, to my mother, Betty Flaisher Corman, always my inspiration in so many things.

ABOUT THE AUTHOR

A practicing psychotherapist for most of her working life and a closet writer all of her life, Alexandra Kivowitz, PhD, grew up in New England and never really shed its sense of place, of its flora and fauna, or its mores and cadences. The inspiration for trying to bring a nineteen-fifties progressive childhood to life in fiction came from having, over the years, known adult survivors of the McCarthy period.

She lives in southern California with her husband Charles and a part-time dog named Maple. *Eavesdropper* is her first novel.

🍃We Grow Our Books in Montpelier, Vermont

Learn more about our titles in Fiction, Nonfiction, Poetry and Children's Literature at the QR code below or visit www.rootstockpublishing.com.